2.25

The Body in the Bog

Anyway Books® Works by John Nicholas Datesh

The Girl in the Coyote Coat (novel)*
A Need Apart (novel)*
Same book, different title
The Nightmare Machine (novel)
The Janus Murder (novel)
The Moscow Tape (novel)
The Last Three Minutes (novel)

You Could Call it a Christmas Story (short)
The Pro Station (short)
The Final Equation (short)
Reruns ad Infinitum (short)
The Very First Blog Posts of All Time (posts)
(on the blog EmptyGlassFull.com)

The Body in the Bog

an Anyway Books® novel by

John Nicholas Datesh

**Published by
Loiseau Media**

The Body in The Bog
An *Anyway Books*® novel by
John Nicholas Datesh

An *Anyway Books* Novel published
by Loiseau Media/Anyway Books
ISBN 978-1-940227-12-2

Copyright 2016 John Nicholas Datesh, Jr.
Cover Copyright 2016 John Nicholas Datesh, Jr.
All rights reserved

John Nicholas Datesh is a
pseudonym of John Nicholas Datesh, Jr.

Anyway Books is a registered trademark
of Loiseau Media

This novel is pure fiction. Ibis Creek does not exist. Its characters, their thoughts, actions and dialogue, are very fictitious

Blog Posts contained herein were used with permission of Loiseau Media

The Body in the Bog

Introduction

Some white thing floated peacefully on the Ibis Creek Condominium Bog, Friday morning, July 24, 2013.

It caught Sybil Foster's eye, but she dismissed it as an egret or ibis or stuffed garbage bag. She was more concerned with water lapping at Bermuda grass, not twenty feet from her lanai.

In Naples, June and July comprised the rainy season. Those of 2012 and 2013 filled the Ibis Creek natural Preserve to the brim and more. The Preserve was designed to collect drainage from the developed part of Ibis Creek. Apparently, it did too good a job, resulting in a swamp. A fellow Ibis Creek owner, Ian Decker, named it the *Bog*.

Ian also coined the phrase *Bog Creep* to describe Bog overflow that washed up on the Bermuda grass behind the first floor units' lanais. The *Creep* had peaked at seven feet of grass in mid-July, retreating to a foot around the rim of the Bog.

Bog Creep was a threat to first-floor units like Sybil's and Ian's. As such, it was ignored by the Ibis Creek board and Collins management ignored, as they did most things. It seemed to Sybil that only her minor rule violations stirred Collins. None of the board members owned first-floor units.

Nonetheless, Sybil took several photos of the minimal Bog Creep and attached them to an email to the Board and Collins without further comment. She copied Baron Abbott, the developer of the complex and the Bog. Her iPad took decent photos. As she swiped through her photos, the white feature became hard to ignore.

She swiped back through the sequence. It was not a garbage bag caught by one of the Bog's tree stump. If it was an egret of ibis, it was a damned big one.

It suddenly occurred to Sybil that ibis and egrets waded; they did not float.

Sybil trained her still excellent vision on the white glob. Whatever bobbed in the water had a garish red tie.

Chapter 1

James Joseph Amos looked at the Ibis Creek Call Box. He touched the Windsor knot of his loose Ralph Lauren tie. JJ did not know Ralph Lauren from Calvin Klein, but he had some of the latter, too. Mara Collins had helped him buy them. He deemed her taste as much better than his own or that of his estranged wife, Sally.

In the past, JJ had only his lesser Calvin's because Ibis Creek deserved no better. That night, however, he had worn his best Lauren tie. He had a meeting with Mara at the high-end Pelican Paradiso. More importantly, he had a later meeting with divine destiny at the despised Ibis Creek.

Despite his limited sense of irony, JJ appreciated that Ibis Creek was God's chosen vessel of his destiny, to be a partner and litigation *Summa Lawyer(tm)*.

Ibis Creek did not promote itself as a lower upscale gated community. Its PR emphasized the gate more than the scale. To JJ, the gate seemed more designed as an eyesore than a barricade. The entry side had a dual barrier arrangement: Right and left tubular poles responded first. They were designed to protect the more expensive gate doors from ramming. They often did.

For most residents, the opening sequence was triggered by a window decal with a bar code. The alternative procedure relied on an apartment-style Call Box. The Call Box took either a four-digit Vender Code that directly opened the gate; or a three-digit dial code that called a resident to remotely open the gate.

An associate with Ibis Creek's law firm, Sanders & Tilden, he had access to the firm's Vendor Code. JJ had used it once. JJ had not forgotten it. Whatever the shortcomings of his brain, it had a one-time memory, for words, numbers, faces, photos and signatures that it heard or saw clearly.

As his mentor Nolan Sanders praised it, JJ's brain was ninety-eight point-one percent memory. Nolan was also the first person to describe his *gift* as dyslexia.

JJ had always accepted his parents' designation of his unnamed condition as a *gift from God*. That gift spared him the sin of *humanism* and worse, *intellectualizing*, God's business not humans."

"Look where it got Eve," they told him. "Probably New England."

As a child, JJ had always been reluctant to leap or dream high.

The gift had two technological weakness: First, JJ could better read characters on small displays of cellphones. Those virtual letters did not jitter so much as float and just up and down, not three-sixty; second, he could understand words spoken to him.

The latter led to the revelation that changed everything. Mara gave him the *Puff Magic* app that converted text to speech. With Puff Magic, God, through Mara, had opened a new *path* for him. In his case, the path was very steep.

As a result, JJ could *read* legal case headnotes, pleadings and discovery documents. He did not need Sally or anyone to read them to him. He could draft anything and hear how it sounded, empowering him to put together, on his own, phrases that sounded right enough. Within weeks, JJ Amos developed into an average Sanders & Tilden lawyer.

JJ had a new power to track down minutia in the Ibis Creek v. Abbott defect case, so long as he knew what to look for. It was something he was not looking for, however, gave him the opportunity to accelerate upward on his path.

It was thanks to Mara, too.

From a young age, JJ had accepted the existence of the *Holy Spirit.* He also believed he was not elite enough to meet up with Him. He had also had heard the term *Spirit Guide* – presumably a delegate of the Holy Spirit – so he took Mara as *that* for him.

He was blissfully unaware that the normal definition would have required Mara to be dead.

JJ always used Mara's Vendor Code to activate the Ibis Creek gate. That use seemed particularly appropriate on July 23, 2013, the day he would secure his destiny.

Preoccupied with what was to come, JJ stopped too far from the Ibis Creek Call Box. Not tall to begin with and mostly trunk, JJ had short arms, legs and index fingers. He had to poke his head and shoulder out the window to begin carefully keying in Mara's code.

He hit the first three keys and hesitated. This final key would be the last one he would ever use at Ibis Creek. He savored the glow of God's grace and hit that key. The Call Box flashed *Invalid Code.*

On another day, JJ's frustration would have gotten the better of him. There was a reason, a part of the *Plan*, he just knew it. He pulled his arm back inside the car to consider his next step.

He had hit one or more wrong numbers, a seeming normal mistake. He stared at the Call Box keypad, trying to settle the numbers. They jumped from one level to the other, as usual, but JJ was not concerned. Early on, JJ's mother had drilled him in touch typing, so that he would not be confused by keyboards or typewriters or, fortunately, touch-tone keypads.

He just needed to collect himself. JJ did not believe in talismans, but if he had, it would have been the Windsor knot in his tie. That was where his hand went.

It struck him immediately that he had found the reason for the keypad error. He had refastened his collar button but had forgotten his tie was still loose.

At first, it shocked him that he had forgotten something so important.

At Blue Martini, thirty minutes earlier, he had received Kami's message. He hurried to his car and slipped the knotted tie over his head. As he drove to Ibis Creek, he did not give the tie another thought until his keypad error brought him up short.

Blue Martini, Mara and his favorite, was the perfect place to wait for his message. It was a classy spot but very casual. He always undid his tie before going in. That night, he knew he required a perfectly knotted tie and had outdone himself. His knot that evening was too perfect to undo. He just carefully worked it down the tie just enough to allow him to slid it off over his head.

Upon getting and listening to the message, he left half of a second beer and hustled to his Mercedes. His mind whirred with scenarios of what would happen next. Sorting through multiple scenarios was new to him.

Once seated, he flipped his collar and buttoned the top button. He slowly put the loose tie over his head and prepared to tighten it. Another text alert interrupted him. He called it up and immediately ran Puff Magic to convert the text to words. Messages that night were far too important for guesswork.

"Are you coming or not?" the iPhone asked him.

He quickly touch-typed, *Yes*, his loose tie forgotten.

Even over the twenty-minute drive, JJ spent the time in his soul. He was *that* close.

It was not until his misdial on the Call Box keypad that he realized that he had to execute the key part of the plan. God rarely acted directly in the temporal world. It would be up to JJ; thus, projecting calm and professionalism mattered. The next half hour was everything.

He believed that God planned his misdial, to give him the time to check his tie, to help him focus.

The knot still felt perfect. Once he had parked at the far end of the Bog, he would check it in the visor mirror and retie it to perfection if necessary.

Confident, JJ stretched three fingers onto the keypad. He closed his eyes and entered the four digits of Mara's Vendor Code.

The gate arms vibrated as they moved slowly upward. The gate doors creaked as they inched open. While he waited, JJ gently slid the perfect Windsor knot back into place.

He believed Nolan Sanders' code: *A professional who dresses like a professional feels professional and gets professional results.*

Dealing with a treacherous amateur over the next minutes, JJ's professionalism would rule. His suit and tie would defy the hot, muggy night. Kami Cabrera would not dare retreat from his righteous demands.

JJ removed his second phone, a so-called *burner* iPhone from inside his suit jacket. Initially, he had bought a no-name burner phone and sim card at a Circle-K, as Kami suggested. Naturally, someone like her would be familiar with subterfuge. He found its Sprint reception adequate, but its microphone and speaker were horrible. More to the point, it would not run Puff Magic.

He turned to Hugh Barrett, a collection client with even more experience in the dubious than Kami. Hugh recommended a flea market and an unlocked GSM phone.

"Get an iPhone 3 at a minimum, for sound and your app. You can get a burner sim card from that Circle-K for an AT&T private-label carrier," Hugh told him. "The service is the same as AT&T. All you need to register it is a zip code. If you want to be extra covert, don't use your own." Hugh did not ask why JJ, an upright lawyer, had need of a burner phone. All he did was wink at JJ.

JJ had a vague idea what the wink meant, and it reassured him that Hugh has put him on the right *wrong* track.

The iPhone was only for his extra covert dealings with Kamila Cabrera. Normally, he would never use a secret phone. He certainly would not use an Apple product or anything else that glorified Eve.

His first Bible lesson was that the *Tree of Knowledge* belonged to God. Celebrating its fruit, the *Apple of Truth*, was meant for the Bible and prayer. The iPhone's logo even had Eve's sinful bite in one corner. It was a small bite considering the size of the sin. JJ did not know what to make of it.

What mattered to him was that, in service to the Lord, a bit of sin was okay, as long as the mic and speaker were good and it was Puff-ready.

He smiled. He had not needed Puff Magic to recognize Kami's signature. Signatures were pictures, not text. He knew hers from her mortgages and whining letters to the Ibis Creek board. She created a nice, flowing, memorable image. In that way, his previous *scut work* in collections had provided him with a jolt on his path.

God, forever efficient, was not into wasting His chosen's efforts.

JJ called up Kami's text from Blue Martini. He stared at the see-sawing letters. Kami had not signed the text, but she did not have to. She alone had the number...

That was wrong: Her rental manager, Marty, had handled the exchange of secret cell numbers. That meant Marty had it, too, knew it was just for JJ and Kami.

JJ keyed up the conversion program and listened to the computerized voice. "You win. Behind Maria's lanai. 11:59. Come as you did before."

By Maria's lanai, Kami also meant her own. She had always owned the unit. An unmarried blond named Maria Suarez rented it from Kami, against County and Ibis Creek rules. Ibis Creek had never received a rental approval application from Kami, not once.

Over several months, JJ's late night strolls along the Preserve gave him proof that Maria, not Kami, lived in the unit. Under the Ibis Creek rules, Kami could not have a friend live in her unit. Under her Collier County agreement, Kami had to live in her unit.

Kami did not. Maria did.

While JJ was appalled at the series of different men friends Maria hosted, Maria's morality – however flawed – was not the point of his investigation at that time. It was about Kami's.

He had already curtailed his surveillance when rumors of a peeping Tom reached Mara. Fortunately, she did not believe the rumors, but Claire Hunter had called the Sheriff to investigate. Even the cursory inquiry secretly upset JJ. He had been doing his duty as a collection attorney, not peeping on anyone.

JJ transferred the used iPhone to his left hand to activate its *recorder* function. He increased the volume as he spoke a few words. The iPhone would easily record the coming transaction through his jacket without a hint to Kami.

JJ returned the iPhone to the right inside pocket. His official smartphone, a Samsung Galaxy SIII using was in the outside breast pocket. He had removed its sim card and tucked it his business card case, safely in his car. Hugh Barrett had told him that cellphones could be tracked, even when off, if they still had their sim cards installed. "Better to be safe, JJ," Hugh said, with a raised eyebrow version of a wink.

The Samsung could still divert Kami's interest, if any, from the iPhone.

He smoothed the lapel and pulled on his collar with two fingers to test fit. He gently tightened the tie's Windsor into position. Ready, JJ pressed the accelerator and passed through the white gates. Though Kami's unit was on the left side of the complex, he turned right. He planned to park well away from her unit and walk the rest of the way.

Once parked, he turned off his headlights. The water in the Preserve reflected only the few lights remaining on in bordering units. It was less a Bog at its north end than soaking wet woods. It was quiet, overcast and very dark. No one would see him.

He turned the lapels of his dark suit jacket up to limit the exposure of the white shirt while he walked. When he approached Kami, he would turn them down again. He checked his knot in the visor mirror. It was excellent.

He set his brogues on the wet grass, confident in his footing and his path. He knew the back lawn probably better than any resident at Ibis Creek. He buttoned the button on his coat and smiled.

James Joseph Amos began to walk carefully yet boldly toward his destiny.

~ ~ ~

At 11:58:17 PM, a car stopped at the Ibis Creek Call Box, catching the corner of Claire Hunter's eye. She kept it on the periphery as the usual routine followed: The Window slid open. A hand came out, followed by a bright, white sleeve. The hand backed up. A blurry face appeared as the man reached farther, a frequent maneuver.

Not until Claire saw the man's hand tap three keys on the pad and stop. Three meant a phone call to a resident and, assuming the guy was not a cheat, a legitimate buzz-in.

Hooray, legit, she thought.

Suddenly, he reached forward and punched, hard, a fourth key. Claire frowned. That meant he used a four-digit Vendor Code. Very few codes should have worked at midnight. Of course, Collins was Collins.

Her next thought made her hungry. Even Domino's and Papa John's had to call residents to get in the gate.

To Claire, improper knowledge of a Vendor Codes was a misdemeanor, using it a felony. She noted the time on a Post-It and wrote the term *coder*. She waited to see the car move.

It just sat there.

With a sense of satisfaction, Claire realized the idiot had typed an invalid code.

He fiddled with something inside the car and took another try, with an odd technique. He placed three fingers of his left hand on the keypad and turned his head away. His knuckles moved four times.

He must have used that Vendor Code so often he did not need to look.

Claire seethed as the gate began its glacial opening routine across a second camera's field. Claire focused on the screen. The visitor finally rolled toward the matching yellow/black banded arms that protected their expensive, fragile gates.

A low-resolution camera captured all Call-Box users' license plates. Claire typed a note on her laptop for the Florida tag number, SFD 552, which was not clear enough to detail the divider of the plate number. The standard divider graphic was a Florida orange. The coder's plate had a something else. She just noted it was an extra-cost, specialty plate with a tag frame from Mercedes-Benz *of Naples*.

Claire shared her observation with her blogging sidekick, Ian Decker. He was the one who had hacked the gate camera, though he denied *hacking* anything. Whatever the term, Ian had gotten Claire camera access after she had lost her board seat and she used it every other day.

Ian emailed back his *shock and dismay*.

She knew that Ian believed in irony above all else and did not feed that conceit. He had enough of that in his mystery *works in progress*, itself an ironic term, in Ian's case.

She watched the gate open on the four-camera screen. The time went to 00:01 as the car moved forward. Claire yawned and wondered why she bothered to watch the gate. Since she had led the Ibis Creek clean-up a couple years ago, sparked by two fatal ODs and the fatal kitchen knife incident, not much happened of interest anymore.

Chapter 2

In Ibis Creek Building Two, Unit 107 at 3:45 AM, Sebastian Decker paced in front of the six windows crowded onto his twenty-eight inch 1080p LCD monitor. Five windows represented his scattered work ethic, but only the sixth had his attention. He listened to the Google Voice recording again.

"Hi, Ian. Did you get my text? I need a favor." Evie's voice said before a pause. "Yes, I know it almost four AM, but I know you are awake. Call me back."

He was right: There was a second slight hesitation.

"At this number."

Numbers not recognized by his contact list did not ring but did merit an email alert via Google Voice. He had intentionally buried both the text and email alerts under one of two adjacent novel windows. Only after moving one did he see the taskbar's alert notice.

At that hour, the alert could only mean Evie had called him. Unknown numbers had become standard for Evie over the previous year. She was not paranoid. Many of her Wall Street clients, neck deep in SEC and DOJ investigations, were extremely so.

He tossed back the last bit of his second Bourbon and put on his headset. He clicked on the dial icon. "Ten to one, you're in a stretch limo, champagne-tipsy and using your date's phone to call your ex-husband."

"It's called a burner."

"I didn't need to hear that."

"The phone, Ian," Evie said. "But it's sweet you still think of me that way."

"You called a fiction writer."

"Call me crazy, but I still believe." She took a deep breath. "Sorry. You will get it done. It's important."

"I know. But I'll still call you crazy.." Ian's writing was even more important to Evie than to him. She needed him to write and often admitted it. "So, who was the SEC flogging tonight?"

"My night could have been dinner after a Tony-nominated musical. Actually, it was supposed to be."

"Bill for the bastards!"

"At eleven hundred an hour and a six hour catered meeting?"

"I'll bet the meatloaf was great," he said. "What can I do for you?"

Evie did not hesitate. With Ian, it was not necessary. "A small favor…"

"And?"

Everyone at the firm knew Evie, among others, still used Ian for unbilled research. She always had. Some matters, however, were not so upfront.

"QT."

"Hence, the secret burner."

The expected laugh did not come. "It's a way of… compartmentalizing."

"And during a federal investigation."

"We call them Administrative Inquiries. Okay?"

Ian felt the nagging disappointment that came when a door closed on their familiar, easy banter. Evie's could not share her securities work, but her response disappointed him anyway. He opened a third Writer window for notes. "Okay. I'm ready."

"You remember that I asked you about Ibis Creek foreclosures a while back? This is a follow-up."

Evie had asked Ian to do some research for her on Florida condo law for an unnamed client.

She continued, "With all the foreclosure sales at Ibis Creek, the same..." She stopped and sighed. "Let's just say that I need to know, for absolute certain, if anyone can buy one of your bank-foreclosed condos without getting approval by the board?"

"The quick answer is... Wait a second, Evie."

"Don't ask that question. Please."

"Okay. I'll skip to the answer: These guys can't get approval from the board."

"They'd rather not buy if they have to," Evie said something, off the phone. "I'm here. I mean in front of the building. About the favor..."

"If it takes me an hour, I'll have lost my internet connection. Do you need a memo on it?"

"No, no," she said, quickly. "This is *way* off the books. I'll call you later on my better burner."

"You do know burners are intended to be disposable?"

"I like that one," she whispered. "It is my special *Ian and Evie* phone."

"That's romantic as all hell, but not very covert."

"Oops. Make it my *Ian and Sim... mara* phone. I always liked that name Simara. It's very sexy. Bye."

"It wasn't supposed to be," he said. "I'll call you around 6:00 AM. Bye."

Ian watched as Skype closed the call's window. Much as he treasured her voice, he did not like the way it conveyed those keywords, *way off the books*.

Simara, though, was a nice, if cutting recovery. Simara was one of his first characters. The *mara* part was coincidence, but Evie knew of Ian's fascination with the allure of Mara Collins, if not the woman herself.

Ian put aside his unease for the moment. Instead, he called up his highlighted pdfs of the Ibis Creek Condominium Declaration and Chapter 718 of the Florida Statutes. Whatever off-kilter interest Evie's clients had in Ibis Creek, it had her uneasy.

First, though, she had asked him for a favor. That always came first.

~ ~ ~

Barton Abbot's father had insisted on beating sunrise with a cold swim in a granddad-dug lake on the family's Ohio soybean farm in Millville, Ohio, not far enough from Cincinnati. Barton had gone in chilly water with him most days after age four. They had kept at it until Barton went off to Kent State, near Akron and far enough east to establish independence while keeping the in-state tuition discount.

In the forty some years since, he still had a thing for the water, if not freezing his ass off. Also, he had never needed an alarm or a sunrise to open his eyes.

At 7:03 AM, he finished his third coffee when Leah Kaline's email arrived. *Barton, guess what Sybil says we have in our Bog this morning!* she wrote.

He may have loved water, but he hated that *Bog-shit* from the first moment he had heard it. He also and its jag-off Pittsburgh author, Ian Decker. Barton kept a printed version of Decker's blog post mocking Ibis Creek's construction defects. Part of it amused him the part about the architect and contractor dead on.

Decker's post came before Ibis Creek sued his company, NEBSIC Development, LLC, for *alleged* construction defects. Alleging meant guessing and that was the best they cheapskates could do: *Proving* the real defects – which were neither particularly defective nor Barton's fault – would have required expensive testing that the stooges on Ibis Creek board of the Association would never fund.

He had just read the latest pdf of the toad JJ Amos's muddled motion in Ibis Creek's lawsuit against him, and the others involved in building Ibis Creek. Barton was used to lawsuits, but that one had hurt from two years before it was filed.

Of all his projects, Ibis Creek was supposed to be his golden child. He had not hired architect Bill Mochyn to design a perfect project, just a first-class C+ grade condominium. Almost immediately, Ballasta Engineering had informed Barton that Bill's sub-lofty design aspirations were too *lofty*, not enough *sub*. The contractor bidding proved Ballasta right.

The subsequent, cheapening, fell under the term *value engineering*, Ballasta's specialty. By the time the County had fussed over every detail, the damned Chinese had made every builder in Florida miserable. Ibis Creek, as approved, guaranteed multiple bankruptcies. With a few informal, under-documented adjustments, Baron's contractor, Burkle Lehane, had built Ibis Creek to within eighty-seven percent of its valued-down specifications.

During the construction, Ballasta and Burkle Dehane surely had Barton's best interests at heart: A developer needed his sleep, his profit and his deniability. They did not know that Barton had a couple well-placed moles cluing him in on every modification. None cost him minute's sleep.

He remained well-rested until a Category Three hurricane named Wilma came onshore in 2005 with Ibis Creek in its sights. Barton quickly dumped most of his non-joint assets into offshore trusts. He need not have bothered: Ibis Creek's concrete block walls and terra cotta-dyed concrete tile roofs easily out-performed Mother Nature's winds and her Preserve's trees, half of which fell flat.

He handed over an Ibis Creek that had thumbed its nose at Wilma.

Instead of gratitude, he got a lawsuit.

Barton was a hands-on type. He read every pleading, motion and order in the case, the morning of July 24th being no exception. That day's incoherent motion was penned Tilden Sanders' JJ Amos. At least, Graham Chapman could string together paragraphs about railings and window bucks, whatever they were.

JJ was barely a lawyer. Somehow, he had gotten, over his head, into Ibis Creek v. Abbott. Months before, Barton encountered JJ in the second day of his deposition. Graham Chapman, the equally bad lead Ibis Creek attorney, called in sick – or "still washing piss out of his pants," as Barton's lawyer put it – and JJ subbed. JJ provoked Barton into several loud disagreements punctuated with *you dolt,* both on and off the record. JJ had kept asking the same question, repeatedly, perhaps in hopes of getting a favorable answer. He did not even reword the questions.

Barton knew that JJ's educational background best suited him to barking at ambulances or hounding late-paying Visa cardholders. He had never expected JJ to be so effective at resurrecting the many dead Ibis Creek delinquent accounts. JJ brought in hundreds of thousands in bad account, a cash deluge that kept the defect lawsuit afloat. He had come to wish that the roofs would, as claimed, blow off in a hurricane and sink six feet into the

Bog, while JJ Amos was service notices on doors beneath them.

At that moment, he would have put bog-meister Ian Decker under the falling roofs, too.

Leah's email had mentioned Sybil Foster, one of his Ibis Creek spies. She hated the board as much as he did.

Barton emailed Leah back: *I'll take a risk: 3 feet of water?*

Literal Leah emailed right back: *No, I think it is 4.7.5, but not that.*

The negative annoyed Barton, as he preferred *Yesses. Fridays.* Leah had an annoying habit of using decimals, too, but she was too effective at procuring Cuban cigars to sack. He was composing a suitable rejoinder when another Leah next email, with photos attached, preempted it.

Leah wrote: *Maybe, it is a rare Naples East Bay Shore White Ibis!*

Intrigued by that impossibility, Barton looked at the photos that included a tree stump with a shirt and tie.

~ ~ ~

For half an hour, Ian shifted to mining his dialog with Evie for nuggets he could use in his books. Occasionally, he flicked back to his foreclosure-themed sequences. He was mired in his fictionalized favorite lien foreclosure: The *JJ Amos – Kamila Cabrera* case made no sense to him in reality, but he was hoping to spin into something vaguely believable for his book. He was still spinning, mostly over JJ's uncharacteristic behavior in the case when he looked up to find 7:02 AM staring him the face.

Ian had nailed down Evie's answer in a few minutes but allowed her time to get home and nap before placing his call to her *Simara* phone.

He felt ambivalent over Evie's appropriation of the name. He had thrice killed and restored Simara as a central character in his lone half-finished Science Fiction novel, years earlier. The name of his first female character had an iconic resonance for him, and Evie knew it. Still, it was a nice hit.

"*Write what you know*. The first rule," Evie had reminded him. "You know less about creating women than God did. And you know nothing about the Crab Nebula."

He got no answer on two tries. He called Evie at her personal cell number.

"I couldn't get Simara."

"I think I told you that the second time you killed her." Her yawn sounded forced. "I must have dozed off." Her voice was clear and normal. She had not been dozing. "Let me call you back. You can bill me the usual rate for the last hour."

"My usual rate explains why I'm here, and you're there."

"And yet our souls are still connected," she said, using her teasing tone. "Must be through the Crab Nebula."

Ian typed away, but only to make the sound of keys.

"Your phone is very sensitive." She laughed, without its usual tinkling. "I can't wait to read that line. Will *my* character get to remind your character of the *Crab Nebula*?"

"You and I are not characters. I promised you to Leo," he said, of Claire's husband and his aspiring *comrade in yarns*. "The truth is I can't duplicate you. You don't even photograph well, I'm told."

Evie hesitated. "You can use that line, too. If it is not too sweet for your hero. I will call you right back."

Evie called on a different burner. "How does Simara sound."

"It is your voice, so it sounds... the way you sound."

"Thank you and that was informative."

"It is much better than the other one. Do they have that at 7-Eleven? I might buy one. Samara seems to like it."

"Please don't, Ian. No one is watching you," she said. "So..." She let the word hang.

"I believe my assignment was for a *yes or no* opinion," he said. "So. *Yes*. That's all you need, right?"

"That's it. Thanks." She added, her voice flat. "I owe you."

Ian then knew Evie was highly distracted. She would never owe him anything. "What is it?"

"I'm tired."

"Evie, I –"

"I love you, too." She sighed. "Oh, shit. You didn't say it."

"You can't help showing off your insight. It's embarrassing," he said. "But I was going to thank you again for the granite counter tops."

"You're welcome. And..."

"Of course, I love you. No, *too* required."

"Thank you. There's something you should know."

"Uh huh."

She waited. "I have a source. At Ibis."

"You what?"

"I can't say more than that," she said quickly. "But they have... kept an eye on you for me."

"No more email for Claire."

"No, not Claire –"

"Leo. Who is obsessed with you, you well know."

"Leo barely knows me."

"It didn't stop me."

Evie gave a one-note laugh. "My, you are sweet, tonight... this morning. But, no, not Leo. It's a client. And, therefore, I can't tell you."

"Your clients are billionaires."

"Not all of them and I have no idea how much... Jesus, I tell you too way too much."

"I do need a burner of my own," Ian said. "Next time you're here, you can say 'Is that a burner in your pocket...'"

She said nothing for a moment. "Sorry, I was fanning myself." Her laugh was almost back to normal." By the way, there is something in the water at Ibis Creek."

"Tell me about it."

"An owner reported it. Her name is Sybil."

"She is an early riser.

"Well, fortunately, she saw something. In your Bog. You –"

"It's not mine. I just named it."

Evie made a sound, air rushing in, a gasp. Evie breathed audibly for a heartbeat or two.

"Evie, come on."

"All I can say, Ian..."

"Is?"

"I'm *so* glad you hate swimming."

~ ~ ~

After Evie hung up, without further comment, Ian pulled up the Ibis Creek Director Message Board. Exclusively intended for director and manager access, the passwords had not been changed since before Claire's term on the board. Owners could use the system to alert the board or Collins about things to be ignored in a hurry.

Sybil had seen something white – something wearing white – on the Bog's surface. Something red decorated the something white.

"It's a tie." Ian jumped from his chair and charged into his second bedroom. JJ Amos immediately sprang to mind. Perhaps, there were other fools who would wear a white shirt with a red tie, outdoors, late at night or early morning, in Naples, but Ian knew JJ would.

He changed into something disposable. He had plenty, the closet full of *northern* clothes from his Pittsburgh days. He tried but could not throw most out, a testament to Evie's good taste.

From the bathroom, he grabbed a couple of the towels she had picked out for the condo.

It annoyed Ian that he felt a little ashamed about his conclusion, but it had to be JJ Amos. JJ simply could not do anything informally or half-decently. That included, Ian would wager, tread water.

Chapter 3

Up to his waist in goo, Hugh shooed the white bird from the protruding stump that had snagged the body's upper sleeve. He did not want to hurt the Condominium's stubborn namesake.

On closer study, Hugh realized that the bird's bill was tan and straight. Its elongated *S* of a neck announced it as an egret. Hugh liked egrets. He agreed with Barton Abbot that the standard white ibis – often seen on a beach, soaked lawn or a McDonald's drive-thru – looked strange with their orange legs and curved beaks.

The unruffled egret rewarded Hugh by repositioning three toes one inch to the left.

"Either help or get going." Hugh found that comment worked reliably on people.

The egret unbent its neck for a last look down at the body, then at Hugh. It then took wing so gracefully, that Hugh had to watch it, as relief from the floater's awkward bobbing.

Dueling squawks interrupted his thoughts. Two turkey buzzards sat atop utility poles on either side of the Bog. The vultures waited for Hugh to deliver their breakfast over to some dry land. The big redheads had less use for floating carrion than Sibyl Foster. Wading in six feet of water was for taller species. They preferred road-side asphalt, both as a solid runway and a place mat.

Hugh preferred blacktop, too, though for different reasons. He had grown up in a Jersey suburb and associated grass with enforced mowing for a *lousy four bits* a lawn. To make his summer job worth something, he had taken to raiding the occasional street-side mailboxes on Social Security check day, while cutting a neighbor's lawn.

Much as he hated grass, he had, as an adult, *volunteered* for some green work, along Virginia state roads. The point, at that time, had been to get out of *the yard,* not on one. He had done two tours in Federal prison for the offense of getting caught.

He no longer did lawns, pruned trees or raked mulch. He contracted with others to do that for him, principally his near friend and quasi-partner Jose *Chiky* Gomez.

Chiky's was the first of four small landscapers in Collier and Lee Counties around which Hugh – or rather Hugh's Caribbean trusts, based in Nevis – built Quadrant Landscaping. The trusts housed Hugh's secret assets and supplied what Hugh and Jeanie, his second wife, called *suitcase cash*. One way another, the cash came into Florida in someone's suitcase, usually by private plane.

Hugh had learned not get his hands dirty. Aside from a dunk in the Caribbean Sea, he rarely got his feet or his hips wet. He was chalking up a new experience, he thought, as he finally gripped the back of the white collar with one hand and the belt with the other. He initially considered the tie lying on the back of the shirt as a handhold, but he turning the body face-up did not appeal to him.

The sleeve finally tore away from the stump. The belt and the collar button held.

Ian Decker had joined Chiky on the bank of the Bog. Ian looked from Hugh to the towels over his forearm and back. He threw them down and began to wade in. Chiky hesitated but followed until the water reached his crotch.

He slowly inched backward until the water was at calf-level.

Though Hugh would not have worried about Ian Decker being chin-deep in anything, he knew that Chiky could handle water at most from a sprinkler or an *Aquafina* bottle. Chiky had given up on his lone foray outside of landscaping, Rookery Bay Pools, LLC when he had been forced to work in the deep end. He sold his Limited Liability Company for peanuts it to another LLC owned by a certain Nevis-based trust. Half of the new LLC was sold to an undisclosed fourth party, named Royal Collins.

"I swim like a grouper without the gills," he told Hugh later.

"Groupers are bottom feeders, Chik."

"Si."

Hugh waved Chiky back. "Get up on the bank, Chik. I'll float him over. Ian, stick close to the... what do you call it? The shore? The bank?"

"The Ibis East Bog Shore?" Ian guessed. "We're in an unofficial lake."

"Okay. I'll need you to help push him up onto the east shore. Chik, you can grab him there. He weighs a ton."

"Who is it?" Chiky happily pulled himself out of the water.

"I can't tell, but it looks like he's wearing wool slacks and an Oxford shirt," Hugh said. "I think the tie is orange."

Heartened in a dismal, petty way, Ian said, "Sybil said it was red."

"From a distance, maybe."

"So, Hugh, looking for a lawyer?" Ian asked.

"Not hardly." Three federal attorneys continued to clock overtime to revoke Hugh's *supervised release* and to search his couch for buried treasure. They could not even identify how much he had sunk into his Caribbean havens. His asset-protection lawyers Hugh was happy to pay.

"I suppose not." Ian had discovered, tracked and fictionalized Hugh's most colorful frauds. Hugh had inspired him more than anyone – Evie excepted – therefore, Ian had grown to like his version of Hugh Barrett, Scoundrel. He had kept the truth about Hugh's past close, sharing it only with Claire and Leo Hunter. He had run the character and plot line by Evie, under the usual and transparent pretense that had made it up on his own. Most of their old habits ignored the divorce decree.

"Nonetheless, Hugh," Ian said, "I think you've got another one. JJ Amos."

"No shit."

"I think so. White shirt. Call it a terra-cotta tie with a red crosshatch. Wool suit."

"Damn. Sounds like JJ?"

As Hugh guided the body to the shore, it let loose some noxious gas and sank a little deeper.

"Now, it sounds like JJ," Ian said.

Chiky let out some relaxed air himself. Three of his undocumented workers had not shown that morning, but bandanas were not ties and jeans were not wool. All of Chiky's regulars for his southeast Naples crew had checked in with him by 7:00 in the Ibis Creek clubhouse parking lot. On most other days, they met up at Quadrant's office, but Ibis Creek was on a bus route.

"Shit!" The deep muck sucked off one of Hugh's socks. He had refused to chance his expensive Mephisto loafers, braving the water in his socks.

At that, Chiky warned him about snakes in the Preserve. "But not very big ones."

"Now? You tell me, now?"

At that moment, Ian arrived. "The snakes are usually on the surface. Your socks are safer than your wallet. That's kind of ironic, isn't it? Considering."

It was not until the second sock oozed off that Hugh started worrying about his wallet's grand and his iPhone buttoned into his back pockets. "Thanks, Ian."

"You forget, Hugh. You *are* my hero." Ian nudged Chiky back. "Get up on the grass, Chik. We'll need you and your guys to pull him up from there."

"Jean. Juan," Chiky called as he knelt on the grass. His crew came forward. Upon getting the 7:10 call from Hugh, Chiky texted his two most trusted men – one Haitian, the other Dominican – from their pruning duties around the back of Building Seven. Its Unit 105 had a bank foreclosure notice on it. Jean had muted his cellphone ringer to peek in the windows of 7-105; consequently, it was not until he eyed his cell screen to start an update for Chiky that he saw Chiky's *Meet me at the Bog behind Building 8.*

A minute earlier, Mara Collins had phoned Hugh about Sibyl Foster report. Mara had scheduled Hugh for that morning's monthly landscaping tour. "Sybil's in a tizzy over something white in the Preserve. Let me know what brand of trash bag it is, please."

Hugh's first thought had not been *Glad or Hefty* but whether one of Chiky's immigrant lawn mowers had slid into the Preserve without the required documentation or company shirt. In either case, his wife and partner Jeanie would be livid. Hugh loved Jeanie, but she did have priority issues.

Long before he heard the whoops of several Sheriff's cars, Hugh knew he would be the first interview in any investigation of JJ's suspicious death. Detective Lieutenant Gabe Hubble and his people seemed unable to grasp of the import of the term *White Collar Criminal*.

A cautious man would have stopped short of a rescue. Mara, as was her way, had requested a report, not action. Hugh had felt sure that the body's movement came from the wind, leading him to hesitate, if only for a moment. It had not seemed right to leave the guy in the water.

"Pretty early for you, Ian," he said.

"I was still awake," Ian replied. "Trying to finish that chapter with you as my hero."

"You're still on Chapter two?"

"Your character needs a believable one-eighty." Ian reached for the body. "A work in progress."

"Easy, Ian," Hugh said, as he pushed the body closer. "He may not hold together very well. Use his belt."

Ian hooked the belt and tugged. The body held. "I think we're okay."

Hugh eyed a long, congealed gouge in the head. "That must have hurt like hell." He pushed. Ian pulled. When they had the guy close enough, Chiky took over the belt and the three of them rolled the body up the bank. Jean and Juan helped Chiky finish the job onto the grass.

Even a cursory look at the bloat above the tight collar said that the *job* had begun several hours earlier.

The red of a buzzard's head flashed onto a branch of the nearest pine. Fortunately, the nearest pine branch was a hundred feet away and forty feet above the water.

Hugh waved at the bird, with no effect.

Ian pinched his nose. "I liked him better under water." He waved the odor toward the Bog.

"Don't do that," Chiky said, nodding to the vulture. "To him, that smells like steak."

"More like *brisket*," Ian said, once they had rolled the body to its back. "No offense, JJ."

"Too bad." Hugh sighed at the certainty that no one would miss JJ, except, *perhaps*, his estranged wife, Sally.

"*Jerky*," Chiky said, thinking aloud of a beef he thought best applied. "Not steak."

"So you knew him," Ian said.

Chiky shrugged. "He worked for the boss here. But everybody has *familia* he ran out of their places. Me, it was Raul, my cousin. He had one at Pelican Glades. Raul went back to Nicaragua to stay out of court." He did not add that he had helped some Bolivian buy Raul's unit after the 5th 3rd Bank finished its own three-year foreclose lawsuit.

"That was JJ at his best."

"Sad to say, Ian, if it's true."

"Sad to say, then."

"He was a hard man," Chiky said. "Not now, so not sad."

A voice boomed from a few yards away. "Should have known you'd be in the middle, *Mr.* Decker." Rich Basehart was once the tallest deputy in the Collier County Sheriff's department. Several inches had since slipped down to his waist and slumped shoulders. His patrol encompassed the south end of East Naples, including Ibis Creek. He often attended the association's board meetings and liked to sit near Claire and Ian near whenever Mara wanted him to add *presence*.

"Anything to help."

After waiting for several sirens to stop one at a time, Deputy Basehart addressed JJ. "Dandy much, guy?"

"He's a lawyer. JJ Amos," Chiky said, distaste masked. The distaste was for the intrusive deputy. Chiky was over JJ.

"Hello there, Chiky. Barrett," Deputy Basehart said. He looked at JJ's body and chuckled. "Hmm. *Land Shark.*"

Ian refused to laugh until he knew whether the deputy meant the old Saturday Night Live skit or the Jacksonville-brewed beer. "One too many, maybe."

"You're not that young, Decker. The Land Shark. You know, SNL."

"Good one," Ian admitted. He regretted the comment as he watched the deputy's big head nod triumphantly. "If you need a preliminary ID, Hugh, Chiky and I all know JJ Amos, and that's him."

Hugh helped out. "It looks like he, JJ, has a nasty gash. On the right side of his head. Near the back. He must have…" Hugh stopped to consider the possibilities for the first time. Until that moment, Hugh assumed JJ had slid into the water and hit his head, but the whack could have come first. "He hit his head in the water." Hugh much preferred the accident theory to keep the detectives out of it. "It must have knocked him out."

"Makes sense, Barrett, but I've got to secure the scene," Deputy Basehart said. "What's left of it."

Ian could not resist. "Great. Now, we'll have your *superiors* all over the place."

The Deputy shot Ian his standard *intimidation* look. Ian returned it with a smile.

Two EMT techs sauntered toward them. One carried a black body bag. Behind them, came two firefighters and two more deputies, all greeting each other casually as if it were more first-responder reunion than emergency. Dispatch had designated the morgue as the victim's next stop.

Hugh recalled his promised report to Mara. He checked his back pockets, relieved that his wallet still in place, as was the iPhone. The latter was less useful. "Deputy

Basehart, would you please call Mara and let her know what happened. She and JJ worked together, often."

The deputy nodded, but said, "Can't do that. We don't know what happened. Or do we, Barrett?"

"I meant, that it was a body, and it was JJ."

As Chiky steered Juan and Jean clear of trouble, Ian and Hugh headed toward the gap between the two buildings. Ian glanced back and clicked his tongue. "Round up –"

Hugh sighed and stopped. "Don't say it."

"No offense, but you *are* the usual suspect," Ian said. "And Sanders Tilden is the crew that covered your ass last year."

"Interpreting the truth is not covering anyone's ass." Hugh glared at Ian. "It's what you guys get paid for."

"As if." Ian held up his hands to signal the end of the debate. "I mean it was in the paper, you, your pal Sanders and a Federal judge. And JJ was your collection guy. Basehart doesn't need the imagination he doesn't have to look at you."

"Nolan Sanders is *one* of my lawyers, yes," Hugh corrected him. "Friend? Who has a lawyer for a friend?"

"I'm hurt, but touché."

They watched the EMT's roll the body onto the open black bag and peer at JJ's head wound.

"Did you have anything going with JJ?" Ian asked.

"Minor stuff, collections." Hugh squeezed his temples, though he recognized Ian's tone as benign. "He handled them for us, until early this year. It's funny, he was as sophisticated as a dog with a bone. But don't tell him it's not his bone." Hugh had admired the way JJ used his limited capacity to put the fear of God into management companies stalling payments to up their kick-backs. Not that JJ knew about the latter. "At the beginning of the year, though, he got this weird bug about improving himself."

Ian grimaced. "Like that could happen. He's with Sanders."

"I thought you had a hand in picking them."

"*Mea culpa.*" After Claire and Ian had deposed a prior board, he had consulted in the search for a new manager and law firm. Royal Collins had come in first. "Ibis had a thirty percent shortfall in assessments and Sanders' collection work was recommended by every management candidate we talked to. JJ's doggedness, as you put it, was frequently mentioned." He shrugged. "When Collins took a cursory look at our four hundred grand in past dues they refused to sign on without Sanders. And then, bingo, we got you, too."

"You got *Mara* and me. Admit it. That's a sweet two out of three."

"I'll have to look *sweet* up in my dictionary."

"I know JJ did the job," Hugh said. "Ibis always pays on time, these days."

"It took a while, but JJ got most of the money. I didn't like his tactics or his ethics, but I can't argue with the results."

"I think ethics are all about somebody else's hindsight, Ian."

Again, they looked at JJ, his tie sliding slowly across the black bag, as a new, tinny siren neared.

"Oh, fuck," they heard Deputy Basehart say, sparing them further reflections on anyone's version of hypocrisy.

Deputy Basehart set his shoulders when the siren cut off. Portable sirens lacked resonance and were the hallmark of the plain-clothes deputies or the detectives. "Shit. It would be Webster," he said, as a smiling woman in a light gray suit approached.

Chapter 4

Detective Nicolina Webster had been slim as a girl, but police academy training and gym time had transformed her body but had not made her any taller than her five foot six inches. While not physically imposing, she normally walked with an aggressive posture and gait. For the wet Ibis Creek grass, she clipped her stride in half.

She knew the layout of the complex, having worked several cases in uniform: Three break-ins, two domestics and a drug overdose. In her second year as a Collier County Special Crimes, she had handled a suicide, by pistol, at Ibis Creek. She responded to a few more domestics and a couple odd-ball complaints about a black bear eating Chinese food. Because she knew Ibis Creek, she had even gotten a peeping Tom, even though she had moved to the General Crimes Bureau.

The peeper, late the year before, came to her with barely enough vague statements to justify detective review. She immediately farmed it out to a rookie Special's detective. She unofficially followed up with a text to the rookie who replied that nothing had come of it.

When the latest Ibis Creek call came in, her Bureau's boss, Lieutenant Gabe Hubble, called her.

"You get a body in the lake. Ibis Creek. You've worked it, right?"

"If it is the one down Naples East Bay, they don't have a lake."

"I hear it's in the middle, Nicolina. You'll find it."

"How?"

"That's in Basehart's territory. You can't miss him."

"Oh, yeah. He'll be the guy blocking out the cell tower."

So informed, Nicolina had prepared her best, toothiest smile for red-necked Deputy Basehart. She beamed it at him from forty feet away. She rarely smiled on the job, she had one just for the old-school, white uniforms, like Rich Basehart. Much as he had improved through the Sheriff's diversity training, he struggled to keep a sneer at bay at the sight of Latins or females who outranked him, as plenty did. Deputy Basehart was a so-called Community Deputy, more PR flack than crime-fighter.

Maybe, she thought, all cops were, anymore.

"Hello, Deputy Basehart." Nicolina had once employed a discernible Cuban accent when addressing the likes of Deputy Basehart. As a proud second generation Cuban-American girl, she had liked to mimic her grandmother's accent. After a while, she dropped the affectation because both Hispanics and whites resented it.

Even Brandon, her former husband, had wearied of her ethnic pride, among other things.

She held out her hand because she knew the deputy preferred a polite wave from women.

Deputy Basehart grumbled, "Detective," but returned her firm shake weakly. "Looks like an accident to me. Fell in and drowned. Name's JJ Amos. Not a resident. He is… was the collection lawyer for the association. Nasty piece of work. They say."

"I know the name." Nicolina had focused on three things as she approached: Deputy Basehart towered over her and still seemed to think size mattered; the EMTs had the body under control; the scene was not marked off by yellow tape. Because she had not yet looked beyond the body, the word *drowned* surprised her. She did not leap to that conclusion from the fact that the body was soaking wet. It took her another second to see what lay beyond the body. "Where the hell did that come from?"

"He fell in."

"Yeah. I mean *what* he fell in." Gabe Hubble had mentioned a lake, and there it was, where the Preserve used to be. She had seen the Preserve as trees, bushes and rampant weeds. She also knew the so-called Ibis Creek was a figment. "I thought Barton Abbot was too cheap for a lake?"

"Mr. Abbot planned for one, but the County said no," Deputy Basehart said, expert that he was in his Community Patrol area. "Last June 2012, it didn't drain very well. This year's worse. It might as well be Karen."

Karen Street, off Bayshore, flooded every time it rained for fifteen minutes.

"You were last here the summer before," Rich said. "That one was normal. Last year, this year, not so much."

"Yeah. I remember last June. Half the streets looked just as bad." The water rippled and leaves moved very slowly right to left. She turned her head clockwise by degrees and let the breeze blow her black hair as a weather vane. She wore it just long enough, mid-neck, to pull back into a ponytail, which she had forgotten to do in the rush to get out the door. The breeze was blowing west, left.

The flat blades of grass between the body and water were extra flat. She pulled out her iPhone from her purse and tapped on it. "The grass is a mess. What size shoe do you wear?" She raised both eyebrows to let him know she was kidding.

"That's need-to-know. Sensitivity training and all that."

Nicolina had never considered Rich Basehart comic, but she laughed at that one. He inched up in her esteem. "Now way the EMTs did that."

"A couple of guys dragged Mr. Amos out." Rich nodded toward Ian and Hugh.

"Noble." Her index finger moved about the virtual keyboard. "But not for us."

Deputy Basehart watched her Cuban hair shifting in the breeze above her shoulders and blocked any further thought with his sensitivity training. "I wouldn't have expected it."

The words caused her to glance up from her phone. She had to arch her neck. At six feet seven, he had over a foot on her. "Yeah. What little *scene* we have here would be a waste of tape."

The statement reminded Deputy Basehart that he had not ordered marking the accident scene with police tape. In his position, he was rarely in charge of a suspicious death scene. "My thoughts exactly, Detective."

"Any sense of the timing. When he went in?"

"Mara Collins, the manager here, told me that he was with her until 10:00 last night." Basehart hastened to add, "She called me. I'm the Community Deputy here."

Nicolina nodded but was not pleased. "Yeah. Fine. I'll talk to her later."

"They were at a meeting until then. Pelican Paradiso. You know it?"

"Yeah. The nannies are all from Columbia. The University, not the country."

"And they make too much to live here," Deputy Basehart agreed. "Anyway, Mara said she went home. Mr. Amos was thinking of stopping at Blue Martini like they did after most meetings. No matter what, though, he couldn't have gotten here before 10:30."

"Good work. We've got the start of a window." Nicolina returned to browsing the weather data she had retrieved. She bookmarked the page. "All night, from that point, from 10:30, the wind came in from the east, in the low teens. It shifted from the northeast a couple times, but it was always blowing toward the Gulf."

"Like now."

"Yeah." The trees were thick at the east end of the Preserve and thinned out westward. From where they stood, they could see all the way across the Preserve. "The entry point has to be to our right, but not too far."

"Okay," Deputy Basehart said. He had not considered the wind and the trees. "There are a lot of trees to come through. Mr. Amos, I mean."

"That's what I'm thinking, too." She let Deputy Basehart have his part. As she studied the pattern of the ripples through the trees and undergrowth, the likely avenue emerged. "On the other side, the north side, about half way to the right from here. The pines are thinner and sparser. They get less light, sunlight. Let's get your guys to secure that area." She doubled down on her disarming mode. "What do you think, Rich?"

"With these conditions, Detective, I think it's an accident." Rich's attitude responded to the respect. "But we got here too late. They'd pulled him out already."

She followed his eyes to the two men behind them and finally studied them. She recognized only one, the handsome one, but him she knew immediately. "Hugh Barrett? Why does that make me think *crime scene*, huh, Rich?"

Rich smiled at the familiar address. "The other one is almost as much trouble."

"Can't be."

"His name is Ian Decker. He is one of those condo commie retired types."

Nicolina could not stop the double-take. The guy looked pretty average, taller, perhaps, than Hugh, thicker trunk.

Rich Basehart caught her reaction. "He doesn't look like it, but he's all new shorts and sandals, and *we got rights* kinda bull… stuff."

"Got it: Bullshit. We all know the type." Nicolina gave Rich is due. Condo activists were the bane of the Sheriff's Department's community contact center. She recalled a certain Claire Hunter, lurking around Nicolina's Ibis Creek investigations. Somehow, Claire had gotten her direct email address and showered it with dozens of messages for the ensuing year. "I take it the Collins girl needs you to keep Decker and Claire Hunter in line?"

Taken aback at her accurate guess, Rich admitted, "At some meetings, I had to lend a hand. She and Decker stir things up."

Nicolina reassessed Ian Decker using the roughly similar Hugh as a reference. They both had medium brown hair. The holistic type, Nicolina did not pick apart men's features. She saw Ian as not bad looking, if no Hugh Barrett. Ian was enough thicker and taller than Hugh that he should have seemed the bigger of the two; perhaps, his unassuming air offset the differential.

She had trouble seeing Ian Decker as upsetting a board meeting enough to spur Mara Collins to call in a Deputy Community Liaison, like Rich Basehart. "I'm surprised Mara any needs help. Especially with any male."

"Maybe." He lowered his voice. "Unless he's gay."

Nicolina did not get that vibe, but the *Mara Effect* would neutralize most straight guys. "Yeah?"

"You wonder. Anyway, you know the type," Rich said. "Wasn't up to it, not in the real world. Now, he thinks he's a tiger in his own jungle." Rich added, with a laugh, "He calls himself a writer instead of a real estate agent. There's that."

"Two points for him."

"Anyway, I took care of him and Claire Hunter a couple times. That was enough to calm things down. You remember what she's like?"

"Yes, I do. I even kept some of her emails. In case, I have to shoot her." Nicolina gestured toward Ian and Hugh, to come forward. Then, she sneaked a half smile for the deputy. "I'd appreciate it if you would secure the scene over on the mid-northeast side, Rich, Those two civilians have screwed up this one so badly, it's toast. We'll start getting more onlookers after breakfast. And get some shots of the grass before you walk on it, okay?"

"It looks like there is part of his shirt torn off on a stump, too. In the water."

"Good. Take a few shots of that, too. We can get someone from CS to wade in later. No one else is going into that much water."

"On my way, Detective," Rich Basehart said in his official voice. He pointed to a couple bored deputies and led them away along the side of the Bog.

"Nice to see you again, Hugh," she said, with a delayed smile. "And thanks so much for compromising the scene."

Hugh shook her hand. "Yeah, June, July and I all apologize, Nicolina."

Ian raised an eyebrow at the exchange. "Ian Decker. I helped with the scene." He held out his hand.

"Hello, Mr. Decker. Deputy Basehart had some nice things to say about you." She shook is hand firmly and held his eyes long enough to establish her authority. She did not like that appraising look in his hazel eyes, a look that said he was analyzing details. "But he chose not to. Detective Nicolina Webster."

Ian had already evaluated her from a distance and as he approached: She was attractive, completely filling out her suit, more with sinew and grit, he guessed, than anything else. He focused on the intensity of her eyes, her best feature. "Basehart must love you, Detective."

"He might surprise you." She turned to Hugh. "Any observations? Or did you just go for a dive?"

"Now that you ask," he said, "the grass looked normal."

"Undisturbed?"

"Chiky was due to cut it today, but not at that hour. As a professional," he said, with a smile, "I immediately its length. And how wet it was, for cutting."

Nicolina drew her finger across her high forehead to keep from laughing. She knew Hugh and grass were estranged. "That does help." She hesitated before asking, "When did you get here? To Ibis, I mean?"

Hugh smiled. "About 7:00. I'll be on the gate camera."

"You, Mr. Decker? Did you notice anything?"

Ian took a moment. He decided to leave out everything before he left his lanai. "Mostly, that Hugh had taken off his shoes. And that Chiky Gomez acted like the water was caustic."

Nicolina had known Chiky Gomez for years, originally as an observant, civic-minded friend of the Department and purveyor of cigars. He was Hugh Barrett's main contractor for Quadrant, which meant there was likely more to Chiky than she would ever learn. She would interview him after Hugh. "And when did you get here, Mr. Decker?"

"A little after Hugh. I saw Chiky coming when I left my lanai." Ian waved toward his building. "I live in Building Two. Unit 102."

Nicolina glanced down the lawn toward Building Two. "Still an early riser, then?" Nicolina asked. "Deputy Basehart said you were retired."

"Only from a previous life."

The comment carried a tinge of regret, whether real or feigned. That she could not tell, annoyed Nicolina. A clear left ring finger reminded her of Rich Basehart's *gay* remark. She was still unsure.

She had watched the way he studied her from afar, but his interest seemed exactly that, *study,* more detached curiosity than any human being would like.

"You can tell me about that later," she said, her eyes back to skimming across the water. The deputies had emerged from the cover of the pines on the far side of the Preserve. "You guys knew Mr. Amos."

"More than enough, but not very well."

"Until a few months ago," Hugh said, "JJ did most of my collections work." To his finely tuned ear, that statement sounded too entangled, Hugh added, "Not lately, though. He was getting too fancy for scut work."

"Personal?"

"No, though he was in the middle of a divorce. Not messy. I think he wanted to handle bigger cases. Litigation, he called it, as if collections were not."

"JJ was passing collections to a couple junior guys at Sanders Tilden, "Ian elaborated. "He seemed to think our construction defect case was his ticket. It is, nominally, a twenty million dollar case."

Hugh smiled but said nothing.

"You sound skeptical, Mr. Decker."

"Does the phrase flim-flam cover it?" he asked in Hugh's direction.

Hugh grimaced.

Nicolina raised an eyebrow at Hugh. "He's deferring to an expert. Help me out, Hugh."

Hugh cleared his throat for effect. "Exaggeration is not flim-flam. It is litigation."

"Uh huh. Do either of you know what kind of car he drove?"

Each man shook his head.

"High-end, but used," Ian speculated. "He's only an associate at a cheap law firm."

Hugh said, "Mara would know. Mara Collins."

"Of course. Good. I have to talk to her anyway. She called it in," Nicolina said. "Mr. Decker, would you wait for me in your unit. I have a few more questions for you. Routine."

"*Routine* usually includes one fewer detective."

"And, Hugh, will you wait for me… in the Clubhouse?"

"Chik and I have a walk-around to do, but we can both be there in half an hour," Hugh said.

"Good. I'll talk to you first since you'll be closer."

"Closer?" Ian asked.

Nicolina ignored him. "Anyone else help you two?"

"Juan and Jose, Chiky's men," Hugh answered. "They helped with JJ, but that's it."

"Okay. I'll catch them last."

Ian gestured to the far side of the Preserve. "You think he went into the Bog over there?"

She shook her head at the unfamiliar term. "I missed that. What did you say?"

"He went into the water," Ian began. "We call it *The Bog*."

Nicolina detected the note of muted pride and wondered if Deputy Basehart was on to something. "And whose fault is that?"

Ian shrugged.

Hugh looked slightly more bemused and innocent than usual. "I just prune it."

"I can't imagine humility forbids, Mr. Decker."

"Naming rights *are* available." Ian knew he had struck the wrong tone. "Sorry. Yes, it, *Bog*, is mine."

Nicolina took the apology with a nod but kept the mental note: Smart-ass. "When I need to simulate how Mr. Amos got over here, I'll be casting a substitute. What do you say, Mr. Decker?"

"Yeah, Ian," Hugh said. "You still have white shirts, for sure."

"Some with pineapples."

Unsure, she looked at Ian for a moment before she laughed. "Pineapples would be fine, but more to the point, Mr. Decker. How did you know to come over? I mean how did you find out about the float... Mr. Amos."

Ian played it half-straight. "I saw Sybil's message on the website, about a swimmer in the Bog. It didn't sound too healthy."

"Good call, Mr. Decker."

~ ~ ~

Assured the Bermuda grass was not as slippery as it looked, Nicolina stuck with it. The back lawn was the shortest way to walk around the Bog, a fitting name as she now saw the extent of it. Staying behind the buildings, she walked east to the end of the Bog. A sidewalk lay between the grass and the Clubhouse parking lot. She used the pavement a few yards after ducking under the crime scene tape. Obviously, the deputies had recognized the possibility that JJ Amos had entered the stretch of grass backyards from the far end parking area beyond the sidewalk.

For a suspicious death, it was a pretty big scene they had roped off. She approved, even if her own suspicion was *accidental drowning*.

The Preserve better deserved the term *woodsy* than *boggy* at its east end. The close-packed, thin pines blocked any view into or across it. Across the parking area lay the Ibis clubhouse and pool area, both off-limits after 10:00 PM. On either side of the Clubhouse-Pool area sat twin dual story villas. If the hurricane shutters meant anything, Snow Birds still owned all four large units. Absent Snow Birds made lousy witnesses.

She surveyed the parking area separating the Preserve from the Villas, Clubhouse and pool. The lot was far enough away from the condo buildings that few residents parked on it after the pool and Clubhouse closed. She saw several recent-year, mid-range models and, from the look of it, a new Land Rover. The magnetic *Quadrant Landscaping* sign on the expensive SUV disclaimed Hugh Barrett's *personal* ownership.

Nicolina smiled at Hugh's artifice. She had to give him credit for driving a functional vehicle, instead of the V-8 roadster or Bentley both of which the Feds confiscated up in Virginia.

With a quick swipe through the Department of Motor Vehicle site, she found that JJ Amos had purchased a *pre-owned*, dark blue 2011 C-Class Mercedes that February. He had owned a Honda Civic before that. JJ surprised her with a tan/blue, *Helping Sea Turtles Survive* specialty tag, number, SFD 552. For lawyers, she expected a vanity plate like *ICU ISUEU.*

She had seen no car that color in the Clubhouse/pool lot, the surest place for JJ Amos to find a space late at night for his swim.

From her previous experience with Ibis Creek, full-time owners, relatives or tenants occupied less than seventy percent of the units in the main buildings; in summer, fewer. Even so, there were not a lot of free spaces at night, many residents opting out of their narrow garages and carports. Tenants tended to take the most convenient parking or use garages for storage. Ibis Creek had an unusually high tenant percentage, the curse of the failed flipper, more of them under water than its Preserve.

Not empathetic by nature, Nicolina sympathized. She and ex-husband Brandon ended up as flipper-landlords, as well. As an ambitious young couple, they had bought into the promise of an eternal rise of 2000's Naples housing prices. They had become landlords of two units in the same way as most Ibis Creek landlords: Picking 2006 to buy with more optimism than sense, not to mention the appeal of one percent down, adjustable rate mortgages with a complimentary toaster oven.

Like so many enthusiasts, their sure-fire investments had torpedoed the value of both their marriage and the asset pile they had to split. Hers was still down thirty percent from their purchase price. She did not care about Brandon's.

She resented relying on needy tenants, especially in the summer when half of Naples went north and half the air-conditioners went south. She hated selling at a loss even more. The rents were not bad, at least, just the renters.

Ibis Creeks tenants had proven useless witnesses in her prior investigations in the complex. Of course, accidental overdoses rarely made involved noise and, at Ibis Creek, at least, were truly inside jobs. Voyeurs, if any good at it, stuck to the shadows.

Nicolina looked down the edge of the Bog. It was not completely straight, but she could see most of the deputies, if not Rich Basehart. Well beyond, they had strung more yellow tape, using the near side of Building Seven as the perimeter, marking a broad, empty scene.

Even wet Bermuda grass did not hold footprints long. She followed the deputies' tracks close to the buildings, skirting the planted areas adjacent to the lanais. It was doubtful that anyone would have walked so close to the lanais after dark. In fact, it made little sense for a non-resident like JJ Amos to be behind the lanais at all.

From her new angle, Nicolina could see Rich Basehart loom over a deputy crouching to take photos with his phone. Deputy Basehart waved Nicolina toward him. "We were right, Defective."

Another deputy pointed to the grass between Nicolina and Deputy Basehart. "The grass doesn't show much, but the edge there does. By the water."

Several chunks of turf were torn.

"That tree." Deputy Basehart pointed toward one of the few thick pines jutting out of the water. "That looks like blood residue."

Nicolina aimed her cell camera and zoomed in. A line of reddish color had survived the rain. "The angle is possible. If he slipped." She keyed a speed dial. "It's about a match for his head wound."

She listened to the ring until her boss, Lieutenant Gabriel Hubble answered. "Hey, Gabe. I'm at Ibis Creek. That floater. I think we have the accident scene. We have an ID, too. He's JJ Amos, an Ibis lawyer."

"Accident?"

"Looks like. I need a couple CS techs. A tall one and one who can snorkel."

"You're in luck. Rain makes for a slow night if you don't do traffic. See you later."

"Hold on, Gabe." Nicolina muted her phone and redirected it for a couple quick photos. "Rich, send a couple guys to check for the car." She gave him the information. "I didn't see it in the back."

After Deputy Basehart had headed off to search the north side himself, Nicolina did a slow three-sixty. She refocused on the stained tree, a fit if JJ Amos had slipped and toppled into the Bog.

She activated the phone's speaker. "One thing doesn't fit: Why he was here?"

"If it is an accident, Nicolina, it doesn't matter."

"Yes, *Sir*."

When the Lieutenant did not respond, Nicolina said, "I mean, I'm not sure, yet."

"I know what your *yes, sirs* mean."

"Amos lives an hour north," Nicolina explained. "He was at Pelican Paradiso until 10:00. That's twenty minutes north. And, maybe, at Mercato. This is the wrong direction and..."

"And?"

"He's behind the buildings, which seems... *furtive* to me. And..." She hesitated, waiting for something to crystallize.

"*Furtive* isn't enough?"

A thought, maybe two, hung just out of reach. "Hey, that's your call, Sir," she said.

Chapter 5

Lieutenant Gabe Hubble's General Crimes' desk was housed ten minutes from Ibis Creek. He had one of the few wood desks and an office in the Criminal Investigations Division's cube-filled corner of the Collier County Government Complex. He put Nicolina on speaker as he exited the parking garage and turned right to Route 41.

Between Tampa and Miami, 41 carried the name *The Tamiami Trail*. Like the many fairly recent migrants, Gabe called it *41* because it was shorter.

"The deputies found his car," Nicolina said. "It's a dark, late-model Mercedes. I had the plate. I'm headed to it now."

Gabe got lucky and the light at 41 and Bayshore. "I'll be there in a minute. You may as well wait for me."

"Okay."

"There is a traffic cam at Bayshore and 41. May as well get the videos. That can wait 'til I get there, too."

Nicolina told Gabe that JJ Amos's Mercedes was parked in near the northeast corner of the complex. "They are wrapping it up for us now."

Gabe could hear Nicolina's quickened breathing. "Take your time, Webster. I'm passing The Real Macaw now."

She blew out some air and the phone's mic picked it up. "Good Happy Hour. Use Shoreview to cut over to Naples East Bay. Some of the other *views* are down to one lane."

"More new sidewalks."

"Nonstop Beautification."

The Bayshore/Naples East Bay area, south and east of Naples, itself, once hosted a very popular hooker, gun shops and bail bondsmen enclave. The County Commission had included the blighted neighborhood in Collier County's redevelopment agency (the CRA). Oddly, the County Commission delegated itself the CRA. According to the dissenting North District Commissioner, "it is just wasting my constituents tax dollars buying lipstick for someone else's pig."

The CRA renamed the two main drags, Kelly and Albright, to Bayshore Road and Naples East Bay Shores Boulevard, as a part of the still pending make-over. Gabe had come to Naples well after the transformation had begun. The old names *Kelly* and its less infamous twin *Albright* were historical artifacts to him, but, in his first Naples years, much of their legacy remained.

The re-branding – creating *Naples East Bay Shores Village* out of *that shit hole around Kelly and Albright,* from that same Commissioner – had happened before Gabe's arrival from Pensacola. The gentrification *talk* continued but seemed to him more forced than hopeful.

His left turn onto Naples East Bay Shores brought him to the boulevard-style planting that was still trying to justify the new names. It was getting there, in his opinion, and reminded him of another new creation in the area.

"Have you talked to Hugh Barrett, yet?"

"Briefly. I admit it made me wonder."

"Not his style."

"That's true," she said, "Still, I will check to see if JJ Amos still has a balance in his 401K."

Gabe turned left again and stopped at the Ibis Creek entry Call Box twenty feet from the gate. "What's our code?"

Nicolina told him and he keyed in the four numbers.

"Did Amos have one?" Once the security arms started to rise, Gabe nosed forward. It took another few seconds for the gates themselves to open. "Man, gates are boring."

"They've helped. It got better with them. And, yes, Sanders Tilden supposedly had a code. I have the Collins people pulling the gate logs. They have video, too."

Gabe passed through the gate. "Which way?"

"Left. You'll see us at the end of the north drive."

"Call about that traffic cam, would you?"

Nicolina assured Gabe she would and hung up.

The speed limit sign that Gabe ignored said 14 miles per hour. The speed bump sent his head into the headliner. He resolved, again, never to risk life in an association.

The area around the Mercedes looked like the Sheriff Department parking lot, with marked cars and CS vans double and triple parked. Few legitimate spots had opened up on the side. A flatbed had beaten Gabe to the scene and was repositioning itself to lift the Amos car and take it in when released. Gabe saw open slots beyond the jam but could not reach it. He simply added to the pileup.

Nicolina approached his car as he got out, her strong features skewed in annoyance. She waved Deputy Basehart over. "Still no keys?"

"Not in his pockets, no. If it's in the water..."

"Lieutenant, you know Deputy Basehart, right?"

Gabe did not usually interact with community liaisons like Rich Basehart, but the deputy covered the area close to the Sheriff's offices and was always around. Gabe shook the deputy's hand. "Yes, I do. No keys, Rich?"

"We haven't found them."

"No cellphone, either," Nicolina added. "They may be in Amos's jacket. It's in the back seat of the car..."

With a nod toward the flatbed, Gabe asked, "He's got a drill if we need it?"

"With that year Mercedes, we may." Nicolina stared at the Amos car. "Rich, will you give us a minute, please. "

Deputy Basehart shrugged and walked, slowly, away.

Nicolina used a stage whisper. "Sorry to have wasted your time, Sir, but it looks like a tragic accident."

Gabe took the cue. "Well, I'm here, so let's open the car."

She held him in place with a squint over her sunglasses and waited until the deputy picked up his pace. In a true whisper, she said, "Basehart is more territorial than most."

"Got it. What don't you want him to hear?"

"My uncertainty." She took a breath. "I want it to be an accident. I know Basehart does, too. This place has had its problems – The whole area has – but it has gotten a lot better, and Rich likes to claim half the credit."

"We do," Gabe said. "And our boasting has cost three vice and two robbery spots. We have more cars than cops. Even when real estate comes back, those cars will still sit."

Nicolina nodded and segued into a shake. "It feels off. As an accident. That's all."

"Furtive."

"Yeah. In a white shirt after midnight? Leaving his dark suit coat in the car? How furtive is that?"

"It's a condo. It's easy to fall asleep after an Early Bird dinner."

She gestured toward the buildings. "Not here. They have a lot of younger people, some in their twenties. Tenants, mostly. And there are some very nosy neighbors who stay up very late. JJ Amos knew that, them."

"You have someone in mind."

"I do," she said, turning to walk. "But the point is that Amos had to know it, too."

Gabe considered Nicolina's comments as he followed her. She was a good detective, with solid instincts. She had gone through a change recently – likely the divorce – that made her erratic personally but not professionally. Though he reserved judgment, he would not bet against Nicolina's take on a case.

Gabe and Nicolina walked under the yellow tape, held high by two deputies. He walked around the Mercedes, taking in its unmarred exterior condition and its sea turtle license plate. He met Nicolina at the driver's window. Inside, a dark suit jacket was half off of the back seat, carelessly thrown. There was nothing else, no briefcase, no files, no phone.

Through the back window, he saw that the car had the expected key-less ignition. Such up-market cars locked automatically when the key fob was beyond a few feet from the sensor and unlocked the driver's side when within range. Gabe matched Nicolina's speed in putting on the blue gloves always in their pockets. Before he called over the flatbed driver, he hesitated. Though knowing better, he tried the door.

The door hit him in the knee.

Gabe just stood there. As did everyone else.

"That shouldn't happen." First to thaw, Nicolina reached around Gabe to flick open the door locks and the trunk. She opened the back door and grabbed the jacket. She raised a set of keys with a Mercedes key fob from the left outside pocket to eye level. She turned her attention to the jacket pockets.

"This had to be a quick visit." She patted the upper pockets. "Nothing." Then she patted the lower pockets "His cellphone is here, too." She dropped the keys back into the jacket pocket and retrieved JJ Amos's smartphone. She feigned a throw to Gabe.

"Your case."

She turned on the Samsung. They all waited while it booted. "It needs a password." She looked at the screen. It had a faint outline of a box. Once her face was framed, an error message came up. *Not recognized.*

She started walking. "The car can wait, Lieutenant. Deputy Basehart secured the scene, please."

Rich looked at Gabe, who barely nodded before he set off after the detective. When he caught up with her, he asked, "What's the hurry?"

"JJ still here."

"And?"

"For sure, he's no Helen of Troy, but he's got a face that can launch a thousand apps."

~ ~ ~

Despite the facial recognition software on JJ's smartphone, his face failed to launch anything but an error message and the virtual keypad. Even the text was gone. His features had ballooned to new dimensions above the tightening shirt collar. At least, the tie was loose, all the way to the breast pocket.

"That button was not sewn on in Bangladesh," Gabe said, impressed with the collar's hold.

"I hadn't counted on ratio discrimination," Nicolina said, ignoring him. "Hell, I figured the eyebrows would be enough."

Jj had long, flat, dark eyebrows, just over his eyes, suggesting an overdose of Neanderthal genetic material.

Gabe retrieved the evidence bag with JJ's wallet. From the driver license, he read off the birth date. He brought a spare bag for the smartphone.

Several combinations of the digits failed Nicolina, as well. "Damn. Who doesn't use their birthday for a PIN?"

"Maybe the autopsy will dry him out some."

Before Nicolina deposited the SIII phone in the extra bag, she called over a tech from the ME's. "Would you unbutton his collar?"

The young man gave the flesh hanging over the collar. "It won't be pretty."

"I'll look away, promise."

The ME shrugged. He pushed up the overlapping skin and tried to grip the button. He looked up at Nicolina, then Gabe. "This is necessary, right?"

"Absolutely," Nicolina said, "maybe."

"It's hard to –" The button-hole gave way. JJ's swollen neck pushed against button number two. The tech opened that one, as well.

Though JJ's face relaxed sum, Nicolina said, "Press in on the sides of his face? Just a little."

The tech hesitated until she showed him the cellphone screen. "Oh. Oh, okay."

After a couple misses and gently increased compression, JJ's face opened the lock screen. His home screen popped into view.

Nicolina smiled at Gabe. "I am *so* after your job."

"Congratulations, Detective. You just proved to me that we should all stick to PINs."

Nicolina searched JJ's calls and his GPS history. Both were unusual. "His GPS is deactivated his GPS. He uses facial recognition but turns off his GPS?"

"A man who knows where he's been." Gabe was not sure if he had GPS on his own phone. He used the one in his car on occasion, but not on his phone.

The tech said, "It saves the battery to keep it off."

"His call log shows no calls between 9:00 and now. Nothing," Nicolina said. "It's like a dead zone."

The phrase did not register with either Gabe or the tech. The latter asked, "Is the cellular radio on?"

"Is the what?" she asked.

"You know. The cell service. Like airplane mode."

Nicolina felt the blood drain from her head as if it had not helped lately. "Oh." She checked the top row of the phone's display and saw the airplane icon. "Why the… He had his cell service off, too?" Her voice rose half an octave in exasperation. "Oh, shit. It says *No Service. No sim*."

The tech looked confused. "He pulled the sim card. That's just weird."

"My job is *so* safe," Gabe said.

"The guy's a God-damned lawyer, Gabe. You don't expect a lawyer to go that damned dark."

"It's small." The tech held two fingers half an inch apart. "A micro sim. Cardboard."

Nicolina ground her teeth. "And here I searched the jacket for something bigger than a postage stamp." The blood had rushed back into her face.

Gabe watched her for an extra moment pass before he made the needed concession to her recently short fuse. "You're right. It's smaller than lint."

Nicolina squeezed the offending smartphone. She appreciated Gabe's gesture and took a breath. His job was safe, she thought. She unzipped the body bag further and searched JJ's pockets. "It's a waterlogged mess in there, but I don't feel anything. Maybe, it floated away." She zipped the bag all the way closed. To the closest EMT guy, she snapped, "You can remove the victim, now." She shot Gabe a challenging look.

He responded first with a relaxed smile. "Me? I'm just here for the job security."

She felt her anger burst with a laugh. "Wait." She handed the bagged SIII to the CS tech. "Who uses sim cards, anyway?"

The tech misread her question as real. "All phones have them, but CDMAs, like Verizon..." He let the explanation at that once he read her face. He headed off.

"The lawyer in the dark, in the *dark*?" Nicolina said.

Together Gabe and she watched the EMTs roll the body away.

Gabe asked, "Can I go now, Detective Webster?"

Nicolina closed her eyes briefly and then looked at him. "Sorry. I just hate sim cards," she said with a smile. "But no, Lieutenant, sir. You are tasked with an interview."

"Barrett?" Gabe nodded. "I'll need another evidence bag for my wallet."

"Oh, no, you don't. I like Hugh." She felt her spirits rally all the way back from her own darkness. "You get the... What's a bigger pain than a dead lawyer?"

"Any other lawyer?"

"Shit. That's truer yet," she said. "I was going for the more relevant *a retired one*."

Chapter 6

Halfway along the Bog toward Ian Decker's unit, Gabe saw a standing figure watching him approach from a lanai. Once Gabe came within twenty feet, Ian opened his lanai door and waved Gabe in with a tablet.

"I was hoping to talk Cuba with Detective Webster."

Gabe opted a form of honesty. "She thought you might not annoy me. As much. I'm Lieutenant Gabe Hubble."

After they had shaken hands, Ian said, "Come on inside. It's still wet out here." Ian led the way into his living room.

His bedroom door was cracked open to their left. Like many condos, the dining area was open to the living room with a bar-like divider shielding half the kitchen. Another bedroom and bath were visible from where Gabe sat on Ian's couch. Everything seemed shades of off-white, rust, green or brown, but chosen by a decorator. The appliances were real, not faux, stainless, the sixty-inch LCD TV was black. Nothing looked especially inexpensive.

Taking a lounger adjacent, Ian said, "I was half punchy as well as wet. I didn't get any sleep, and a guy I thoroughly disliked was dead," Ian said. "I'm not usually annoying under such circumstances. Tell her I'll be better next time."

"Webster is a good judge of character, but how did you figure she was… of Cuban descent?"

"Genius is as much a burden as anything." Ian gestured with the tablet. "*Google* is more so."

"One good google leads to another, doesn't it? Or twelve." Gabe found the search engine more useful when a subordinate ran it. "So, what else did you learn in the last half hour?"

"Not to call a cop of Cuban descent the *H-word*."

"That would help." Gabe voiced a thought that had been lurking. "Or leave ancestry out of it. Webster's hot and cold on it these days."

"I don't expect to need that advice…" Ian began. "Will I?"

"Did you push Amos into the water?"

"No, I…" Ian stopped, taken aback. "Did anyone?"

"Maybe you should remember my advice," Gabe said. "It's a suspicious death until it isn't. It's Detective Webster's case, and you are part of it."

"Then it won't hurt if I show you something." Ian fiddled with the tablet. He enlarged a window with a four-pane view of four shots of the Ibis Creek gate. "This is the entry-gate video feed, live."

Gabe watched two cars approached in the right entry lane. That gate opened for the first, then began to close. Once the second car approached, the half-closed gate began to open. Another car approached in the left lane. A fourth followed very closely. "You watch this?"

"Watch this third car," Ian said.

The third car pulled up to the Call Box. The driver leaned out to hit three buttons. She sat back and waited. After a few seconds, the gate opened, and she drove through. The fourth car shot trough behind her. In both cases, the third camera pane showed the cars' license plates.

"That's just now," Gabe said, disappointed.

"It's not much help and, no I don't watch very often. Only when someone tells me to." Ian enlarged another window with a chat dialog. "A friend of mine keeps one eye on this feed from 10:00 through 1:00 AM. Even when she watches TV."

"Like last night?"

"As you can see from our *chat*," Ian said, "she saw a Mercedes just before midnight. 11:58, in fact."

In one window, Ian had a chat client open. Gabe saw the exchange between Ian and someone named Claire.

"Claire and I – Claire Hunter, across the Bog from here – We were chatting, briefly, around midnight," Ian said. "Starting at 11:59. As you can see, she had just seen a Mercedes at the Call Box."

"Amos's Mercedes?"

"She didn't know it at the time."

"I should be talking to her next," Gabe said.

Ian handed Gabe two business card, one his own and one Claire's. "She does some freelance appraisals now and then."

Gabe looked at both sides cards. "Yours says you are a lawyer. With a Florida ID. I thought you had retired."

"Some fates you can't escape. I'll always be a lawyer. It's like being a felon," Ian explained. "I would prefer to give you my novelist card, but I believe optimism, when printed, is bad luck."

"Back to the video."

"Yes. Any owner can view the live feed from any association camera. We have them at the gate and at the pool and in the Clubhouse. As far as we know, Claire is the only one who can't resist. There are four cameras covering the front gates: One for the driver at the Call Box and one that catches the plate. Another shows the entry gates, and the fourth shoots the exit gate, which is like filming a horse's tail as it leaves the barn."

"Anyone can watch?"

"Live, yes," Ian said. "The camera system records the videos and stores them on a DVR in the clubhouse. Owners can view the whole array, as you saw. Claire watches for people running the gate. It must be for fun since Collins never does anything about what she reports."

"Fun?"

"As in paint-drying fun," Ian said. "It gives her a reason to chat with me at midnight and me a reason to interrupt my work."

"Work? At midnight?"

"The optimism I spoke of? I am working toward earning that novelist business card. Four times over. I just started another book. Starting is easy. The end starts out easy, too. It's the in between that gets you and usually screws up the ending."

"How much have you made writing?"

"The price for half a novel is not very high."

"Gabe looked around him, indicating the condominium. "I assume you have a nice trust fund."

"If I did, you couldn't get at it without, say, a few hundred miles and some tiny umbrellas."

"Sorry."

"One sites one's trust fund on Caribbean islands."

Gabe wondered if Ian and Hugh Barrett shared Caribbean banks, but returned to the main topic. "So. Anyone can replay the gate video. Say, at high speed?"

Ian hesitated. "Do you have confidential informants who are not scumbags?"

"No, but maybe Webster will vouch for you."

Ian laughed. "Okay. The truth is that only…" He hesitated, to choose his words. "It's not me. Only Claire has administrative privileges. She can take you to the spot on the DVR. All I can do is take you to Claire."

"I find that hard to believe."

"I found the Administrator's page, but she has the password. I didn't want it."

"Why not?"

"All I'd do is play videos all day."

"How did you do your part?" Gabe asked. "Finding the page?"

"As often as the statute allows – the condo statute – Say, every month or so, I ask to inspect Ibis Creek official records," Ian explained. "After the usual fight with Mara Collins – she's the CAM in charge here…"

"Yes. I know of Ms. Collins."

"She thinks the records belong to her, so we squabble every time," Ian continued. "Then I scan records, including invoices for the most mundane things. Such as the gate service contract, the equipment and the DVR."

"So you know what the DVR costs. How does that help you?"

Ian held out his hand for the tablet. "I know the model number. Hell, I know the serial number, which helps." Once Gabe returned it, Ian tapped and swept with his right index finger. He waited for Google Drive to return a file, opened and showed it to Gabe. "That's the manual to the DVR." The tablet extended, Ian did a quick search of the manual. "The Admin site is right there. Just add Ibis Creek and stir."

"Do me a favor," Gabe said. "Get me a copy."

"I'll email it."

"And the video, too."

"That will have to come from Claire. We'll need your email address to do that."

"A video will be too big for my mailbox."

"It's only a few minutes. It'll be a gigabyte or two."

"I'll need the whole evening," Gabe said. "Figure 6:00 until dawn."

"That download will be a big one. Come on." Ian led Gabe toward the hall of his condo. "Hold on." He ducked into left front bedroom-office and sorted through a batch of USB drives. He picked a 64-gigabyte drive, still in its package. "Claire will copy it onto this. It cost twenty bucks, so she refuses to buy one. Hers are only two gigs."

Gabe turned over the drive several times, with suspicion. He waited for the quid pro quo that always followed. The silence became awkward as Ian waited along with him.

"You see the package. It's new." Ian said, pointing. "It is even says *guaranteed virus free.*"

"We have a protocol for externals USBs. We keep an old laptop to check them."

"Let's got get that video, then."

Gabe still hesitated. "In exchange for?"

"In exchange for? Twenty dollars is a rounding error for that trust fund you think I have." Ian was neither surprised nor annoyed. "It's a favor, Lieutenant, not a contract. Let's get over to Claire's. She will take us right back to 11:58 last night."

~ ~ ~

The Hunter condo was directly across the Bog from Ian Decker's, a ten minute at an ambling pace. Gabe and Ian took it in five. As they went, Ian briefed Gabe on the Hunter history as he knew it.

After her divorce and a winter of shoveling snow on her own, Claire moved to Naples from Delaware. She had long been a successful real estate appraiser before the move. She had a natural sense of value and a compulsion to be forthright.

Upon moving south, she studied the market in Lee and County Counties. With her divorce settlement, and bought into a small partnership to learn more. Her partners frequently dealt with Leo Hunter's mortgage brokerage. Unlike many in his business, Leo was conservative, but the marketplace required him to initiate mortgages when he knew better. Still, his exposure was lower than most when the S&L meltdown peaked in the early 1990's. At that time, he acquired several brokerages then on the ropes. He came to know the newly arrived Claire as brutally honest in her appraisals, refusing to inflate numbers to please buyers, banks and other mortgage brokers. By 1994, the real estate and mortgage market began to rise again, and Leo's operation boomed.

Leo knew booms do not last. He saw Claire as a hedge against the usual Florida real estate fever. He guaranteed her as much business as she could handle if she went out on her own. Claire jumped.

Neither had purely honorable motives.

Leo admired Claire's mixture of enthusiasm and honesty as much as her wavy red hair. It was a close call. Claire knew the market was heating up, and her appraisals reflected rising values, accurately, in Leo's mind.

Their relationship crossed over to personal, despite the complications of the business conflict. Their intimacy had remained closeted to protect the legitimacy of Claire's valuations. As time passed, they chaffed under the veil of secrecy. Leo's conservatism gradually infected Claire's valuations. They both knew the fever would break at some point. Leo lost mortgage business by hundreds of thousands in face value as he refused to write what his competitor, including banks, cheerfully took on.

Claire other clients' demanded ever higher appraisals to allow banks and brokers to lend more. Wall Streets appetite for mortgage-backed securities demanded more mortgages each month. Claire's appraisals were always *too low.* In 2006, Claire and Leo stepped back.

As they liked to tell it, Claire finally declared, "Let's retire so you and I can sleep together in public."

That declaration had triggered one engagement and two disengagements. They sold their businesses to feverish competitors and their individual condos at the peak and rented for a year. Many of the buyers were invited to the wedding.

"Seriously?" Gabe asked. "To the wedding?"

"I wasn't here then, but the buyers are friendly again. I've met them. They had some lean years, but the heat is on in Naples again. Clair and Leo rented here until 2009 when the prices were near the bottom."

"What about you? When did you buy?"

"Evie and I bought a few months later," Ian said. "Even as a tenant, Claire had kept track of the goings on here. As a recent buyer herself, she came over and introduced herself. I think I was assembling the TV stand and not very well. She gave me some excellent tips. Evie and I bought them a couple bottles of wine more expensive than we ever had at home. Claire knew the price and insisted we get half of our investment back."

"How was it?"

"Better than I'll ever drink again."

"I meant the *sharing.*"

"Leo found out I was a terrible carpenter and frustrated novelist. I found out he was a frustrated playwright and not much of a plumber. Different as they were, Claire and Evie hit it off immediately. We all did."

"All because Claire was retired enough to pay attention," Gabe said. "Good thing for you and me."

"It was nice to have friends already when I moved here."

"You traded one ex for two friends."

Ian's smile faded. "No offense to Claire and Leo, it wasn't much of a trade." He rang the Hunter's doorbell. "But, yes, it helped a lot."

"We can talk about *you* later," Gabe said. "Evie, too."

"Sorry. She can't help you," Ian said, as the door opened. "She's only been here four times. For a total of a month."

"If you're talking Evie," Claire said, "No wonder you took so long."

"You just heard half of our entire conversation about Evie," Ian said. "This is Lieutenant Hubble."

Claire extended her hand and gave Gabe a solid shake. "Ian emailed me about JJ. I realized, right away, that it was him at the gate. At midnight. His name did come to me, but… At midnight?"

"Why would it?" Ian agreed.

"I have the video queued up. The website kicked me off twice. It doesn't keep you logged in forever. Come on in."

Ian waved Gabe ahead of him. When Gabe was even with Claire in the foyer, he showed her badge. "Investigations run at their own speed, Mrs. Hunter," Gabe said. "And Mr. Decker was one of the men who pulled Mr. Amos out of the water."

"And with Hugh Barrett, no less," she said. "Hugh doesn't usually get the soles of his expensive shoes wet."

"He was the one who went in, Claire. I just helped him."

"Seriously?"

"Yep."

Claire looked at Gabe and then Ian. "I was expecting your *attractive detective*?"

Ian massaged the bridge of his nose. "You mean my attractive *female* detective."

Claire pretended to give Gabe an appraising once-over. "Of course, that is what I meant."

"Detective Webster is interviewing some others involved in finding Mr. Amos," Gabe said. "I'll have to do."

"I'm sure you'll… By the way, call me Claire. I'm sure Ian told you I loathed JJ but it's still a terrible thing," she said. "If only the board could keep the Bog… the Preserve drained properly. I've been telling them it's dangerous from day one, but especially starting last year. We got the Bog for three or four months. This year is almost as bad." She turned and escorted them to the living room. "We can sit in here. The lanai is too small for four. Sit. Lieutenant, grab that chair. It is the most comfortable." She pointed to an oversized, dark red leather recliner. "Ian will if you don't. He thinks it is his."

The first floor of the two-story *townhouse* had a layout similar to Ian's, with only one bedroom and a den. It had larger great room and kitchen large enough for a breakfast nook. A loft covered the entry kitchen and dining area. Unlike Ian's place, the unit had bold, coordinated hues and twice the furniture.

"I do not," Ian said to Gabe. "But I will gladly lend it to you." Ian took a small upholstered chair nearby.

Claire stepped onto the lanai where Leo sat, still in a world of his own making. With a red pen in his hand and lap full of fur named Dovey in his lap, he was editing the latest stage directions for the second act of his play. Claire had to clear her throat to get his attention. Leo turned his head with a wince, and his eyebrows shot up. "Oh. Hello, Ian. Who's your friend?"

"Come into the living room, Leo. Lieutenant Hubble is here about JJ Amos." While Claire waited for Leo to get Dovey off his lap and himself off his chair, she glanced at the top page of his play. "I don't know who is slower," she said. "You or Ian."

"I guess I am," Leo said. "Ian's halfway through three novels. I have half each of five acts."

"Four," Ian said. "Remember, I started the fourth in the series two weeks ago."

Claire grabbed an open laptop from the lanai table and stepped carefully off the lanai and over to the living room sofa. Leo and Dovey followed, the former weaving neatly between the sets of feet. She sniffed at Gabe's shoes while she waited for Leo to make his lap available again. When Claire sat and put her laptop in her own lap, Dovey reversed course. She leaped onto the sofa, strolled onto Claire's keyboard and looked at the screen.

"For God's sake, Dovey," Claire said, nudging her gently toward Leo. "She always does that." Once the cat had moved on to Leo's thighs, Claire used the touchpad to open the window with the video.

"It's a matter of principal," Leo said. "Newspapers, books, bills, dialog. If you want to look at something, Dovey will wake from a dead sleep to sit... That was a poor choice of words."

"We're not exactly in mourning," Claire said, as she put the laptop on the coffee table and turned it toward Gabe and Ian. "I have the Call Box camera's video paused at 11:58. You see the front of the Mercedes hood, the grill."

"Logo and all," Ian said.

"Ready?"

Gabe nodded.

"Here we go." Claire hit *play*. "I tried to get the camera's upgraded, so don't blame me."

Once the video started, Gabe saw an image of the Mercedes move forward until its driver's window was even with the Call Box. It was not possible to see the front of the Call Box. A white-shirted arm reached out of the window, coming up short of the keypad. An ill-defined face then appeared with a reddish streak on the white shirt. Claire paused the video. "I didn't notice last night, because, well, I didn't notice, then. The color's washed out, but that's a guy with a blur of red. It's a loose tie. Not very JJ, a loose tie."

"And you can see," Ian said, leaning forward to point. "You can see the eyebrows. Right? JJ."

"Yes. They are fairly distinctive. Go on."

Just before Claire resumed *play,* she said, "You see four pushes of the keys, even from this angle. Some people are subtle about pressing the keys. JJ isn't."

The hand jerked slightly, but definitely, three times and stopped.

"What the..." Ian caught himself. "That's only three, Clair. It's a phone code."

"Be patient."

The hand pressed hard and hung there, waiting. Nothing happened.

"What's taking so long?" Gabe asked.

"Wrong code," Leo said, not even watching. When Gabe looked at him, Leo added, "We've watched it twice while we were waiting for you. Claire, three times. I had work to do."

"Must have been," Claire said. "The gate would have started already. That tells you he's a coder. A phone call and buzz-in take forever."

The hand withdrew and went towards the throat. The fuzzy image made it impossible to tell what the driver was doing for the next few seconds, but a hand hovered around his neck.

"Here it comes," Claire said, as the arm came out again. "A second try. Weird, but it is still a code."

Three fingers reached for the Call Box. The face looked away. It was easy to see four slight but distinct movements of the fingers. After the last of the strikes, the face looked back at the Call Box and then receded with the hand and arm.

Quickly, Clair switched to a four camera array screen.

Finally, the car rolled forward, and the license plate came into view in one pane. *Mercedes Benz of Naples* read the sedate tag frame. Gabe paused the video, too late, catching only the tag's colors of sand, its central graphic and last three characters, *552*. "Sea turtle," Gabe said. "No need to back up. That's him. He's inside by midnight. That starts our timeline."

"Sanders Tilden," Claire said, "is sea turtle crazed. Among other things."

Ian pulled out his packaged USB drive. His toss skewed toward Leo. Dovey leaped up and swatted it back toward Ian.

"Ouch." Leo looked at a drop of blood on his leg.

"Ursula," Ian said, "that was unnecessary."

Dovey narrowed her eyes and returned to Leo's lap.

"Sebastian," Leo said, grinning. "Your aim was too tempting."

As Ian retrieved the drive from the floor, he conceded. "It's my five iron elbow."

Claire explained to Gabe as she freed up the drive. "Ursula is her real name. We only use real names to scold."

Gabe stifled a laugh. "My mother did the same thing with me. The whole family, including the dog."

With the USB drive firmly in place, Ian said, "Claire, Lieutenant Hubble needs twelve hours downloaded: 6:00 PM to 6:00 AM."

"I wish I'd known that," she said. "I only downloaded ten minutes. It will take a long time, Lieutenant."

"Call me *Gabe*," he said. "As Ursula knows, it's hard to stay formal in a place like Naples."

The other three nodded approval.

"One last thing," Gabe said. "Do you know if Mr. Amos had any real enemies? I get the foreclosure enemies, but anyone else?"

Claire stiffened. "I thought it was an accident."

"Most likely, but we can't rule out other causes at this point. It is a suspicious death."

Leo cut in. "He liened a lot of units here. He collected a lot of money for us, but those on the other side of the liens were not happy."

"And," Claire snapped, "he was lazy about it."

"How so?" Gabe asked.

Clare took a breath. "We had a lot of delinquencies. We turned them over to Sanders who turned them over JJ. They knew we had three hundred thousand we weren't getting in. With the costs of the lawsuit – our suit against Barton Abbott and his incompetent builders – money was running out. Collins even suggested bankruptcy for Ibis Creek. Despite all that, JJ did nothing for six months. Until I squawked. I was on the board then, been elected because we were broke."

"It's true," Ian said. "Until Claire said Ibis would have to stop paying Sanders' Defect case invoices did JJ take serious action on our collections."

"Yeah, he blocked me from Sanders' collection website."

"That part is true, too," Ian said.

"We were paying a lot more in dues. More than any association this size. For a four-stroke lap-pool and a treadmill."

"When JJ did start collecting, with our high dues, we had enough money to keep the Defect suit going," Ian added. "I heard Barton Abbott was furious with JJ. Abbott figured our delinquencies would break our will to continue suing him."

Leo looked at Gabe, smiling. "So, you see, Gabe, you'll have the longest enemies list story since Nixon," he said. "And these two rank up there with Barton Abbott."

"The only time you can lump me with that asshole," Claire said, "and make me proud of it."

Ian shrugged. "*Proud* is an overstatement. As of today."

"I'll pencil all three of three in," Gabe said. "But I doubt the list matters. It's more likely his estate will sue Ibis Creek for a slip and fall."

Claire raised her eyes, "So, it's better for Ibis Creek if someone pushed him."

"That's one way of looking at it," Gabe got to his feet. "But no so much for the someone."

"Don't look at me," Leo said. "I was asleep."

"Oh, great," Claire said, "Why is my alibi is always asleep?"

Gabe looked at Ian. "You?"

Ian hesitated. "I guess I vote for *the slip and fall.*"

"Maybe, we shouldn't give you that video," Claire said, with a big smile.

"You don't have to," Gabe said. "I'll get the whole DVR from the Collins people eventually."

"They'd have to find it first," Claire said. "Good luck with that."

"The DVR doesn't matter to us, anyway," Ian said.

"No?"

"Nope. We were already inside the gates. Along with almost a hundred other people, half of whom JJ threatened or sued outright."

Chapter 7

As Nicolina Webster headed to the Ibis Creek Clubhouse, she watched Mara Collins walk slowly from her car to the main entrance. Mara's normal confident, jaunty walk was noticeably absent that morning.

Nicolina had first met Mara while still in uniform on a robbery case at another complex managed by Collins. Mara had just scored her license as a Community Association Manager but had acted, if not dressed, the part of a seasoned pro.

That was not fair anymore, Nicolina thought. Mara had always dressed like a seasoned pro, currently for a different profession.

As Nicolina approached Mara – and Hugh – in the Clubhouse great room, she saw that Mara still liked to wear skirts. With those legs, skirts were no-brainers. Her legs were crossed, as she sat on the arm of the couch next to Hugh, but mid-blue skirt almost reached her knees. She wore a form-defining white blouse that on Nicolina might have looked whorish. On Mara's slim body, it looked perfect. The push-up bra was tame and, in Nicolina's opinion, legitimate.

She acknowledged that Mara, at thirty-two, had come a long way. Nicolina had a file on her from earlier encounters.

Born in Rochester, New York, Mara Owens' parents moved the family to the Fort Lauderdale area when she was four. She was a lackluster student, but her grades got better shortly she hit puberty. Recruited by the cheer squad, she dropped out because it was too time-consuming and the coach too serious. She did not need cheerleader status to recruit popular boyfriends. She also did not *have* to do what it took other girls to keep popular boyfriends, even as older guys came calling. The same applied when she went to Miami University.

Mara Collins possessed no outstanding features, aside from a winning smile. Her medium brown eyes lacked dramatic size, location, eyelashes or brows. The sun effectively highlighted her dark blond hair but did not make it special. She had the lithe build and slim legs that did require accenting. She was average height and, due to her body type, smaller than average.

Part by part, nothing about her was imposing, but the sum was. She had the overall effect, per Nicolina's analysis, of was awash of the *I'm available and I mean available for that but not that* charm.

She married Roy Collins, Jr. and joined the family management business. Roy immediately deployed her in sales –or account acquisition – and later in subcontractor relations. Roy increased his rake-offs thirty percent her first year in that role. When she and Roy Junior split, Roy banished his son to the Punta Gorda office, sixty miles away, north of Ft. Meyers.

If physical appearance, Mara was nowhere near bombshell material, she pulsed with a Darwinian tractor beam for men, an effect that, at best, annoyed other women.

While Mara could not turn her allure on or off, she had learned to dial it up or down, depending on her need or mood. After she had dealt with Nicolina a few times, Mara had admitted to the detective that the inevitable attention was draining. Worse, in her work, she had to deal with a lot of women most of whom dismissed her as a not-quite-empty skirt. "Like you, Detective Webster."

She was more aware than she looked.

Mara and Hugh were talking quietly. Nicolina saw Hugh as a male equivalent of Mara, only better looking, with a similarly nice slim build. For women, Hugh Barrett had *it*. He had a roguish analog to Mara's sultry, except that Hugh was, in point of FBI-proven fact, a rogue.

Hugh had his hand on Mara's thigh, but there was no sensual component at all on either part.

Damn, Nicolina thought, he was so good, so controlled. Most men would have killed to have a hand in that position.

Hugh's radar sensed company and he gave Nicolina a nod. Though Mara had lost Hugh's eyes, she did not react at first. Finally, she followed Hugh's eyes toward Nicolina, only they were blank.

Because of the frequent strain of the Mara effect, Mara had mastered the art of ignoring people while smiling slightly while looking right through them. That was not the stare she gave Nicolina, but her brow eventually furrowed, followed by a wan smile. Mara's red, swollen eyes took another second to almost focus. She looked like a frail, sad girl.

Hugh stood up first and caught Mara off guard. It took her a second to stand, which she did so weakly that Hugh wrapped his arm around her shoulders. He did so on instinct alone, which led him to raise and eyebrow for Nicolina, who nodded back an acknowledgment.

Mara leaned into Hugh before she started and separated. "Hugh. My God. You're still wet."

Hugh's clothes were damp, but he looked as comfortable as ever. "You get a three-fer, Detective," Hugh said.

"Chiky will be back in a second. He won't have much to add, but he knows you have to talk to him."

"Thanks, Hugh. Hello, Mara." She hesitated until she was sure Mara remembered her. "Sorry about Mr. Amos."

"Hello, Detective Webster." Mara's narrow nose sounded full and it was red as her eyes. "It really is JJ, then." The resigned statement came out more throaty, or, perhaps, nasally, than usual.

"I'm afraid so."

Mara opened her mouth but did not speak. She closed it down to a pursed line and shook her head.

"They had a meeting together last night," Hugh explained. "Pelican Paradiso. They were done just before 10 PM."

Mara nodded a couple times as if warming up from a chill. "He asked me to go with him last night. To celebrate his last ever collection presentation." She choked up, having trouble getting words out. "To Blue Martini. Our favorite spot after meetings. All I had to do was go with him. It was the last time…" She got a look of horror in her eyes. "Oh, no. I mean… I don't know how to say it without *last*."

The comment so surprised Nicolina that Hugh clarified. "JJ was finished doing collection work after the Paradiso meeting. He wanted to celebrate. Mara was too tired."

"I see." Nicolina put her hand on Hugh's arm. She rarely made contact that way, but Hugh invited it in a way she understood. "Please, Hugh. I want you to stay, but let me ask the questions. And let Mara answer."

"Sorry."

"Go on, Mara."

"It was to celebrate. You're right." Mara looked at Hugh with filmed eyes. "It was a big deal to him… not the end so much… It was a start, the beginning of something new.

He was done with collection work. *Done with the scut-work*, those were his words." Tears started flowing. "Oh, no. Scut-work. That was *mine*. I called it that." She looked anxiously from one to the other. "But what I said was that what other people called *scut-work* had kept Ibis Creek solvent, kept its lawsuit going. It was all because of JJ's collections."

"I've heard that," Nicolina said. "Ibis Creek would have had to drop the Abbott case. Correct?"

Hugh nodded.

Mara nodded with him. "Absolutely. And I told him there would be no Abbott Defect case without him. He was the foundation of it. I told Nolan Sanders that, too. JJ was the only reason the Abbott case existed. That he deserved to litigate the Defect case, as least as number two." She shook her head. "Telling him he could, should be doing more."

Hugh put his arm around Mara, again, so naturally. "Mara, I used to tell JJ that it was time to move on; that collection work is the lawyer equivalent of a landscaper with a rake."

"You did?" Mara looked up at him gratefully and eased into his arm. She even managed a small laugh and a pun. "I'm with the *rake*."

Hugh's eyes brightened a bit. "I'm not completely reformed."

"You encouraged him, Hugh?" Nicolina asked.

"Yes, I did," he said. "I didn't know him at all, not outside of his collection work for me." Hugh glanced at Mara but continued to address Nicolina. "I basically told him he could hand off my collection work after January. To concentrate of that defect lawsuit. *Litigation.*"

"It was like a magic word for him," Mara said. She stopped in mid-nod. "It was more than that. JJ was very religious. He felt – *knew* – God wanted him to be more, do... more than *scut-work*."

Nicolina felt her accident slipping away. She hated working suicides, preferring flares of anger to hints of despair, even in herself. "Had he been depressed long?"

Mara's eyes cleared. "Depressed? No, no. I'm sorry. I'm doing this wrong," she said, looking frantic. "It's the opposite. He was upbeat, so upbeat. He had been content, really. Until, I..." She stopped and looked concerned. "Until I started pushing... I started it." She tried to add more, but could not.

"Take a breath, Mara," Nicolina advised. "Two."

Mara took four, each deeper than the previous one

"Okay. Go on."

"I had *convinced* JJ he could be better. I wanted him to be. I convinced Nolan Sanders and Graham Chapman that JJ should be number two in the Defect case. I didn't think Graham was very good. I had to keep my eye on him, but I couldn't. I'm not a lawyer," she explained, rushing, halting, sniffing. "Graham must have known that was why. He was pissed. Stayed pissed at me." She seemed mildly surprised. "To herself, she said, "Maybe, he's..."

"Maybe, he's what? You mean Chapman?"

"He got mad at me and stayed mad." She looked at Hugh. "Do you think he's gay?" she asked if it was barely a question. "Which is okay."

Hugh squeezed Mara a little. "No, Mara. Just because he is a wimp doesn't mean he's gay."

Mara nodded acceptance. "Graham kept saying JJ wasn't ready. That may have been true, but Graham wasn't, either and JJ was older. He had more – I don't know – he was fierce. Graham... wasn't." She looked at Hugh again. "You know what I mean."

"JJ *was* fierce," Hugh said to Nicolina. "Tenacious. Ferocious in his opinions. Unmovable. Being on the opposing side with him was not pleasant."

"Oh, he wasn't with me," Mara said. "Besides, in the case, he would mostly be doing motions and those kinds of hearings to start. I got the idea after my deposition. I was the second one. Graham didn't protect me. He just sat there. He barely objected and when he did, the other lawyers just kept going. He wouldn't fight with them. After that... I guess you could say JJ was more my kind of my guy."

Hugh's eyes shot a question over to Nicolina.

Nicolina asked, "In what way? Your guy, I mean."

With an expression nearing a smile, Mara said, "Not that way. He was my guy at the table. Inside Sanders' strategy meetings. Sometimes, Roy got to sit in, but me? I'm just a girl, right? So. I made JJ my guy."

"Got it. How was that working out?

"Pretty well, except..." Mara rolled her eyes. "JJ got to see how much Chapman was a wimp. Even during phone conferences with the other side. That's just what he was. JJ told me that at his first deposition – I think the defendants were doing one of the board members – the defendants' lawyers, all five or six of them, made fun of Chapman – called him a *Good Chappy* – and his inexperience. I guess they were brutal. One even told JJ he should be doing the case instead."

"That may have been it," Hugh said. "He mentioned a deposition. As a sort of turning point, though he put it in more religious terms. He took that comment as fact. Sarcasm and nuance were not JJ's thing."

"It convinced him," Mara said. "You know, I encouraged him, but when an insurance company *litigator* said that?

When someone he respects tells JJ something, he *really* believed it."

"Like you?" Nicolina asked, challenging Mara with direct eye contact.

Mara flinched. "Of course, he believed me. He started calling me his *angel*. He believed in me and my belief in him. But this guy was an expert. It's like... It was like he heard the voice of God saying I was right." She recoiled. "Oh, God. That's what he said."

Hugh laughed. "JJ, not –" A glance from Nicolina stopped him.

"Yes, JJ." Mara gave Hugh an elbow and recoiled again. "God. You're still water-*bogged*." She rolled her eyes immediately. "Damn that Ian Decker. It just comes off my tongue."

"It's not official, yet," Nicolina said. "But Decker suspected of being an asshole."

"Thank you," Mara said, rupturing her inward tension with a laugh. "He's my nemesis. Claire Hunter is a pain, but Ian Decker's behind it all."

Nicolina wondered if Mara had ever used the word *nemesis* to refer to any other man.

"Do you need me for anything else?"

"A couple more," Nicolina said. "Was JJ here – at Ibis Creek – last night on any business for you?"

With some hesitation, Mara said, "No. You know, though, I have been thinking about it since Hugh told me. I don't think he had any cases here he had not handed off, so he was done for me here. And everywhere else." She shrugged. "Even if he still had a collection case here, why would he come after the Paradiso meeting? I mean, he wanted me to go for a drink after that. This is half an hour away, for God's sake." She blanched after the last two words came out.

"He wasn't upset you wouldn't go?"

"Sure, he was disappointed, but...!!br0ken!!

"But?" Nicolina knew that word meant something interesting was next.

Mara thought, her eyes distant. "I was a little surprised. He seemed so okay with it." She took a few steps away as if seeking an explanation in the small alcove with a set of bookshelves. She stared at them, then ran her fingers over the few audio books. "I had forgotten about them." She turned back, her eyes clouded again. "I bought him some. Audiobooks."

"Audiobooks?"

"After the dictation program, I gave him." She wiped at her eyes "That changed him. Any infatuation became that other thing. I couldn't compete with it, not that I tried. Sally certainly couldn't."

"How so?"

"He said he felt he had to leave her behind. *Spiritually*, for his *Path*, he said. In a way, me – the real me –he left that behind too."

"So, you are saying that none of this, the divorce, none of it depressed him?"

"No. It's like he barely noticed," Mara said. "No, that's not true. He felt sorry for Sally, but not for himself. The opposite was true. He had his new path, some new place within reach," Mara explained. "On this new Path of his, I wasn't a girl, a crush, not a woman to be loved, not anymore." She shook her head and looked at Hugh. "This path thing was different. And I *showed* it to him. I don't know how, but that's what he said. It made me feel different, that someone thought of me that way. He could be so sure, had always been. But..." Some realization made her reflexive.

"But?"

"It was even more. The certainty? It was a whole different level. I kind of envied him," Mara said. "I'll never have that."

"One last question, Mara," Nicolina said. "Can you think of a reason JJ would have inactivated his cellphone at about 9:00?"

"Sure. The Paradiso meeting." Mara seemed puzzled at the question. "He always turned it off for meetings. So do I?"

"Me, too," Hugh offered. "Dinner. Drinks. Later..."

"TMI, Hugh," Mara said, her spirits lifting a little further. "Why do you ask?"

Nicolina generally avoided divulging too many details of a case to witnesses. The *dark space* in JJ Amos's night was a close call. She decided to withhold it for the moment. "Nothing. We just noticed that JJ' turned his phone at 9:00."

"Oh, okay."

"Yeah. No big deal."

~ ~ ~

Once Nicolina had released Mara, she quickly debriefed Chiky Gomez, who had reappeared. Nicolina knew Chiky fairly well.

Chiky, born in Honduras, one of three sons of a Honduran father and Nicaraguan mother, was a child of the cigar business. His father converted the family farm to cultivate tobacco wrapper in the early 1960's to take advantage of the Cuban embargo. He sold the farm and went on to become a manager of a tobacco rolling shop. Chiky was an accomplished roller by the age of twelve, the year the company sold out, and his father moved the family to Tampa for the same job with the acquiring corporation and a lot more money.

In Tampa, he acquired his nickname from his peculiar addiction. When boys playing baseball his age, including his brothers, were pinching or chomping tobacco, he was exclusively into Chiclets. He outgrew the addiction and shortstop but not the name.

Since Chiky was too young to work in a US plant, he cut lawns and did yard work for some of the tobacco company executives. Later, he returned to cigar-making for a few years, but, unlike his brothers, he decided outdoor work suited him.

In a wave of consolidation in the tobacco business, Chiky's father took an early retirement buy-out. He moved everyone but Chiky back to Honduras to join his own brother's cigar import/export business. The buy-out allowed him enough to stake Chiky's purchase of a small lawn service outfit in Ft. Meyers. Chiky ran the business well for a few years, supplementing his income with what he liked to call cigar *distribution*.

The distribution involved importing cigars with fake labels and switching the labels back to the originals. Getting Cuban cigars was difficult as well as illegal, but Chiky's tobacco connections kept inventory in Tampa. Normally, the cigars came in with his family's Honduran labels and were reestablished as Cubans. On occasion, Chiky may have put Cuban labels on his family's cigars, but they were, in his mind, indistinguishable and more legal than Cubans. Americans were connoisseurs of labels, not cigars.

One of the latter, a bush-league real estate lawyer – pretending he was playing at the AA level – wanted some Cohibas for a grand opening he was throwing in his new office building. Since it was Nolan Sanders and his level of clientele, Chiky decided to relabel and re-wrapped the Hondurans – not especially well – as Hondurans. He would use a wink and a whisper to convert the Hondurans to Cubans.

Nolan Sanders introduced Chiky to Hugh Barrett, fresh out of prison and maybe wanting lawn service for two houses. In jocular, smoky small talk, Chiky let on that he could do more by buying out some competitors. "That just takes money."

Hugh and his new wife and not-so-new secretary, Jeanie, and Chiky soon became thick as thieves. While Hugh, himself, was deep in debt to the DOJ, his trust – secure thanks to the Caribbean island of Nevis – had untold riches. The trust set up several limited liability companies, one of which bought Chiky's business for twenty-five thousand in cash, a ten-year exclusive subcontractor agreement and a yearly vacation at a Trust-owned villa with a wonder view of the Caribbean.

Instead of a solid landscaping company, Chiky ended up as the beneficiary of his own Nevis trust, seeded by two-hundred thousand in cash the DOJ only suspected that Hugh had ever possessed.

As Hugh's trust acquired more small landscaping companies, aided by Chiky's advice, Jeanie Barrett's company, Quadrant, moved southward. The Barretts and Chiky moved to the Naples area.

Chiky's vacations in Nevis usually included a week-long trip to Tegucigalpa, Honduras, to see his extended family. The visit enabled him to participate in the family cigar business on the export side.

Chiky was not one for office work – Jeanie Barrett helped out – so he worked with his main crew almost every day. He worked at a lot of complexes in Collier County. This access he converted into a scouting operation. He served several investor groups, feeding them information about pending foreclosures. The Bolivian group fronted by Auggie Martin – Chiky was one of few who dared call Marty that – and a pool of Sheriff deputies were his favorite information customers. This was so, even though the latter wanted too many free cigars balanced by the fact that they, like Nolan Sanders, didn't know Cuban from an excellent Honduran. Corporal Rich Basehart was a prime example.

Nicolina Webster was not like that in either respect. She knew her cigars. Before her ex had become her ex, she paid full price for the Cubans. Chiky found Nicolina nice to look at – even though her coloring was a shade light for his taste – but intimidating as hell.

His side-businesses in cigar distribution brought him into a circle of very rich men who liked cigars and, Chiky had proven, liked the illegality of Cubans more than the cigars themselves. He arranged with his father to transship cigars legally imported into Honduras from Cuba. He had standing deals with several rich guy assistants who bought Hondurans and put Cuban prices on their secret expense sheets. Leah Kaline, the Executive VP of Ibis Creek developer NEBSIC, was a frequent example.

He also kept Sheriff's deputies in high-quality Honduran product.

"Mr. Barrett called me over. I was afraid it was on of my crew," Chiky said to Nicolina. He and Hugh maintained a formal front when on the job. "Better JJ Amos." He crossed himself. "I'm sorry I said that. Better to keep that inside. Today."

"Anything else?" she asked.

"I helped pull him onto the bank." He shrugged. "I didn't know him good. What I did, I didn't like."

"Thanks, Chik."

To Hugh, Chiky said, "I know he was sort of a friend of yours, but he put out a lot of people I know."

Hugh clapped Chiky on the back. "Not for me, he didn't. You know that. You okay to keep going, today?"

"Sure, boss. Unless Quad and Mrs. Jeanie have bereavement pay."

"If we do," Hugh said, "you sort of disqualified yourself just now."

Chiky chuckled on his way to the door. As he went out of Hugh's eye-line, he made a smoking gesture to Nicolina, who slightly shook her head. She had never smoked the cigars. She had not had to use her Honduran cigars to placate any superiors in months. Gabe did not smoke.

She had always declined Cubans from Chiky, as a little too risky unless she was close to being fired for being an *uppity Cuban bitch*. The reputation persisted, even if the rep had become hollow. She had not let on.

When it was just Nicolina and Hugh, she asked, "Okay, What can you tell me?"

"I knew Amos, used him, but I had nothing to do with what happened to him."

"Are you saying it's not an accident?"

"Are you?" he asked, calmly. "Should I get one of my lawyers in here?"

"Well, Hugh, one of them…" she began. "He just departed."

"I have more," he said. "Lots more."

Chapter 8

Over time, Hugh Barrett had had five teams of real lawyers and Sanders & Tilden. He had needed all of them.

As an audacious youth, he had disdained lawyers for his early zero-equity mortgaged properties – he did not exactly own them – but his subsequent Ponzi investment clubs required a lawyer to draw up agreements Hugh never intended to honor. When the schemes began to rake off too many dollars to shuffle off the Caribbean on vacations. His second firm of lawyers had deported most of the cash before investors set the Feds on him.

His third law firm handled his defense and managed to plead him down to three years. Loyal wife Lauren struggled on her bookkeeper's salary, allowing only a couple brief vacations in Saint Kitts and Zurich. Switzerland was so private then.

Once Hugh was released, early for excellent behavior, he ran a tech company – for Lauren – with several offices, each littered with expired student visas. Officially, only Lauren owned Boson's Mate Computer Services. He did claim credit for finding it for Lauren, if only because he found it through his reputable money-parking lawyer in 2005.

The previous software whiz of an owner gave up Boson's Mate inexpensively, with a check for twenty-five thousand dollars and a plane ticket to Zurich. Grigore Popescu had tired of Virginia and an Inspector General's sniffing. "I speak not good your language to understand those clueless sons of bitches," Grigore admitted.

Grigore's abrupt departure made for an awkward transition. While neither Hugh nor Lauren had been aboard to cheat the government, they also did not know *Java* from a cup of coffee. To them, the company's name was an immigrant's misspelling of the nautical *bosun*. Grigore's playful quantum mechanic reference did not occur to them. Fortunately, Grigore's few employees knew the bit and software because Lauren and Hugh referred to bits as X's and O's.

What Hugh had lacked in computer networking expertise, he had compensated with good lawyers and his ability to manage – much better than Grigore ever had – people who could hack and fix software belonging to others. Government IT bureaucrats, who had never appreciated Grigore's accented technical gifts – at least not nearly as much as his generosity – found Hugh a welcome replacement.

Hugh knew even better than Grigore before him, that bureaucrats with big budgets required performance, yes, but also wining and dining and tippers. So, Hugh, with deeper, if distant pockets, offered more in service; more in responsiveness; and more in college tuition than Grigore could afford.

Boson's Mate's business grew so quickly that Lauren hired a pretty, savvy UVA dropout named Jeanie Simmons to take over the intricate scheduling of their on-site programmers to allow Lauren to take over from Hugh handling the flood of money in a more effective manner. He had taught her well.

Lauren and Hugh had both enjoyed having an inexpensive actual American in the office and on the phone. Jeanie had enough computer skills to make more sense of the IT lingo that her employers could. Jeanie was smitten with Hugh, but Lauren had long embraced that inevitability: Hugh's inherent appeal to both men and women was the Barretts' meal ticket, which is not to say they did not love each other in the bargain.

The Great Recession beginning in 2008 had crimped budgets in governments and businesses, forcing Boson's Mate to trim much of its goodwill thank-you's.

"I like you, Barrett. I do. But, those kids are still in college. [Insert competitor here] seems more understanding of education than you." It was true: Lauren and Hugh did not have college bills or children, but they did *understand*.

That kind of understanding had forced the re-purposing of cash Lauren had earmarked for her dream Cape Cod vacation cottage. It also frustrated the prospect of a decent, new boat.

"Sorry, Lauren," Hugh explained, "but just because an adage is old, doesn't mean it isn't true: You have to have cash to make money."

Lauren understood. "Hugh, it is hard work running our employees' Savings Plans, and they are not returning what they should." Lauren had her own sense of *return* and who should get it. Discrete and loyal Jeanie deserved a piece of the management fees, too. "It's not like they ever ask about them," Lauren said.

Hugh nixed any looting of the principal of Savings Plans. "I am not my uncle," who had done exactly that as his own ticket to prison. Hugh wanted to be more evolved and less apprehended. "Besides, it's not very much. I think I can tweak our cash flow some."

Boson's Mate's had had a million dollars tied up slow-paying accounts receivable. Its business had depended on reliable but squeaky governmental paymasters. The frustratingly slow collections had driven Grigore back to Romania.

After taking over from Grigore, Hugh fixed the cash flow problem in a few months. Hugh reanimated several defunct LLCs to act as Boson suppliers. Gradually, he built up a deluge of billings, with millions in payments circulating among banks in Alaska, Hawaii, Florida and Virginia. He had used his cash flow magic before but on a far smaller scale. He used one of the Grigore's Ukrainian import to write a program to control the timing of the check kiting.

Hugh felt he was only doing what economies and their bankers had done since forever: Using a little money to create a lot of money; it was how economies grew.

The tightening of 2008, though, changed everything. It forced Hugh to ramp up the flow into a thirty million dollar whirlwind of checks, possibly more as he lost track. He did so in seemingly tidy monthly steps, all without worrying Lauren. When Hugh realized that 2008's bottom had become 2009's ceiling, he also realized that slowing down the money cyclone meant evidence would fall out and drop on Citibank's head.

Lauren had always siphoned cash from the Boson's Mate seemingly flush accounts for their personal accretion – such had been the point of the new array of Caribbean trusts – but, ignorant of Hugh's acceleration, she adjusted to the steadily climbing float by an extra ten million dollars. She believed the wealth was almost real and her twin Florida mortgages sustainable.

She also borrowed from the Boson's Mate's Employee Savings Plans to buy a Bentley and finance improvements to the Naples mansion, both, she was sure, would only increase in value.

Hugh would come to rue his second basic mistake: Cheating Citibank instead of *being* Citibank.

He would suffer even more for the first: Trusting Lauren with the Savings Plan and assuming she would not to siphon off *for herself* three million in Boson's Mate's fast moving worthless checks.

For many months, Hugh's white-collar criminal lawyers wrestled with the FBI and IRS investigators and, then, with Federal prosecutors and judges. In the end, his team finagled a sweet deal for him: He would pay, as restitution, every cent of his millions in *known* assets. That wealth included his confiscated Bentley and fishing boat and the net proceeds from the jointly-owned Naples mansion and Cape Cod house. He had to spend spend eighteen months in a country-club prision. Seventy-five perecnt of any subsequent income earned over fifty thousand a year and of any aquired assets would go toward more restitution. Second worst of all, Jeanie and Hugh had to testify against his beloved Lauren. Jeanie got immunity for her contribution.

When sprung, Hugh married Jeanie and moved into her four-bedroom condo in Naples. Neither had a job, but Hugh pledged to go as straight as life's curvy roads allowed and find something.

Despite his time for planning, Hugh emerged from prison with no real plan. He had gobs of ocean-view money, but it was not as readily available as it might have expected.

A zealot at the FBI headquarters had raised a fuss with the Nevis Ambassador about access to private trusts on the Caribbean Island, purportedly set up by or for Hugh and Lauren Barrett. The Nevis diplomat had suggested the Special Agent ask half of Congress the advisability of such a precedent. The Special Agent dropped the inquiry from Duluth, Minnesota, but the embarrassed FBI kept an eye on every dime Hugh had in-country and he had to account for everything that officially came into his household in a monthly probation report.

Hugh had a record and nothing for a resume, but Jeanie had gotten a decent job as an assistant in a small, stand-alone title company recently formed by a real estate closing lawyer named Nolan Sanders.

Jeanie ran things so effectively for Nolan that the title company quadrupled its monthly underwriting investment. That success allowed Nolan to concentrate on hiring associates for his law practice. He established ties with Simon Tilden's condominium law firm in Bonita Springs and an asset protection firm with offices in Palm Beach and Antigua.

Shortly after Hugh left prison, Nolan merged with Simon Tilden and moved into their new Vanderbilt Beach Road headquarters building, with a long term lease. The building was owned by Mule Key LLC, with a managing member named Roca Secas, ownership a trust in Nevis.

It was only natural that the sale of Hugh and Lauren's Naples mansion, the one owned in all but title by the Federal Government, was handled by Sanders & Tilden.

When Jeanie and Hugh attended the Sanders & Tilden's opening day Champagne, paté and cigar party, he felt aimless. He knew he could get no job and would have to buy one with money he did not legitimately have. He just needed the right opportunity.

Not halfway into his Cuban cigar at the Sanders & Tilden party, that opportunity shook his hand with enthusiasm.

"This is Chiky Gomez. He's the man," Nolan Sanders said, indicating his cigar, "responsible for these beauties."

He whispered, "Attorney-client privilege? Forget the label... They are really Cuban. Cohibas."

Hugh started. Going straight was nearly impossible, he thought, even in little things, "Very nice."

"Chiky, meet Hugh Barrett. He has a couple houses for you if you can fit them in."

"I would like to."

"To be honest, Hugh, Chiky learned to wrap... cigars as a boy. He is wasting his talent in landscaping, but he is great at that, too. He is as good as anyone around here. We've worked on buying a competitor or two for him, but no luck so far."

Chiky knew Nolan was being kind. "I do need to be bigger. To get some bigger HOAs. And keep them." He needed money for big Home Owner Associations, mostly to kick back to management companies or directors. A small operator did not generate enough profit for that. "That's expensive," he said with a laugh.

Hugh chuckled back, but the thought had taken root. "How much bigger?"

Chiky recognized the look in Hugh's eye. The man was serious, so he explained to Hugh that there were many, many small landscaping contractors in Naples. Most of the Homeowner Associations were too big for the small operators. He left off the part about kick-backs. "I know a couple ready to sell tomorrow." He shrugged. "All it takes is money. And not that much each. I could build a big business."

"Hm."

Nolan looked at Hugh and saw the glint of more business.

As Hugh and Chiky would later laugh, the largely legitimate Quadrant Landscaping, LLC was born over doubly fake Cuban Cigars.

~ ~ ~

Nicolina let Hugh go through the *rescue* in the Bog, without interruption. It bothered her that she admired his voice and the way he minimized his role. He graciously exaggerated the contributions of Chiky and Ian Decker. So, when he was done, she overreacted with a sharp, "Why not wait for us, damn it? You screwed up my damned scene."

"That wasn't the scene," Hugh said, mildly. "I saw you, and your boss, over at the real scene. Gabe got himself down here pretty fast."

"He likes mucking up my scenes as much as you do."

"Or maybe he's met Mara before?"

"You can stop now. She's gone."

"For you, maybe." Hugh flashed one of the smiles that made him Mara's equal on the other side. One too many of which helped put him in prison for a while and kept him on the Sheriff's radar.

"Last I looked, you were happily married."

"Happiness does not mean we couldn't be happier."

"Spare me, Hugh." Nicolina made a note and spoke it out loud. "Once a con man... Finish that thought for me, why don't you?"

"And now a reformed lawn man." Hugh waited for Nicolina to write down his words. When she didn't he, he gestured writing. "You spell that *L A W N*."

"No need to write it down," she said. "Who can forget organic fertilizer that deep?" She flipped back a couple notebook pages. "Speaking of which. What you said about Amos? About your sage guidance. It sounded true, so I assumed it wasn't. I shouldn't do that, even with you."

"My story about telling him to move on?" Hugh held up crossed fingers. "That was for Mara's benefit. She was down on herself. Like a single drink with her would have saved his life."

"Maybe it would have," Nicolina said. "Any part of it true? Your little pep talk to Amos?"

"Sure. JJ did my collections work. Sanders and I... well, we did a lot of things together... below your pay grade. Still do," he said. "But JJ was as thick as Bermuda grass, Nicolina."

She stiffened at her reaction to his use of her first name. Damn, he was a natural boundary-jumper, she thought. "Try that again."

"Detective Webster. Sorry."

"Thank you."

"That was unfair of me, the *grass* comment. But JJ lacked the... what? Flexibility to be either a good lawyer or a good Nolan Sanders lawyer. His mind was already made up. Any topic he knew about – and there weren't many of those – was a matter of principle."

"That's pretty rough."

"I'm not sure it is," he said. "Still, I'm good a sizing up people. Used to be."

"Except wives."

"Oh, I knew Lauren was crooked," Hugh objected. "That's why I loved her. "

"She stole millions of your stolen millions."

"She thought I had stolen more than I had," he said. "I'm not sure whose fault that was."

"Must have been hers. She's still inside."

"Lauren is very a proud woman. I like that." He cocked his head to convey the compliment to Nicolina.

"I'm sure the Feds are happy to have her." She gave him an inquiring look. "Do you and..." Wife number two's name eluded her.

"Jeanie."

"Do you and Jeanie... Jeanie was her best friend, right?"

"We were in business together. Very close, but friends?"

"And Jeanie? She is the jealous type."

"We digress," he said. "What your should know about JJ..."

"Is?"

"He really did tell me Jesus was leading him."

"Verbally?"

"I don't think so. Symbols. Signs." He added, seriously, "Mara became part of it. Maybe, the fist part."

"So, you're saying it's all true? Come on, Hugh."

"He once told me he was not worthy of direct contact." He shrugged. "I admired him, some, for that cock-eyed humility. He was proud enough to get the Word, but not quite up to a face-to-face. That was JJ. In November? By January for sure. Not much before that, not with that certainty."

"And he quit your collections."

"Directly? By the end of January, yes. I did say, *Good for you,* but I wondered if it was."

"Not as it turned out."

Chapter 9

In the shadow of her front door, Sally Amos brushed matching locks of brown hair away from her red and brown eyes. With tips too damp to stay behind her ears, the hair flopped forward when she nodded to Gabe and Nicolina. "Thanks for coming up so soon." She dabbed at her eyes with unevenly red nails. "Maybe, now, this nonsense stop."

She was on the short, stout side. She wore loose jeans and green cotton shirt that accounted for half the appearance of her figure. Her face also lacked definition but it was swollen and flushed over light skin and freckles. "I didn't even like him much... As of yesterday."

Nicolina had phoned the new widow, and Sally had surprised her by asking for an immediate interview. "I am Nicolina Webster. This is Lieutenant Gabe Hubble."

"We are sorry about Mr. Amos," Gabe said.

"He was too solid," Sally said. "Like a tree stump."

She caught the look in their eyes and misunderstood. "I mean, that was him. Just so solid. I used to think of him as a tree stump. All the way..." Sally tapped her forehead. "I'm glad for your visit. Once I knew you were coming, I managed to get off my..." She arched an eyebrow. "My lanai and make some coffee. It doesn't sound like much... It's Costco. Please have some. I made a lot."

The aroma of freshly brewed French Roast deepened as she led them past the dining area of the subdivided great room. Sally's eyes pleaded. "I don't want to drink alone." Suddenly, she emitted a nervous giggle. "Oh, that sounds like I offered you all some Wild Turkey. Which we never had. But maybe should." She winced. "I'll be getting out. This afternoon. I hope."

Nicolina rescued Sally from another run off sentence fragments. "Thanks, I will have some coffee," Nicolina said, despite vying for jitters champion with Gabe on the drive up. "Lieutenant?"

"It smells too good not to. Thanks."

The house was a small, cottage-style affair. Given the location and the area's low cost per square foot, Gabe and Nicolina had expected a more elaborate place. The dim, spartan room had an inexpensive sofa, chairs and tables, very few nick-knacks. A few discount store prints dressed up the ivory walls.

On the way up, Nicolina had checked the County deed site. Sally had owned it before marrying JJ Amos a few years before. The groom had just graduated from law school, which explained his moving in. Sanders Tilden did not pay raw associates enough for a new house.

Off-white plastic plantation shutters were closed over the windows until Sally cranked one open. The room lit up. She did as well. "Damn." She winced again. "I've been cussing a blue streak all morning. Pent up, I guess." She read the neutral expressions of her guests. "Pretty tame. *Angel Blue*."

"Yes, ma'am," Gabe replied.

"We're used to Navy," Nicolina agreed. "And up from there."

"JJ didn't like swearing." Sally's speech remained halting, uncertain, but the pitched had dropped. "Neither of us, really. The way we were brought up." She laughed, the giggles gone. "Sit. I'll get us some damned coffee."

After an exchange of glances, they sat side-by-side on the sofa. Leaning into Gabe, Nicolina whispered, "I expected a nicer place. I mean, this is kept nice, but Amos had been a lawyer for a few years."

"Maybe he was waiting to make partner. That would take some money. To buy in."

"Or saving up for kids," Nicolina speculated. "Sally seems like mom material," she added with no emphasis.

Gabe just nodded. *Child conversations* had become eye-rollers or eye-darters with Nicolina since her divorce. Occasionally, she combined the eye-roll with the question *to become what*. Gabe assumed that meant either something gloomy about the future or simply *get the hell off my cloud, Sir*.

After a brief silence, Nicolina said, "Does she have any friends or family who could come over? She's pretty broken up."

"We'll ask, but, judging by her accent, she's not from here."

"People follow family down here."

An increasing number of residents had taken to Naples while visiting parents or grandparents. Frequently, a divorce or job loss had freed them to make the move. It was far easier to move to even the most pleasant town if it was familiar territory. That had been true of Gabe.

Sally returned, placing on the coffee table a woven bamboo tray and three simple, white ceramic mugs of coffee. The set was completed with a bowl of yellow sweetener packets and a creamer. "We don't have sugar and the half and half is no-fat. I hope that's okay. We..."

"That's fine," Nicolina said.

"We were always on diets. All the way back to when..." She started to tear up. Then she mixed in a laugh. "It is pretty sad when you cry about a lifetime of enforced dieting."

Still standing, Sally took her coffee black and sipped it. She put it down, added some half and half and tore open two packets. "You know, I hate black coffee. I always have. Still, discipline..." She took her coffee, sat in the closest chair and raised both eyebrows. "Discipline just sucks."

"Amen," Nicolina said.

Sally smiled at the affirmation and then at Gabe. "Okay. I'm ready." She began with, "I threw him out of the house about eight months ago. He was cheating on me with Mara Collins."

It was not what they had thought, Sally clarified. "Not directly. They weren't even friends, not really. Even JJ realized that."

Sally did not hold Mara at fault, directly, though she knew Mara was aware of JJ's thrall. "She couldn't help it. She was that way. But she kind of tuned him, too, because he was her tool..." She blushed. "You know. Useful, I mean. First, in collections. He brought in the *past dues* like crazy. He had always managed to scrape by – we did – so he had no sympathy for sob stories. Mara called him her *leg breaker*. But that was only a figure of speech. JJ wasn't like that."

Nicolina nodded and made a few notes.

"As a compliment?" Gabe asked.

"A lot of her associations were running out of cash until JJ came along."

"Like my HoA," Nicolina said. "My sympathy dried up, too."

"But that was not the big deal, for Mara," Sally went on. "The big deal was the lawsuit Ibis Creek filed against Mr. Abbott, the developer. Mara wanted a seat the firm's conference room table. It's fifteen, twenty million. Hurricanes blowing roofs off. Walls falling down. Or *out*, JJ said." Her brow lift underscored her skepticism. "Lives at risk. Catastrophe!" She waved her hands.

Gabe said, "It's still going on, right?"

"The suit," Nicolina said. "Not the catastrophe."

"Yeah. Well." Sally smiled at Nicolina. "Mara knew that as long as the lawsuit went on, Nolan Sanders would call the shots for the board. She had brought Sanders in originally, but for collections, not millions in construction damages. She and her father-in-law were used to controlling the board of directors. That was how it worked. But the board was listening to Sanders and Chappy who Sanders had just brought in. Chappy was younger than JJ but had worked on those kinds of cases."

"Chappy was Graham Chapman?" Gabe asked. "Head of litigation."

"JJ didn't like that. He said defense lawyers called him a good *Chappy* but I don't think anyone else did. JJ liked it, so probably Mara did, too. JJ said she didn't like Chappy, either but didn't think he was very good. Didn't think he was strong enough, tough enough."

"They were rivals," Nicolina said.

"They weren't supposed to be. Sanders Tilden didn't have a litigation department before they hired Chappy," she explained. "They had real estate, title work, closings, trusts and association law. Collections were part of the Association Department. JJ was the senior associate for collections and did some association rules enforcement, too. You know, when he said he would sue someone, he usually did. And he wouldn't take less than the full amount or their units. He was so bull-headed that way. About everything."

"I hate to ask it in this way," Gabe began, "but was he confrontational when he was bull-headed?"

"Oh, yes. People would get mad at him because he didn't like…" She considered. "He wasn't very good at listening to other people. *Accepting*. That's more it. He was not *accepting*. Of anyone else's reasons for things. He called them all *excuses*. I can tell you that from personal experience. For sure."

"That must have tough for him," Nicolina observed. "Lawyers live on excuses." She smiled. "Personal experience. And double for sure."

"JJ believed what he believed," Sally said. She had to think again of how to put it. "Come down to it, he didn't like outside interference. It's a strength in a way."

"Most people aren't up to it, Mrs. Amos," Nicolina said, dourly. "They don't know enough. Personal experience, again."

Gabe hesitated at Nicolina's tone.

"I meant me," she said, glancing at him. "Not the Lieutenant here. He's the listener."

"What about Mara Collins?" Gabe asked, finally. "Mr. Amos listen to her?"

"Ha."

"Ha, as in *yes*?"

"Every *sweet* word." Sally put her shaking hands out, palms parallel to her thighs. "See that. I do this sometimes to see how I react to things. I have Anxiety. Not bad, not panic attacks, but the name alone can give me the *quivers*." She watched her hands steady. "Because of her, JJ he wanted to be more than what he was." The eyebrows raised. "He believed he was more than that."

"You didn't agree."

Sally sighed. "The truth is... well, we don't believe in being too smart. Not *intellectual* smart. You know? Not *Tree of Knowledge* smart."

Gabe and Nicolina did not *know* and checked with each other, drawing dueling blanks.

"The Garden of Eden." Sally took on an abashed look. "The Serpent and the Apple. Knowing things is more for God than man. And woman, too."

"Oh... Of course."

"Call me modern." Sally laughed. "I apologize. I'm not a proselytizer. JJ and I kept our faith in Jesus and the Bible to ourselves." She took a breath. "Anyway. In a way, JJ was smart, but mostly in retaining whatever he learned. I think it was less because of the *apple* and more because it had been so hard for him to learn things in the first place."

"How so?" Nicolina asked quickly, to keep the Serpent at bay.

"Well... He couldn't really read," Sally said, reluctantly. "He didn't admit it, but I'm sure he was dyslexic. I used to have to read cases out loud to him. That's how we met. Mr. Sanders hired me to read to him. I was a History TA at Coast of Paradise when JJ was at the law school. I teach History there now, 1980 through 1988 and the Covenant with America."

Gabe and Nicolina nodded but stole glances at one another. Neither had heard the 1992 Contract with America called a *covenant* before.

"JJ said he liked my voice," she sadly. "It was very sweet. And it surprised me. He didn't look like he would be sweet."

"That's quite a nice cover," Nicolina said.

"I learned a lot," she said. "Mostly, that I didn't want to think like that. Like a lawyer."

"Amen."

"For about a year, JJ used a computer program. It read to him." Sally's eyes took on a wistful look. "I have a much better damned voice."

Caught off-guard, Gabe and Nicolina laughed.

"But it changed everything. I mean, it really, really changed him. A man named Sebastian *something* told me about it. It's funny. It was at a reception for Ibis Creek last year. JJ hated Ibis Creek, but we had to go. I had been reading to JJ up to the last minute... before we left. I said I had a headache, because of that."

"Sebastian told me all about the program for dictating, *Dragon* was the one he used, he said. It could take dedication but it could say words. I mean, words already written. He said lots of lawyers used it, which I think he lied about. Because he said I should tell JJ that but not mention him, Sebastian. You know how someone is sayings something without saying it and somehow tells you they are?"

"Sebastian Decker?" Gabe asked.

Sally looked horrified. "Decker? Oh, no. It couldn't have been."

"Why not?"

"JJ absolutely hated a lawyer named Ian Decker who criticized everything. He lived at Ibis Creek." She searched her mental picture of the reception. "The two of them stayed clear of each other." She shrugged. "I don't know. Maybe, I was kind of embarrassed and didn't notice. Sebastian was good looking and was nice to me."

"Can't be *that* Sebastian," Nicolina said with an edge. "On both counts."

"I thanked him, but he said I should just think of it as a little favor."

"Yes, that's Sebastian Decker," Gabe said.

"Then that's really funny. He wrote the name of the program down. *Puff Magic?* He said something about a dragon and some apostles... And Mary, I think." She shrugged, embarrassed. "I didn't know what he meant."

"I think it's an old song," Gabe explained. "Before our time."

"Not Decker's," Nicolina added. "He's a retiree."

"Oh. Okay. Well, he had a little notepad he had in his pocket," Sally continued. "I gave the name to Mara. I knew JJ would listen to her. He never listened to me... Except when I read to him." She teared and wiped her eyes. "Mara looked at the note and said she would get it for him." She shook her head. "I thought that was nice of her. Even though I didn't like her. He had it installed the next week at Sanders Tilden. On his laptop. After a month, he had it – or something like it – on his tablet and his phone."

"He spent all his time at home listening. He had thousands of documents from the Ibis case and he could finally read, you know, listen-read, them. I made him get earphones."

"Interesting," Gabe said.

"He called it a Godsend," Sally said, her posture wilting. Her voice did, too. "And he meant it."

"Sounds like a great thing."

"It helped him learn to read a little better, too." She put her hands out again. They were vibrating. "He didn't need me to read for him. We barely talked anymore." Tears began to form. "He started to believe that the program was a sign that he was ready for... that God was readying him for more. I'm not sure what it was, exactly, because, little by little, he stopped... We just didn't talk anymore." She leaned forward and whispered, "We stopped, you know, having relaxations."

"Was that ever a problem?" Nicolina asked. "Before?"

Sally leaned back. "We were Christians, *so...*" She sighed. "But, not really problems."

"How else did JJ change?"

"He didn't really change, I guess. He always believed. It's just he believed *more* in himself, *more* about himself," she continued. "I was not *more*. Not *more* enough." She got up from her chair abruptly and hurried from the room. "Sorry," she called from the kitchen. She returned with a box of tissues. "Forgot."

Sally stood beside the chair and looked at. "I used to sit in this chair and read to him. He got it from me. I'm a hateful person." She looked at Gabe and then fixed on Nicolina, intensely. "I liked that. Have you ever felt that way?"

Nicolina ran her fingers through her hair, a tell of hers, that she was holding back. "You bet. It didn't pan out."

"From the beginning, it did. He couldn't be a lawyer, couldn't function without me. Maybe, he was just a collection lawyer, a bottom-feeder," she added, harshly. "But it the two of us. Me. I know now that I didn't love him, and he didn't love me. We needed each other. Which was good. Love isn't out there for everyone, right?"

"I'm no expert, am I, Gabe?"

"No one is."

"Or maybe, it is. I thought we were where we were supposed to be. Then, one day..." She sucked in a huge breath, held it and let it out. "We weren't. A little *knowledge* and it's gone. Poof." She made an explosion gesture with her hands. "The knowledge wasn't the program. You know, that wasn't it. It was knowing we were *false*, indulcing our *needs*. That is closer to sin than love. For us."

"That sounds difficult."

"It was, but I'm saying Mara Collins didn't really matter. Every man, every woman has... fascinations. Usually, they are, for me, George Clooney or a first love. Mara was like that, even if she was in an office with him sometimes."

"It didn't matter before. And then, it did. But it didn't."

"Are you saying they had an affair," Gabe asked, drawing the dimmest of looks for Nicolina.

"No, sir. She isn't."

"I wish they had," Sally said. "I wish it had mattered. What mattered was the apple. The knowledge. The knowledge was that our love wasn't. Love, I mean."

"That's a harsh judgment, Mrs. Amos," Nicolina said. "Did JJ feel that way? Was he angry?"

"No. I'm sure he didn't bother feeling that. I could say that he was limited, but I'm not sure that was ever true. I feel liberated somehow, too…" Sally stopped on to something else. "This sounds bad of me. It's not about his dying, but we were moving on. He wouldn't tell me much, be he was excited. It bothered me a bit, but I was at least as happy for him. It was something important, he said."

"But you don't know what it was?"

"Would Mara Collins know?" Nicolina asked.

"I doubt it. He said he had to keep it to himself." She thought about it. "No. It was that God had given him new reach and had shown him a new path. That's how he put it. Shown him a new path to fulfillment." She sighed and said, "It's sad."

Nicolina nodded. "That he didn't make it?"

For an instant, Sally Amos looked confused. "Oh. No. It's sad that I won't know if he was right about God."

Chapter 10

Gabe sat in front of his computer, laughing. Nicolina brought him his second cup of afternoon coffee, hoping he would stop. "Gabe," She Whispered, "we Only Handle The Unfunny Criminals."

"It's official business," Gabe said. "I wanted to get a handle on this Ibis Creek Construction Defect Case. It's at the heart of most of JJ Amos's actions. Ian linked us to a cloud drive with several hundred of things on it. The last amended complaint and Abbott's answer put me to sleep."

"Don't I know that."

"I thought I'd skim Claire Hunter's blog as a break." He hesitated. "*Ibis Crock*. She is relentless. She rants about JJ, but board members come in for worse. Ian's are less detailed and more fun."

"The very word that describes our job?"

"They are also more informative. This is Ian Decker's longest." Gabe explained. "From a couple months before the Abbott Defect lawsuit was filed. It explains a few things. You have to read it."

"To understand the case?" Nicolina asked, rhetorically.

"That," Gabe said, "but mostly why he is unpopular at Ibis Creek."

"No," she said, as she began to walk away. "I've read some Decker. As much as I can stand."

A Killing in Heron's Beak Brooklet Kingdominium Or All Parody is Local Book One – Part I

In a land pretty close by.
Down the block, even…

There was a mighty Empire that stretched beyond imagination to the Snow Countries of the North and nearly to Cuba in the south. Figure about eight days as the sea turtle paddles. In the Empire, a rich, ambitious Bishop – whose Bishopric saddled several parishes, Prefects and their prefectories – relentlessly followed his dream. More than gathering more riches or even rising to princehood, the Bishop yearned for Kingship, First Amendment be damned.

So, the Bishop purchased a small kingdom and chased out the few vagabondsmen, hookers, vultures and alligators using just the force of his hard-blowing voice and some well-placed treasury.

And, like that, he declared himself a King, keeping the title of Bishop, in case the Kingdom went belly up.

The Emperor did not hear the new King amid the din of twelve hundred other similar declarations directed his way, being on his fifth cup at a Tea Party that day.

The new King searched Empire Records online for weeks and finally gave his nascent Kingdom a positively musical name: Heron's Beak Brooklet, planning to pump water back and forth in the scenic ditch adjacent to his new Kingdom. And, besides, what other name was left?

The King envisioned his Kingdom as a kind of large hedge-walled realm with an inviting Welcome Gate since that was like his own castle and every other one on Gordon Drive. First, he hired a laid-off engineer to diagnose with terminal myopia to be his Royal Building Code Enforcer, because someone amenable had to do it. Then, he proved his seriousness by hiring the small but respectable architectural & engineering firm, Piglittle & Piglittle, LLC to realize his vision.

Piglittle & Piglittle, LLC was the remnant of the storied Piglittles Three, Inc. The third Piglittle brother had become disenchanted with the firm and moved to Reality Bites, far away in an Empire near New Jersey. He had tired of his brothers' unwavering faith in and specification of certain building materials.

He, this third Piglittle, spent years trying, in vain, convincing his brothers to combine their materials to build buildings no one in the Empire could afford. He finally conceded and receded to Reality Bites, a place where people paid their money for houses made of the dung bricks he so loved. Unfortunately, he had the same obsessive gene as his brothers. He became too enamored of the Northern style using something called basements and soon designed nothing but two-story dung brick basements.

Hence, it was only Piglittle & Piglittle, LLC that designed the new Kingdom. The two brothers had once squabbled over the relative merits of straw-only construction and stick-only construction. ("Brick, you can use the hell up where it snows," said both Piglittle brothers together. "We don't need dung bricks here!") Thanks to the yang of their departed brother, they had fused their yins and now designed truly elegant buildings with premium, flexible stick structural components and organic linseed-oil-treated straw floors, walls and roofs that the King knew, from experience, repelled water and single-malt Scotch.

The King, a utilitarian of Scot descent, had hidden his doubts about paying for sticks that bent for high-rise buildings. But, if you want the Piglittles, you took bendy sticks as well as whiskey-safe straw. The King and the Piglittles settled on the brothers' favored materials but separated the Kingdom into many squat, rectangular buildings instead of one tall swaying one.

"With hedges of figs, and grass imported from Bermuda all over the place and a matching pink gate, it will look grand," the King told the Piglittles with his powerful voice blowing a half ton of straw onto the recently tarred street. The wise Piglittles did not disabuse the King of his notion that the new grass would not, in color, match the gate.

The King hired a master builder, von Buffy, who had been using sharpened stakes and mallets long before the Piglittles even sniffed through a straw. And let the sensitive Piglittles know it. Von Buffy had built for the King's (when only Bishop) several glorious cathedrals in strip markets, where strips of everything – some very valuable booty – were purveyed around the stalls and poles of the markets.

The Piglittles and Von Buffy vied for the King's favor and, for a time, the Piglittles prevailed.

Book One – Part II

The King's vision developed, on paper, and looked more colorful and elegant than any two mobile homes next door to the Kingdom. Trouble began, however, when the Piglittle-specified structural support sticks failed under the Von Buffy mallet technique. Von Buffy had imported rough mercenaries to keep costs way under his official guess and because the skilled ones were off building or hanging about strip markets. The Kingdom had no remaining inhabitants more skilled or even larger than a gecko. Unfortunately, Von Buffy could only afford daily mercenaries held to a less stringent standard: Somewhat larger and stronger than a gecko but with eyelids; but no more skilled and unable to walk on walls and ceilings to do the wiring or ductwork properly.

Despite that failing, the mercenaries, encouraged by the King's hard-blowing voice, and Von Buffy's piecework wage, roughed in the weakened sticks for buildings, seeming a triumph of the King's will. Unfortunately, the King was resting in one of his royal saloons when all the straw was being tied to the sticks with Grade-G string and... you'll see.

Ironically, just as the King began construction, several menu items of some foreigners from farther than even Hawaii suddenly required more and more straw that tasted like chicken. Much more and more. Trillions of pieces of Grade-A and even Grade-B to Grade-F straw and sticks were suddenly being bound into bundles with Grade-B string and placed in 40-foot shipping containers. Just when all those materials should have been available for Heron's Beak Brooklet for a budgeted price.

In a desperate conference, the Piglittles expressed their horror. Von Buffy was demanding they approve inferior straw and clumsy, pointy, mallet-worthy stakes, since "the good sticks are over there, and the dung bricks are all in Reality Bites, thanks to you know who."

There was nothing for the King to do but halt construction or approve ungainly, rigid stakes and straw you could smell for miles but wouldn't feed your least favorite goat

The King thought long and hard, agonized, to be honest. Heron's Beak Brooklet had made him a King, a title that would be forever his, in the Empire's pubs and its courts. King! No matter what. Also, he mused, in some other Empires, Kings who overstayed were often offed in the big Public Square.

It was a long, seemingly endless blink of the King's eye, but it was decided. "Put two other buildings where we planned that big Square."

Heron's Beak Brooklet was to be finished with a warranty, that being a promise dressed up as a fact, that the sticks, stakes and straw would hold together.

Sneezing became a Capital Offense.

The King, with the Piglittles and Von Buffy beside him, beheld his vision that day when his Royal Code Inspector, nose held, sealed the certificate of completion. So proud was the King that, while he noticed the grass did not match the pink of the gate, brown was close enough. The straw sparkled in the morning dew in a breeze gentle and soothing. Upon feeling which breeze, the Piglittles did dare open their eyes. Yet, the buildings still stood.

Now, the King thought, the easy part.

It was February, long before the yearly naming of breezes began.

Unnoticed, the Piglittles moved to Tampa in May.

Book One – Part III

Following Empire tradition, the King declared a Constitution, hired a scrivener to cut-and-paste together—a process ironically much like his buildings – a body of laws, the Royal Edicts of Governance, the Regs, for short. Pursuant (in scrivener-speak) to the Royal Edicts of Governance, the King installed a Privy Council in a Privy of a Clubhouse. These elite members were privileged and had keys to the executive privy, the only one that actually flushed. Which also explained their titles, the Privies. The King easily filled in the first Privies himself.

The Principal Privy was called the Main Tributarial Vassal, or MT Vassal. He or she also presided over meetings as the Beaker of the Clubhouse. In the early days, the MT Vassal was truly the King's personal Privy, dedicated to receiving the King's most thoroughly processed inward thoughts to be spread about the cork boards and fig shrubbery of Heron's Beak.

Using his Royal slogan You gotta Trust Me on This, the King quickly assembled suitably trusting people, half with down payments, for his Kingdom. The King called these buyers Half-Full-Beakers, but only in private; Once titled, they were called FullBeakers. Those not fooled the King called Half-Empty-Losers.

As much as the King knew about building a kingdom, he was a little vague on running one. The singular exception was the need for a Royal Heron's Beak Brooklet flag, which like all flags, would have a design to die for. He, himself, photoshopped the flag's crest: A relieved, skinny white bird that appeared to be dropping something onto a field of stagnant water. The King told his subjects."If you squint, he's swimming. Trust me."

Again with the trust me.

And – this being a fairy tale – they all did.

As Empire custom had it, the King hired more, more mercenary mercenaries to administer his kingdom as orderly as any other kingdom in the Empire. They were called the Dickensian Administrative Bureaucrat Heads, but, in a land of nicknames, the BeakHeads for short. The first BeakHeads' action was to shelve the Regs securely under the Executive Privy so that they may receive their regular – and irregular – due.

Best of all, the King could levy taxes, originally called His Majesty's Due. This gave the King cash to complete his prioritized Bucket List, which he called the Bucket of

Privies. Eventually, these taxes were doubled and were called the Frickin' Dues in Heron's Beak-Speak.

Early on – at that fateful construction meeting, in fact – the King planned to turn over the governance of Heron's Beak Brooklet to his subjects, the FullBeakers. As Creator of all things Heron's Beak, with the title eternally his, the King left the day-to-day shoveling of matter to the Privies and the BeakHeads.

Thus, the King, by Royal Edict, amended the Regs and declared the Kingdom Heron's Beak Brooklet, a Kingdominium and turned the keys to the rosy Welcome Gate to the MT Vassal/Beaker of the Clubhouse and his loyal Privies. Though the King kept several stake-straw abodes there, for show and to let, the King left Heron's Beak forever behind him, spiritually, physically and, most important to him, legally.

Only, the last, not so much.

End Book One

~ ~ ~

A few hours after finishing Ian's blog post, Gabe officially clocked out without again suggesting Nicolina read the piece. She had always been confident in her assessment of people and things but she had become rigid lately. She had decided on Ian Decker and would not change her mind: If he was not a suspect, he was useless.

Gabe disagreed, finding a surprising rapport with Ian. He could not put his finger on it but, because of it, he found himself driving down Bayshore to meet Ian. After half a mile, he turned left into the parking lot of the Real Macaw. He had eaten there a dozen times and liked the place's Key West feel and its similarly styled menu. It was early, 5:15 PM in an August, so there were plenty of spaces in the small lot.

He used the side-lot entrance, walking past the small stage that would later have a singer on it and the outside restaurant tables. He glanced at the Real Macaw's real macaw, sitting on its perch to the right. The bird ignored him, its right eye focused on one of the bar tables with its sole occupant. He walked up the three steps to the bar and stopped at that table.

"Ian, thanks for meeting me." Gabe shook Ian's hand and sat across from him. "What are you drinking?"

"Ah, the interrogation begins," Ian said. "And during Happy Hour."

"I'm off duty, so, no, this is two guys with a common interest having a drink."

"But the common interest is a person," Ian said. "Which is me, if I'm not mistaken."

"Formally, I suppose you are."

"Call me Sebastian, in that case."

"All right, Ian. I will." Gabe signaled the waitress, pointed to Ian's drink and held up two fingers.

"I didn't tell you what I was drinking."

"Bourbon smells like Bourbon, unless it is Jack Daniels, and I'm guessing your trust fund pays for a good one."

"Makers Mark, today, but, as Webster thinks, I'm shifty. Tomorrow, it may be Grey Goose."

"But you only shift around the top-shelf."

"At home, I drink wine aged in cardboard."

"That would surprise Detective Webster."

"Does she like surprises?"

"No."

The waitress brought two neat Makers Mark and, with thanks, left them alone. The bar was never crowded off-season, which was most of the year. It was never empty, either.

Gabe sipped his Bourbon. "I hope you don't mind, but I've done some googling myself."

"Be careful. It is addictive. You're looking at the poster child for relapse."

"It is routine, and Detective Webster has decided you are not a person of any interest. She has busy researching anyone else." Gabe explained. Before Ian could comment, Gabe added, "She's been in and out of a funk for the last few months. I don't know why, but her tolerance level is off by the fifty percent you fall into. Don't take it too personally."

"I'm used to it," Ian said. "I'm the guy whose the law firm only wanted only the better of the two halves of my marriage. And I was there first."

"Genevieve Decker. Her name doesn't show up as much as yours. She needs better PR."

"No one blogs about what she does."

"Only convictions and big penalties make the New York Times I suppose," Gabe said. "And, then, there's you. You defended a dog. And made page four of the Chambersburg *Public*. Out of eight."

"I wasn't supposed to make a paper," Ian said. "But I was never partner material, anyway. I managed to survive on the goodwill of my single contribution to the firm: Evie. I identified and recruited a true star." He raised his glass. "You may as well toast to Genevieve Decker, now, Gabe. When you finally meet her, you'll have the first one out of the way."

They clinked the glasses and drank their toast.

Ian pulled a USB drive from the breast pocket of his pale orange Hawaiian shirt. "Here you go. As I told you, Claire and I have requested emails and other correspondence from the Association. We've gotten a lot. This has every email we ever got that have JJ as an addressee, including those on which he was just copied. Some should have been off-limits, as privileged, but Mara refused to spend much time on Claire or me and wanted to bury us in records. She dumped tons of emails on us without looking at them. I guess she didn't know anything more about *search* than she did managing."

Gabe gestured with the USB drive. "How many? How much time do we have to spend?"

"Eight hundred and thirty-four."

"You counted them?" Gabe asked, surprised. He realized how foolish the question was. "Never mind. Any file manager does that."

"Claire and I use our right to inspect records all the time," Ian explained. "Collins claims we are doing to harass them, but we are compulsive information hounds."

"*Information is power*," Gabe intoned. "It's true in my line of work."

"In mine, too. The lawyer side. Information can shake granite buildings," Ian said. "In the condo context, that *power* is enough to drive, I don't know, an LED candle? Maybe, two."

Gabe laughed and pocketed the USB. "We should have a fair amount, soon. It is hard to tell. The problem is that he was a damned lawyer."

"A familiar phase."

"Sally Amos brought us JJ's personal laptop, but there wasn't much on it. We hope to get more after Sanders Tilden has reviewed his office laptop. Ibis Creek's board hasn't helped much. Mara Collins gave us some. Mostly, we got emails and texts from JJ's phone. Sanders can object to them later."

The phone had a wealth of emails and texts to and from Mara Collins and very little else.

From JJ's Sanders Tilden laptop, the firm did release a limited number of personal emails. JJ did not use a tablet very much, and it was owned by Sanders Tilden, too. Gabe hopped to encourage Nolan Sanders to expedite the confidentiality review when meeting with him.

"We have learned that JJ Amos did not like you or Claire very much," Gabe said. "He had pdf copies of everything the two of you wrote on Claire's blog, *Ibis Crock*. That was public, so we got all of those. We didn't read through them because they were not sent to or by him. They are not his words."

"I doubt he listened to them himself or understood them. He didn't have a sense of humor," Ian said. "I didn't use real names in my Blog posts. Claire can't help being direct. She was rougher than I ever was, naming names. I don't use words like greedy, unprincipled, unethical, bumbler or incompetent very often. Especially when they are understatements."

"You consider yourself a satirist?"

"I wanted to be Jonathon Swift when I grew up," Ian admitted. "If you've read my posts, you know how well that worked out."

"I read a few. I learned all about the Abbott construction defect case from the *Heron's Beak Brooklet* condo association. Your disguises are the equivalent, in my business, of Ray Bans and a Jaguar's ball cap." Gabe added, seriously. "Still, it is background and may help when I interview the Sanders people tomorrow. I might use it to get a rise out of Sanders."

"I don't know, Gabe," Ian warned. "They will threaten to sue you, too. At the least, they'll shove you out one of those two-ton doors."

"I saw the threatening letters," Gabe said. "Certified."

"Yes, extra scary." Ian shuddered for effect. "Actually, they did scare Claire. We suspended the blog for a couple months."

"You threatened to *hit beak*," Gabe said, deadpanned. "Webster stopped reading at that point."

"Some death threat," Ian said. "Though JJ's reverse-dictation program probably made it *hit back*. Those programs have less sense of humor that JJ."

"Sally said that came from a guy named Sebastian," Gabe said.

"Hm."

"You're named Sebastian."

"Only when scolded. Which Claire will do for a year if you tell her I did that," Ian begged. "Sally seemed so... beleaguered. She had to read to him." Ian shrugged. "I thought it might help her by helping JJ. It was a favor to Sally, not JJ. Trust me."

"You told her not to mention Sebastian."

"In the immortal words of my generation: *Duh*."

Gabe studied Ian for a moment. "Isn't it ironic, then, that JJ, in the Sanders lobby, tried to punch you in your *snotty nose* six months ago. That's a quote from one of his emails. You might have mentioned that."

"Right. Because he meant *snooty*."

"And?"

"And he wouldn't have known the difference. Unless Sally told him. Or better yet, Mara, but neither one of them was there to help."

"Ian, he took a swing at you," Gabe said, annoyed. "You didn't think physical violence was relevant to the investigation?"

"I had forgotten about it. I will admit, it caught me by surprise. It wasn't like him." Ian waved his hand. "But seriously, he telegraphed it, and his eyebrows are longer than his arms."

"You weren't concerned?"

"Only that he'd sue me if he fell down. No, even in this shape – or because of it – I outweighed him by thirty pounds."

"You don't seem very tough to me," Gabe observed. "And I'll bet JJ thought the same thing ,"

"There you go with that *thinking* accusation, again."

Gabe switched gears. "Maybe, you weren't concerned because you have a concealed carry permit. What do you carry?"

"I plead the Second Amendment."

"You had one in Pennsylvania, too. I checked."

"I only carry the permit. My Smith & Wesson M&P 40 is too damned heavy," Ian said. "But it was a gift from a friend with a dog and a big backyard. Everyone is Western Pennsylvania has at least one gun."

Lt. Hubble knew of that area's hunting long tradition and popular deer season. Still, he gave Ian a skeptical look. "You don't strike me as a hunter."

"Only for information. And golf balls. So, I was in the woods, often."

"That explains a seven iron, but why the 40?"

"It sounded four times scarier than a 9."

"To JJ, maybe?"

"He wouldn't have known that."

They went silent and drank more Makers Mark.

"It sounds like you find me interesting," Ian said. "I thought we were past that. Unless, JJ's tie wasn't that red to begin with."

"I found you interesting enough," Gabe admitted. "I'd like to know how reliable you are."

"Like Webster hasn't weighed in on that."

"She's suspicious that you retired awfully young," Gabe began. "And into a condo Evie and you bought together. Sentimental doesn't fit."

"Price per square foot isn't sentiment. And why does a single writer need more than thirteen hundred square feet?"

While Ibis Creek was no luxury condominium complex and had had its problems, it was just outside a very expensive town. Gabe had not quite solved the Ian Decker puzzle with a few phone calls to Pittsburgh detectives who referred him to a couple local lawyers. He had put together a brief, Swiss cheese profile of Ian.

Ian Decker appeared to be well off by Naples East Bay Shores standards, outside of ritzy Windstar. He and Evie had purchased at Ibis Creek for reasons unknown. They had had enough money to afford something nicer than Ibis Creek, perhaps even in Windstar.

Ian had been a trust and estate lawyer with a large firm in Pittsburgh for almost a decade, though, as he had admitted, probably was never partnership material. His wife Evie had found her niche in the Securities Law Department at the same firm. She outshone Ian by several megawatts. Shortly before their divorce Ian left the big firm and hooked up with a two-lawyer estate practice. The couple first came to Naples in late 2008 but held off buying anything for another year.

For whatever reason, they had homed in on Ibis Creek. Gabe had the impression, Evie drove the buy and, with her background, she had to have known prices had not bottomed in 2009.

Then came the divorce. Genevieve ended up on Wall Street beating up on the SEC and Ian on Naples East Bay Shore Boulevard taking on a thesaurus. The public part of their divorce proceedings showed total assets over four million. It didn't hurt that Evie had become a partner just before the firms' merger with an even bigger, New York-based firm, the one that spirited her to New York for good.

Ian had no need to work or to shop at the Courthouse Shadows Walmart as Gabe's wife Suzannah had learned to do.

"Securities law," Gabe said. "New York's big jump from Pittsburgh."

"Evie became a very good securities lawyer more quickly than anyone expected. She had always done some work in New York. You know? The place where they shuffle all those securities like Crazy Eights. It's the place to be."

"Not for you, though?"

"Too many delis."

"I wondered it you had a secret to keep," Gabe said, reading Ian's eyes. "Maybe, an extra benefit from your wife's access and expertise, say." Lt. Hubble said. "Maybe, JJ Amos found out?"

"Insider trading?" Ian laughed. "JJ wouldn't have understood *trading*. Have you ever seen a prospectus? A million words and thousand esoteric concepts? JJ? Better you look at Hugh Barrett. Did you know he has Nolan Sanders as a managing member of his landscaping LLC? Quadrant itself. Along with Jeanie, of course."

"I didn't, but I'm not surprised," Gabe said. "Lawyers always start up companies that way."

"They don't stay after a year or two."

"Hugh is always looking for an angle, but he is not a physical guy," Gabe said."Any more than you are."

"Thank you. I feel better being classified with a twice-convicted felon, but I agree."

"I don't see either of you whacking a guy. In your case, you'd just annoy him to death?"

"Webster, again?"

"Webster, again." Gabe finished his drink. "The Medical Examiner says it looks more like an accident."

"Whew."

"The head laceration came when he went into the water. The contusion matches up with a tree trunk... more like a stump. He probably slipped and hit it. It was bad enough to knock him out. For sure, the ME had a cause of death as drowning. The most likely scenario? JJ slipped into the Bog..." Gabe sighed. "Damn it. That sounds unprofessional as hell."

"I typed it and couldn't shake it. Tell Webster I'm sorry."

"Now that I've seen the place, I can't argue the point. I guess it dries up by October."

"It does," Ian said. "I have come to prefer it over what my friend Phil Bass calls the *Graveyard*. As in where trees and real estate values go to die. The values you know about. And, as you've seen, many of the trees where JJ fell in were damaged by Hurricane Wilma in 2005. It is much worse on my end of the Bog. Fortunately – or unfortunately depending on who you ask – Ibis Creek was about seventy percent built then. The structures that were up stayed that way."

"What's unfortunate?"

"One is that our lawsuit predicts everything Abbott built will fall down in the next half-Wilma."

"Your *sticks and straw* description?"

"It was and is our biggest claim," Ian said. "But how do we prove something will collapse in a Category Two hurricane when a *Three* skipped through it for some trees?"

"What did JJ think?"

"He swallowed the idea of *The Three Little Pigs, Part One* like it was from Moses." Ian polished off his Bourbon.

Gabe waited until Ian had finished. "Have you ever slipped on that Bermuda grass back there?"

"No, but I have no reason to go out on it."

"It is not as slippery as real grass."

"It may depend on the shoe."

"He was wearing standard oxfords. Leather soles," Gabe said. "Not new. Very scuffed up, so they shouldn't have been as slippery as, say, new shoes or any urethane."

"You know your shoes."

"You haven't been divorced that long. Suzannah, my wife, may know how to tan leather." Gabe waved for the check. "Is there any reason you can see for JJ to drive down to Ibis Creek when his home is the other direction? At 11:30?"

"No. That's just weird. I think he came to an Ibis meeting once," Ian said. "It was too far. Not that he was needed. Chapman did the Abbott lawsuit updates, and there were only a few of those. Mara did a better job of keeping us posted than Chapman did or JJ could have. And she was as informative as a cheerleader."

"Damn."

"I take it back." Ian had recalled an oddity. "We had something called a Town Meeting more than a year ago. I don't think of them as meetings at all, but Chapman and JJ were both there. It struck me that Mara went overboard giving JJ credit for bringing in the money that kept the Abbot lawsuit afloat."

"I gather he did."

"He did, and Mara said we would not have to increase dues because of it. The applause pissed off Chapman – it was his show – and must have been heard in Abbott's office. He always knew what went on at our meetings and kept expecting us to run dry."

"That was the last time? For JJ?"

"Chapman one other time since. Not JJ. Sorry."

"Until we figure out why he was at Ibis, we're stuck with a suspicious death."

The waitress brought the check. Ian offered a ten. Gabe shook his head. "My interview, my bill."

"Gabe, you drank a Bourbon," Ian said, smiling. He knew the price of Real Macaw's top shelf drinks at Happy Hour were not bad. "It can't be official. You can't let me pay it, either, me being a person of passing interest. How about we just split the damage?"

"Fine." Gabe fished out his wallet and put a ten on top of Ian's. "I should thank you for your help with the video. Mara didn't seem pretty clueless about the details."

"Pretty, you've seen. Detail-oriented? Not that I have."

"Unlike Claire and you."

"I'd say *guilty*," Ian said, "but that seems like a pretty bad idea."

Chapter 11

Nicolina parked in a loading zone near the Sanders & Tilden offices, housed in a modern, one-story building. It was an out-parcel in a shopping complex, connected to two restaurants, typical of North Naples. She and Gabe exited the car and reached the double doors at exactly the same moment.

"We are on the same page," Gabe said.

"Coincidence. It does happen."

They simultaneously pulled on each of the elongated, brass spiral handles and entered side by side. Gabe said, "See."

The most striking aspect of the fair-sized lobby was a mural of sea turtles flopping from a beach to the water. The colors matched the license plates of most of the cars in the building's lot, as well as JJ's. The mural covered the wall behind the receptionist's sand-colored desk.

The second most was the pretty, perky receptionist who greeted each by name. "I'm Gail. Mr. Sanders reserved conference room two for you." Gail and led them to a small conference room halfway down a paneled hallway. Gail and the paneling were thin and honey blond with lighter highlights. The conference room had three walls of soft green paint and one mostly of windows with a tinted view of Vanderbilt Beach Road.

Several Naples beach scenes hung on the long wall opposite the windows with one of a Loggerhead sea turtle on the adjacent wall. The bamboo veneer table, with its six matching chairs, were several cuts above Home or Office Depot.

"Mr. Sanders has arranged for those who worked closely with JJ to meet with you. He will be in shortly. His 9:00 AM ran long. Can I get you some coffee? Or bottled water?" She frowned slightly and then smiled. "You can have both."

"Both would be great, Gail," Gabe said. "Thanks."

After Gail had left, Nicolina asked, "What if I just wanted one?"

"I asked for both to avoid this conversation."

Nicolina took in the paintings. "I like this guy. He has a place in Crayton Cove and seems as into sea turtles as much as anyone outside this firm."

"Pricey?"

"For a collection and condo law firm? I'd say *a bit*," she said. "You and I can afford a couple prints. But not of the turtle."

Gail had knocked on the open door before she entered with a tray of coffees, creams, sweeteners and waters. She bent forward and lifted the bottles from the tray. She looked up at them. "Mr. Tilden insists on spring water." She moved the ceramic cups next. "The coffee is made with it, too." Gail glanced over her shoulder, where her boss waited and admired her performance. "Sorry, Mr. Sanders." She shifted left to clear a pathway.

"Not at all, Gail." Nolan Sanders wore dark gray suit slacks and an open collar blue-striped shirt. He was as thin as Gail, six feet and eighty percent bald. He waited for Gail to straighten before he offered his hand first to Gabe. "Lieutenant Hubble. "He hesitated until Nicolina held out her hand. "Detective Webster. All set, Gail?"

Gail's eyes flicked between the guests, each of whom nodded. "Looks like it."

"Thank you, Gail." Once she left, Nolan gestured toward the chairs and closed the door. "I have another room set up for you if you want to interview our staff separately."

"We'll see. It might speed things up," Gabe said. "But we'd both like to hear your overview of Mr. Amos."

"I have known him the longest." Nolan took the chair at the head of the table. "I met him during his senior year at Divine Ascent College. He was in a law course of my own design I taught there at the time: *A Spiritual Guide to The Law*. It was an attempt to the Bible and our current Law. JJ came up to me after one of the classes. He thought I was too flexible. That amused my partners here. I liked that stubborn streak. I helped him get into Coast of Paradise Law School despite unimpressive grades and no LSAT. That's the legal equivalent of the SATs. It rewards test-takers with a... *flexible* bent. Coast of Paradise is about real-life results, not multiple-choice aptitude. I was, still am, an adjunct professor there, but with limited time lately, I teach only an elective: Florida sea turtle conservation law... as you might guess."

Nicolina interrupted. "Do you mind if we record the interviews?" She held up a candy-bar style MP3 player. "This has a surprisingly good microphone."

"Not at all."

"I love that turtle painting," she said, "but let me repeat one question, first." A narrow blue ring lit up on the tiny device before Nicolina asked, "JJ... Mr. Amos went to Divine Ascent College where you met him, correct?" The small screen showed several bars of volume. She nodded to Nolan.

"Yes. JJ came from a *very* strict Christian background. That is one of the things I look for," Nolan said. "I think morality underlies the law and ethics. I am in the minority of lawyers in that regard."

Gabe and Nicolina knew that about Sanders & Tilden, having reviewed files on each lawyer and the firm website. "Having Coast of Paradise nearby must be a godsend." Gabe sighed. "That's an observation, not a quip."

Nolan pinched his brows. "I know you are thinking, *That's why it is such a small firm.*" He let the comment simmer before he laughed. "And it is true. Simon, Simon Tilden, and I are very selective."

Coast of Paradise University was the recently relocated and renamed school with a brief history of accreditation challenges. It had been established as by a wealthy lapsed Evangelical Christian, Thomas Moore. Publicly seeking redemption, Moore cashed out most of his regional cable empire to consolidate the remaining divisions of online education into the forward-looking Indianapolis Christian Cloud University.

During a year of feuding with that city over real estate tax exemptions for the school, he negotiated favorable terms with the State of Florida, Collier County and Amazon, allowing him to move the college to the Naples area. As the majority of students attended online using Amazon Web Services, Coast of Paradise got by with leased office space vacated by the County. With extra space, Moore started the law school from scratch.

Nolan Sanders used his influence at Moore's Coast of Paradise Law School to get untested JJ into the school's first year. Accreditation had come a week before JJ graduated. LSAT results were optional. Moore, himself, had tested poorly academically.

"Aside from an unusually good memory, JJ had a dogged quality, a moral certitude, that made him stand out for me." Nolan tapped the table top. "I just knew I could mold him into an effective collection lawyer."

Nicolina said, "I guess you did. He wasn't very popular at Ibis Creek."

"Those who enforce covenants rarely are."

"According to your organization chart," Gabe said, "JJ didn't work directly for you."

"No. I head the real estate department. Simon heads the association law department and, until recently, that included association collection work."

"Which is now under Graham Chapman."

"We hired Graham a few years ago to build a litigation practice," Nolan explained. "He was, is, young, but he is a whiz at civil procedure. That is motions and the like. Neither Simon nor I excel in that regard. Graham is lead counsel on the Ibis Creek construction defect case. JJ joined him on that case about a year ago, more for seasoning than anything. JJ kept most of his collection work, just helping Graham out on research and drafting. It is our first big case defect case and, because of it, we had two more in the pipeline." Nolan amiable expression dimmed. "JJ started off quite well, but after a while, we all observed a change in JJ. A good turn, I thought. Simon and Graham didn't agree."

Nicolina made her first note.

"How so?" Gabe asked. "We understand he had the backing of the Collins people."

"Yes. Mara, mostly. She doesn't hear *no* very often. Graham tried it, and it didn't work. Mara started being..." Nolan rubbed his chin and looked out the window. "She was pretty up on the case, suggesting JJ be more involved because he was less expensive than Graham and had the more... aggressive personality. Graham took offense. I think he thought she should just be pretty and leave the case to him."

"I understand, of course," he continued after another pause. "The case is Graham's baby. Still, the Collins company sends us a lot of business and Roy defers to Mara completely on Ibis Creek and several other associations we represent. Simply put, she has clout. So, I interceded and gave JJ a bigger role in the Ibis-Abbott case and a small, support one in the newer defect cases. Even before that, JJ had begun to shift work on his collection cases to his two subordinate associates, even without clearing it with Simon or me."

"How did Chapman feel about that?" Gabe asked.

"It led to a blow-up at an associates' meeting. Neither Graham nor JJ was a partner, so our partner meetings missed the growing tension between them. Or, rather, I set it aside as normal, healthy jostling for billable hours. We all live and die by billable hours. Bonuses are based on it. So is the partnership track."

Nicolina asked, "Was Amos a hurdle on Chapman's partnership track?"

"Not remotely, but he may have thought so. He thought JJ had Mara undermining him behind his back. Which is funny."

"Why?"

"JJ did not have Mara do anything. It would have been her idea. Frankly, she felt Graham failed to measure up to the defense lawyers during her deposition. All of them were experienced insurance lawyers, much more than Graham was. Mara demanded that JJ handle her second day. To make her more comfortable, I agreed. I don't think Graham quite got over it, but he did allow JJ to handle some depositions and lesser motions. I think he did it to keep Mara off his back."

"So, there was some bad blood," Gabe said.

"Not so much against JJ. Graham was angry with Mara." Nolan waved his hand. "That wouldn't, didn't, last, so I didn't worry about it."

"I see. So JJ and Chapman were all right?"

"JJ had a quality that forced you to forgive him. Even make him a sort of a protege. I am sure that was true with Mara. Graham tried after that confrontation, but could not get there with JJ."

"So, let me get this straight," Gabe said, "JJ was winding down his collection work at Ibis Creek, to concentrate on its Abbott case, on the more complex litigation cases."

"That's right."

"And JJ was here before Chapman?" Nicolina asked.

"About two years, yes."

"You brought Chapman in to head up these big litigation cases."

"Yes..." For the first time, Nolan looked troubled. "What are you inferring?"

"It seems like you are describing a rivalry, if not a blood feud," she said. "Did they confront each other? You know, *toe to toe*?"

Nolan Sanders straighten stiffly. "If you are suggesting anything but an accident, we should adjourn this interview for the time being."

Gabe nodded. "We have to consider several angles, Mr. Sanders. Accidents often involve more than one person. A shoving match, for example."

Sanders' hard expression dissipated. "Graham Chapman couldn't shove JJ if he drove a car at him." He laughed. "Graham weighs about half what JJ does..." The laugh died. "Did."

"Was JJ physical?" Gabe asked. "He looks like he was capable."

"Don't be absurd."

"He took a swing at Ian Decker."

Nolan pursed his lips white. "I heard that he was provoked. Have you met Ian Decker?"

"Oh, yeah," Nicolina said, to ratchet down the tension. "It's a matter of time…"

"Thank you."

She followed up on the goodwill. "We have one question that comes before any others, Mr. Sanders: What was JJ Amos doing at Ibis Creek in the middle of the night?"

He sighed as relief set in. "To that question, we have no answer. We have been asking it since we heard. He did not like the place. A couple owners were very unpleasant."

Gabe nodded. "We've heard."

"Maybe Mara knows. She was closest to him."

"She doesn't."

Nicolina asked, "Wouldn't his wife have a better idea? Of what JJ was doing?"

Nolan looked at Gabe and Nicolina in turn. "Unfortunately, no. She had barely spoken to him since their separation."

"Was Mara involved in that?"

"I talked to Sally a few times. Mara's name came up," Nolan said. "Not the way you think."

"I think a one-sided *crush*," Nicolina said.

"Initially, I would agree. She paid a lot of attention to him, and he may have misinterpreted. But something happened, and he stopped seeing her that way." Nolan took a deep breath. "He thought of her as what I have to call his *Spirit Guide*, initial caps."

Under other circumstances, both Gabe and Nicolina raised their eyebrows, Sally Amos had alluded to the altered relationship. "Is that a Christian thing?" Nicolina asked.

"It is more of a *Seance* thing," Nolan said. "JJ sometimes misapplied words close to what he meant."

"Had he ever called her, Mara, that. To you?"

"He did. About nine months ago." Nolan responded to their expressions. "Oh, God, no. Not that *nine months*. I can't imagine Mara having... uh... relations with JJ. I *have* tried, but I can't see it. Sally said she couldn't, either."

"According to Sally," Gabe said, "That might have made it easier to take."

"I think so."

"Can we talk about access to documents?" Gabe asked.

"Frankly," Nolan said, "JJ was so dedicated to his work that almost everything we have reviewed has to be off-limits. We have sampled less than ten percent and have found almost nothing we can give you. His communications with defendants in his case, we have compiled for you – except for collection settlement talks of which there are precious few. He did not like settling those cases – but no one communicated with him significantly about non-legal matters. Ibis Creek, for example, never did. He and Ms. Collins had some exchanges that were personal and those are included. They informed part of my contributions today. As I said, they were certainly not intimate in content. More along the lines of her advice to him and religious philosophy from him."

For a moment, the three of them sat in silence. Finally, Gabe said, "That may help give us an understanding of his frame of mind. That's what we are after." He did not reveal the extent of such communications he already had. "Could we see Graham Chapman now?"

Nolan nodded several times and finally chuckled. "See him? I think that would be very good idea."

~ ~ ~

While waiting for Graham Chapman, Gabe and Nicolina made notes from the Sanders interview. Gabe stopped first.

"If suicide was an option," Gabe said, "it is looking more unlikely all the time."

"Agreed. And Ibis Creek would be the last place he'd go for that."

They heard footfalls approaching and fell silent. Nicolina finished her writing just before Graham Chapman entered the conference room.

The first thing they noticed about him was how jittery he was. He was average height and slight. Like Nolan, he wore no tie, a good thing since the collar of his baggy shirt looked two sizes too large for his thin neck, which supported an over-sized head. His face was pale but red.

"Hi. Nolan said you wanted to see me." The words came out in a rush.

"Yes," Gabe said. "I am Lieutenant Gabe Hubble. This is Detective Nicolina Webster. We are interviewing people who knew JJ Amos." He pointed to the recording device. "We have to record this interview."

"His death is still categorized as suspicious," Nicolina said.

"It was an accident, everybody says. He fell in that water," Graham said, looking flustered, back and forth at them, three times. "At Ibis Creek, right? That place is a mess. I've warned them to post signs around the Preserve because it is slippery. And they have had three slip and fall cases already – mostly bogus – but the insurance company is not happy..." Graham paused, but not for a breath. He was thinking. "I know how they think, insurance companies. They pay out for anything –" The words ran together in a blur of syllables.

Gabe held up his hand, and Graham stopped. "Are you saying there were other instances of people slipping on the wet grass? Near the Preserve?"

"No, not there but that was where JJ was –"

By sitting back, Gabe signaled Nicolina to take the lead.

"Mr. Chapman," she began, "we need to know how the other slip-and-falls happened? Were there any near the Preserve. The Bog as they call it."

Graham sneered. "No one calls it that. That's that Ian Decker character. He and Claire Hunter make it impossible for me to run the place… I mean the case. The case. Mara Collins runs it, and she has her priorities misplaced if you ask me. You know about the Abbott Defect Case. That's mine. I mean, I'm the lead attorney, right? JJ was my subordinate. Mara made him my second chair, not that I needed one. I made him my left-hand man." He grinned. "And I'm right-handed if you see what I mean."

Nicolina smiled. "That says it all. Thank you."

Graham nodded vigorously, then opened his mouth to speak. Nicolina cut him off.

"Was Mr. Amos pissed off when you were hired?" she asked.

"Oh, yeah. Like he could do my job."

That answer preceded a flood of sentences on JJ Amos and his *you know, like angels* Nolan Sanders and Mara Collins. He had problems describing both, mercifully stumbling over his words. He did not respect or like either, but he knew his boss was his boss and that Mara was Mara.

"It doesn't sound fair," Nicolina said, all sympathy.

"Fair? It's not fair," Graham said. "But it's the law, you know. The law firm. It's not supposed to be fair. It's the survival of the…" He paused for seconds, a rare occurrence Gabe and Nicolina savored. "Survival of the Species.

The lawyer species especially in litigation. It's different from real estate or collections. Those fit enough for it, have to have the mind, the feel for it. You have to know insurance companies the way I do. JJ wasn't fit for complex litigation against insurance companies. A construction defect case is all about outsmarting insurance companies, not bulldozing mortgaged houses."

There followed five minutes on the Ibis Creek-Abbott Defect Case.

"Sixteen million dollars!" Chapman said. "And that was for starters. I got it up to twenty. JJ Amos in a twenty million dollar case? He was great in a sixteen hundred dollar case against a bunch of... Hispanics." He paused. "My secretary is Hispanic. She is very good."

Gabe reentered the conversation. "So, you do not feel Mr. Amos was depressed or suicidal. Correct?"

Graham looked shocked. "Not a chance. He thought he was going to take over my case over and hit the big time. My whole department. I couldn't talk him down from that. Nolan tried, but Mara kept getting in the way. JJ wouldn't listen to me. His mind was made up. He doesn't think after that. He just takes what someone tells him – someone like Mara Collins – and that's the end of thinking. One of the defendant lawyers told him he should take my case, and suddenly he was *God's Gift.*". He sneered again. "He believed an insurance lawyer! Come on. Right?"

"That jibes with what we've heard," Gabe said. "His emotional state was good."

"Too good. Way too good, if you want to know the truth."

"Thank you, Mr. Chapman, Gabe said, standing and offering his hand. "You certainly understood Mr. Amos."

"I sure did. He was an okay guy, underneath." Graham launched himself verbally and physically. He shook Gabe's hand, his hand weak and vibrating. "A bit too religious, too moral, even for here, if you know what I mean. We are all *saved* in this firm. Nolan doesn't hire anyone else. And charitable. We are all in Nolan's charity. And other ones. It's a good way to give back and get the right kind of clients."

Nicolina had stayed seated, as a back-up. Once Gabe opened the door, she rose and shook Graham's hand, extra firmly, dragging him toward the door. "You have given us a true perspective on JJ Amos."

Graham winced and then grinned. "Be happy to. We weren't friends or anything, but I knew him well from working with him. He was okay, in the end."

"We can't keep you," she said. "Mr. Sanders said you were crazy busy."

"Right. I am. He keeps on top of everything."

Gabe patted Graham on the back with enough energy to get him through the doorway. It did not fully work, as Chapman stopped just beyond and turned back.

"JJ may not have been litigation material," Chapman said. "But I have to admit there would be no Abbott Defect case without him."

"You mean, the money," Gabe said. "The collections he brought in."

"Over three hundred thousand over a couple years, most of it paid to us. In our fees and experts, I mean." Chapman waggled his head. "Abbott thought we'd be dead two years ago. He didn't take us serious because Ibis had no money and lawyers can't work for free."

"So, Barton Abbott was not JJ's biggest fan?" Nicolina asked.

"He hated him." Chapman shrugged. "Abbott was like that. He came to a couple depositions – a party can do that – interrupting, mouthing off so bad his own lawyer had to send him out. For the second day of my deposition of Abbott, I was under the weather, so I sent JJ. Abbott knew JJ pulled in the money to pay us, so JJ made him crazy during the deposition." He grimaced. "Thought you should know."

"Thanks again," Gabe said.

Chapman nodded and walked away. Gabe closed the door and put his back against it. "Jesus Christ. I'm exhausted."

Nicolina collapsed against the table, laughing. "I thought Decker talked too much. I'll have to apologize."

"You have to say Ian was right about another thing."

"Yeah. Barton Abbott and JJ. Not a mix made in heaven."

"It sounds like we need to do some background on him."

"Screw that, Gabe. Let's blitz his office."

Gabe sighed. "I want to talk to Ian first. To see what he has."

Nicolina counted to three in her head. "Of course, you do, Sir."

"You can apologize, then."

"And distract him," she said. "That would be wrong."

Chapter 12

Ian Decker usually relied on news accounts for his normal blog posts. For posts about Heron's Beak, he used a variety of sources available to him as an owner and lawyer. For the Barton Abbott pieces, he used several Naples Daily News stories, but mostly excerpts from depositions in the Abbott Defect case.

He did not acquire the depositions directly – the board and Chapman simply declared everything involved with a lawyer's name on it – including, probably, the phone book – as privileged. Though withheld from him in records requests, various motions posted on the Court Clerk's website had long parts of depositions attached. The depositions were those of Barton himself; his *majordomo*, Leah Kaline; personnel from the companies involved in building Ibis Creek: contractor Burkle Lehane; engineers Ballasta; and Pridd-Baw; architect Mochyn Design. A couple County Building officials contributed material to Ian.

Planning to spoof the whole story as a series of blog posts, Ian soon realized that Claire would never agree to post a comic novella.

Therefore, what he emailed Gabe Hubble was his original draft for the epic post, names unchanged. In their phone exchange, Ian begged, "Please don't give this to Webster."

"It's her job to know these things." Gabe had not read the piece at that point. He waited until he and Nicolina had returned to the office. While she made an appointment to see Barton Abbott, Gabe read Ian's *background story.*

From his earliest days in Millville, Ohio, Barton Abbot loved water. Nearby Hamilton was annually lauded for its fine municipal tap water. As an Eastern Ohio entrepreneur, he brought in bottled tap from Hamilton as Abbott's Western Natural *for his restaurants. His patrons loved the taste of the western water enough to pay for bottles like it was French wine.*

Beginning in a town near Akron, Ohio, Barton got his hands wet in the restaurant business, literally, washing beer glasses in a Kent State college bar. He moved up to tending bar at an Akron neighborhood saloon. From there, he built a dining fortune catering to its remaining tire unionists and middle-manager families. He spread his restaurant formula gradually north and into Cleveland, where he and Alice eventually moved to a Lake Erie penthouse.

As more people lost jobs, Barton's modestly-priced food business boomed. Soon, he and Alice became rich enough to winter in Pelican Bay, Naples. To make the stays deductible, Barton purchased the building housing a small but authentic French bistro on Naples main drag, Fifth Avenue. As authentic French Bistros tend to do in Naples, the owners defaulted on the lease and traded the restaurant for tickets back to Avignon. Barton and Alice were delighted to leap up in class, from Fried Iowa Meatloaf *to* Boef Bourguignon *because they owned a building with a kitchen.*

In time, Barton learned what his predecessors had. Naples drew rich mid-westerners, like himself. Most of them, Barton included, wanted mashed potatoes with their New York Strip, not Veau au Poivre Vert avec Pomme Frites.

Their bistro was down for a second count... until Alice convinced Barton that bistro *was French for* café *with food and that half his customers thought it was Montanan for buffalo.*

Barton renamed the place The Abbey Bistro and Café *to clarify things for everyone and put Bison burgers on the menu.*

A quick study, he learned that the plebeian term main drag had no place in Naples. Its main street was Fifth Avenue or, to the initiated, just Fifth. Alice had convinced him to replace Café, as redundant at best and inaccurate otherwise. The French on the menu was largely in American and the green pepper sauce flowed like – and exception to the translation rule – Eaux de Semi, *fresh from Hamilton by Semi trailers.*

Alice had the sense of humor and Barton the sense to open four more in Southwest Florida.

Much as Barton had loved running his fancy bistros, he had found owning the commercial buildings housing them more rewarding. The hours, if nothing else, were much shorter, and there was no till to temp employees. While he kept his five The Abbey Bistros, he spent the profits buying the stucco walls enclosing eighteen competitors on Fifth Avenue and its renewing rival, Third Street, or just Third.

In 1998, Barton noticed that his bistros had far more commoners coming in than he had projected. He had raised his prices, successfully restoring The Abbey's exclusive bistro-ness, but he had begun thinking: As Naples grew, his bartenders, wait staff and paid building managers had begun earning just enough more money to live closer to Fifth and Third than Everglade City or Estero. Not everyone had inherited or earned enough wealth to live on Naples' Gulfshore Drive or in a ritzy highrise north off Tamiami, but they had to live somewhere.

Barton had cut his teeth serving the low-to-middle income market. That niche in the Naples area had become a chasm since no one cared to look. North had become too expensive. The East had less appeal as too far from his market's workplaces. He focused on the southeast border of the long, slender estuary called Naples Bay.

That sodden strip of land, anchored by Albright and Kelly Roads, had originally been platted for mobile homes but also had become home to half the pawn, bail, skin and gun shops in Collier County. In 1999, the County had undertaken to reclaim and rename the area. By 2001, Kelly Road had become Bayshore Road, Albright Naples East Bay Shores Boulevard and the whole area Naples East Bay Shores Village.

Despite its name, Barton determined the Village was the place to build his condominium complex. It would not be for boaters, art collectors or people who could shop on Fifth and Third. He would dedicate half of his development for Collier's working folks. He had planned the other half for Midwesterners not quite rich enough to buy into Naples on the top three rungs of the real estate ladder.

The site Barton gradually assembled, by 2001, fronted on recently landscaped Naples East Bay Shores Boulevard, roughly between the County Courthouse and the planned Naples Botanical Garden and Hamilton Harbor Yacht Club beyond. Upscale Windstar was a neighbor as were the guaranteed to be gentrified mobile homes.

To the east, the County had created a marketable amenity called Sugden Regional Park, with its Lake Avalon, sixty acres of fresh water pond with little sailboats and narrow beaches.

Barton timed his drive from the parcel to Fifth Avenue at ten minutes at the speed limit, which no one drove. It was perfect.

The Body in the Bog 151

In 2002, Barton's engineers and architects had designed the basics of the 300 mid-rise unit development. Thanks to his Affordable units – contractually designated for those whose work actually ran Naples and was, therefore, poorly compensated – Barton was within the County's density requirements. Drafting the land use and watershed applications had begun.

Barton knew he had to dedicate the middle of the complex to a natural element. He assumed that term would allow an attractive pond – water being very natural and one of his specialties --created by backhoes and bulldozers. The grounds' design would funnel rain water hitting roof tiles, sidewalks, automobiles and asphalt, by pipes, directly into the County storm sewer system.

The County killed both the lake and the stormwater scheme. Barton gave up his pond for a central Natural Preserve to actd as a catch basin. The basin, in turn, would filter surface water before it got to the County stormwater system.

Barton's contractors, Burkle Lehane, had layered ton after ton of sandy earth onto the surrounding acreage so that the buildings footers would start well above the preserve/basin.

Having established a good depth for it, his civil engineers assured Barton that the Preserve would handle any amount of runoff. They had not guaranteed it in writing. It turned out that the Preserve did handle the runoff by becoming, in later summers, a marshy bog.

The previous owner had dedicated – been forced to give away to the County – an easement on its east end for a drainage trench for collection and absorption of surface water. Barton had assumed the trench would be enough, leaving his pond out of the equation. Failing that, Barton requested a release of the easement and failed again. It was all about water in a state surrounded by it.

It amazed him that the County wanted to keep a scrawny bit of water that never moved – except up and down – as proven by the sight of the same beer cans until the County scooped the thing.

Barton Abbott was the man who turned a French Bistro into an American Bistro and tap waters into d'eaux. He set those translation skills to work.

He had his engineers pencil in a narrow extension of the ditch all the way to Haldeman Creek, which fed – and the wider part of which received no credit for actually being – Naples East Bay. The extension had to be narrow enough to be ignored as a non-navigable waterway, beneath the notice of the Corp of Engineers or the interest of Florida or the County. Even with the aid of a pencil, the water did not flow, but Barton's creativity felt vindicated. His project had its marketable water feature, a scenic canal.

It did not, however, have a marketable name.

Alice shuddered at his first choice. "No, not Abbey Heights on Naples East Bay. It's eight feet above sea level. And overlooks half a gallon of water in a tenth of a moat, not Naples Bay, East or West."

"I need something unique, special, Alice."

"That means not Pelican Abbey. Or Pelican anything." She laughed, but she had a point. "Not Pelican point, either."

For inspiration, Barton took to walking the half-cleared property, sometimes alone, sometimes with an engineer or two. One July day, Barton observed a dozen white birds, their skinny orange legs half into the trench's stagnant shallows. Barton watched as one bird had turned its reddish-orange face toward him before it gave him a droopy-beak profile.

"What are those in the canal? Egrets?"

Abbey on Egret Canal? Barton thought but kept to himself.

"No, Mr. Abbott. Those are ibis," said the civil engineer with him that day, a fellow who did double duty as the environments engineer. "They have shorter necks and those curved beaks. Egrets' beaks are straight and not orange. Neither are their legs."

Curved Beak, he thought, of Ibis Beak. Barton laughed out loud as genius struck again. "I've got it: Ibis Creek!"

"Except, sir, there isn't one," the engineer looked puzzled. "Oh, the ditch... Er, the canal?"

Alice called it worse, every time it came up, so Baron was not annoyed. "Everybody and everything deserves a name. How much to rename it?"

"Rename that? You can't."

"Money can do everything."

The engineer nodded. "I meant it doesn't have to be renamed. I've lived with maps of this area for two years, and not one shows a name for things like this. In submittals, we just call it the drainage easement."

"How about you start calling it by its name," Barton said. "In everything you guys submit from this minute on, it is Ibis Creek."

Barton Abbot decided to budget $10,000 to officially name the slender body of standing water but found no takers. The State and County water people never recorded names for the small rainwater collectors in Collier County. With that official shrug in his pocket with the unused cash, Barton put the name to Alice.

"Ibis Creek Condominium," she said. She repeated, an octave lower, the said, "I love," she said.

The simplicity of the name delighted him. That he had created it from nothing brought extra satisfaction.

Barton Abbott was no fool, however. He realized that the less fevered of his prospective buyers might want to view the dirt they were buying into and notice Ibis Creek was not the burbling stream the name implied. He concocted – and heavily edited – its history, as well.

Millennia ago when the Tamiami Native Americans roamed the Tamiami Region, a rushing creek fed Haldeman Creek and Tamiami Bay (as it was called then) much of its majestic waters. Over time, the Conquistadors, phosphate miners, Corps of Engineers and distant bureaucrats re-directed much of the water. That and rising property values caused the ambitious Natives to move to the Oklahoma and leave the creek to the Naples East Bay Shores White Ibis and mankind We honor the history of this gift of nature with a long-term plan to restore its full northerly flow and provide the amenity of a sparkling water view.

Barton's PR satisfaction plummeted into dismay when he first saw the mock-up of the Ibis Creek marketing materials. The graphic of the creek looked subtly misleading, but his logo included a full body picture of a buzzard-red face scrawny white bird with a weird curved orange beak. In short, it looked like an American White Ibis.

"No frickin' way," he said. "Where'd you learn to draw? Kindergarten?"

"It is an actual photo of an ibis, sir," the graphic designer said. "I took it myself."

"They sure don't look that ugly in person."

Abbot stared at the logo for days afterward. He walked the property with a camera. He ignored a few dozen ibis. He did take five nice shots of a large solitary egret, its rich gold beak feeding a yellow gold loop around is eye. He emailed the best close-up to the designer with Photoshop instructions.

The designer immediately called him back. "I don't understand, sir. It's very pretty, but it's an egret."

"It is the head of the Naples East Bay White Ibis. Photoshop it onto your bird. This head is solid gold, as in marketing. I like you original neck. Keep that, but this is the face of Ibis Creek."

"Pardon me, Mr. Abbot. It's not an ibis."

"According to you, maybe. But you had to look it up, right?"

"That's true."

"If it'll make you happy, give the beak a little bend – only the slightest – and make its gold on the orange side, but still gold. Maybe a touch of red to the yellow gold around the eye." Barton envisioned how perfect the logo would be. "We will call it the Naples East Bay White Ibis. If anyone wants to find one, they can forget Gordon Drive or Port Royal. They'll have to come to Ibis Creek with their cameras. And their checkbooks."

Barton next speed-dialed his attorney and ordered trademarks for Naples East Bay White Ibis, under waterfowl, and Naples East Bay Ibis Creek Condominium. His lawyer filed to reserve the corporate name Naples East Bay Ibis Creek Condominium, Inc. and its fictitious nickname of Ibis Creek Condominium by the end of business.

Seemingly aware they had been supplanted via technology and registration, real ibis shunned the property, giving Ibis Creek owners no reason to question the creator's stately Naples East Bay White Ibis.

In his many trips to Ibis Creek Condominium, Barton Abbot had never again seen a competing ibis, except as he drove past the McDonald's drive-thru. He usually detoured *to disperse what he considered lesser versions of the species. His annoyance at the birds abated once he realized that no Naples East Bay White Ibis would ever be seen pecking at fries like a beggar.*

"What have you done, Barton?" Alice teased him when she saw the completed logo.

"It's a Glamor Shot, Alice. I did every damned ibis in this country a favor."

He believed that he had glorified the ibis until he saw the logo on paperwork for the lawsuit Ibis Creek filed against him. When his rage abated, he wondered if birds could manipulate karma.

Against his better judgment, Gabe insisted Nicolina read Ian's description, with, "If half of this is true, we will be dealing with a hell of an ego."

"We already are," she retorted.

"Just read it. Please."

When Nicolina had finished, she sighed. "I'll give him this: Decker is brutal. Did the Tamiami Indians really move to Oklahoma? Or is that a myth?"

"The Tamiami Indians are as real as the Naples East Bay White Ibis."

"Creative." Nicolina mulled the history over and understood Gabe's meaning. "Oh. Do you think it took Abbott six days to build his world?"

They sat in silence until Gabe said, "If JJ Amos kept that Abbott Defect case afloat, he made one hell of an enemy."

~ ~ ~

Faced with their impromptu appointment request, Leah Kaline, Barton Abbott's right arm, fit Gabe and Nicolina in very quickly. "Barton is not in this office today, but you're in luck. He has a leasing office in his new strip center a couple miles down the road from your offices. He will be there the next few days."

Barton Abbott had concentrated on buying existing buildings at first but entered the building frenzy before he started Ibis Creek. His latest venture was a large strip center on Davis near Santa Barbara. The complex was being built by Burkle Lehane, the same contractor being sued by Ibis Creek. It was almost completed and ninety-five percent *available to lease*. With his *do it yourself* spirit, Barton set up his own a satellite desk in the center's leasing office and had another Abbey Bistro being installed next door.

Though the center was only half stuccoed, the leasing office had a finished, if spartan look that they could see through the huge lightly tinted windows. Inside, they saw two closed pressed wood doors in the back wall. All three engineered wood leasing agent desks sat empty. There were no visitor chairs. The walls had layouts of the various parts of the strip center.

An attractive sixty-plus secretary in maroon jeans and a white blouse rose from her similar desk and greeted Gabe and Nicolina.

"We are a work in progress, accent on work," she said as if reading a script. "Ms. Kaline said you'd be coming. Mr. Abbott will be off the phone in a minute."

"Thank you," Gabe said. "We didn't expect a busy man like Mr. Abbott to see us so quickly."

She looked at him, smiling. "We are in the gearing-up stage."

Nicolina broke off and studied the drawings. "Lots of space."

"We don't expect to take up too much of Mr. Abbott's time."

One of the doors opened. "You can take as much time as you need, Lieutenant Hubble," Barton decreed. "Trying to lease in this market is mostly waiting for return phone calls." He looked at the secretary. "Pat, transfer anything coming into Leah, will you." His deep voice carried.

Barton Abbott was about average height, five foot ten, not much of it neck, and build, though fifty-eight years had packed on a few extra pounds. His large head still sported some light brown hair. He was no impressive until you saw the look in his mild blue eyes. The look was *welcome to my lair*. He waved a meaty hand toward Gabe. "I moved two of... the only two guest chairs in for you."

To Nicolina, still at the wall schematics, he said, "See anything you like, you can get it cheap. Today only!"

She turned and walked toward him, hand out. "Maybe, I'll be back next month."

"I get that a lot." He shook her hand with one solid movement. He did the same with Gabe's.

They followed him into his surprisingly large and equally surprisingly empty office. He had a larger version of the leasing desks and a mesh-style manager's chair – both from Staples, Gabe recognized – with no file cabinets or credenza. A laptop sat on the desk, next to a simple, two-line phone and that was about it.

Barton watched as the two visitors sat and discretely scanned the room. "I'm not burrowing in. This space is for a retail store, not me."

"It is very generous of you to meet with us on such short notice," Gabe said. "As we told Ms. Kaline, we are following up on the death of JJ Amos at Ibis Creek."

Barton forced a frown. "Sad, but you know, it figured."

They looked at him, surprised at his attitude.

"How so?" Gabe asked, evenly.

"Not his dying," Barton clarified. "His dying at Ibis Creek. Of course, he would do that. It's like he's screwing me all over again. Indirectly, like before."

"Before?" Nicolina asked. "You mean helping finance the defect lawsuit, you mean?"

Anger lit Barton's eyes. He banked it before he spoke. "I can't even explain to you what this lawsuit means to me. The accusations."

"We're trying to put a profile of Amos together, Mr. Abbott," Gabe explained. "We can't explain his death at this point. He was becoming more involved in the Ibis case, as we understand it."

"He'd done all the damage he could," Barton said. "The money was all in. The bad accounts. The board ended up owning ten, but they were getting first class rent." He narrowed his eyes at them. "That's proof Ibis Creek was what I wanted it to be, despite…"

He hesitated, his focus inward for a moment. "You don't know what I planned originally. Or why. You should have seen the original design. It was going to be special. Special, but not out of reach. We had almost half the units priced within the range of working people. I had people working in my restaurants who couldn't buy or rent within thirty miles unless it was in some old studio or a trailer. That wasn't right. It made them late."

"We understand the goal," Gabe said. "The so-called Affordable units."

"The County had that program," Baron explained. "Still, does, but who talks up their flops? They encouraged developers to build some part of condominium complexes for… I don't mean to be uppity, but for people like your deputies and secretaries. Hell, I started out as a working stiff, waiting tables." The thought calmed him down. "Better a bus boy than a farmer, that I gotta say."

Gabe and Nicolina exchanged knowing looks. She said, "Been there."

"Mine was a Navy bar," Gabe added.

"And what you could afford? To live?"

"Three Roommates."

"Two."

Barton beamed. "Exactly. Without people like us, then, the whole country would shut down. In the meantime, condos here are going up with studios at eight hundred grand."

Neither Gabe nor Nicolina disputed his point.

"Ibis Creek was not going to be a *Port Royal* palace," he said. "That wasn't the point. But, even so, with this State and this County? We had to make sacrifices. I wanted a lake, but I got to keep the look of nature. I was pissed at first, but the trees gave me something different, more fitting in a way."

"Wilma didn't help there," Nicolina said.

"Let me get back to Wilma," Barton said. "Pre-sales went well. Material costs were going up, so we had to rejigger…" He stopped. Something had him stymied.

"We understand," Gabe said. "We were both here."

"I even bought a couple to flip," Nicolina said. "They had to substitute… *down*. Cheaper appliances, more carpet, less tile. We were still lucky they got finished."

"Okay, so you know," he continued. "They call it *value engineering*, but we had to do it or rebid the whole job. The Affordable units would have been impossible to bring in at the target cost. It was still going to be great, just not *as* great. I okayed a lot that hurt and believe me, I kept my eyes one everything Burkle Lehane was doing. Not to say I didn't trust them – They are doing this place for me, too – but we got half of the building shells up… And bam! Wilma."

"She ended up at Cat 5," Gabe said. "Not here, but before, in Yucatan."

Barton nodded enthusiastically. "A terrible, tree-killing best friend."

Both Gabe and Nicolina were taken aback by Barton's tone and phrasing. Then, they got it.

"The buildings were not affected," Gabe said.

"Even better, all those flattened trees showed she had given Ibis Creek her best shot," Nicolina added. "And the buildings were just fine. Right?"

"It's funny that a disaster can be a miracle selling point," he said. "I guess not everyone was impressed. We had a terrible time selling the Affordable units. Even at our low prices, with the County putting in down payments and second mortgages. We cut every deal we could think of. There was *a lot* of pressure. We had to sell them to keep things on track. The program required X number of units below that affordable price. Based on some average income formula. No way around it."

"We understand the program," Gabe said. "We understand it stalled out."

"Did it ever. I admit, the County and I were kind of fucked." He shrugged. "Pardon my French. But we were, The County had made a big deal of the program. I did, too. And it was important to my vision. So, we had to be flexible… let's say, with the build… tolerances. "

"Plywood, two-by-sixes, toilets," Nicolina said. "Trust me. I went through it."

"So, we had to bend again. Both the County and I were little lax on enforcing the terms of the Affordables law. Live-in owners only? We couldn't find even half the number needed. We tried. I even got jobs for some with my contractor and subs, my restaurants, you know, to give them the income… "

"The income to qualify?" she asked, with a smile.

"In those days," Barton said, "it didn't take much. Any job would do, but the County insisted on real jobs… Legitimate jobs. I arranged for that."

"That was generous of you."

Barton started to respond but stopped. When he spoke, his face was somber. "No. It wasn't. I admit it. It was part of a deal I made with a couple small groups of investors. The group would supply whatever mortgage was needed, at a higher interest rate, but the applications required jobs. I think the plan was to sell the mortgages for a premium based on the interest rate. Or get the money out fast after refinancing. I'm not sure what they were up to."

"The County was supposed to require jobs, too," he continued. "Well, it didn't matter. The buyers had to have jobs. Some did. Some didn't."

"So you and Burkle Lehane made sure they had jobs."

"In one case, I had to place both the wife and the guy she married, her fiance. She was single on the deed and original mortgage but was married when she refinanced. Quick turnaround, in her case. There went two of the jobs, but they were good workers." He stopped again, frowning. "She was one who never lived there, as the County required."

"How did that one work out?" Gabe asked.

"Kamila Cabrera? She is still an owner. She was a good girl," Barton said, sourly. "But after I turned over Ibis Creek to the owners, they let her get behind on her dues, and she couldn't catch up. Especially after she refinanced with Orion Bank for more money than she paid, but her payments adjusted at six months. I think she expected to refi again or sell. Whatever her plan, she couldn't afford the new payments, even with her job with Lehane – she worked for him – and he let her go a few months after this place was all finished. It wasn't a permanent job. No construction job is."

"Quick turnaround and bad luck." Gabe conveyed no judgment. "One of many?"

"Over half the Affordables. Two-thirds," Barton admitted. "She did part-time work for a while – temp, secretarial, I think – so, she didn't make much. And she was too far behind."

"I guess you do what you have to do," Gabe said. "But a lot of them didn't pay their mortgages or their association dues."

"As it turned out. They didn't pay a lot, and condominium associations live on dues," Barton agreed. "My Ibis Creek was going broke. And it was partly my fault. And the County's."

Nicolina looked at Barton hard. "And you get pissed at JJ Amos because he, almost alone, fixes the damage, the financial damage you did," she said, with a deliberate edge. "By collecting the three hundred thousand in shortfalls you helped create. If not for you and your games, Ibis Creek could have sued your ass without JJ Amos."

Barton Abbott did not wilt. He glared back. "The buildings are fine. Wilma proved it. JJ, money, whatever. There may be a warped breezeway or two but structurally? He just didn't get it. He was very rude – no, he was abusive --in my deposition. He kept asking about this defect or that defect. I kept telling him there *are* no defects. Dolt. I think I may have called him that. I was so pissed off."

Gabe let Nicolina get in one more shot and watched Barton.

"One defect," she snapped, "is that JJ Amos is dead."

Barton slumped but kept his head up. "I'm sorry. I am," he said. "And you are right. I was wrong to be so angry with him for the money he got in. But the buildings are solid. He refused to accept my word. He even said it was sinful to lie under oath, for Christ's sake!"

"He accused you of that?" Nicolina asked. "Of lying under oath?"

"He kept saying it was a sin to lie, which is the same thing," Barton said, still seething. "The lies were coming from Nolan Sanders, Mara Collins and the board, and they all know it."

Gabe stayed Nicolina with a hand on her arm. "What about JJ?"

There it was. Gabe saw it. Nicolina saw it. Barton Abbott's eyes flickered with regret. "He was just stupid. That's the truth. He just believed what they told him." He blinked the reaction away. "He didn't understand real life, construction, development. He didn't understand insurance. He thought something was *something,* and it was *nothing.* He didn't have the smarts to let it go, I guess."

"Any one *something* specific?" Gabe asked. He sensed there was one issue that rankled Barton Abbott. "One that stood out for you?"

Barton made a show of searching his memory. "No. No. I meant that he went down some list and thought each item was a big deal."

Satisfied that he would get no better answer, Gabe looked at Nicolina but stood to signal her the interview was over. "Detective Webster? Anything for you?"

"No. You've been very helpful, Mr. Abbott." She stood, as well.

"Thank you," Gabe said.

Barton stood up slowly, his movement oddly controlled. He shook both their hands. "I doubt I can help any further, but just let me know."

"We will." Gabe let Nicolina go out the door first. They both thanked Pat. She gave them the cheery smile of ignorance.

Not until they were in the car did either of them speak. Nicolina finally said, "I may have gotten a bit too hot."

"You did. Thanks."

"Yeah. Something's off. His emotions are all over the place."

"He ran from anger to pride, to defense, to what?"

"He's got a problem with something that's *something*, right?"

"Maybe more than one," Gabe agreed, "but I think I saw *remorse*. If you can see that at all. You got to him. Nice job. You made him see that he.... maybe not alone, but he's responsible. For all the somethings, including JJ's death, however it happened."

"Caused, maybe. But only indirectly." She put her head back and sighed. "Do we care if he's remorseful? That and two dollars get you a Grandé of latté."

"We got something." He laughed. "I hate to keep saying that, but we got a piece of something."

"Do we need pieces of Barton Abbott's psyche? We need JJ's."

"Unless they're related more closely, that's true," Gabe said. "Let's get some caffeine wisdom and try to put vibrate what pieces we have into something coherent."

"Now, you're doing it on purpose."

"It's his fault."

"By the way, do not let me get Lemon Meringue Mousse," Nicolina said. "It might be fatal."

"It sounds kind of good."

"Yeah. Damn it."

Chapter 13

Gabe and Nicolina huddled back at the office to distil the interviews about JJ Amos and merge it with their other interviews and Nicolina and Ian Decker's background research.

Between the two of them, they had interviewed the very few people who knew JJ Amos well and several who knew him just enough to fill in the picture of him. The gist was that no one knew the current JJ in any depth, probably because there was no well of personality to plumb. Not even Mara, Nolan Sanders or his wife knew what, if anything, lay under his stubborn, God-oriented veneer.

They had reports from other detectives of interviews of his parents, his last bartender at Blue Martini, the attendees at the Pelican Paradiso meeting and Ibis Creek owners. Taken together, they felt they knew the barest of basics, which Nicolina bulleted:

JJ Amos Profile

JJ was thirty-four and nearing a divorce with no children.

He believed, to a fault, in God and Jesus Christ.

He believed, to a fault, in Mara Collins, though supposedly he was no enamored of with her.

He was convinced he was onto something for himself, his much better so-called path.

His had come to believe that his divorce was part of the something and Sally was not.

He had a plan of some sort to reach a milestone on that path.

His plan had something to do with being a first-rate litigator, probably beyond God Himself.

He worked for a firm well stocked with religious outliers.

He seemed to be a dunderhead but was unmeasurable not that dumb.

He was dyslexic.

He had acquired a text-to-speech capability that had an outsized impact on him.

He believed Mara blessed him his new-found ability (though it was an Ian to Sally to Mara parlay).

He had a spectacular memory for things he wanted to hear.

He had specific bad relationships with Chapman and Abbott.

He was despised by foreclosure victims, some of which were frauds anyway.

Despite it all, he was definitely not depressed.

To the contrary, he was enthusiastic, upbeat, on a high.

He had great faith in the Abbott Defect case.

He may have had extra faith in a certain something about the case.

"Maybe, he crashed from his high," Nicolina posited. "The higher, the lower and all that."

"In a few hours?" Gabe shook his head. "Mara claims he wasn't even upset she stiffed him for a drink. No, he was still up, still high."

"Okay. So based on what we have," she said. "Let's speculate. Here's my narrative, not Decker's."

~ ~ ~

James Joseph Amos eventually resented his God-given talent for brow-beating immigrant and other marginal condo owners into paying their past assessments. He also extracted the legal limit of eighteen percent interest and attorney fees usually larger than the actual debt. JJ was very good at his job and, for a time, satisfied with it. At some point, late in 2012, he came to believe he was destined for what he saw as greater things.

He believed this despite the fact that he was not much of a reader or thinker. His favorite teacher, Pastor Bishop's wife, loved him because he did not endlessly ask *why*, not about anything. When she told him something, he took it on faith and could not seem to forget it. To him, the *why* was Tree of Knowledge stuff. That story was burned deeply and shallowly into his brain.

Though not self-aware, JJ understood that learning was easier for him by ear than eye. Books were the devil's work and that fact JJ could see if others could not. He best acquired knowledge by being told and skill by repetition. He became a very good touch-typist by keeping eyes averted from the keyboard or the results of his typing.

Naturally, but unintentionally, intimidating as a boy, JJ had *borrowed* whole sheets of homework from the bookish, who began to write up a second scrawled set just to give away.

He remembered the Cliff Notes summaries his mother read him and the things tutors told him to the point he could sound like he understood each written word that he could not read.

His aptitudes explained why his guidance counselor in high school had recommended a Christian college for JJ. His parents had been very Christian and read the Bible to him endlessly.

The guidance counselor, fooled by JJ's memory of words, had further recommended that JJ definitely consider becoming a lawyer.

Through four years at Divine Ascent College, JJ determined that God had a *Jacob's ladder* tailored to him. He liked God over all else because he was often told that God valued him all the more if he was not good at anything. He just had to believe enough in Jesus, donated money and did not persecute anyone who did not deserve it.

One anecdote related that JJ regretted not being named Meeky so he could have inherited the earth when God died.

Nolan Sanders took him under his wing and even hired Sally to read to him through three years at Coast of Paradise University Law School and marry him. JJ joined Sanders & Tilden right out of law school and became the most feared and content small-scale collection lawyer in Collier County.

Somewhere along the line, Mara Collins happened to him. Unlike most men – and even Mara – he resolutely believed Mara was God's gift. God took a little time but He used Mara to revise JJ's plan, big time. Only God and JJ knew the plan. Jesus, too, of course. Mara knew part of it, but not that God's design exceeded her own infiltration scheme. Otherwise, she was as clueless as anyone.

When JJ believed in something, he was unmovable. He knew a secret celestial plan when it was revealed to him, and no one could change that plan. Maybe, that was why no one else needed to know.

He certainly didn't tell anyone or leave a message for anyone, either.

~ ~ ~

Nicolina and Gabe conducted a follow-up interview with the person closest to JJ Amos.

They met Mara Collins at the Collins office. A less distraught Mara shared more about her own thoughts of that night than JJ's.

Yes, JJ told her he was wrapping up his final collections career and its last presentation at 9:55 PM at the Pelican Paradiso meeting. She had some concern that Nolan Sanders would want JJ to continue collections and JJ would refuse and scuttle both his career and his utility for her.

In a casually self-critical manner, Mara admitted that she had only pretended to have seen that *more* in JJ. She knew he was an effective collection lawyer, but wanted him involved in the Abbott Defect to keep her apprised of the lousy job Graham Chapman was doing. She truly did think JJ could do no worse at litigating the case than Chapman.

If JJ was bowing out of his life as collection attorney at that last meeting at Pelican Paradiso, he made it count. She had never seen him more confident, reciting her embellishments of his dues-collecting. He had problems lying, so Mara had emailed him a few fibs to add in for maximum effect.

She had come realize he could hear better than read; because of that, she knew she had helped him by giving him Dragon Dictation and making him feel astute in using it.

"I wanted him to give it a serious try," she said. "I felt bad that it was Sally's idea but... I was the one he listened to."

The ten Medicare-eligible men at Pelican Paradiso liked JJ's big finish, the Mara-added fiction about how he, and Collins, saved their association from bankruptcy. She personally congratulated JJ on closing out the last fifty thousand dollars of Paradiso delinquencies, emphasizing JJ's employment of threatening letters and a dozen foreclosures. The owners applauded them both.

After their association meetings, JJ and Mara would often go to Blue Martini. Occasionally others would go, but Mara preferred debriefing JJ on the Abbot Defect case there. She was well aware how much JJ liked being seen in public with her, so it was also a reward for his loyalty.

She had intended to go that night, as well, but Paradiso was her third meeting of the day. She did not have the energy and an Ibis Creek meeting with JJ was less than a week away.

It was a fluke, she assumed, but JJ had backed in next to her car, so they were very close as she made her final decision to skip the drink. She did not sense tension or desperation of JJ's part

She flicked his dark orange-on-orange tie and added, "Next to you, I'm way under-dressed."

He surprised her by loosened his tie, removing it and throwing it carelessly into his car. "Who wears a tie to Blue Martini?" His tone was jocular, not needy. She heard the latter in the past.

"You have," she said. "But I meant... I left my bustier at home." Servers, all female, at Blue Martini wore bustiers.

JJ's dark brows could not bend, but they did twitch. "You don't need one," he said without irony. "Customers don't have to wear them."

Mara laughed and went coquette on him. "Are you saying I don't need one?" She immediately regretted it.

JJ realized his gaff and blushed. "I meant you're too pretty... too good for that."

Mara gave him the slightest, carefully innocent curtsey. She did not want him to misunderstand. "Thank you. It's nice of you to say."

She waited for a response and, thankfully, only got the cheerful nod she wanted. At that, she smiled and climbed into her car. She gave him a smile and a wave.

Until days later did she realize that his usual smile for her turned not into a look of disappointment but one of determination. That may have been why she did not feel bad at the time.

Nearly home, she felt disappointed in herself. The night was very significant to JJ: He was done with one thing and on to another much more important to him. She knew that he considered her some sort of *spiritual guide.* It was that undercurrent of pressure fed her fatigue and led her to bail on him. She did not feel like anyone's spiritual anything. If he had doted on her before, he had elevated her to a higher pedestal where the air was precariously thin.

"I know that's not who I am. I wish."

All things taken together, she doubted – even selfishly hoped – JJ would not go to Blue Martini without her. The thought that he may have just gone home on his big night distressed her less than his being at the bar alone, without her.

"I'd never been anyone's S*pirit Guide* before."

She couldn't let him down. She did not wait for a red light after that realization. It was too important to wait. She could get him before he got home.

Her texting while driving was dangerous, but something told her to look up before she sent. She saw a white Ford 250 coming right at her.

Good God! She thought after skidding to a stop. Then she laughed and pulled over.

"Whose guiding who, right?"

She edited her text to JJ. It was 10:42.

Just got His message: Celebrate a Grand Finale! Text me back. I'll meet you. XO

She had never closed a text to him that way, with an *XO,* the universal symbol for *Hugs and Kisses.* She rarely used it with anyone, but it had never seemed appropriate for JJ. Yet, she actually added another XO. To the date of the interview, she did not know why she did that. She cried relating that final *send.*

"That made me cry," she said. "I was a little mad later that he didn't text me back. That makes me cry, too."

"You shouldn't," Gabe said. He gestured for Nicolina to explain.

Nicolina did. "Do you remember I told you JJ had turned his phone off before the Paradiso meeting?"

"Yeah."

She put her hand on Mara's. "Don't feel bad about it," she said. "We have confirmed that JJ never turned it back on."

"His battery was dead, maybe?" Mara asked, hopefully.

"It was fine. He pulled it out." Nicolina omitted the missing sim card as too complicated or too devastating, she didn't know which."In short, he could not have responded to your text."

Mara's eyes filled. "He never saw it? At all?"

"No. He couldn't have."

"But why?"

"We have no idea? Do you?"

"Me? No." Mara laughed and cried at the same time. "I just thought he just didn't need me anymore. That he didn't need anyone on that fucking *path* of his. It hurt."

After leaving Mara, Gabe and Nicolina compared their takes. Neither had expected the levels of Mara's vulnerability, her conflicted reaction to her last text and his failure to return it.

"I hate it when people like her surprise me," Nicolina said.

"We're pretty jaded," he replied. "But half of me kept thinking how she shouldn't feel so bad about a text that went nowhere."

"She didn't know. Until just now."

"Maybe, we helped her on that score."

"Not in my job descriptions, Lieutenant."

They continued to mull over the interview, increasingly certain that JJ was waiting at Blue Martini for a text he wanted and that they could not find. The text was beyond *wanting.* He *needed* that text but he did not need to be at Blue Martini.

That text, for some earthly reason, was to send him on his real path, to the one place he needed to be: Beside the Ibis Creek Bog.

Chapter 14

For a few minutes after listening to Ian's report on his Happy Hour meeting with Lieutenant Gabe Hubble, Claire had nothing to say. She did render a variety of facial expressions. Finally, she said, "Damn it. Sebastian Decker was my top suspect. Now that you are pally *Ian*, I have to start over. And change clothes." With that, she went into the master bedroom to change for the Ibis Creek board of directors meeting.

In the few days since JJ's body's recovery, Claire had focused on the same issue as everyone else: JJ Amos had no business being on Ibis Creek property after dark. Claire was not tapped into the Ibis Creek swimming pool-based gossip klatch that served as its newsletter. "I get burned too easily at the pool. In more ways that one. Yet, she knew JJ better than all the klatchers together. She had clashed with him for six months while a director.

She could not envision him cheating on either his wife or the love of his life. No one at Ibis Creek would invite him over for a drink, except, maybe Claire, herself. She would have happily mixed him a drink fancied up with the right ingredients. "Where do I buy rat poison?"

"Rat poison," Leo asked. "Call Pelican Bug-Away. They are already here all the time."

"That's not the problem."

"Home Depot, then. Why?"

"Just thinking," she said from the bedroom. "About JJ."

"Don't expect and *RSVP*," Leo said.

"I'm thinking a party for Mara, Roy and Kenny Becks. Throw in Joyce Becks, too."

Association Kenny Becks and his wife Joyce had once firmly supported Claire's rebellion. Kenny had since fallen prey to the Mara Effect, and Joyce had on IQ point more than her husband.

"JJ wasn't that bad."

"And he drank beer," Ian added. "Besides, Claire, you have to give him some credit for collect a lot of money for Sanders Tilden's fees." He held up a stop-palm. "No need to say it. You badgered him… In a good badger way."

Claire did not respond, preferring only to *think* ill of the dead. In her view, anyone could have collected the many delinquencies, with her and a cattle prod.

Both Leo and Ian had agreed to the latter often enough.

By 2009, offers of cheap mortgages – any mortgages – had dried up, giving *flip flop* a new meaning in Florida. Condo values plummeted fathoms under loan balances. When an owner faced losing a unit to a bank, association dues had priority zero. Boards of directors, just retired, regular folk, had not volunteered to be prosecutors. Ibis Creek was no different.

Except that, Ibis Creek had Claire Hunter. Claire knew what was coming and had the empathy of a barracuda. Her director campaign brutally focused on the huge amounts uncollected, with a Claire-subtle undercurrent that Affordables were cheating owners who paid in higher dues. She was elected – carrying Kenny Becks and Phil Bass along with her – to ramp up to *really* ugly and get the money first and ask later.

It took her half her one-year term to harass block-headed JJ Amos into action. When she did, JJ, with Mara's and Kenny's approval, retaliated: JJ canceled her access to Sanders Tilden's collections-monitoring website. Fortunately, like-minded Phil Bass kept an eye on the suddenly motivated JJ as he crushed delinquents by the dozens.

Phil, unlike Kenny, remained an ally and friend.

Claire and Leo had contracted to buy their Ibis Creek unit while it was still in the footers-stage. Though they knew better, the price per square foot seduced even cynics.

That same incentive – albeit at crumbled prices – enabled Evie to talk Ian into their buying at Ibis Creek. "It may get cheaper, Ian, but it is already cheap for the size. If nothing else, it can be your writing retreat...

Claire envied Evie's accuracy and her decision to live elsewhere.

Ibis Creek was to be on the leading edge of the gentrification of the Naples East Bay Shores Village. Instead, it became a cash-bleeding orphan. Not far from Ibis Creek, another developer razed a large apartment complex for a sure-fire mixed-use project. The uses turned out to be a mix of weed growing and weed selling, though the latter selling was more mixed than that. There was no other market or money.

Financing, like sharks, died when it stopped circling.

Sort of like JJ, Claire thought as she dressed and steeled for battle in her personal Condo War.

~ ~ ~

Condominiums comprised certain fundamental elements: Common Elements, Limited Common Elements, the condo units and Condo Warriors, like Claire. The first three were designated by state statute and the condominium's Declaration of Condominium, the latter a constitution similar to – if less italicized than – the Ibis

Bogger's Heron's Beak *Royal Edicts of Governance*. The language of any Declaration, to stay under one hundred pages, could not have spelled out every possible combination of facts that owners, managers and lawyers would later incite all-out war.

Common Elements were everything not part of the defined condominium units. The units were apartments owned by individual owners, not a single landlord. Limited Common Elements were Common Elements designated for the exclusive use of a unit or that vaguely that served only a single unit. In perhaps 50 percent of the time, such distinctions were very clear, depending on the age of the lawyer who *cut and pasted* the Declaration.

Condominiums were like the municipalities or real life. They were ruled by a board of directors elected by unit owners who cared about one or two things they actually cared about and little else. Most owners did not vote at all, especially at Ibis Creek. This indifference resulted from their being landlords or Snow Birds – or Snow Geese, Canadian Snow Birds – who did not live anywhere near the Condominium. Some paid no attention because they were accustomed to living in apartments with no say at all.

Boards were filled with unpaid owners lusting for the power they never had or too naive to realized the first type would dominate the board. Boards then hired managers, usually outside management companies – like Collins Management – to do the dirty work of running the condominium. Such managers were analogous to a town manager, the executive branch of the Federal Government or one's parents.

Condo Warriors were like the loyal opposition in politics, with the accent on opposition. Some of these brave or whacked out individuals simply hated their boards;

others took issue with one or more board decisions; some thought dues and fees were ridiculously high; many found management companies impossible to deal with; a very few combined all of the above.

Claire Hunter was not whacked out, but she had an innate dislike of messiness and disorder. Unlike most Condo Warriors, Claire had a siege weapon named Ian Decker. Ian was a native born iconoclast, a skeptical outlier. More importantly, Ian had the ability and the time to research any issue as a favor to Claire. It was a big plus – for her, not him – that he willingly deferred his own writing to help out. They formed a formidable pair of barbarians at the Ibis Creek gates.

Claire, Leo and Ian walked together – with Claire, as always, a stride in front – to the Clubhouse for the board of directors meeting. The lot had a few cars in it: Mara's, manager Jenny Moreno's, a 2012 Mercedes E 350 with the familiar Quadrant sign magnetically affixed to the front doors. An unfamiliar silver, larger but older, Mercedes S-Class sat next to Hugh's.

Ian spotted Gabe Hubble's car, as well.

"Has there ever been a lawnmower in that trunk?" Claire asked of the Quadrant car. "Does Hugh own anything?"

"Maybe. Jointly with the Feds," Ian said. "But you know that."

"You like Hugh," Leo said. "Don't pretend you don't. It is unseemly."

"Everybody likes Hugh," Ian agreed. "He surprised me with JJ. I'm not sure I would have gone into the Bog for another lawyer."

"Amen," Claire said. "And, yes, I admit Quadrant has done a good job with the flower beds and the hedges."

"Except for killing more of the grass." The sad state of the Ibis Creek grass was a pet peeve of Leo's. "How can anyone kill Bermuda grass? It's criminal." He hesitated, contrite. "You know what I mean."

"The criminal is a fungus or dog pee or something," Ian objected.

"Yeah." Claire nodded. "Besides, who calls stealing from banks criminal, anymore?"

"Hugh just forgot the second half of Robin Hood's ethics." Ian checked the plate on Gabe's car to be sure it was a Sheriff Department car. "Lieutenant Hubble is here, too. To give us all an update on JJ, I presume."

"If he knows more than he told you at Happy Hour," Claire said, "you need to add more booze."

"I'll try that." Ian opened the Clubhouse door.

Claire went right in, but Leo made it only halfway. "I've been thinking," Leo said.

"That's not good." Claire took his hand and dragged him inside.

Once inside, Leo gestured toward the far corner of the foyer and led them to it. "Maybe, he was doing what you two were accused of doing."

"Harassing Collins and the board," Claire said. "That's bullshit."

"Extortion? Ian said. "I got that one for demanding statutory damages for their withholding records and delaying record inspections. JJ was part of the reason –"

Leo shook his head. "I don't he meant that." He opened the door to the cramped when empty exercise room and ushered them into it. Still, he whispered. "Spying."

Ian and Claire both stopped and looked at Leo, stunned, then, each other.

"Where'd you come up with that?" Claire asked, forgetting to whisper.

Ian followed Leo's example. "Leo, he barely knew were Ibis Creek was."

"Still."

"Damn. What do you think, Claire?"

"I think Leo's…" She stopped mid-sentence. "Damn. I guess it would explain…" She looked in both directions. "Not very much. Mara doesn't live anywhere near here."

"Spying," Leo said. "What if JJ was spying. Not peeping."

"Claire's right. Spying on whom? Why?"

Leo frowned at Ian. "You're the one with all oddball conspiracy plots. Mine is the tragedy of love gone wrong."

Claire rolled her eyes. "You two! What happened to *who the hell done it*?"

"I am a dramatist," Leo objected.

"Oh, good Lord."

"We don't know if anyone *done* anything," Ian said. "And we don't know JJ was either peeping or spying. I don't think it matters. All it does is explain why he was there. It's not like he was kidnapped. Let's kick this *spy* theory around ourselves before we run it by Gabe. I'll come over after the meeting, and we see what it could mean."

Leo nodded.

Claire made a disapproving face but finally nodded. "You always come over, anyway."

"You have wine with corks. Mine lives in a box." Ian pulled out a small notepad from his pants pocket. His Costco Tommy Bahama knock-off had no breast pocket. "Oh, shit. Claire. A pen."

"This," she said, presenting him with a choice of three, "is how novels remain unfinished."

He ignored her long enough to jot down *exorcise room*. "It's for a post." He showed her what he had written.

"That's just dumb enough to be an Ibis Crock truth."

Leo glanced at the pad before it went back into Ian's pocket. "I can't read your handwriting, but I'll bet ten bucks it's another pun."

"Think more Kenny Beck's malaprop."

Claire sighed. "Fish in a damned barrel, Ian. Can you shoot, say, the side of a barn? One with Mara Collins in front."

Ian let the Mara comment pass as completing Claire's *Baker's Dozen* for any given run up to a meeting. "I am barn-certified, thank you very much."

"You can show us later. Time to find a chair." Claire said. "We don't want to miss the National Anthem."

Leo opened the door, and they crossed the foyer, passed through the short hallway and breached the great room. Leo stopped and nodded toward the small bookshelf nook. "I still don't see a single Hemingway, Faulkner – "

"Or Decker," Claire added. "Shocking."

"I appreciate the company, Claire. Now, I'll be permanently blocked."

Several rows of party-service chairs had been positioned with the usual upholstered furniture moved aside. Ever optimistic president Kenny Becks looked pleased with the turn-out. He looked less so when he saw Claire, Leo and Ian sit at the pool end of the third row. He immediately looked down at some papers on the board table.

"I didn't read the agenda," Leo said. "Is Lieutenant Hubble on it?"

"Not by name," Ian said."It just says *update on accident*."

"Look at this turnout," Claire said, annoyed at the unusual numbers. "Don't these people know it's August?"

August of any year was the lowest ebb of the Ibis Creek population and interest.

"For once JJ Amos is sexier than replacing than fixing the Jacuzzi heater."

Claire and Leo looked at Ian with dismay, as did a few owners in his vicinity who had shown up only to complain about the cold spa water.

"I mean, fixing townhouse door lighting," he said, without glancing and apologetically.

Ibis Creek meeting agendas contained few memorable items. Most owners attended out of concern for only one issue, usually dog poop or water temperature. Claire and Ian were rare in that regard. Leo fell in the middle. He usually came with Claire and Ian for moral support. For once, he had his own issue.

"You made it on," Claire said. "Good luck."

"Righteousness needs no luck," Leo propounded. "Though luck is more likely to help here."

"I'm with you, Leo," Ian said. "We need more light, not less. Your bulb is an important –"

"It is not my bulb, damn it. That's the point. You said so."

Ian had, indeed, researched the issue. "And I'm right."

At the end of each of the twelve four-story buildings, Barton Abbott had affixed on a pair of two-story units that the promotional literature designated as luxury townhouses. The title came with a bit of snob-appeal, the appropriate pricing and a couple vintage-style fixtures per floor. The Hunter's – or, in Leo's mind, the not-Hunter's – left, first-floor carriage lamp was dead. It had been for weeks.

The missing light had no effect on the Hunters. Usually, it combined with its right-hand mate to cast an interlocking shadow that made it harder to unlock their door. Still, Leo was a man of principals, and one was symmetry.

Jenny had passed the issue up to Mara, who had decreed carriage lamps to be the townhouses' problem, not the associations.

"Bullshit," Leo had been grousing since.

"Well," Claire said, "their shadows only affect our doorway."

"Not true. There is less light on the sidewalk, a very common element."

Mara remained steadfast in her disinteres. Jenny had to field Leo's weekly emails, replying, finally, with a certified form letter: "I'm sorry, Mr. [name field], the declaration says the [LCE field] is a limited common element and your responsibility." Jenny had been new to Collins forms at the time.

Leo even tried the added danger of "slipping on dangerously unseen dog poop" to no avail.

In fact, the lamps provided half the light preventing residents stumbling on a heaving sidewalk and its piles of poop. The other half came from lights under the garage eaves, most of them out, as well.

Though the lamps were nowhere near the Bog, Leo whispered to Ian, "Bad lighting. Good for spies. Bad for spies on foot."

Ian held an index finger to his lips, but Claire had heard, and her eyes narrowed.

"Claire, don't," Ian begged.

"Jesus. Okay. I won't."

"Okay, everyone," Mara Collins called out. "Grab a seat, please. We want to start on time. As usual, we can't take any audience comments during the meeting. There is a lot to get through."

Claire bristled, visibly. "Oh, Mara. By Florida statute, we are not an audience. We are participants."

Leo put his hand on Claire's arm. He did that a lot at meetings.

"Yes, Claire, I agree," Mara said, with her gracious smile. The smile was for the man standing next to her. "I meant that President Becks will give everyone a chance to speak before adjournment. If you have signed up in advance of... now. The sign-up sheet is on the table in the hall." She turned to Jenny. "Please get the sign-up sheet, Jenny."

As Jenny hurried off, Kenny Becks said, "Comments before adjournment. If you signed up."

The Florida condominium statute guaranteed owners the right to speak on agenda items at board meetings and incorporated that right into all Condominium Declarations. The right was patterned after the open-meeting policy for public meetings. To Claire and Ian, it was the First Amendment of condominium constitutions. Mara's interpretation meant owner could only speak in an empty barn.

Mara and the Beck board also felt that no issue important enough for a vote should be openly discussed at a meeting. Too much superficial knowledge was bad for owners and discussion slowed meetings and delayed cocktail hour.

To its credit, Collins Management had always gone the extra mile to keep owners fully uninformed. Its meetings went quickly. Its savvy proprietor, Roy Collins, had built his business on the theory that discussion with owners cost his staff *time,* and every one of them knew what *time* meant. Mara was well trained in that regard.

"Thank you for your concern. We're working on a solution," was another Collins' mantra that Mara had down. Claire observed that Jenny said the same thing, but sounded less sincere.

Mara looked splendid, even to Claire, as she stood in front of the director table. She wore a conservative teal skirt suit, with narrow lines and a jacket that showed only her perfect neck and served to catch her slightly wavy hair.

"Damn," Claire said. "I hate her."

The sixteen-seat table was a Collins special order. They supplied it, for a slight charge, for all of the associations they managed. There were seven chairs along the far side and two on each end. It was deep enough to put suitable distance between the audience of owners and their elected representatives.

Short, squat Kenny Becks, presidential by default – no one else wanted the job – presided, when Mara didn't. He commanded the middle chair. Two directors flanked him to either side, the other two, a Snow Bird and a Snow Goose, had absented themselves northward.

Site manager Jenny Moreno sat on the Left side of the table. The amiable recently hired manager had much of the Collins Way to learn, as she responded to owner emails the same day.

Jenny was born in Immokalee, on of five children of diligent Yucatan Mayan migrant workers based in the town for years. She had gotten a scholarship to Gulf Coast University in Ft. Meyers, graduating as one of its top hospitality majors. Even so, Roy Collins hired her as one of Mara's subordinate managers on her very first job interview. She was smart, tenacious, spoke Spanish better than her parents and came cheap. Roy believed Mara could convert that tenacity to obstinacy with a little training.

Ibis Creek, like a few other complexes in its immediate area, had a Hispanic population hovering around thirty percent. While their English was decent to perfect, Roy knew that communication was time and time was precious. Jenny's inexpensive language facility meant he could stretch her thin immediately. By the time she became a licensed Community Association Manager, he would have Jenny handling a portfolio of ten Hispanic-intense properties, freeing Mara up to entice more associations into the Collins fold.

Raw, inexperienced Jenny had won over the women in Ibis Creek who felt snubbed by Mara's inattention to them and attention to her of their male counterparts. Roy Collins notice the effect of the combination overcame Mara's major weakness. He planned to have Jenny accompany Mara wherever females had serious clout choosing management companies or running boards. Ibis Creek was not one of those but was more difficult to run than most because of Claire's and Ian's constant intervention.

Jenny owned a dog, so she also had a firm grasp of Ibis Creek's poop plague. Few associations allowed dogs to the extent Ibis Creek did. Most tenants assumed they would be gone before their dog poop piled too high, but owners without dogs had shoes and cholera to worry about.

Once the participants took their seats, Mara glanced back at Kenny Becks and walked to her seat next to Jenny. Kenny called the meeting to order. Kenny always started meetings with a loud but uncertain voice. As he went, he tended to phrase everything as a question for Mara or Jenny or anyone else to answer. President of the board was the highest position he had held since he became an older brother at four and that dominance did not last long. In the ensuing sixty-six years, Kenny had run nothing including his two households.

"There is a lot to get through." Kenny parroted Mara's phrases and soon would Jenny's. Kenny's most current thought was the one he thought he had just heard. Sometimes he simply read what Mara wrote. "You are all aware of the tragedy of JJ Amos's drowning here at Ibis Creek. Detective Hubble from the Sheriff will be joining us in a few minutes for an update. In the meantime, we can proceed with the meeting?"

Kenny was concerned that JJ update would slow the meeting with condolences, although he disliked JJ more than most. JJ had never listened to word Kenny said and had threatened to lien his unit before Kenny assumed his high office.

As with all meetings, Kenny emphasized that all directors make up their minds by email, conforming exactly to Mara Collins' recommendations. Claire and Ian had argued, correctly, that such board decision-making violated Florida's statute, Chapter 718. Kenny suspected they were right, but Mara told him no one cared about boring, long-winded legal jargon, especially busy, underpaid state regulators. Mara's advice, suited Kenny on two points: It came from Mara, and he never read anything with double-digit chapters numbers or sub-paragraphs. He preferred magazines with pictures and captions.

The bottom line for Kenny was that Mara said, "No one knows what the statute says except Ian and Claire, and she only knew because Ian told her It's not a problem."

With Roy's training and her own innate good sense, Mara understood that even good directors had short attention spans. As a consequence, she routinely *buried the lead* and all substance in the last third of long paragraphs. Not even Kenny would not read through the long text, even though – or maybe especially since – they came down from Mara.

A good example was Mara's pre-meeting email to the directors in support of the old business line-item for pool chair replacement: The lowest quote of $6,728.18 from Osprey Pool Supply, LLC, followed by six sentences about colors, types of mesh and pillows. The real reason for replacing the perfectly good chairs had fallen into the third to last sentence. "The chairs are out of warranty. And we budgeted replacement this year."

Roy's preferred pool equipment supplier, Rookery Bay Pools had originally supplied the budget figure and, later, the specifications. Not surprisingly, Rookery submitted the budget number as its bid.

In most cases, Roy's preferred suppliers, like Rookery Bay Pools and Quadrant Landscaping, always submitted last and came in as low bidders. Knowing the other bids in advance may have helped. Invariably, post-award additions drove up the costs enough to cover certain overhead.

In all fairness, Roy got decent bids and rarely took more than five percent. He was not popular with other management companies.

In the case of the pool chairs, though, the preferred supplies lost out to a new bidder. The Board voted unanimously to approve the Osprey quote.

"Want to bet," Claire whispered to Ian, eyes rolling, "that the osprey hatched on Rookery Bay."

"'I believe Osprey is on record as Mara' favorite bird."

"We chased five quotes for the chairs." Mara's own eyes twinkled from Claire to Ian and back. "We had expected better of Rookery Bay, but these other contractors were just hungrier this time. That is why we always get competitive bids."

"The budget," Jenny volunteered, "was $7,500. So we are $800 to the good."

The history of Ibis Creek had proven that low bids almost always exceeded the Collins-designed budget for a given year.

"Super work, Mara, Jenny," Kenny said. "Moving on. I want to insert a guest here, before Hugh, Quadrant, reports on the landscaping." Kenny nodded to Mara.

Mara stood and took center stage, her enthusiasm strained. She looked toward the back of the room and said, "We have the first of special guests, right now."

Like everyone else, Ian looked to the back of the room, expecting Gabe or Nicolina. Neither was present. He did not recognize the tall, trim black man who made his way forward.

"Let me introduce Marty Pinedo," Mara began before Marty reached her. "He is the developer of the homes on Ester View, just up the street from here. Marty's management company also handles several of our rented units here."

Hugh stepped forward to shake Marty's hand making it obvious to Ian, and everyone else, they knew each other on very friendly terms. Ian thought greeting spoke volumes about Marty.

Marty had quite a smile, even next to Mara's. "Thank you. I won't take up much of your time," he said. "I know you have some more important business to attend to."

"Do you recognize him?" Ian asked Claire, in a whisper. "Hugh sure knows him."

"Don't you? He came to a Collier Redevelopment meeting months ago," she said. "You and I have checked out his Ester View project. He's got walls up on three and is promised big things for the whole tract. Thirty houses. He needs CRA density waivers to build that many. He talks a good game, I'll say that."

Marty had continued to talk during their hushed exchange. He explained that he loved the Naples East Bay Shores Village and saw it as the best place for the rebirth of gentrification in East and South Naples. "Yes, we are starting to see large complexes being built, or at least planned, for Airport, Livingston, and Collier Boulevard.

But this is more of a neighborhood already. It just needs to regain its momentum."

He let the audience murmur for a moment.

"We heard that six years ago." Leo kept his voice down.

"We'll be hearing it in another six," Claire agreed.

"Ester View is part of that momentum." Marty had a slight accent that Ian could not place, not that he was good with accents. "He's smooth."

"My company is negotiating with the CRA, the Collier Redevelopment Authority, to purchase some of the lots they own over on Bayshore. The Ester View project will have only *green* single family homes in a small gated community. We have three underway but we the help of your neighborhood's CRA to build out at least thirty more, every one of them LEED certified." He spoke with no particular urgency, but in a commanding rhythm. "We are committed to Naples East Bay Shores Village."

He reminded Ian of someone. "Oh, shit."

"What?" Claire asked.

"Listen to him. Who does he remind you of?"

She listened. "No, I don't get it."

"Keep listening."

Marty continued, "For those of you who don't know LEED is short for Leadership in Energy and Environmental Design. It is not a governmental certification, but an established organization promoting – and certifying – design and construction of green buildings. The certification guarantees our Ester View homes will be environmentally sound, with energy-efficient lighting, low water consumption and recycling. We will use recycled construction materials. We will have energy efficient appliances."

The audience seemed ambivalent, and Marty clearly saw he was losing them.

"From your point of view, you will see the Ester View homes just as upscale as Ibis Creek, but in house form. LEED buyers see the extra value of green building and will to pay the necessary premium, though we're keeping it under twenty percent per square foot. They will be the type of new neighbor you expected when you bought here. To make sure, we have contracted with Hugh's company Quadrant to do the Ester View landscape design."

"Landscape design?" Ian asked, rhetorically. The three of them knew the Barretts knew nothing of design, at least not of landscaping.

"Oh, shit," Claire said. "He sounds like him."

"Who?" Leo leaned in before he got it. "Oh. Hugh."

"Bingo."

"I'm afraid I can't stay for questions after the meeting, but we'll have presentations at the CRA's meetings every step of the way," Marty concluded. "And I hope many of you will attend. Thank you." He gave a little bow and thanked the board and Mara, as well.

Mara let the crowd digest Marty's words until he had left the room.

Ian heard the Clubhouse door close. "Boy. He wasn't kidding," he said to Claire and Leo.

~ ~ ~

Mara began again. "We are starting to see what Ibis Creek started in this neighborhood." She turned toward Kenny as she backed toward her chair. "This village."

"Yes, this village," Kenny said, cheerfully. "That is some great news for our village." He hesitated, appearing distressed for a moment. Then he said, "On to more day-to-day, but a topic of great interest to all of us. Mr. Hugh Barrett of Quadrant Landscaping. Hugh will give us his status."

Leo fidgeted. "He skipped the lights again." Unlike Claire and Ian, Leo could had superb tunnel vision on Ibis Creek issues. At the end of his tunnel, Leo saw only the light of working bulbs.

Hugh Barrett first thanked Mara for inviting him to his fortnightly command performance. He then thanked the absent Marty Pinedo for the kind words. Thanks exhausted, he detailed such items as the difficulties in blowing wet grass cuttings, leveling off the wide border hedges and edging weed-like grasses. For a change, though it mattered little, the excuses doubled as legitimate reasons. Hugh was getting to the unusual problems specific to the Bog when he cocked his head and stopped talking.

Hugh glanced at Mara, who shook her head. She had slumped just a bit in her chair.

He looked at the rear of the room and said, "Mara asked me to introduce Lieutenant Gabe Hubble and Detective Nicolina Webster from the Sheriff's Department. Rich, Corporal Basehart is also with us."

Leo and Claire looked to the rear of the room, but Ian kept his eyes on Mara. Her eyes glistened. She was hiding it well, but Ian could tell: She was – surprisingly to him – genuinely sad. JJ had been more than a tool to her.

Even more interested in her movements than usual, he watched as she rose from her chair, took a breath and approximated the usual Mara. It was an impressive effort.

As if she sensed it, Mara looked directly at Ian for a moment and – as if the mere sight of him helped – she squared her narrow shoulders and became more Mara-like.

Gabe let Nicolina lead the way along the pool side of the Clubhouse. They passed Ian, Claire and Leo, but neither did more than glance sideways in recognitions. By the time they reached the front, Mara and Kenny had joined Hugh to greet the detectives. Hands were shaken, sedately, all around.

Gabe and Nicolina turned to face the audience, but Gabe waited until Hugh and Mara had taken the seats at the right end of the table, and Kenny had returned to his central seat.

"First of all, Detective Webster and I would like to extend our condolences on the loss of JJ Amos," Gabe began. "In an important way, he was a member of your community and he will be missed. Of course, that is not why we are here. Many of you have met Detective Webster and Corporal Basehart. They, along with other deputies have had to interview residents and owners here as part of our investigation into Mr. Amos's death."

Many in the audience looked to their neighbors, but there was no murmur.

"We are charged with investigating any death that is unexplained. That would include even death by natural causes when the causes are not readily discernible. Really, until we have a cause of death formally established, our department has to investigate." He paused and held out his hand as a signal to Nicolina.

She took a step forward. "As of today, we do not have a certified cause of death. We know that the immediate cause of Mr. Amos's unfortunate death was drowning," she explained. "But the circumstances are still unexplained. We have talked to most of the residents on the north side of the complex and have been able to learn a good deal, but we have found no witnesses to the death itself. That is not surprising. It happened after midnight on a rainy night."

"There is no evidence that anyone else was involved," she continued. "We can't say for certain that it was just an unfortunate accident. We don't know. We don't even know why Mr. Amos was here so late on that night."

Nicolina aimed her eyes directly at Ian. We would welcome any insight you have in that regard."

Gabe asked, "Any questions?" Fortunately, he did not have to wait long for the ice to break. "Mr. Decker."

"You know we have a gate and gate camera," Ian said, lobbing a softball. "Did you learn anything from that."

"Yes. Mr. Amos came in just before midnight. He did not have a bar code. He did not call anyone from the call-box. He used a Vendor Code," he added, "which confirms the time of entry as Midnight. The visual of him is not very clear, but the plate established that it was his car."

"You're getting soft, Decker." Claire leaned toward Ian. "You already knew that."

"No one else was going to ask a question. Right?"

"I was intimidated," she whispered. "Until you started."

Ian had a bad feeling about an uncorked bottle.

Hugh Barrett asked, "We didn't screw up your scene did we? I didn't want to leave –"

"Detective Webster."

Nicolina smiled the least lethal smile in her arsenal. "Normally, we prefer an undisturbed scene, but, no, Mr. Barrett. It was too wet to make any difference at that site. Also, we established that you were not at an actual scene. Except for your altruistic efforts. The entry point – the place where Mr. Amos entered the Preserve – was on the north side several buildings east of where you recovered him. You did the right thing." She lasered Ian again. "And Mr. Decker, too."

The audience seemed to be hushed or repeating the term *entry point*. Gabe redirected the conversation. "I understand that JJ Amos was very aggressive in collecting for Ibis Creek. And he ruffled some feathers."

A few nodded, but that was all.

Gabe looked at Mara. "And he did not check in with anyone at Collins?"

"No, Lieutenant." Mara managed to sound definitive, her look did not match her voice. "Also, you have all of our collection information. The board is set to waive privilege later in the meeting, on collection matters." The next words she visibly forced out. "That's mostly what JJ did."

Nicolina leaned forward. "Thank you, Ms. Collins. That would be very helpful."

"We want to do everything…" Mara began before stopping, pressing her lips together.

Hugh leaned into her, his hand slipping behind her back. "It's fine."

Her posture improved, and she nodded without looking his way.

"Anything," echoed Kenny, not to rescue Mara but to sound in command. "A terrible accident."

Claire's hand shot up.

"Uh, Claire," Ian whispered.

"Kenny says it's an accident," she said. "Can we feel safe?"

Ian shrugged when Gabe looked at him. Gabe could feel Nicolina sizzle as he turned his attention to Claire. "We are still investigating, but *accident* is the most plausible. We can't put anyone else at the scene. But," he emphasized, "we can't say. We simply cannot explain what he was doing at Ibis Creek at that time. I wish we could."

"We just want this terrible accident over with," Kenny said. "I'd like to move to waive privilege on anything to do with JJ."

Mara began to stand, but Hugh subtly restrained her, whispering, "It's not important."

"Second," came four other voices.

"Unanimous," Kenny declared.

"Oh, boy," Ian said. "That was way too broad."

"Anyone else has anything for us?" Gabe asked. "I realize this is painful and the more information we can get, the more quickly we can close the case."

Mara took half a breath. She and Hugh stood up together. Mara said, "Thank you both. I think it is time to…" The sentence just stopped when Claire stood up.

"Claire," Ian and Leo said together.

"I do have something to contribute," Claire said.

Nicolina tried to vaporized Claire with a look, not knowing it would never work. Mara just looked away. Gabe did not flinch. "Go ahead, Mrs. Hunter."

"About what he was doing back there? At that hour?" she said. "Obviously, it was a little late to post an eviction notice."

Ian whispered, "God damn it. Not here."

"Maybe you don't know," Claire pressed on. "We have had a report – more than one, several – reports or a peeping Tom – "

"A what?" Gabe stared at Claire in disbelief. He turned to Nicolina who shifted her eyes from Claire to Ian.

"A peeping Tom," Claire repeated. "Ask Mara. Or Kenny. They as much as accused me."

Mara stiffened with every word, but she said nothing.

Kenny becks said, "It was just a rumor. Months ago. Nothing came of it."

Gabe said, "Thank you, Mrs. Hunter – "

"That's crap!" Mara finally snapped. "You vindictive bitch –"

"Mrs. Hunter," Hugh said, firmly. "Why don't you meet with us after the meeting?"

Gabe was still processing. "That would be very helpful." He half-turned to Nicolina and raised an eyebrow.

Nicolina gave Gabe a *don't go there* look. "It was nothing."

"When was it nothing?" he asked through clenched teeth.

"Last year."

"We can explore that later, detective."

"Thank you, Lieutenant. Thank you both," Mara said, stepping away from Hugh's support. "Let me see you out." She turned back to Kenny. "Let's take a ten-minute recess while I escort our guests out."

"Everybody. Let's take a ten-minute recess."

Half of the residents headed off to the restrooms. The meeting had only consumed thirty minutes of the meeting, but it had clenched most of the bladders in the room. The remaining owners stood but said little.

"Ms. Collins?" Gabe put his hand on Mara's elbow for just long enough to make his point. "Walk us to our cars, please."

"It was nothing, Lieutenant. It was months ago."

When Hugh began to follow, Gabe froze him in place with a look.

"Whoa." Leo whistled quietly. "He's pissed."

"He didn't know," Claire said. "Ha."

"There was a better way." Ian shook his head. "Hadn't we agreed?"

Claire wrinkled her nose. "It made her look bad. Kenny, too."

"That's not always the point."

"It is to me."

As Mara, Nicolina and Gabe walked past Claire, Ian and Leo, Mara straightened and kept her eyes front, denying Claire any grin of triumph.

Gabe nodded to Ian. "A favor?" Then he added, "Wait a second. Then meet me just outside."

Ian did, uncertain of Gabe's intent. It did not take an *empath* to know Gabe was barely controlling a bad case of fury.

Once they were outside, Gabe let Nicolina and Mara continue. He stopped Ian.

"What do you know about this peeping Tom shit?"

"Not much," Ian said. "I know there were reports in the fall and winter last year. I know that Kenny Becks, a couple other directors wanted to lynch Claire and/or me for it. Mara, too."

"Interesting."

"Not really, the descriptions – to the extent there were any – had a body type nowhere near Claire's or mine," Ian went on. "Way too wide for Claire and much too short for me. It was wishful thinking."

"Wishful thinking?"

"If I didn't tell you already," Ian said, "we are pariahs here. Dissent is the Devil's voice at work. Anyway, after I pointed out the descriptions angle – in clear legalese – the accusations just swam around in the gossip pool. There weren't any reports after that."

"I'll want to talk to you more about this," Gabe said. "As a source."

"I can be a veritable fount."

"That, I've noticed," Gabe said, with a slight smile. His anger had cooled. "Thanks."

"Sure," Ian responded. "It seemed harmless enough. At the time."

"That was then." Gabe nodded and turned to join Mara and Nicolina, standing at their cars.

Nicolina detected that Gabe's anger had abated. "I didn't directly handle that case." she insisted. "It was Vice. And Amos's name wasn't anywhere near it."

"Because it wasn't JJ," Mara agreed, emphatically. "No one even thought of it. Really, Lieutenant. That's just Claire Hunter – "

"That's just Claire Hunter giving us a reason he would be here," Gabe said. "It is the one damned fact that's been missing."

Mara glared at Gabe. "It couldn't be JJ. No way."

"And why couldn't be?"

"He wouldn't. He…" Mara wanted to explain, but held back. "He just wouldn't."

Nicolina supplied the withheld explanation. "Because of you. Because he literally only had eyes for you. That's the truth, isn't it?"

Mara stood fast, but tears trickled down her cheeks. "I know how that sounds."

"I don't blame him," Nicolina said.

"When it started, the reports?" Mara said, recovering. "That was before."

Gabe's impatience gave way to his hunter instinct. "Before? Before what?"

"Before he changed?" Nicolina asked.

"Yes. Before that." Mara said, mostly to herself. She stood straighter and set her shoulders."So, it could not have been him."

"We need all of the call-box log-ins," Nicolina said. "Do they go back that far?"

"I don't know. I don't keep track of that."

"Who would?"

"The vendor. I don't even know who that is," Mara said, defensive. "I don't handle that."

Gabe said, quietly, "We'll need you to find out. He used your code, didn't he? JJ."

"Did he? I didn't know that."

"Did you ever come here at night?" Gabe asked. "I get the impression you didn't... didn't have to come here often."

"No. I didn't. I'm the senior CAM. The property manager comes here on a weekly basis. I mostly come for meetings."

Nicolina saw Hugh standing not far off. She waved him over. "Go with Hugh, Mara. "

Mara nodded.

"Can you drive her home," Gabe asked Hugh. "Or to the Real Macaw or something."

"Of course." Hugh took Mara's hand and broke her inertia. "If we stop at Real Macaw, we'll see how it goes."

She started to follow until he let her pass. Then she stopped and turned back. "He *worshiped* me. Yes, I know that. I knew that. And, yes, I used that," she admitted. "But I was good for him. I helped him feel better about himself. It helped him change. It wasn't the same after that." She considered what to add. "It was better. He was his own man. It was kind of... admirable." She nodded at the last word. "Funny, but I did admire him after I understood what he believed."

Gabe and Nicolina watched Hugh and Mara until they were safely driving away.

"Whew." Gabe took a deep breath. "Admirable."

Nicolina said. "What just happened?"

Gabe looked at her. "What just happened is Mara Collins saved your ass."

"It wasn't anything," she said. "Peeping toms? Come on, Gabe. It didn't even occur to me."

"You didn't go over the incident reports?"

"Yes. No. I skimmed them. But I gave it to, what's his name, Chuckie Montrose at Vice...

"You gave a rookie in another bureau the key to our DB case."

"A DB accident case," she said. "And since when do you abbreviate dead body?"

Gabe ran his right hand over his face. "Jesus, Nicolina."

"Listen, the report had a statement from Mara," she said. "She said it was probably Claire Hunter or Ian. She said they nosed around all the time, especially Claire."

"Which could put one or both back there."

"Oh, no you don't," she snapped back. "You aren't going to tell me you suspected Ian Decker for one God damned second. Or Claire, either. Don't try to sell me that shit."

"It's a line of thinking," Gabe said, conceding the point. "It would have gotten us thinking." He laughed. "It would have made me look less like a clueless asshole."

She smiled. "That never occurred to me."

"And, you know what?" he asked her. "For a minute there, I was thinking of you back in uniform."

"I'm sure you were. Can we get in the car?"

Gabe took the driver seat while Nicolina circled the car for the passenger's side. Once she had drawn the seat belt harness over her chest, she said, as if wistful. "I did look damn good in a uniform."

"I can't comment on that."

"Yeah? Don't worry," she said. "I threw it the hell out."

Chapter 15

Gabe and Nicolina drove back to their offices. On the way, she and Gabe decided Blue Martini offered a perfect place for an off-duty, post-argument nightcap. She checked her notes. "The bartender who served JJ was Suzie, with one *z* and an *ie*," Nicolina read. She started to tap out the phone number. "Obviously, JJ must have been feeling extra spiritual, as in martinis and bustiers. It's one thing to go with someone like Mara, but he only had God as his wing-man. Figure that one."

"Hm."

"Is Suzie working tonight?" Nicolina asked into the phone.

"Sure. I'll get her," said a helpful receptionist. "It's not that busy, yet.

"No..." Nicolina took the cue from Gabe's nod. "Yes. I just need a minute. It's..."

Gabe shook his head. "Don't spook her."

Nicolina spoke into her phone. "Yeah, it's pretty important... I was there the other night and left something."

During the pause, Gabe said, "Good. I know she was interviewed, but we don't want her to hear you're a detective second hand."

Nicolina asked, "You want it on speaker?"

"Yes. To get a sense of her."

She tapped the speaker icon and held up the index finger on her free hand. "Hi, Suzie. My name is Nicolina Webster."

"Hi," Suzie said. She would have sounded perky, but she had a throaty voice that Nicolina categorized as appealing to men. "You left something?"

"No, but I'd like to come by to chat. I'm a detective with the County. I know you talked to a guy – "

"Yeah," Suzie said stretching the word. "About JJ Amos? He said that was all."

"At the time, it was. We are close to wrapping the case, but something new popped up. You could shed some light on it for us. Let me emphasize it is not about you, okay? For that matter, I'm technically off-duty."

"Okay," Suzie sounded less wary. "I'm here all night."

"Great. See you in about half an hour. I'm thinking a Blue Martini, in fact.

"If we have anything, that we've got."

"Good. Bye."

"Bye bye."

Nicolina tapped the red *end call* icon and looked at Gabe with a satisfied look, not one seeking approval.

"So, we are *technically off-duty*, are we?"

"I am. Unless you are a complete asshole, you won't let me drink alone."

"Do we dare take both cars?" Gabe asked, raising an eyebrow and smiling. "Can you drive after one of those blue things?"

"I'm not bringing you back here so you and I can both drive back up north," she said. "And I can have two of their martinis and drive five minutes home. I'm not sure about an hour round-trip with you at the wheel."

~ ~ ~

During their separate drives, Nicolina and Gabe mulled over, in parallel, what they had learned. By the time they parked in the Mercato open lot across from Blue Martini, they were on the same page again: They left their jackets in their cars, their Glocks already locked in their consoles.

"JJ was not much of a drinker," Gabe said. "We know that."

"From what I gather, Amos liked Blue Martini because Mara told him, once, it was the place to be," Nicolina said. "She talked him into a blue martini once – "

"Pretty but dangerous."

"The results are less pretty. I went through my first two, much too fast. They do gown so easily when you're an innocent. I start talking as cogently as Graham Chapman and almost as fast," She said. "In his case, JJ could manage two sips. Mara took pity on him and sent a bustier to get him a Budweiser, so she's nicer than she looks."

"Very nice, then."

Nicolina held her tongue until they had reached a fresh-faced hostess at a stand in the open entrance to Blue Martini. Straight ahead was the outside bar. To the left was the dark interior, with another bar and a space for dancing or a band. The covered, open-air right sat forty or more at high and low four-tops. All the servers were women and all wore the trademark bustiers. There were several bartenders at each bar, most women, all in white shirts and black slacks.

Nicolina asked, "Could you point me to your bartender named Suzie."

The girl looked at the outside bar. "She's all the way at the end."

The bar was about half full, so were the outside tables. They took adjacent stools at the end of the bar. Suzie came right over.

"You're the one who called?" she asked, in that throaty voice. She was average in every way, except for the voice, a quick smile and alive brown eyes.

"Are you that good," Nicolina asked, "or are we that obvious."

"A little of both." She explained, "I don't recognize you but you came over to my station like you seriously meant it."

"We don't," Gabe said. "Seriously. We just need of few of your… observations." He discretely showed his badge. "As Nicolina told you, we are off-duty. I'm Gabe Hubble."

"Nicolina Webster."

Neither extended their hands and Suzie did not invite the formality.

"I think I told the other detective what I remembered about Mr. Amos."

"I know," Nicolina said. "I reread his notes before I called."

Gabe interrupted. "Let's order a drink. Just to prove our status." He picked a beer he could see behind Suzie. "I'll have a Corona."

"I'd love a Blue Martini," Nicolina said, "but I'm not *that* off-duty. I'll go with a…" She scoured the line-up of beers. "A Labatt's Blue."

Gabe did not have to ask why Nicolina passed on the Mexican instead of the Canadian. She liked exactly half of NAFTA. He did say, "I haven't had that in a long time."

"Corona is barely beer."

Suzie returned with the bottles and glasses. She glanced down the bar. "Okay, I have a few minutes."

Nicolina started. "You served JJ Amos that night. Did anyone else serve him?"

"No. He sat to the left of you. It's my station."

"I take it he did not have a martini."

"No, wait." She pulled a receipt out of her pants pocket. She handed it to Nicolina. "I pulled this for you. It's his tab."

"So, he stuck with beer that night." Nicolina handed the receipt to Gabe.

"He was working on number two, but he left half of it. Gabe studied the bill. "He was here 10:22 to 11:32."

"He's a slow drinker," she said. "But a good tipper. That night anyway. I never saw him drink at the bar before. At least not mine. I did recognize him. He's distinctive, blocky and his eyebrows are low to his eyes. But he didn't come in alone, as far as I can remember. Sometimes he was with a few others, but almost always with... what?"

She sought the right word. "Let's just say, you couldn't miss her, even in the dark. He usually came in with her. Mostly, just the two of them. I couldn't see the attraction. You know? He didn't look like much, for sure."

Gabe and Nicolina let Suzie pause again without comment. "She did have him wrapped – Like she should, her being her – Wrapped as in hanging on every word. She did have nice legs and, you know what, she had nice lips. Kind of made her face, I think. You notice too many things like that after a while in this job. What makes people work, their features. It passes the time, too."

"Her name is Mara Collins," Gabe said.

"Yeah, yeah, Mara. Collins? I know that name. Real estate or something." She laughed. "Like, who isn't? I did talk to her here, a couple times, but she was never at the bar, either. Unless she thought the server was too slow. Not often, though. For someone like that, she seemed pretty nice."

"Yeah, she sure does," Nicolina hedged. "So, he didn't finish his second beer? What a waste?"

"Maybe a third. He waited a while to order it, too," Suzie continued. "He didn't want to order it. I may have been too pushy, but it was a good night, so the bar spaces were full. We had both the Marlins and the Ray's games on.

They were on the road, so it was big screen-to-big screen baseball, even that late."

"It is hard to choose when you live in Naples," Gabe said. "Rays or Marlins."

"He didn't talk much but asked him. He said he liked both," she said. "It was kind of funny. He said it was like a sign. Because of the name changes. He said they were *born again*. And I said, 'How do you pick? They on at the same time a lot. He didn't seem to know that, which is funny for a baseball fan. If he has a TV."

"Devil Rays to Rays and Florida Marlins to Miami, right?" Nicolina added, "They were born again in a way."

"You got it."

"Designated hitter or not," Gabe said. "I'm surprised you remember. You are good."

Suzie nodded. "I am, but not that good. It was kind of strange. He was different. That's why I remember. Preoccupied. Not chatty, at all. Except about the *born again* baseball. Really funny, though is he didn't use his iPhone until the end, even though it sat on the bar the whole time."

"Any of that was unusual?" Gabe asked.

"Oh, yeah, yeah," Suzie said, with a frown. "Nowadays, everybody's on their phones, even when they are with someone. Guys who come in alone, can't take their eyes off their phones. And look at the girls in the place. Myself included." She smiled. "Well, I'm not like them, but, hey, guys, look up! You know. Thanks a lot, Steve Jobs."

Gabe smiled. "What we are missing. It's sad."

"He means," Nicolina said, "you're pretty."

Suzie laughed the comment off. "It was nice of him to not say that." She took another look down the bar. "Hang on a sec." She went down her section asking if anyone needed anything and came back. "Everyone is like him,

Mr. Amos, tonight." She gestured at her other customers. "Two of the guys are here alone. See how they keep their phones on the bar."

She looked at the TVs both games were on commercial breaks. "See, that one picked it up. He's probably playing Angry Birds." The other solo picked up his phone and tapped the glass. "Or texting. No one leaves the phone on the bar for long," she added. "He did. Mr. Amos."

"He had it on the bar the whole time?" Gabe asked. "He didn't pay any attention to it?"

"I didn't say that," she said. "Not at all. He looked at it a lot. More as the time went on, but he didn't pick it up during the TV commercials like everyone else. Or play with it, not at all. That's mostly why he stuck with me."

Nicolina said, "So, he was waiting for something. Is that what you're saying?"

Suzie nodded. "After I talked him into the second beer, he didn't even sip it for a while. He kept watching the phone like it was supposed to do something on its own. He barely looked at the TV." She took a breath. "He looked angry, then worried. Back and forth. Finally, he typed a short text. I was watching him because he seemed so upset. Another funny thing: He could type without looking. Who can touch-type on a phone? He seemed to avoid the screen. Weird." She sensed a customer needed another drink. "Hang on. I'll be back. He just wants a beer."

After Suzie had walked away, Gabe said. "He was waiting for something."

"Sure sounds like it. And he was getting pissed."

"Something important." Gabe watched Suzie fill a draft and sipped some of his Corona. "Something to take him to Ibis Creek."

Nicolina kept pace. "Canadians can make beer," she said. "JJ had to have driven there straight from here if he left at 11:32 plus."

"Something from Mara, maybe? A belated *Congrats*?"

"It doesn't feel right," Nicolina said. "Waiting for Mara, I mean."

Suzie was back. "Sorry. Hey, you aren't drinking any more than Mr. Amos did."

"You are fascinating," Nicolina said.

"Seriously?"

"Seriously," Gabe agreed.

Suzie seemed pleased. "Good. You know, I felt sorry for him. He was so upset. That's it. Not so much mad," she said. "He finally got something. His phone buzzed. Vibrated. I was right there, and it looked like a text. But he stared at it like it was in code or something. Like he couldn't quite get it."

"He was dyslexic," Nicolina explained.

"Oh," Suzie said, with sympathy. "I have a cousin like that. We thought he was dumb. Surprise! He's a physics professor, now." She frowned. "Gee, I feel bad. I asked him if he needed glasses. No wonder he looked at me funny."

"What happened next?" Gabe prodded.

"He hit a couple times on his phone and lifted it to his ear. How weird..." Her eyes opened wide, and she put her hand to her mouth. "Oh. He had text-to-speech! That's a great thing for a guy like that."

"When was that?"

"Just before he left. I mean, literally. He looked up and me and smiled," she said. "Like he'd hit the Powerball. He slapped a twenty on the bar for a tab of twelve bucks. I'd remember that, too."

Nicolina asked, "Did you hear anything? From the phone?"

Suzie hesitated. "I'm not a snoop. But I do have a good ear." She pointed to her right ear. "This one. The left, not as much."

"And you had your right ear pointed at JJ Amos." Nicolina mimed the action.

"I only heard one word, which is so common here, it's not worth mentioning."

"We'll take it."

"Just the word *lanai*."

Gabe and Nicolina exchanged looks. They were both disappointed and exhilarated.

"Thanks, Suzie," Gabe said, after a moment. "You were very helpful."

Nicolina corrected him. "He means you are one amazing bartender."

"You're not going to finish those beers are you?"

Gabe gave Nicolina another look. "I think we will, thanks."

"Good." Again, she knew she was needed elsewhere without hearing or seeing anything. "Back to work." She strode to a couple at the far end of her station."

"Well," Gabe said, taking a sip of Corona. "That confirms something."

"Or three." Nicolina took a long drink.

"One thing bothers me." Gabe drank some more, not wanting to ruin the moment. He did anyway. "He sent a text and received a text. So he wasn't one hundred percent dark."

"Could he have some some way to delete it?" Nicolina shook her head. "No. He had a second sim card."

"Okay," Gabe agreed. "let's pass the *why* for the moment. At least, it fits the timeline. JJ Amos was waiting for something and, once it got it, he went directly to Ibis Creek."

"Yeah. Non-damned-stop," Nicolina agreed, "right into Ian Decker's Bog."

"So, the texts get us closer to why he went there," Gabe said. "And we're no worse off with the second sim card: For JJ, it has to be done in secret."

"One answer."

"Yeah?"

"You aren't going to like it," she said.

"I don't like *n*ot hearing it, already."

"It's a sim card to Heaven."

"You were right. I don't like it."

"It gets worse, Gabe."

"Of course, it does."

"I'm not serving a warrant on Heaven. Are you?"

"Maybe later."

Chapter 16

Gabe had no friends who were not cops or husbands of his wife's friends. Perhaps, that explained why he reluctantly began thinking of Ian Decker as perilously close to a friend. He understood it was a slippery slope to a bad idea, but Gabe's mitigated the negative with the perception of Ian as a resource, not a suspect or a source.

He knew he was right about that.

Ian had an easy generosity and willingness to share what he knew or could find, with no expectation of a return. It struck Gabe as odd at first, but it made Ian's company relaxing. Attempting to analyze it had gotten him nowhere beyond a hackneyed examination of his own flaws.

He also found his own rhythm fell into sync with Ian's minutes into a conversation. To varying degrees, he had that with Suzannah and with Nicolina Webster, but he had spent far more time in their company.

Gabe did not share any of the above with Nicolina. At the other extreme, Suzannah seemed pleased, but, then, she had not met Ian.

Gabe and Ian met for a discrete lunch at La Pinata in Naples East Bay Shores Village, on Bayshore. La Pinata was a new, good Mexican place, sparsely occupied for late lunches. Nicolina did not eat Mexican food any more than she would drink Corona and the tacos were excellent. Gabe had taken both into account when picking the lunch spot.

Afterward, he had disclosed an abridged version of the Suzie interview, he took a bite of his second taco and waited until his mouth was mostly empty. "So, as of now..." He finished swallowing. "I'm stuck with JJ Amos as our official peeping Tom." He did not sound pleased.

"He is your official *former* peeper."

"That's right and that's the good news," Gabe said. "I can't justify keeping his death active – my boss, the Chief of the Criminal Investigations Division – is sold on accidental drowning, if only because we are low on resources right now. I've got two detectives on vacation and one on Family Leave. He made it clear I have to use *resources wisely*. That's his term for *not one hour*, Gabe."

"How about the peeper case?"

"That's easier. It's a no-harm, no foul case that is technically still in the Vice Bureau with their file number. They had trouble finding the file to share with me," Gabe said. "It's safely in bureaucratic limbo." Gabe took another bite. "I can do anything I want with it as long as I keep it quiet and don't set off bells asking for a warrant. I can help out a fellow bureau. Can I put my Chief's *precious* resources into a suspicious death case that he sees as ninety-nine percent accident? Nope."

"I admit, it doesn't look very suspicious, anymore."

"No, it doesn't."

"So. Have you gotten any further into Limbo?"

"Some. We've seen Mara's code being entered at night on a few occasions in January and February this year. 2012's data was erased as too old. It was purged in March. Collins never bothered to review access reports the way they are paid to, let alone print them out. At best, they occasionally ran a search for an abused Vendor Code..."

"But not Mara's."

"She was the one approving the searches. It never occurred to her. Why would it?"

"Meaning you have nothing from all from last year?" Ian asked. "Shit."

Gabe went on to say that Mara had accounted for her whereabouts in most of 2013's entries. The gate cameras' DVR had been overwritten, as it was every month. "Abbott bought the DVR used –"

"Even though the specs required *new*."

"You know that, don't you?"

"I didn't know he chintzed us on a used one."

"Anyway, my IT guy says it was okay for 2006. Ibis Creek's board upgraded the cameras to 720p HD a couple years ago –"

"That was all Claire."

Gabe shook his head. "Well, tell Claire, she should have had the DVR upgraded, too. At 720p, my guy says they use up eight times as much space Ibis has on the DVR."

"Tell Claire? I'm not doing that," Ian said. "You can, but you have nice eyes. You should try to keep them."

"Thanks. I don't hear that enough."

"The upshot of all this is that JJ's death case is closed."

"Not technically," Gabe said. "I had Webster put it in our slush pile, inactive investigations, with a tentatively accidental death on it. Subject to subsequent information. Nicolina is not totally convinced, either, but we're at a dead end."

"You have a slush pile? Do you put novels in it?"

"It is a virtual slush pile, and we frown on pure fiction."

"Mine isn't *pure*."

"Can we stay on topic?"

"Okay," Ian agreed. "What about the two texts at Blue Martini?"

"For me, that's the rub," Gabe said. "One of them. A warrant turned up no activity after 10:42 PM. Mara sent him a text about meeting him, as a second thought. She felt bad that she had let him go alone. His last collection presentation was a big deal to him, and she realized later she should have celebrated with him."

"And she was the one who encouraged him."

"Survivor's guilt, maybe," Gabe said. "She had inspired whatever JJ thought was his next big thing. He called her his *Spirit Guide* if you can believe that. And, yes, I know the internet definition,"

"She doesn't strike me as *medium* anything."

"She said he interpreted almost everything in religious terms," Gabe continued. "More and more lately."

"Makes sense. If God had had a decent civil litigator, Cain and Able would still be in depositions." Ian watched as Gabe finished his taco. "Maybe he texted God and God got back to him. "

"That's as plausible as anything I've got." Gabe sighed. "Nicolina can buy it, the peeper angle, me, I can't. Not for a guy hooked on Mara Collins."

"And sees once or twice a week," agreed. "What about the *spying* angle? For JJ, I mean."

"On what?"

"Illegal tenants? For his foreclosure cases?"

"Would that amount to much?"

"Just some additional threats he could throw at them."

"Then, it's a bit late for last month? I can see that for last year," Gabe said. "But the whole point of that night was that he was out of the collection business.

"True." Ian shrugged. "So spying doesn't seem as plausible as peeping."

"Which is fine," Gabe said. "The *peeping* file is active. I'm keeping the *accident* file in my desk drawer."

Ian laughed. "Because Webster doesn't want it?"

"I keep telling her I want your input on it, so, no. She doesn't want it."

Ian gave it some thought. "Doth she protest too much?"

"About some things, not about you." Gabe laughed. "Besides, what do you care? You're still stuck in the past."

"The past being prolog."

"There!" Gabe said. "*Glib* drives her nuts."

"Oh, come on." Ian laughed. "Everyone likes Shakespeare. He has depth."

Gabe conceded the point. "She probably likes *Macbeth*. Parts of *Othello*. We've never discussed it."

"How does she feel about mystery novels?"

"Unlike some, we get paid for mysteries," Gabe said. "Mostly for writing *The End.*"

"That part, I start with," Ian said. "As you know, I get stuck in the middle."

"Do you dislike that as much as I do?"

"No. I'm used to it," Ian said. "I get hung up on subplots. Like *The Most Peculiar Case of JJ Amos versus Kamila Cabrera.*"

Gabe looked at Ian and grimaced. "Kamila Cabrera. Barton Abbott mentioned her specifically. As one of his Affordables."

"Kami? Really?"

"Yes. He got her a job with the contractor to justify her mortgage," Gabe said. "Her husband, too."

The surprised expression remainder on Ian's face. "Her husband? Which one?"

"What do you mean, which one?"

"She's on a learning curve. She had three. Has three." Ian closed one eye, as he thought. "That would have been 2006. Auturo Guillen. He didn't last long and probably wasn't meant to."

Gabe let his head droop enough so that he had to roll his eyes up to look at Ian. "Why do I keep getting this feeling I should take you with me wherever I go?"

~ ~ ~

Kamila Cabrera was not an obsession for Ian. That was Claire. Ian simply found Kami as more mythic than Barton Abbott's Naples East Bay Ibis.

Kamila Cabrera was the name on all of the Ibis Creek paperwork: Deed, Mortgages. She had four of those: A first with a private lender; two subordinated ones with Collier County; and a refinancing mortgage with Orion Bank that she turned in a hurry. She had two marriage licenses with the same name and two divorce actions. After the second divorce, the records showed that Kami Cabrera had vanished.

She had not, but she may as well have, as far as Ian was concerned. JJ Amos filed his lien and foreclosure case against Kamila Cabrera with the Collier Circuit Court, but service of the complaint kept bouncing back as unsuccessful. Somehow, JJ served it himself in March of 2013. That is what the publicly available records and not so publicly available records told Ian.

Of all of JJ Amos's many Ibis Creek collection cases, pretty, diminutive Kamila Cabrera presented his – and Ian's – toughest challenge. When Claire first enlisted Ian's search prowess, Kami seemed a standard Affordable-Program buyer at Ibis Creek. Originally, she borrowed one hundred percent of her purchase price, thanks to Collier County. She refinanced her first mortgage with Orion at ninety percent of a fever-inflated value. All told, she netted twenty thousand dollars in cash with a higher monthly payment.

Despite that windfall, Kami fell behind her condo assessments payments shortly after the refinancing. She claimed both she and her husband had lost their jobs. Later she claimed divorce and a new, lower-paying job.

The board of directors – some themselves struggling in the recession – did express sympathy and nothing else. Kami was *a good Ibis Creek neighbor*, they decided, even though she had never been an Ibis Creek neighbor and had slept in her unit twice, for a few hours on a chaise lounge, back in 2006. For the next several years, the board did send occasional late payment letters to good-neighbor Kami and dozens of other owners. That was as far as it went.

According to their agreements with Barton Abbott and Collier County, Affordables could not be flippers. They were supposed to live in their units, which meant no rentals, either. Barton Abbott was out of the picture and the board did not care. The County pretended its Affordable program worked perfectly at each election.

Deep as the Mortgage-Backed recession went, few in Naples expected it to last beyond 2008. Even Ian did not. As a result, the board assumed delinquents would catch up in 2009. That year was worse. Uncollected dues passed $300,000, twenty-five percent of the entire year's budget. The maintenance fees soared another fifteen percent for a second consecutive year to cover the shortfall from the likes of absently neighborly Kami Cabrera.

The board's dismal, if idealistic, performance on collections from these delinquent owners – and Kami Cabrera, specifically – first frustrated and then infuriated Claire Hunter. At every board meeting, she attacked the board for its costly laxity. The directors countered by banning owner comments at board meetings, ignoring the statute that forbade such a rule. Claire began her Ibis Crock blog soon after that. Her strident posts and subsequent campaign emails eventually landed her at the directors' table.

The incumbents, cowed by the unimaginable mandate, put Claire in charge of monitoring collections, a de facto one-eighty from passive forbearance. Claire had already memorized the list of delinquents, dubbing the worst eighteen Super Deadbeats.

Kami ranked fifteenth in amount but fourth in Claire's mental list. Kami twice pleaded in person, with sobs, sob- and job-stories. The cute, little, young ingenue, with her accented English and sad smile, won every heart, except the one. The board voted four to one to offer her one deferred payment plan and then another.

In her answer to JJ Amos first collection letter, Kami wrote, "I thought *deferred* means I pay when my job hours are more. My tenant lost his job and pays only a little when he can" The letter had the unit as her address, which inflamed Claire.

"Another damned Bolivians," Claire observed. "Do any Bolivians still live south of Ibis Creek? Like in Bolivia?"

Ibis Creek accumulated a disproportionate percentage of Bolivians immigrants, exclusively in its Affordable units.

"Kami's not an immigrant," Leo observed. He found Kami appealingly waif-like. "She said she was born in Disney World on a vacation."

"There are no hospitals in Disney World." Claire pushed JJ to sue Kami and the other Super Deadbeats immediately upon taking her board seat. JJ promised action. After six months of brush-offs, Claire enlisted Ian. "How are you at non-fiction fictions?"

From the County Deed site, Ian confirmed that Kami had used $30,000 in County money to purchase her Affordable unit. In Ibis Creek records, Ian found that Kami had breached the County financing terms by leasing her unit a month *before* she had closed on it. Leah Kaline approved the improper lease application, the last Kami ever submitted.

Leah's boss, Barton Abbott, had an Affordables quota to meet. The County had a PR quota to meet.

Ian's information sent Claire into a full-blown lather.

Soon after, Ian found another interesting tidbit: Kamila Cabrera had racked up two very real Bolivian-national ex-husbands – Auturo Guillen and Mateus Duarte – by the time she had reached twenty-two. On the Marriage Certificates, Kami was listed as Florida-born. In her Ibis Creek purchase application, she described her nationality as Bolivian. Each marriage lasted under thirteen months. Kami and Mateus divorce in early 2012.

Ian put off flat-out telling Claire about the marriages for a week, for obvious reasons injury. Instead, he dropped several prefatory hints. When he ultimately shared the two short-term Bolivian immigrant husbands, Claire surprised him and beamed.

"I knew it!" Claire felt her being right was the natural order of things."

"She was an international con artist before she fleeced the County."

"Or she is an unrepentant romantic," Leo suggested. "Like me."

Leo's comment came before Ian mentioned that newly second-married Kami purchased at Ibis Creek only in her own name, not jointly. Leo retreated before a Claire glare. "Okay. I repent."

"She and a guy from my old haunt, Providence, just bought a place together. Javier Gomes," Ian said. He did not say how long – and badly – he had searched for the deed. "The deed and mortgage, from January, listed them both as single. They were married a few weeks later, in Sarasota."

"Providence, Bolivia, I'll bet," Claire snapped.

"I didn't go to college in Bolivar, Claire."

"Too bad. You'd have more friends in Ibis Creek than Leo and me –"

Leo said, "Sorry, Ian, but I chose Evie in the divorce."

Ian nodded. "Me, too."

"You are sad specimens, you two."

From that day forward, Ian drilled into JJ's Ibis Creek liens beginning with the Kami Cabrera case. She simply stood out. Ian quickly retrieved her Ibis Creek deed and mortgages from the County site. He had skimmed them several years ago, as part of Claire's campaign against deadbeats.

She purchased in 2006, while portents of the mortgage implosion remained obscure. She borrowed $21,000 from Collier County and received the usual Affordable expense deferral from the County to the tune of $9,000. Those two liens included language that required Kami to live in her unit or pay off the Collier County loan and pay the deferred development fees.

As Ian previously learned, Kami secured a purchase money mortgage with some private outfit named Western Dry Rocks Key Funds, LLC. Within four months, she refinanced with Orion Bank, an overly aggressive local FDIC-insured bank. The Orion mortgage paid off the Western Dry Rocks mortgages and brought Kami's borrowing to one hundred twenty percent of her purchase price of $140,000.

She did not pay off the County as agreed.

The first time around, Ian had paid little attention to the odd name of the first mortgagee or the addendum to the mortgage. Everything seemed the same: Fifteen to thirty years, some with balloons, most with six-month adjustment – increases – to interest rates and payments, blah blah boilerplate.

The second time, he went over Kami's mortgage, he read the entire mortgage. When he reached the mortgage's clause transferring all rents to the mortgagee, *i.e.* Western Dry Rocks, he reread it. Given Kami's pre-closing rental, that provision suggested that the lender knew about the improper rental. After the last page of Riders, he knew: Kami was more slammer than a planner. Attached at the end was a lease executed thirty days before the date Kami signed the mortgage.

Over time, Western Dry Rocks funded nine Affordable mortgages in Collier County, Kami's being the only one Ibis Creek. Each mortgage had the same arrangement, a pre-closing lease attached with rents assigned. None of the Western Dry Rocks' mortgaged units were permuted, by Collier County's program, to be rented.

The following day, Ian turned his attention to JJ's cold-hot-cold pursuit of the chronically delinquent Kami Cabrera.

The pre-Claire board not liened Kami, giving her payment plans she never met. For Claire, Kami was high on the Super-Deadbeat hit list. Skimming past emails, Ian confirmed that it had taken JJ a full six months to cave to Claire's increasingly strident demands.

In his emails of the time, JJ flatly dismised Claire's approach of immediate liening and foreclosure. He argued that Ibis Creek would be lucky to get payment plans. Otherwise, the delinquents would simply stop paying completely. While Ibis Creek could foreclose on a delinquent unit and get title to the unit, it would take time. Cash was needed more immediately to pay Abbott case fees. Also, the remaining bank mortgage prevented an outright sale.

Banks had again began foreclosing their mortgage and would take units like Kami's out from under the association.

Claire knew the negatives and argued back that the point of liening and foreclosing was deterrence, discouraging future delinquencies. "Foreclose and take the damn Cabrera unit!" she wrote. "People will get the message that sob stories won't work anymore!!! And if we can get rent for a month, great!!!"

Finally, in June 2012, Claire prevailed, if briefly. JJ liened and sued to foreclose on Kami's unit. The next week, he retaliated by deleting Claire's password, blocking her director access to the Sanders Tilden account-tracking website. The move, which he denied, depriving Claire of current information and neutralized her pressure. It took months for JJ to own up to his sabotage. He had cut Claire off with full Collins and Kenny Becks approval.

Even without a torrent of Claire emails, JJ followed his filing against Kami at a more normal speed. He met deadlines and refused to grant extensions. Claire had, in fact, succeeded to start the clock on Kami Cabrera's time at Ibis Creek.

Ian read through everything JJ filed with the Clerk and the records he obtained otherwise. It became clear that JJ had reacted to Claire a bit earlier than they had known. The problem was that certified mail notices to Kami came back unclaimed. JJ could not effectively serve Kami.

Attached to JJ's complaint, Ian found copies of collection letters, return-to-sender envelopes and proof that Kami only made five payments on two payment plans over two years.

As standard procedure, JJ included the last tenant he knew of for Kami's unit, her second ex-husband, Mateus Duarte. Late in 2011, JJ added tenant Maria Suarez as a party. Neither Kami nor Maria submitted a lease application to the board. The board and Collins did not notice.

By February 2012, JJ had used two different service of process firms to verify that JJ had used all reasonable means to find Kami and serve her with papers. The second process server's affidavit claimed that a tenant named Maria Suarez lived in the unit. A notation indicated that the tenant said she paid her rent to "Mgr. early 40's? nmd Auggie." He could not find Kami.

JJ was free to use legal advertisements as official notices. He procured a default judgment. A month later, he filed a motion for Summary Judgment that would have led to a foreclosure sale and most likely Ibis Creek ownership. That ownership would allow the association to rent the unit until Fannie Mae, as successor to bankrupt Orion, finished its own glacial foreclosure process.

Then, in March 2013, JJ stopped cold. The only actions he took after March were to reschedule his own summary judgment hearings. Kami never filed a piece of paper with the court. JJ just stopped.

Always tracking Ibis Creek collection cases, Ian knew JJ had pulled up. At the time, he had not cared. He also knew that JJ was bringing in junior associates, but did not realize that JJ had dropped out of all the other cases. The dockets of the cases did not note the fact, either.

Of twenty active cases, JJ kept only one case, filing in early July to reschedule his summary judgment hearing for mid-August.

JJ kept Kami Cabrera's case.

Kami's unit was not very far and visible from where JJ went into the water.

Ian stared at his computer screen's display of the Kami case docket.

He called up the Fannie Mae foreclosure on Kami's unit. After Orion's bankruptcy, Fannie Mae had taken over the Cabrera mortgage. Eventually, Fannie Mae began foreclosure proceedings. Its lawyer no valid address for Kami, either, using her unit address and then suspending action. Fannie Mae had tons of mortgages to foreclose, and Kami's was among the smallest.

Ian fared no better than JJ, Fannie Mae or the process server. He, too, found that Kami's real estate tax records listed her Ibis rental unit as her address, as did the Ibis Creek owner roster. Several web phone-address services returned the same. Ian tried each married name with no success.

After trying dozens of combinations of names, Ian learned only that each of the two ex-husbands addresses in Collier County under a combination of names. Wikipedia informed Ian that Bolivians used dual surnames with a father's followed by a mother's. When married, the husband's name replaced the mother's. Transferred onto rigid US official First-Middle-Last forms, the names were sometimes reversed, hyphenated, ignored or even combined into a single word that was then truncated.

With Kami's suspicious marital history, she very likely tied a third knot but not in Collier County. Ian could not bring himself to start over for neighboring Lee or Dade County.

He could bring himself to head for the beach at Central Avenue, the easiest drive for him.

~ ~ ~

Ian's favorite beach was 34th Avenue South, with its wind-break. On still or breezy days, he frequented more convenient beaches at Central or the avenues just north of it, First and Second North.

When he referred to a *beach*, Ian meant a public access point to the long, continuous Naples beach. It lay immediately west of Gulfshore and/or Gordon Drives. Each *beach* was served by an avenue's access and parking area. Gulfshore and Gordon had such accesses almost every block from Lowdermilk Park down to his favorite at 34th. The latter required extra driving and Ian's idea of planning, not a sudden impulse.

Evie aside, what had sold Ian on Naples had been the many *beaches*. He had never seen the like of it.

It was 5:15, 85 degrees and cloudless. The twelve mile per hour wind was a Naples-qualified *nice breeze*, so he went to Central. Twelve mph would generate surf enough to drown out the echoes of the mysterious Kamila Cabrera.

She kept him company as he drove up the nicely landscaped Naples East Bay Shores Boulevard and cut over to Bayshore at the small sports saloon that boasted a new name, theme and proprietor every other year. Nearing 41, Tamiami Trail East, Ian had to brake for three Ibis jaywalking over to McDonald's.

He made the drive northwest on 41 toward downtown Naples more often than any other – excepting the opposite direction to Walmart and Publix – and he barely noticed passing by the auto service shops, hourly-rate motels, empty retail strips and franchises, dominating the road. Approaching the Gordon River, the view improved, with the Naples Bay Resort and the Bayfront complex dressing up either side of 41. Linked to Bayfront by an underway tunnel, touristy Tin City was as quiet as expected on an August day. Touristy or not, Ian liked Tin City's hyper-casual restaurants for their river views.

Since Ian needed neither women's shoes, artwork nor expensive dining that afternoon, he swung right at Fifth's entrance and headed north to Central. He turned left at the 7-Eleven and drove slowly toward the beach. As usual for off-season, he found a parking spot ten feet from the beach. He hauled out his chair and orange and yellow towel from his trunk. He did not feel citrusy, so he swapped for his Gulf blue alternative.

Ian lifted his cellphone and, as usual, wanted to leave it and its temptations into the trunk. Almost as if Kami had intervened, he pocketed the phone and firmly closing the trunk lid. In three minutes, he plopped into his chair, closed his eyes and let the sun, breeze and surf sounds wash over him.

Nowhere Girl Kami was in the mix.

With a sigh, Ian retrieved his cell and draped his shoulder with the blue towel, which cut the reflectivity of the cell's glossy screen. He activated the data stream and pulled up the very Collier County Deed search page that driven him to the beach.

He promised himself three insanity-defining searches, maximum.

On the sixth, he entered *Cabrera* in the Last name field and *Kamila* in the First Name field. He caught the last name misspelling and deleted it. Even though he could see the Last Name field was empty, he could not stop his finger's rote tap on the *search* button.

Kamila proved such an uncommon name, Ian gaped, embarrassed at a result that shredded his self-image as an ace researcher.

Atop the familiar list of six Kamila Cabrera entries for Ibis Creek and her marriage certificates, the name Kamila appeared three times, but not as Cabrera. It was Kamila Mende. The three entries all dealt with the January 2013 purchase of a home in Mangrove Hammock. The two-year-old development, upscale, but not outrageous, included condos, single-family houses and a golf course. It sat a bit southeast of the intersection of Collier Boulevard and Immokalee Road, several daunting miles beyond Ian's comfort zone.

The deed listed Kami as co-owner with Javier Gomes, both unmarried. The address given for Javier was in Venice, Sarasota County. When he googled Javier, a Venice address showed up, as well as the newer Naples one. A third was in Bristol, Rhode Island.

He found their Mid-February marriage certificate Sarasota County, too. The County indexed her as Kamila Mendecabrera. The certificate, itself, showed her as Mende Cabrera, with Florida as her place of birth. Javier's was Rhode Island.

Feeling the quarry within reach, in reality, Ian put his phone on speaker and told it to "dial Gabe Hubble's cell." The phone apparently heard the surf and the wind and dialed nothing. Taking the cue, he canceled the speaker, held the mic close and said, "Call Detective Webster's cell."

She answered with a curt, "Hello, Mr. Decker. To what – "

"Hi, Detective Webster. Have you found Kami Cabrera, yet?"

"Since I don't know who that is, no."

"She owned a lanai near the spot where JJ Amos went bathing."

"Oh. Right. And didn't live there. Ever. I'm not sure she lives anywhere."

"She does and I'm going to take a run up to see her," Ian said, a bit too satisfied for an ex-ace. "I thought you might like to come along."

"I mightn't."

"Just a thought."

Nicolina's sigh was audible over the breeze, putting it around fifteen mph. "I'm sure I appreciate the thought... Sebastian, but, I know Gabe told you, JJ Amos's death is on hiatus."

"He'll be glad to hear it." Ian bit his tongue an instant too late. He had plenty of time to savor the flavor. "Uh, Detective?"

"I will pass your wisdom on to Lieutenant Hubble. He is so Job-like."

"You are nearly so. Thanks."

After another pause, she asked, "Do you know how shitty it is to call a desk from a beach? Which one is it?"

"Central."

"Hm. I haven't been there."

"Try it. I'll be here."

"Good point. Bye."

Ian dumped the phone into his shirt pocket and slumped in his chair. He reassessed his, and JJ's, preoccupation with Kami. She had burrowed under his skin, as a glaring signpost on JJ's pathway.

JJ had gone after her hard, as he should have, but then backed way off. He let her case slide, but unlike all the others, he did not hand it off to younger associates. Kami Cabrera Mende was different, personal.

Kami Cabrera mattered, he was sure of it.

He closed his eyes and imagined his route to Mangrove Hammock. His cell's vibration caught him at about Davis and Santa Barbara. In the mirror finish of the phone, he could not make out the name, but he knew. "Lieutenant Hubble."

"Webster said she wants to apologize," Gabe said.

Ian let his skepticism rule. "Did she really?"

"She said she wants to but just can't." Gabe laughed. "What did you say to her?"

"Mostly that I found Kami Cabrera."

"Mostly? It's hard to be a *major dick* with a *mostly...*" Gabe hesitated before he added, "Actually, she doesn't call you that anymore. She made a new three-letter word. She calls you an *Ian.*"

"I get that one a lot."

"Oh. She forgot to pat you on your hopefully sunburned back for finding someone we weren't looking for."

"You had to write all that down? Or are you paraphrasing?"

"She sent me two texts."

"How ironic of her," Ian said. "Just what we are looking for in JJ's case."

"Out of curiosity, how did you find Cabrera? We looked."

"Do you know how many Kamilas show up in official Collier County records?"

"Two?"

"About half that."

"And you went *smug* on Nicolina?" Gabe laughed. "No wonder she was not impressed by your feat."

"Yeah. There's that."

"I've stowed my jacket and my Glock. I'm putting on my sandals right now. See you in a couple minutes."

By the time Ian finished skimming for emails, Gabe was flipping open his chair. "Did you ask Webster to go with you?" He wore a short-sleeved white shirt and khaki slacks.

"It was her case. I thought she'd be interested."

"She *is* charged with ignoring it." Gabe sat, adjusted his sunglasses and kicked off his sandals. "We've got to keep not meeting like this."

"You don't write me up as a CI?"

"I'd like to think of you as a secret friend."

Ian said, "A step up from *imaginary*. Like Kami is for me. Like the peeper was."

"The Peeper case will be, too, in a couple weeks. Your board is satisfied JJ was the guy and doesn't want to hear about it anymore. It is yesterday's embarrassment, and they want it closed before it gets into the papers again. They sent Nolan Sanders in to see me. He wants it closed, too."

"Damn. Does he have any clout?"

"I just waved Mara's statement in his face. The one that insists the peeper could not possibly have been JJ," Gabe explained. "That and my promise to keep it quiet finally sent Sanders away."

"Mara Collins and JJ Amos. It is so strange," Ian said. "She's not the smartest person I've ever met, but how could she think of him as litigator material? He couldn't read."

"What do you think of Graham Chapman?"

"Point for Mara."

Gabe filled Ian in on the latest they had gleaned from new material from Sanders Tilden and the degree to which it matched and elaborated on what they knew.

Sanders Tilden had released a decent number of emails and texts JJ sent from his work laptop. There were a few to Sally late in 2012 that reflected JJ's indifference to their break-up. He was neither angry, resentful nor sad. If anything, they reflected a *where I'm going, you can't follow* quality worthy of *Casablanca*.

Almost all were with Mara. Early on, as they already knew, the texts and emails between them showed how well she *worked* him. She admitted as much to Nicolina and Gabe. The new emails reinforced JJ's *Spirit Guide* role for Mara. After March, she increasingly tried to bring him back to earth, back to her. "To see her as a person, a woman. It didn't work."

"Jesus. As a woman, she's hard to miss," Ian said. "How religious can one guy be?"

"Religious enough. Gabe paused to make another point "Religious enough to think his destiny ran through Ibis Creek, a place he hated."

"That's like slaying a dragon, maybe?"

"Good analogy."

"But before he went on his *quest*, he did not see the fair maiden's XOXO? That sucks."

"He couldn't have. Not without a sim card," Gabe said. "He might be alive if had seen it."

"I doubt it. He had to meet his dragon," Ian sad. "He's a saintly cavalier savvy about sim cards and Mara almost gets herself killed trying to be a true friend." He shuddered. "Evie and Claire are right: I'm a shit judge of character. Present company excepted."

"Thanks for that."

"But why would he do that? With the sim?"

Gabe shrugged. "We don't know. One reason to pull a sim and battery is to avoid tracking."

"Oh, great." Ian away and then back. "Does this sound like a closed case to you?"

Gabe shook his head slowly. "You want to know where we found his sim card? In a business card case, buried in the middle. The case was in the Mercedes console."

"He *really* hid it?"

"Or maybe, it was just safe in the card case. It had a snap clasp so it wouldn't fall out." Gabe gestured such a closing with his hand. "Based on his phone records, Mara and he talked at least once a week and they met almost as often.

They used text and email, which I guess JJ could read better. She kept hers very short. His were longer. After he got into text conversion? That's when the tone of his texts and emails changed." Gabe gave Ian a knowing look. "Mara, the *Spirit Guide begins to appear*."

"Shit. I his wife a little favor. Text-to-speech is so *run of the mill*," Ian said. "As favors go, it barely registers."

"Maybe so, but we could see just how much it transformed his view of himself and her. She had given him something God wanted him to have. His emails were personal to her, not as the Ibis Creek manager, really, so Sanders let us have them. I think he wants the answer as much as we do."

"I'm on the same page as Nolan Sanders," Ian groused. "I'm shocked he gave them to you. They deem their coffee maker manuals as privileged."

"They weren't really about the case, about nothing the defendants didn't have. He started emailing Mara details about the documents of the Abbott Defect case. He quoted from Barton Abbott emails. Burkle Lehane emails to the engineers. He had a new view of things. And you'll hate this…"

"I'm not too happy right now."

"He started sounding like he really understood some of what he wrote."

"If God was helping him replace Chapman," Ian said, "I'm fine with it."

Chapman wasn't. He got a little bitchy about JJ's over-involvement and *divine mission*, as he, Chapman, actually called it."

"So JJ finally gets ambitious and he goes for the *Stairway to Heaven*?"

"And, to him, all because of Mara Collins. Because of Mara *guided* him there, to his new *path*," Gabe said. "His favorite word. And, though he mentioned other defect litigation, the Abbott case... the Ibis Creek case is obviously necessary for his *path*."

"This is beyond me."

"By April, JJ began to write more about the Abbott case, but more vaguely. In June, you saw him make another jump," Gabe went on. "Mara tried harder to tone down the destiny talk, to bring him closer to earth, to take on some collections for her."

"He turned her down?"

"He said, wrote, 'Sorry, You know I must not' but she tried one more time with the same result. By that time he had honed in on something – just as Sanders said – and she was not part of it. She'd lost him but she didn't know it."

"Maybe, her guidance wasn't needed anymore?" Ian asked. "

"We believe that's it."

"If that something didn't work out, he could have crashed."

"If so," Gabe said, "it happened within a few hours. And..." He left to Ian to finish the thought.

"The two texts, again."

Gabe nodded. "But not by themselves. He was still feeling fine when he left Blue Martini."

Ian ran a hand over his eyes. It happened at Ibis Creek. That's what you think."

"Or on the way from the bar to Ibis Creek."

They sat and watched tiny birds peck at the sand, running in and out with the surf.

"That's a lot of work for not much," Ian said. "Is that I'm doing chasing Kami Cabrera?"

"I don't think so."

"You don't?"

"She's his only other connection to Ibis Creek as of July," Gabe explained. You have any other candidates?"

"No."

"Me, either. She's part of this somehow."

"Gabe, Lieutenant Hubble, are you telling me to leave Kami to you?"

"No. I am not," Gabe said, with a firm head-shake. "The case is in a drawer. Still, two last texts have disappeared, but Bartender, Suzie saw them. She nailed the text-to-speech, JJ listening to a text. We didn't prompt her."

"Which has what to do with Kami?" Ian asked. "Wait. You think she sent the text?"

"No, but she may know something. As I said, she's a link we have not accounted for, yet. I want you to talk to Kami Cabrera – or whatever she calls herself – because my ass is stuck in that drawer."

"I came here planning on it."

"When you say that, I assume you have a plan."

"Maybe I overstated it."

"So, you just plan on showing up on her doorstep?"

Ian rocked his hand in mid-air. "Yep. As in 'I'm Claire Hunter's lawyer and I'm gathering information on her Peeping Tom complaint at Ibis Creek.'"

"Where she's never lived."

"Kami's tenant, Maria Suarez, complained about the peeping Tom," Ian said. "That's my foot in Kami's door. Since Claire was accused, from the start, of being the peeper before it was called that. I had Claire sign an engagement letter for me to represent her legal rights inside ibis Creek. I have it my car."

Gabe laughed "Since Claire was named, you can talk to tenants and owners. Will you mention the prevailing theory is that JJ Amos was spying? Gathering intelligence."

"Let's go with *intel*."

"Right. And he needed intel for... what?"

"Leverage. Pressure," Ian suggested. "For a settlement. It might explain why he held off extra filings."

"A kind of blackmail?" Gabe hesitated. "Wait a second. You said he named a tenant in his lien foreclosures. So, he had known for months about her renting."

"Yes."

"And his other cases were no longer his concern."

"True."

"He had no reason to pressure anyone on July 12th," Gabe said.

"And we could barely find a few defects in the dark." Ian held up his hand, palm out. "He had everything he needed for Kami's case. It was open and shut. He even had a default."

"Damn it."

It took Ian a few seconds of frustration before he said, "But why not close her out? He kept the case alive himself, putting off the final hearing. Why would he do that?"

"Sounds more like reverse blackmail," Gabe said. "She had something on him?"

"Were they trading? Or are we just sun-struck?"

"Only one way to find out."

"Gather some intel," Ian said. He started to get up.

Gabe restrained him with a look. "Be careful, Ian. I'm sure Kami's not dangerous, but... "

"But," Ian continued, "her intel may be."

Chapter 17

Before his trip north and east in search ofr Kami Cabrera, Ian stopped off to deliver a post to Claire. He decided to physically deliver it on a USB drive. Claire would have a harder time rejecting it face to face.

To save time, he walked imes as he walked around the Hunter unit to its lanai. As expected, Claire hacked away at her laptop. There was no other way to put it, but he did not... in her presence. Chardonnay splashed near the rim of her stemless glass. Engrossed, she did not hear him approach.

Leo, in his usual corner chaise, with his usual sheets of paper crowned with Dovey, did. "Hi, Ian."

Claire looked over at Ian with a skeptical glare. "Well?"

He tossed the USB in the air. "Aren't stemless stemware gauche."

"They are, but the stems keep breaking out here. Now, Dovey thinks they are birds."

The USB went up in the air, again.

"Okay. I get it. I won't want to use your latest," she said, her mood grim. "But I'll have to use it. I need a stopgap."

"Why? You are much more prolific that I am."

"I'm not as forgiving as you are," she said. "I've been trying to write something nice about JJ Amos for Ibis Crock. For two God damned hours."

"She has managed twelve words," Leo said, with disapproval.

"That's not true. I have typed *he wasn't so bad*. A hundred times, like I was a kid at a blackboard." She got up and unlocked the screen door to let Ian in.

"I wouldn't know," Ian said, taking the chair next to Claire once she was seated.

"Me, either," Leo agreed. "And all those boards have been green for fifty years."

"Progress," she said, with a laugh. "Phooey!"

Ian glanced at the WordPress window she had open, with its two paragraphs on JJ. "You know, the more I get to know him – belatedly, I admit – the less JJ seems like the self-righteous asshole we thought he was."

"Keep that to yourself, Buster," she said. "I like my *dear departed* JJ Amos as he is."

Claire's words, as usual for those incorporated into Ibis Crock – or any blog, as far as Ian was concerned – comprised a reflection of the writer more than the truth. He did not offer that wisdom to Claire.

"I'm trying to give him some credit for helping Ibis Creek financially," she said. "I'm leaving my contribution, the ass-kicking out. I gag on every word. Which, by the way, beats throwing up."

"Mr. Amos's *unfortunate* death," Ian read. "That must have hurt.

"I started with your pal Gabe's official *undetermined* but thought it lacks verisimilitude."

"That word is for fiction," Leo said.

"And that's not fitting. I thought it was *not* undermined: It was an accidental slip-up by a peeping Tom."

Ian hesitated, unsure of what he should disclose. "They aren't sure."

"Aren't sure about what?" Leo asked. "I thought he was spying or peeping on people."

"Yes. We're almost sure of that."

"Are we?" Claire snapped. "Sorry. I guess, I want everyone to know for sure it wasn't me."

"There is not enough evidence to be one hundred percent sure."

"Hopefully, you write with more conviction than you talk. Give me that thing. Please."

Ian handed her the USB drive. Claire plugged it in. After a second she opened it.

Ian interrupted her. "Let me set it up, first."

Claire closed her eyes. "All right."

"Evie liked it," he said. "Very much."

She said, "I've asked you not to mention that name –"

Leo chimed in with an often-made declaration, "Genevieve Decker is my muse."

Even Dovey gave Leo an annoyed look and raked his knee with a paw. "I mean, she is *too*, Dovey," Leo added.

Claire sighed. "And we never tire of your saying so. And I keep reminding you that Evie, as a muse, is taken."

"Not legally." Leo mused.

Claire looked at Ian. "I'm not sure everyone got that memo."

"It was a decree," Ian said. "And it's impossible not to see Evie in the renamed *Evelyn* character."

"I didn't like the name *Carla*, anyway," Claire conceded. "It rhymed with Mara."

"So it did." Leo had already admitted that transgression.

"Can I now read what I am paying so handsomely nothing for?"

"Remember, Evie liked it," Ian lied.

Evie had not seen the draft, but would approve when she did. She was disheartened when Al Gore sold his carbon-free cable channel to oil-rich Qatar's al Jazeera. None of her clients got to handle that *total sell-out* by the presidential candidate turned environmentalist filmmaker and cable mogul. It was yet another reason for Evie to regret voting for Gore in 2000.

"Leo, bring Dovey over here," Ian said. "She'll want to read this, too."

Cats Save Naples East Bay Shores Village; Vermin Not So Much

It has been reliably reported – al Jazeera, I think – that cats are fighting global warming by killing virtually anything which emits under twelve milligrams per year of vile carbon dioxide.

Hey, it adds up. Like, their really fast breathing.

Exactly like that.

This is a great service, for which we pay our cats too little homage.

Billions of birds and tens of billions of mice – and other critters that make you jump on a chair – are gone. They can no longer exhale the key greenhouse gas – in the aggregate of megatons – to melt all of Greenland and flood your Paradise Coast condo. They are dispatched with barely a licked whisker.

Where's their movie?

And, yeah eat your vole-like heart out, al Gore.

"No way." Claire buried her nose in Dovey's mane but looked at Ian. "No Medal of Freedom for you, Dovey. No Pulitzer or Chardonnay for Sebastian Decker."

"It doesn't matter," Ian said. "I'm driving."

Leo said, "It's not like you voted for Al Gore."

"How would you know?" Claire had, but claimed the contrary when Leo was in the room. When Leo had a position, it saw Fox News to the Left. "You're driving."

Ian realized his mistake and covered his tracks. "I have run out of Bourbon. So, it is either drive or go without writing tonight."

"Perish the thought." Claire started to get up. "You can borrow –"

"Never lender nor borrower be," Ian quickly paraphrased.

"Hamlet?"

"Polonius," Leo said. "And you misquoted, Ian. Badly."

"Writers!"

"After I restock my Maker's Mark, I promise to write *Cats Save Naples East Bay, Book Two*?"

"Stay home," she said, with a smile. "I beg you."

"I can't have you writing another post using my name," Ian said.

"That one cleverer than this cat food thing," Claire said. "The cost of sub-prime beef is crazy. Even at Costco. It had to be written."

"It read like chicken."

"He's right, dear."

Leo's sacrifice inspired Ian to hurry off the lanai and concentrated on a place called Mangrove Hammock and its mysterious Kamila Mende Cabrera Gomes.

~ ~ ~

Like many in the Naples area, Ian had experienced his new life in a small rectangular grid. Most of Collier County was laid that way, with the diagonal gash of Tamiami Trail East ruining the geometry from Fifth Avenue southeast toward the Miami part of Tamiami.

Kami and Javier Gomes lived in what Ian considered *The North,* as in north of Vanderbilt Beach Road. East-west Vanderbilt, with Mercato's pivotal Blue Martini, as well as an upscale movie theater, bars, restaurants, offices and condos represented the top end of Ian's comfort zone. The next major parallel, Immokalee Road, had a Super Walmart to which Ian had sojourned twice. It had felt as if he needed his passport. The towns beyond Immokalee, Bonita and Ft. Meyers, comprised Ian's new *Arctic Circle.*

Ian's familiar territory was limited, bounded by on the west by the Gulf and on the east by Santa Barbara Boulevard. The latter was a frontier. He did not even know that Santa Barbara did not make it all the way to Vanderbilt, at least not under that name. Street names changed all over the Naples area. Tamiami North, 41, was one consistent name-changer, but every other change seemed whimsical. It was charming until the addresses started going backward.

He ventured as far east as County civilization's true eastern boundary, Collier Boulevard as chauffeur for Dovey's trip to the animal hospital on Claire's lap. His normal north-south routes were Tamiami North, Goodlette-Frank, Airport-Pulling and Livingston, west to east in that order. Livingston underwent a variety of name changes on its way toward the Southwest Florida International Airport outside Fort Meyers. Ian stubbornly ignored all the other names on his occasional trips to the Airport.

Gulfshore and Gordon, the westernmost north-south streets lay west of Tamiami, 41, but as residential, two-lane streets, they were not part of that grid. For Ian, for anyone in Naples, the western most boundary was the Gulf of Mexico and its beach.

The more easterly roads were suitably wide and lightly traveled, awaiting traffic growth that stalled with everything else. Ian rarely traveled any of them. He barely expanded his horizon to include Livingstone, mostly to avoid crash-prone I-75 when he ferried Claire and Leo off to visit their adult kids.

On her trips to the area, Evie flew into Naples' small executive airport – the one that gave Airport-Pulling half its name – and did not need a lift.

Ian used *Map Advisor* to locate Mangrove Hammock, nineteen miles away, just southeast of the intersection of Immokalee and Collier. Though he knew the distance and estimated thirty-five-minute driving time, Ian had no feel for distance on Collier Boulevard. He drove the last five miles in the right lane, looking for the landmark mangrove trees.

At the red light on Collier Boulevard at Immokalee, Ian realized several things: *Map Advisor* was not the most accurate mapping app; most varieties of Florida mangroves grew in salty water; the salty Gulf of Mexico was ten miles due west; developments picked names for marketing no accuracy; and that had been Pelican Hammock in the early 1990's.

He could not see Mangrove Hammock. He had not passed it on the southeast corner of the intersection.

Ian took a right, pulled into a strip center and parked. He used his phone's Google Maps to lookup Mangrove Hammock. It was just beyond the northwest corner of the intersection. With his new guidance, he found Mangrove Hammock's tree-marked entrance.

Finding Kami's cul-de-sac would have been difficult without his new map. Thick hedges hid the five-house street. The two lots running along each side of the street had not been cleared of their high underbrush and trees.

The house was a simple one-story, with two large, curtained windows on either side of the front door. The front door itself had two narrow vertical windows running up on each side. A single car garage was attached to the left. It had a separate walk directly from the street. The driveway had a cut over to the walk and was long enough for two cars, but only a white Kia Forte sat on it.

Ian had memorized Kami's plate number, and it was on the Forte. The door to the garage was up, showing a Kia Sorento SUV. A URI decal sat in the middle of the rear window. LinkedIn showed University of Rhode Island grad, Javier Gomes worked as a warranty service supervisor at the local Kia dealership. Ian planned to wistfully relate a couple fond memories of his days in Providence, in hopes of making Javier and Kami more relaxed.

Kami did not have a LinkedIn page. Neither Kami nor Javier had a Facebook page.

He circled the cul-de-sac and pulled up to a high hedge bordering a small four-spot parking area. He got the only available slot. Not visible from the Gomes house, Ian sat for a few minutes, concentrating partly on his approach, but more so on memories from his Providence days. His Brown University years lay, not forgotten but in the deep shadow of Evie, who came along quite a bit later.

Ian put on his suit jacket after exiting the car. Ian had chosen his favorite suit, a casual, natural colored linen-blend, and a lime silk shirt with the collar buttoned down. It had a casually professional look, accent on the casual. He left his portfolio in the back seat.

As he approached the house, he passed the driveway and used the walk both to get a better view and to allow himself to be seen.

Ian saw no light to the left of the front door, with energetic motion through the partly open curtains of the right picture window. He caught sight of a large wide-screen LED TV on the opposite wall. Players hustled across a green field and then stood for a while.

Soccer, he thought, would look good on a giant set, but no good enough for him to watch it.

He hit the bell to the left of the door and stepped back. He wanted to be visible if someone looked through the windows bordering the door. All he saw was off-white tile before the door opened.

Though he had seen Kami only a few times, he recognized her immediately. She was tiny, prettier, shorter and more slender than he remembered. After she cinched the tie of a beach cover-up, Kami slowly raised her eyes to Ian's. She did a double take. Her "Hi" sounded as uncertain as one syllable could.

"Hi, Kami," Ian said with a mild smile. "I am a fellow owner at Ibis Creek."

Her eyes widened and then narrowed in recognition. "I remember you. You're Claire's lawyer friend, Ian. Decker?"

"Guilty. To all of the above." He handed her his card.

Kami looked at the card and smiled. "Your office is in your condo. That's not very intimidating."

"Thanks."

"Okay, that wasn't a compliment," she said. "And your friend is... not very nice. She called me a deadbeat." Kami's voice did not match her size. It had an alto with a musical accent and precise, yet easy diction. Her voice was a pleasure. "I mean, I was, but it was hard to hear someone say it, so often. When I tried so hard." The last sentence came out as charmingly insincere. She waved off the innocent act. "Sometimes."

"It wasn't you. It was the number of..." He caught himself.

"Deadbeats." She laughed. "It's one of the reasons I stopped paying. No one else I knew was. The board was so sweet about it. They wanted to help me. Until… Claire changed that."

"Her argument wasn't with you or any other owner. Not really." Though Ian chosen near-honesty as his strategy, tactical omissions were needed to blunt the cutting edges of the truth. Claire's diatribes, in emails and at meetings, focused primarily and unreasonably on delinquent Affordables, like Kami. "Her problem was with the board. It still is. In fact, I am here as her lawyer," Ian began his *tale*. "She's considering a legal action against the board, against Ibis Creek. It appears that a man in the association's employ was spying on women at Ibis Creek. And the board did nothing about it. Do you know what a Peeping Tom is? A voyeur?"

"Yes." She lifted her shoulders in a restrained shudder, but the gesture was slightly late, intentional.

Ian did not acknowledge her acting. "I know. It's hard to believe Ibis Creek had one."

"It's a nice place."

"It will stay that way if we owners hold the board accountable. Would you consider joining Claire's lawsuit?"

"Side with Claire Hunter? And you sounded so sincere." She began to close the door but stopped. She hesitated further. "Do you know who it was?" She hesitated again, glancing toward the TV. "Come in. We can talk in the kitchen."

Instead of walking directly to the kitchen, Kami turned right, stopping at the mouth of the living room. The room was tiled and big enough so that the LCD screen fit in nicely. It was sparsely furnished, with an Ikea look to it.

Ian noticed a large wood table in the dining room opposite. The style was vaguely familiar, but he turned his attention to the men sat on the living room couch.

They were engrossed in the players watching an intense one-one battle at mid-field. The body language indicated they were not buddies. One was a bit taller than the other, sitting there, the other being the wider.

Kami went no farther. She cleared her throat. Both men looked over at what appeared to be a familiar attention-getting sound. She nodded to the men as she said, "Javier, Auturo, this is Ian Decker." She smiled at Ian. "He went to Brown, Javier." To Ian, she said, "Javier played soccer against Brown. He went to Rhode Island."

Javier smiled, stood and revealed himself to be about five foot ten. He nodded. Auturo did not budge, just narrowed his eyes.

"Auturo is an old friend," she said, with a subtle *get up* gesture.

Auturo frowned at either the remark or the gesture, most likely both, but did stand. He was broad and very short. He appeared very stiff, but he had little length to be limber. He looked up at Ian with a dour expression. He did not capable of a nod or smile. His hands seemed permanently in fists.

Javier stepped forward and extended his hand. "Javier Gomes."

"I saw the URI sticker on one of the cars," Ian said. "I wasn't sure I'd be welcome. Brown had a nice basketball rivalry with URI when I was there. Not that I had anything to do with it."

"Me, either. I played soccer and we beat you a couple times," Javier said. "Good games."

Kami aimed her eyes at Auturo. "Mr. Decker lives at Ibis Creek. He's a... friend of that awful Claire Hunter."

At that double-whammy, Auturo took a step back.

Quickly, she added, "Auturo has collected rent there a few times for us."

"Ibis Creek?" Javier asked, his attitude shifting to defense. "What is your business here?"

"Fuck his business." Auturo's face flushed, his fists tightened. Yet, he took a full step back. "Get –"

Kami halted Auturo's remark with one palm out. "He is not here about the foreclosure. It is something unrelated. I'm still an owner there. I invited him in to talk with me, not either of you. Go back to your match." Her voice had taken a firm tone and was directed at Auturo.

She took Ian's arm, firmly, and led him away from the tension. She held an index finger to her lips as they walked to the kitchen, in the rear of the home. Once inside, she said, "Sorry. Ibis Creek has been difficult for me. They both know that." She gestured for him to sit at a narrow table with two metal mesh chairs.

"Look, I know all about it," Ian said. "Ibis Creek wasn't run very well. It still isn't."

"Would you like something? To drink?"

"No, thanks. I hope to keep this quick."

"You had better start, then," she said with a smile and sat down. "If it is about Mr. Amos, I know he is dead. Marty called me."

"Marty?" Ian had to think for a second. "Marty Pinedo? The developer."

She laughed. "A developer? You know him?" she asked, suddenly cautious again. Then, it dawned on her. "He was at the last Ibis Creek meeting about his Ester Land up the street."

"Ester View."

"Oh, yes. In the spirit of your little Village." She laughed again. "He has little deals everywhere."

"It sounds promising, Ester View and its LEED houses."

"LEED. Yes, he likes that word because it costs extra." She grimaced. "I shouldn't say that. He's been good to me. To Auturo, too. To a lot of people from our country, Bolivia. He finds us jobs – he found me three, I'm an admin…" She inclined her head. "A secretary. I keep to temp work, mostly… Now, only temp work. Javier has a good job at the Kia dealership and would like me not to work." She dropped her voice to a whisper. "But his job is not *that* good. Kia is not Lexus."

"I suppose not."

Using her normal voice, she added, "And I like working." She smiled. "I have time to manage my Ibis unit, but I don't like to. Marty does that. For me and lots of others. He's everywhere and…."

"And?"

"I was going to say *nowhere*. He can just be hard to find sometimes." She shrugged. "He goes back to Bolivia a lot."

Ian feared he had lost control of the conversation, so he fibbed. "I don't know if Marty stayed for the detectives. I think he left before that."

"He had a meeting for his project in Golden Gate," she said. "He already knew about JJ." She tilted her head. "He told me. He said it was an accident."

"It looks like it, now," Ian began. "The detectives believe he was our peeping Tom. That would explain his presence at night."

"Really?" Kami's expression tightened all the way around. "I heard about that…" She stopped and looked away. "My tenant complained once."

"Your tenant? Can you give me her name?" he asked. "I could use a witness or two. For Claire's case."

"It's Maria Suarez. She's been a good tenant for me," she said. "I think the police talked to her already. She was upset about that."

"Thank you. I won't bother her for now. I haven't even filed a case for Claire, yet. I may wait until the police are sure about JJ. He doesn't seem like the peeping Tom type."

"I always thought he was creepy," she disagreed. "So, the police think he was doing... that... when he fell?"

"That's the theory. That he was back behind the northside units, slipped on the wet grass and hit his head. He ended up unconscious, face down in the..." Ian caught himself.

"In the Bog. I know you gave it that name." She relaxed. "Is it that bad?"

"You haven't seen it lately?"

"I stay away from Ibis Creek. I have no reason to go there," she explained. "Marty does everything."

"Yes, it is that bad. The nickname seems less funny now."

"I guess so."

After a slight pause, Ian asked, "How did you find out about Ibis Creek? You were an original buyer."

"That's Marty's fault," she said. "That's what I keep telling him. He was so sure it would be a good investment he got the financing for a large number of his fellow Bolivians, not just at Ibis Creek. Other developments." Kami cocked her head and raised an eyebrow, but kept her eyes locked on Ian's. "Marty made Ibis Creek sound like the best to me. He didn't know what was coming."

"No one did. I bought much later. After the prices came down."

"You were smart. I refinanced for a bigger mortgage to get some money. To pay off some debts back home. All of a sudden I couldn't sell it or afford the payments."

"Enter JJ Amos."

"I was ashamed," she said, "when Marty called... told me. He called it *good news*." She crossed herself, the Catholic gesture seeming automatic. Her mouth turned downward. "And I agreed with him. It's terrible to feel that."

"I won't exactly miss JJ, either."

"I think, now, though, he didn't know his righteousness was so hurtful.'"

"Some jobs are just that way," Ian said. "Some lawyers like their jobs too much."

"He did." Her eyes went dim, and she put out her palm. "I don't want to think about him anymore."

Ian nodded. "I wish I could do the same, but I can't represent Claire and forget JJ. Certainly not now. How about a couple more questions and I'll leave you alone."

"Sure," she said. Then she added with that same knowing look. "Sure you will."

"You never experienced any problem when you were living there."

"I didn't..." Kami caught herself, tensed and then sighed. "You know I didn't live there."

Ian nodded. "Okay. Yes, I do."

"You know a lot, don't you?" she asked. "Like Marty. About people."

"Yes."

"But not *the people*."

"Not many, no."

She kept her eyes on him, for an instant longer and then broke away. "I'm sorry. We all do what we do. Even JJ."

Ian sensed the change in direction. He considered his options and stayed narrow. "JJ knew you never lived in your unit."

"No. I mean, no, I didn't, but yes, he knew. It wasn't a secret. Marty told me no one would care, that it was playing the game. I doubted it at first, but he was right." She gave him a coy smile. "The truth is I did live there for two or three days. I did that to say I lived there, but mostly to be there early in the day for some deliveries. After that, Marty took care of it. He even signed up my first tenant before I bought it."

"You still list it as your homestead for real estate tax purposes." Ian laughed to keep the tone light. "Half our landlords claim that."

Kami shrugged and then sighed. "I know. It's part of it. The game. I should feel bad, but I don't. I had to…" She tilted on hand back and forth. "To lie to get the loan and the condominium. They bent the rules first. Mr. Abbott couldn't sell the small units like mine. And the County wanted to show their program worked even when it didn't."

"I guess I need to talk to Marty?"

She hesitated and then laughed. "Be careful. He will get you to invest in something."

"I don't do that anymore. I was never any good at it." That was all Evie, he thought, and still was.

"Wait." She went to a drawer and pulled out two business cards. She returned to her chair, just the edge of it and handed them to Ian.

The first card read *Martin Pinedo, AMP Financing;* the second, *Martin Pinedo AMP Investments.* Both bore the same address, one on the east-west J & C Boulevard, filled with service companies and dealers and fabricators of materials for the building trades. It lay just north of Costco and Lowe's, paralleling its sister street, Trade Center Way.

"J & C. I haven't been there for a while." Ian's thoughts turned to Evie, again, their shopping for tile and marble on J & C. As with the investing, it was all Evie, Ian to exercise a usually overridden veto. "We bought tile there. Counter tops, too, I think."

"You have to call Marty," she said. "He's almost never there. I guess I told you that."

"You did. Thanks."

She stood and led him out of the kitchen. As they passed they living room, she called, "Mr. Decker is leaving now. I'm not being sued."

Ian waved. Javier waved back. Auturo's reddened face convey his version of *get the hell out*.

Kami laughed a little but said nothing until they were at the door. She opened it, and Ian walked through.

Suddenly she said, "You said *we*."

"*We*? When?"

"About the tile and counter tops." Something in her expression was encouraging. "*We bought*."

"I was married at the time."

She looked at his hand. "And not now."

"Not now." Ian's comment felt incomplete. "Different..." The most accurate word suddenly struck him. "Different *paths*. One to Wall Street, the other the beach." JJ was not the only one with a *path*.

She eyed him at the use of the word *path*. "Fate, yes. It can be hard." She blinked the thought away. "Is it hard for you? Living alone. Without her?" The questions came with beats inserted, probing then hesitating to disguise her interest. "I have never been."

Ian made a quick calculation and made a play for a reaction. "I Just couldn't live there, you know, New York. Lawyers have to wear a tie every single day."

Kami's face did not change, but her eyes widened. She covered quickly with a big smile. "Javier has worn a tie. Auturo? Not since the army. He may have quit because of that." She closed the door part way. "Please pretend I said *hi* to Claire. Bye-bye, Ian."

"She is not easily fooled..." He added a question. "Do you like cats?"

"As a matter of fact. Why?"

"Because Claire has one," Ian said. "She almost humanizes her."

"I don't like cats that much."

"You'd this one. Her name is Dovey."

"That's a strange name for a cat." Kami clearly wanted to shut the door, but could not.

"Not if you heard her. She coos."

Her look was all skepticism.

"It's the truth. And Claire thinks cats are heroes."

"I'll remember that," Kami said. "If I ever think of Claire again."

He waited for her to close the door. She didn't. She kept smiling at him until she turned her head to one of the men who had come up behind her. At that, Ian finally walked to the driveway and down the street toward the small parking lot. Before he reached the corner, he looked back to see her watching him. The shadow of a man was still behind her. She waved and then pushed back to close the door.

Ian realized that the man had been squat and that Javier was too tall.

He drove away with Kami's easy voice in his head. So charming, so smooth. She had inquired into his personal life and brought it out of him. That was a gift, he thought.

He wondered why first ex Auturo had hovered at the door and not her current husband.

Chapter 18

Immediately after visiting Kamila Mende Cabrera, or Kami Gomes, Ian took a side-trip down Ester View to refresh his memory of Marty Pinedo's project off Naples East Bay Shores Boulevard. Since Claire, Leo and he had last seen them, the three original houses had acquired roofs, doors and windows.

They sat on narrow lots, with little space between the buildings. Long ago, the then inheritors of a family farm had laid out lots primarily for mobile home use. Well over half the land in Naples East Bay Shores Village had descended from that family farm and fifty or fewer feet wide.

With the sun setting, Ian had just enough light to peek inside and recall his memory of the basic layout. Each of the three compact one-story designs allowed for three bedroom with decent closets, two baths, an open kitchen and an anomalously named great room. The lanai was barely bigger than Ian's.

The pricing Marty Pinedo had indicated would exceed $400,000, a number that still seemed inanely high to Ian, LEED or not. Ian hoped Marty would get that price, making his own unit more valuable.

Once home, he typed up some notes on what Kami had said. He highlighted the names Marty Pinedo and Maria Suarez as victims of his next visits. He included a list of husbands: friendly *current* Javier Gomes, sullen *ex* Auturo Guillen and absent ex Mateus Duarte to keep a scorecard-lineup of Team Kami. He would flesh out the full official legal names later when he figured out the Bolivian sur-naming conventions, assuming he could.

Ian never opened the blinds in his office, in the unit's den-sized third *bedroom* – Like the Ester View houses, it had a qualifying closet – because the view consisted of mostly stairway to the upper floors. He also disliked the idea of the passersby involuntarily spying on *him*. The building's elevator kept footfalls to a minimum on any day but did not eliminate them. He paid them no mind as they approached, paused and went up the stairs.

Glued to his chair and his monitor, Ian researched Marty Pinedo and revisited Wiki Bolivia well into the night. Therefore, his peripheral awareness took a while to alert him to a shadow hesitating a beat too long outside before heading up the stairs. He dismissed it as an overly ambitious stair-climber's regret.

Later, pouring himself two fingers of his favorite relaxant, in his kitchen, he thought he detected another shape through the angled verticals of his living room sliders. Beyond the sliders and the lanai, the stretch of grass keeping the Bog at bay invited late-night dog walkers and their shadows.

And, he thought, peeping Toms.

He drained half the Bourbon to chase the spirit of Peeping JJ. He topped off with two more fingers to calm his imagination to allow more research. He returned to his office and the subject of Marty Pinedo.

Augusto Martin Pinedo was not an easy google. There was nothing on him in Bolivia where the name Pinedo was common enough. Included in the Pinedo list were famed soccer players and a king of Afro-Bolivians. Ian left those types of Pinedo for later searches.

He *was* all over the Collier County Deed site and corporate name search site Sunbiz. Marty, individually or through one of his companies, was a managing member for a dizzying array of corporations and Limited Liability Companies. LLCs had become the vehicle of choice for most real estate and development outfits. Marty held powers of attorney for hose entities and for dozens of individuals, including Kami Cabrera. Other member or director names in the LLC and corporate filings were predominately Hispanic or, to a much lesser extent, Eastern European.

He had no Collier County marriage license or divorce filing of record. Other records stated that he and Peta Pinedo were husband and wife. She appeared as an agent or signatory on any number of documents.

Marty's main companies were LLCs all named AMP – Augusto finally explaining the *A* – something or other. The most active were Financing, Development and Management, the later function including rental management and rent collection. All the entities lived at the same J & C address and used the same phone number.

Ian imagined that Marty hid something behind his very public face. Evie had long warned him that his plotter's mind enjoyed, too much, even "concocting a conspiracy theory out of the fact of thin air."

From Ian's cursory, three-hour search, into Marty Pinedo, it appeared AMP Financing had been the first of Marty's businesses. He originally incorporated it as a sundries store named Pinedo Sundries, Inc. He later changed its limited purpose to general, its name to Martin-Pinedo Distribution and its form to LLC. It later became Pinedo Financial with a final renaming in 2008.

Under the file name *Small World*, Marty had acquired an LLC that he transferred within a year. He changed its name to Martin-Pinedo Lawn Service, LLC. and then sold the company. The next listed managers were Jeanie Barrett and Chiky Gomez. Naturally – in a small world sense – Kamila Mende Guillen appeared as a manager twice in Marty's long list of companies, Kamila Mende Duarte only once.

Ian sent his Kami notes to his personal Gmail account but deferred Marty's information, as it was in very raw form and might not have fit under the twenty megabyte Gmail inbox limit.

The next morning, Ian reviewed his Kami-related notes and called AMP Financing in an attempt to pin down the famously elusive Marty Pinedo. Mara had landed Marty for that recent board meeting, seemingly a rare feat. He was a favorite absentee at the CRA offices and meetings, once he had their backing and/or subsidies for his local projects.

CRA administrator Louise Baker's reports at CRA Advisory Board meetings usually included the frustrated remark, "Marty seems to be in Bolivia, again." Marty had seven outstanding promises to the CRA still outstanding.

Unlike Louise, Ian got Marty on the first try, although a voice mail intro began before Marty cut in. Ian was so taken aback he forgot to say anything.

"Hello," Marty finally said.

"Sorry, Mr. Pinedo," Ian said. "I was composing a message for you."

"My fault. I usually let all calls go to voice mail, but Kami told me you would be calling. She gave me your contact information and I saved you as a contact last night. I saw your name, and here we are."

Ian detected that slight accent, but it sounded less Bolivian than California. He spoke quickly but with diction that nearly matched Kami's.

"I appreciate your taking my call," Ian said. "I trust Kami filled you in on the reason for it."

"She did. I won't be able to help you much. So it won't take long. If you can come up to my office, now, we can meet in person."

"That would be great," Ian said, surprised again. "I can make it in, say, half an hour."

"Fine. I'll take that time for an errand, but I'll be here when you get here. If I'm not there, wait for me, please. I may be a couple minutes late."

"Great."

"Good. Good-bye."

Marty terminated the call, leaving Ian with mixed feelings. While he would finish with the Pinedo portion of his investigation, Marty sounded convincing about how little he had to add.

As Ian drove north on Airport-Pulling, Ian wondered why Marty did not go by Auggie. In his too brief search on Bolivian names, Ian learned that Martin should be Marty's father's surname with Pinedo his mothers. That assumed the usual South American format. A last name of Martin did not sound Hispanic, complicating the issue.

He wondered how or if Kami had added her various husband's names and how that worked. He believed the most recent, Gomes, should come last. The one thing he knew was that Hispanic names befuddled the index of a rigid computer database.

As with a nice surf, driving tended to send Ian's mind off on tangents.

Turning onto J & C brought back memories of shopping for rigid materials with Evie. Though she had repeatedly assured him of their hefty profits on Citi and AIG stock justified the investment in inorganic finery like granite and porcelain, he had balked.

"Can we get it out in rental or resale?" he had asked, in his mild objection. "Do Snow Birds know granite from roast beef?"

"We may be snow birds, so, yes, absolutely. And women love these kinds of touches. You'll thank me someday, Ian. I promise."

Evie rarely promised and more rarely failed to deliver, so Ian had deferred to her superior knowledge and taste. She had made the decisive, hugely profitable buys of stock anyway.

History had proven Evie right. Granite helped sell Ibis Creek units, if not in price, in speed of a sale. More importantly, Ian found that he liked the granite a lot and did not mind re-sealing of the surfaces once a year. Finishing anything was a treat for Ian.

Ian made excellent time on Airport, traffic seasonally low. He reached AMP's office, in the middle of a strip of small, store-front style offices, in fifteen minutes. J & C and Trade Center had a great many of such efficient strips. He recalled that, according to the Assessment site, the strip was fifteen years old. Neither Marty nor AMP had ever financed or owned the strip or the office space. Marty had a power of attorney for the LLC that did.

Marty had left more fingerprints around Naples than any ten kids on a stainless steel refrigerator.

The names behind the LLC were both Hispanic, but the mortgage was held by a Florida LLC named Sand Key Investments, with a managing member listed as Mule Key LLC. The owners of LLCs were not in the public Sunbiz database. LLCs owning LLCs was common, even if listing one as a manager was not. The structure poked Ian's imagination and then let it alone.

Sand Key had five such mortgages in Collier County at one time or another. All were tied to Augusto Martin

Pinedo, at the very least with him excerpting a power of attorney. Mule Key owned neither mortgages or real estate, but it did have manager status in a few other LLCs.

The research indicated that Marty was a player of some level and that Marty played in a league with an individual or group enamored of the word *Key*.

The office strip's parking spaces were all empty, so Ian took dead in front of AMP's door, if only because the air was soupy that day. The door to the office was locked. The sunlight darkened the heavy tint of the window, blocking any view of the interior. A ring of the bell produced nothing. Ian went back to his car, started it back, and aimed the air conditioner vents at his face.

After thirty blissful seconds, an older, silver Mercedes S-class – obviously the one he had seen at the recent Ibis Creek board meeting – pulled onto the painted line a space and a half from him. Marty Pinedo got out of the front passenger seat. Auturo Guillen got out of the other and walked far enough along the hood for Ian to him holding a small, securely zippered bag, the kind used for cash. Auturo hesitated when he recognized Ian, fixing him with an undisguised glare.

Marty beamed and held out his hand. "Marty," He was a tad shorter than Ian. "Mr. Decker. Sorry. Rent collection day."

Ian shook his hand and looked over at Auturo, who had edged around the car as if looking to avoid a fight he wanted to start. "Ian, please. And I've met Auturo, at Kami's Hey, Auturo."

Marty glanced at Auturo, surprise on his face. "Well, that's... nice. Auturo, you forgot to mention that to me."

"I was..." Auturo began. "Javier and me were watching a match. Javier has the best TV for football." He sounded miffed that Javier had the best of anything, perhaps including wives.

"She does," Marty said.

"I agree," Ian said. "I saw it. Great for a game like…"

"You can say it," Marty said, with a smile that effectively approximated a wink. "I called it soccer until I was ten years old."

"Okay, then. The soccer field looked beautiful."

Auturo lightened up to grim but said nothing.

Marty unlocked the door and waved Ian inside. He then waved Auturo in and pinched his eyes when Auturo hesitated. "Come on, Auturo. The cool is getting out."

Auturo followed orders, reluctantly. He immediately brushed past Ian on his way to a small hallway beyond the large front office area. Ian felt something hard and flat against his thigh. Auturo was not happy to see him, presumably making another point.

"He is in a bad mood these days," Marty explained. "He was a construction foreman – cement forms, that sort of thing – in Le Paz. Bolivia. He had good work, but it slacked off. I offered him a chance to come to Naples and marry Kami during the building boom here. That was 2006. With an American wife, I could get him a green card." The wink-smile indicated he had gamed the system for Auturo. "But by 2007, things slowed down. By 2008 almost everything came to a stop. Were you here, then?"

"We bought in 2009."

"It was even worse by then. My own businesses, too, especially AMP Financing. It was hard. That car out there was repossessed by my company. From a client and friend. Terrible times." He shook off the memory of acquiring his S-Class. "Kami and Auturo? Money strains cause most divorces." He smiled it again.

"Most."

"Auturo and many others went back to Bolivia, or Columbia, Mexico," Marty went on. "They found it worse there. I paid for Auturo to come back. He was loyal to me, and I owed him that."

"Thinks have started to pick up," Ian said. "How are things for you and Auturo, now?"

"As you know, I provide management services for landlords," he said. "That supported me, in truth. It is not what I see for myself, but times dictate, don't they?"

Many people asked questions for information – back in Pittsburgh, every third sentence sounded questioning – Ian sensed that Marty used the form to draw in his listener. Few could have done it with more charm. "So, Auturo works for you?"

"Only occasionally, mostly on rent days. Auturo is my *muscle*," he said with the wink-smile. "He is not tall, but he's solid and such a sourpuss, he can be intimidating to tenants. He was in the Bolivian army for a while. He has remained very fit, very strong."

"I'd give him my rent just to see if he can smile."

"He can. Just not lately." Marty took a seat behind a laptop sitting on modern style desk, similar to those sold in every Office Depot or Staples. A matching credenza behind him held a compact color laser printer. Two spartan chairs were in front. There were two other similar, if lesser, desks with nothing on them. Function, not fancy, ruled in Marty Pinedo's office. More than anything, it looked largely unused. "To the business at hand. What can I do for you, Mr. Decker? Ian?" He gestured for Ian to sit.

Ian did and began his story. "I don't know what Kami told you –"

"Assume she told me very little. It was late."

"I live in the Ibis Creek condominium, as does my client Claire Hunter," he said.

Marty nodded.

"I represent Claire, as her attorney," Ian continued. "Without naming her, the board has clearly accused her of spying on residents at night. Claire is not well liked by the board of directors. She is the ultimate squeaky wheel, hold the grease."

Marty grinned. "Yes. She was very hard on owners who could not afford to pay dues." The grin had been replaced by the winker. "Kami, especially."

"True. Since you are her manager," Ian said, with a nod, "you know Kami paid two or three times in the entire time she owned her unit."

"Her tenants didn't pay. She lost her job. That is why she asked me to help." He wink-smiled, almost daring Ian to contest his tale. "Then, your Mr. Amos sued her. Her lender, as well I, told her not to pay Ibis Creek at that point."

"Naturally," Ian agreed, affably. "At that point, no one does. I doubt I would." He added, "Claire wouldn't, either."

Marty laughed at the postscript. Even his muted laugh was charming.

Ian began to wonder if Naples was some kind of magnet for charm as well as wealth. After all, he lived there himself. "My visit to Kami was just about the peeping Tom case, nothing else. I know she has never lived there..."

Marty wink-nodded, just as effective as the smile counterpart.

"She though you, as her manager, may have heard something," he continued. "And I wanted to ask you whether Kami's tenant, Maria Suarez, would be available to me. I see that she complained last year."

"She emailed me about it," Marty said, elevating his eyes, searching. "And, certainly, you should talk to her. I think she only complained once but was sure she saw someone on the back lawn three times. Maria is laid back," he added, with the smile. "She works in a nail salon not too far from here." He quickly wrote down Maria's work and personal contact information and handed it to Ian.

"She works at a nail salon and is not Vietnamese, "Ian observed. "That's talent."

"Manicura Pelicano is owned by and staffed with Latinas," Marty said. "If you are going today, I can call ahead and make sure she is available."

"Thank you. It won't be a problem?" Ian asked. "During her work day?"

"A couple... clients of mine own it."

"I'd like to go straight from here, if possible."

"Could you wait until after lunch?" Marty said. "Maria has her own clientele. They won't go to anyone else, so she can give you ten minutes or so. But lunchtime is limited for customers who work."

"Fine. What can you tell me about Maria?"

"Very little. She is outgoing but not chatty. She also is very attractive, but in a way that women don't mind. She is a natural blond, which is rare in Bolivia." To Ian's raised eyebrow, he said, with his wink-nod, "So, I'm told. And she has light eyebrows."

"That is a giveaway."

"I believe her ancestors fled Norway."

"For Bolivia? Before World War II?"

"After." Marty shrugged. "I don't believe Maria understands the meaning of the sequence."

"*Collaboration* doesn't mean what it used to."

"Back to Maria. You'll see why, but she has more than a healthy share of jealous men friends. That is why she did not report to me the first two... incidents. Her admirers might have been looking in on her... and her dates, at odd hours." He chose his words with obvious care. "The third time seemed too much, and she contacted me. I contacted your association."

"Do you have other accounts at Ibis Creek?"

"I have five or six, depending on the season." Marty rubbed his upper lip. "No one else said anything when I asked. It was just Maria. Thank God nothing came of it."

"Not nothing, so much."

Marty lost all semblance of his smile. He almost looked mad. He took a deep breath, after which his words came out with deliberation. "I apologize. I meant to Maria, of course. I didn't care for JJ Amos, but he was just doing his job."

"I understand. I had my run-ins with him, too," Ian said. "My list of favorite people? It could be ten times longer, and he still wouldn't have been on it. And vice versa."

"Is he truly suspected of being a peeping Tom?"

"Very likely, yes. Not that it matters, now," Ian said. "Except to my client. Claire is thinking of suing the association for defamation."

"I don't blame her," Marty said, "though that's a pot calling the kettle names, isn't it?"

"She can be brutal." Ian agreed. "As for your analogy: The kettle was, is, in fact, black."

Marty looked at Ian, confused. Then he burst out laughing and slapped his desk sharply, several times. "So, it was, damn it. I need another analogy."

Auturo appeared suddenly, with a scowl that made his earlier expressions seem cheerful. He flexed his left forearm, just above his hip, indicating a death grip on something Ian could not see. Auturo saw Marty winding down his laugh and looked bewildered. "I heard… I heard something."

"I'm sorry, Auturo," Marty said. "I slapped the desk. That's all. Your friend Mr. Decker is damned funny."

Auturo was not the grunting type. With his face, he did not have to be. He relaxed his forearm. "Okay." He turned his left toward Ian and paused, intentionally letting Ian see the knife handle jutting out a scabbard.

Ian's eyes must have given him away because Auturo approximated a smile.

Marty said, "Go on, Auturo." He waited until Auturo had disappeared. "Construction sites often lack box cutters and the like." He rose. "And you saw my cash bag."

Ian rose and shook Marty's hand. "That's the biggest *old habit* I've seen lately," he said, walking beside Marty to the door." At least, since I left the Pennsylvania woods."

Marty's wink-smile showed Ian out the door. "We men, Ian? We do like to measure things."

"Your car's sure bigger than mine," Ian said, as he got in his car. "But you should have seen see my old bag. It was a briefcase that needed wheels."

~ ~ ~

Ian had to drive only ten minutes to Manicura Pelicano, housed in a large shopping complex at Livingston and Pine Ridge. On the way, he ran errands he hadn't known he had.

He could hear the din of conversation through the glass front. The salon was packed. Hispanics were less seasonable than Anglos, but there three of the latter, as well. Maria Suarez jumped out of the brunette crowd, with her long, lean figure and light blond hair hanging just beyond suitably narrow shoulders.

She was puttering around her station, with no client in the chair. The woman next to her whispered something and Maria looked up with large, dark blue eyes. She smiled and strode to the front of the shop, free, sure of herself even at her young age, or because of it. "Mr. Decker."

"What gave me away?" Ian asked, embarrassingly disappointed that she considered him *Mr. Decker*.

"Sex."

Ian ran some responses through his head and chose, "Surely, you get men in here."

"We don't." She inclined her head toward the interior. "It is too crowded for men. They don't like the talk." She had a strong accent, tinged with something else. "Come next door to the gelato shop. It is cool there and fashionable. They won't mind."

The gelato shop was far from empty, but three tables were available. Maria waved at the two women behind the counter. She pointed at the table in the corner, and the women both nodded. "Our salon is half their business."

Once they were seated, Ian noticed that Maria had beautiful hands and perfect nails, only a bit longer than her nice fingertips. He asked, "Can I get you anything?"

"No. I have to eat later," she said. "I have evening clients every week this day. For women who work."

She settled in and showed off her hands. "You were looking."

"Of course. I'm not a manicurist, but those nails are hard to miss."

"I don't do them myself, but thank you," she said. "I can, but I don't want to give my clients any ideas. Some of the other girls are almost as good. They are getting better. I was not as good when I started here. I only did my mother's in La Paz – she had terrible nails. Some medicine she took, I think – so I was better than most, even to start. We rotate doing each other."

She looked Ian's hands and frowned deeply enough that he put them on his knees. His reaction amused her, but she became serious, tapping the table with her tips. "We have a good nail strengthen. From Japan. I can give you some, a sample. No, I must give you one."

"That's nice of you, but my teeth might break."

She laughed and put the elbows of her long arms on the table, curling her hands to support her graceful jaw. "I have heard your name, Ian Decker," she said. "I mean before Auggie called. He likes you. Ibis Creek?" She shook her head.

"Auggie? You mean Marty?"

"I can tease him. We are... friends," she said, with a meaningful hesitation. "Don't you try it."

"With Auturo around, that could be fatal."

Her sunny expression darkened. "No, no. Not with Auturo. He scares me."

"Me first."

She laughed and brightened back up. "So... Marty said you had questions about my... *voyeur*."

"I do. I represent an owner," he began, handing her bare-bones lawyer card. "You may know her name: Claire Hunter."

Her light dimmed again. "She does not like tenants, like me. She wants us to pay our rent to the board, not Marty. So, far, they haven't made me." She shrugged. "I never met her."

"Claire was accused of being the voyeur by some board members," he explained. "I am her lawyer, and we are considering suing."

"I have some lawyer friends," she said. "Not very many."

"Me, either."

She laughed again. "Marty said you were funny."

"It's why I am a retired lawyer."

Maria tossed her hair, to great effect. Then she fingered it into place again. "Not so retired, now."

"I take a case occasionally," Ian said. He added, "I do work for other lawyers, too," as if she had pulled it from him.

"Do you make much money?" she asked, with a sly grin. "I like men like that."

"I can start tomorrow."

Maria could not stop laughing.

"I take it," Ian said, "that I can take tomorrow off."

"I'm sorry." She shook off the laugh. "With the polish remover, we laugh too easily." She laughed. "To answer your question, I know I saw someone behind my lanai… my building, not directly behind my lanai. It was dark, very little moon or cloudy, so I couldn't really see him."

"But you saw a man."

"I think so. He was too square to be a woman…" She thought about it. "He moved like a man. He was maybe my height without heels. A little shorter. Not as short as Auturo, but as wide the shoulders."

Maria was about five-nine.

"Not Auturo, though."

"No, I know Auturo," she said. She looked straight at Ian. "Yes, I'm guessing, but I'm a good guesser. About men."

"How many times?"

"Four or five. Some of them just moving."

"That often?"

"Yes, but over almost a year. With a long time between," she said. "I didn't think much of it, the first times. People walk dogs back there. Behind the buildings, there is lots of grass for the dogs."

Ian recalled his thought of the previous night. "Yes, I'm glad I don't walk out there."

She nodded.

"Marty said you only saw him three times. The same guy?"

"I think so. The same shape." She hesitated. "I didn't want to say anything. It just seemed dumb to see shadows every place. You know, to seem... Suspicious?"

"*Paranoid* is the word I would use," Ian suggested. "Except you weren't."

"Yes, paranoid." She shuddered. She had the perfect body for it. "No, I wasn't."

"We think the voyeur was the lawyer for Ibis Creek."

"The one who is dead," she said. "Marty told me. Mr. Amos. I got certified papers from him. It scared me more than the voyeur, but Marty took care of all that."

"Could it have been him? Mr. Amos?"

Maria looked surprised, her eyes wide. They got narrower as she thought about JJ. "Yes. Him." She started nodding. "Yes. I think it was. Why would he?"

Ian held back. "We don't know. He may have been checking on tenants for his lawsuits. That's why he served you those papers. Tenants are always added as a matter of form."

She nodded again but did not mean it. "It's not fair. I didn't do anything."

"No, it's not, but he had to." With her unexpected confirmation in hand, Ian almost forgot his last line of questions. "Have you ever met Kami Cabrera?"

"Kami. Sure. Most of us know each other. I don't know her. Just to meet. Marty handles my rent. And Auturo. A few times he came, only when my rent is late." She exaggerated a frown. "I make sure I mail my rent way ahead of time. If I can. This time of year? Not slow, but tips are less." She added, "Oh. And Mateus. He once came for rent. He was nice. Not Auturo. He has never been nice. In his life, you think?" And he has his knife when he comes. Have you seen his knife?"

"Not yet."

"Good." She looked at the thin watch on her thin wrist. "I should get back pretty soon. A few minutes." She seemed in no hurry.

"Is there anything else," Ian was in no hurry for her to leave. "Anything about the voyeur? Something odd? Was he wearing a hat? White sneakers, say?"

"No, sorry," Maria said, standing and stretching in the most innocent way. "I didn't want to look."

"Marty said it may have been a jealous guy friend."

"No. I thought that, but I know their shapes. It was not any of them."

Ian tried not to watch her as he stood and then, suddenly sat down. "You know, you didn't ask me how I got here. *Everyone* asks *anyone* that."

"I tend to forget," he said. "I'm just happy you made it to Naples."

Maria smiled. "Me, too. But now I have to tell you."

She told her story as a simple one. In 2007, her aristocratic boyfriend in La Paz, Silvio Morales, moved, first to New York to "work the UN," as she put it. They did not stay long because his project made little headway. Before they returned to Bolivia, they stopped in Naples to visit the Bolivian community in Naples. Marty Pinedo knew Silvio well and acted as consul of Naples for them. They stayed for two weeks. Silvio left, Maria stayed.

"I liked it here," she explained. "I'm not the only blond and am not so tall. I don't want to stand out."

Ian nodded. "Good luck with that one."

She smiled, demurely. "A little is okay."

"What was Silvio doing at the UN?"

She shrugged. "He was a lobbier for coca leaves to be legal. In Bolivia, coca leaves are legal. Religious, even."

Wiki had informed Ian about the coca leaf issue, important to Bolivia. Coca plants also supplied cocaine and were, therefore, unpopular in the US and most of Europe. Bolivians were chewing the leaves and making tea out of them for a thousand years before the Spaniards arrived and took them back to Europe, where, later, they became less humble.

"Bolivian would like to sell coca, but it is illegal. That's how Marty knew Silvio. His mother knew Silvio," she went on. "Silvio didn't succeed. He was easily discouraged. He took a month to ask me out after I said *no* the first time. I said I was busy. I was busy. He believed me, too much. Nobody is busy all the time!."

Once she settled on Naples – and Silvio departed – she and Marty became "better friends." He found her a place to stay – in a Bolivian enclave – and asked her "what other skills" she had. Striking before nineteen and from a well-to-do, Norwegian ex-pat family, she had never needed a real job. "Just boyfriends who did."

"I told him I had experience with nails," she said, with a slight grimace. "I did. Twenty of them." She laughed, a little embarrassed. "I should not be proud of lying to Marty."

"I'm sure he's used to it."

"But, we..." She shrugged again. "He was married, though. To Peta... who is very nice."

A few years after her arrival and success in nails, Marty steered her to Ibis Creek and Kamila Cabrera's condominium.

"There," she said, concluding. "Your turn…"

A woman in a salon smock entered the gelato shop. She waved at Maria.

"No. I have to get back," she said, putting as nice a pout as Ian had seen. "I want to hear yours, but maybe again."

"I can tell you right now," Ian said. "My wife and I were both lawyers. We bought here for vacationing. We got a divorce, and it does not snow here. All finished."

"No." She shook her head, refusing to accept his version.

"Yes."

"Everyone has a better story than that."

"I tried. That was the best I could do. Hence, the divorce."

She pressed her well-defined lips together and slowly stood up. "Men tell me their stories."

Ian tried not to watch the entire time. "I'm sure they do. And I just spilled mine."

"There is *more*," she insisted, standing again. "With a martini? Vodka. Maybe two?"

"I will work something up to tell you." Ian stood and walked with her to and through the gelato's door.

After she opened the salon door, she stopped. "He was blocky. Like he was wearing a jacket. Not a short jacket. Like a suit."

"Like a lawyer."

She looked at his casual clothes. "No like that." She laughed and went into the shop.

Ian had an urge to rush home, change and buy some dry vermouth. He shook his head at himself as he went to his car. He stopped when he saw a big Silver Mercedes with a short guy in the driver's seat.

He called Marty, who picked up. "Hey, are you having me followed?"

"What do you mean?" Marty sounded surprised.

"Take a look in your lot."

"Okay. My lot. You mean... Damn it."

"It's here," Ian snapped. "Not twenty feet from a very good gelato shop."

"They do have good gelato," Marty said. "But the truth is Auturo doesn't like gelato... any more than he seems to like you."

"And I thought we hit it off over that soccer game."

"You called it soccer, Ian. What did you expect?"

"A pass, maybe." Ian kept his eyes on Auturo. "Does he like the beach. I'm headed there next, but I haven't decided which one."

"He doesn't relax much and he is overprotective. Especially of Kami," Marty said. "I will call him as soon as we hang up. If nothing else, I'd like my car back."

"*If nothing else* is not what I was hoping for, Marty." Ian broke off eye contact with Auturo and got into his car. "I'll be down at 34th South in a couple hours. Come on down, if you want me watched."

"Here's the *pass* you wanted."

"Thanks." Ian hung up and waited until Auturo's right hand produced his cell. Auturo read the screen and typed a few characters with his left hand. Ian waited further until the Mercedes was gone, its voyeur with it.

Ian mentally compared the body types of Auturo and JJ Amos, both spies. They had similarities and Ian doubted could distinguish their shadows. He could not envision Auturo in a suit and, more than that, he trusted Maria's sense of shape.

Chapter 19

Ian could have driven to the beach at 34th Avenue South with his eyes closed. He performed the functional equivalent a couple hours after he returned from Manicura Pelicano. Maria having nailed JJ for the peeping Tom, he had turned his attention to researching Auturo Guillen Huerta more thoroughly. He had found the full name on the Clerk's site for a traffic ticket and a dismissed misdemeanor for a fight outside a bar, but nothing else.

Oddly, he felt a letdown, a frustration, with the conclusion of JJ's spying activities. He had been sure, after all, but now he *knew*. Even so, he felt no closer to the meaning of the spying.

He had tried a little Maker's Mark to clear his head before reporting to Gabe Hubble. It had helped every bit as much as expected. He had then tried practicing his report at Claire and Leo to report. He did not like the muddled sound of it. He felt too wound up, unable to clearly convey how sure he was. Gabe would have to wait. The JJ file was hardly smoldering inside Gabe's drawer. It was in Ian's head.

The beach access at 34th was well south of Fifth Avenue and even farther south from the beach at Central. It required another, extra-leisurely ten minutes of auto-piloting along Gordon Drive, home to a string of beach-side mansions. Most were not visible from the road, sparing even the most vigilant outsider from fits of envy. After his first few years of using that particular beach, Ian had ceased to notice much of the splendor. On that day, the tall protective hedges blurred into a wall of green.

He practiced his current mantra: No JJ; No Kami; No Auturo; No Ibis Creek. Maybe a little Maria Suarez.

Not easily smitten or even very observant, Ian expected Maria images to stick with him for a few days.

Still on auto-pilot, Ian parallel-parked in the closest of two remaining slots on the stub of 34th. It took him a while to realize that the engine was still running but not the car. He turned off the ignition, popped the trunk and got out. He clicked his doors locked as he focused on walking toward his trunk. A pair of Brown Pelicans caught his eye before he turned.

They seemed to skim over the short hedges separating the street from the beach and the Gulf. Once they had ducked below that line, he retrieved his green mesh beach chair and a silver cooler bag. The bag contained an ice brick and two Mountain Dew bottles filled with something other than Mountain Dew. Ian had begun working on mindlessness at home, with two shots of Bourbon. He expected it would take more than sixteen ounces of Dewly aged wine, so he brought double that.

He threw his cellphone into the trunk where it could ring as much as it wanted.

34th was as far as anyone could go southward and walk onto the Naples beach without inheriting forty million after taxes. The Avenue amounted to five hundred feet with two houses on the north side and one on the south. It contributed five public parking spaces nosed against the divided hedge that hid the beach and three on each side leading there. Those spots required the County beach sticker displayed on Ian's windshield to park ticket-free.

A dozen paces took Ian through the hedges and into a thirteen-knot breeze off the Gulf. He stopped to squint at the pelicans. By that time, their wings appeared to brush the Gulf's shallow swells. The birds split formation and flapped to circle the low sun. Suddenly, one bird's path collapsed into ambitious headfirst crash into the water. Its head emerged with something squirming in its throat pouch. It arched its neck and gulped without ceremony. Wings partly extended, it lifted from the surface and joined its associate in flight to the south.

Now, *that* was he should try with *his* head, Ian thought.

Ian hoisted his chair and looked over the beach. After the Naples' rainy season, the sun and white clouds dominated the days. Showers came and went quickly. No one was starved for the sun, and the wind was stiff with gusts to 20 miles per hour; therefore, the beach had a middling crowd, which by 34th's standard, meant five clusters of two to three chairs or towels. That number would double to applaud the sun's daily money shot.

Ian wore an oversized, long-sleeved linen shirt, white, over one-size too big sand-colored slacks. To blend in further, he wore tan swim trunks under his pants, in the event he felt moved to go into the body-temperature water. Ian had learned the hard way that UV kept on coming all the way to a Naples sunset.

Ian favored the far right side, where a protruding wall provided a wind break on most days, not with winds directly from off the Gulf. Besides, two couples had a tight chat circle in place. Chatting in the wind required a very tight circle and, Ian knew, the conversation would travel about four feet in that wind. The wind kicked more surf than usual, too, further dampening noise.

He would have preferred being more offset from the access and closer to the beach, but he saw an unusual gap in chairs halfway to the windbreak wall. The opening centered on a solitary stump. Any true Ibis Bog lover had an affinity for stumps – JJ came, unbidden, to mind – that the current beach-goers apparently lacked.

As he neared it, the stump opened its right eye and cocked its head the opposite direction, as if to explain the gap.

Ian immediately realized three things: No stump that size landed on Naples' beach; Brown Pelicans normally appeared more *gray* than the name indicated; proof of that latter rule sat – brown as could be – right in front of him.

Out of respect for the pelican's personal space – and its powerful beak – Ian slowed his approach. When some feathers stirred, Ian backed off two steps. The pelican settled and closed its eye. Ian set up his chair, sat and began his second pelican watch of the early evening. He was confident that the welcome distraction would be short-lived. He could then progress in converting reality into plot devices. Optimistic, he lay a small notepad on his lap, pen clipped to the pages to fight the wind.

An hour later, out cold, Ian was well into celebrating of his renowned discovery of the first petrified pelican on record. He proclaimed it Pelicanus Amosus, which he had trouble spelling even in a dream. The find was as impressive as the pelican was not: Nature and eons had crafted a dull brown statute of a stump, with some dull gray. Ian's 35mm cellphone photos had gone viral, bringing the Smithsonian to his thirty-five hundred square foot Gordon Drive tear-down, in mid-tear.

Ian found that he enjoyed fame immensely.

"Hey."

Ian recognized reality when it spoke to him. Petrified pelicans did not talk, and Ian was too sensitive to consciously name a rock after JJ, apologies to the rock. The *hey* had been his own, as his steno-pad hit his foot. He had dozed off sketching three small versions of the pelican for a planned novel cover. For the extended, wing-flapping one, he had borrowed from Barton Abbott: It had JJ-style short neck. A second drawing featured the stump. The third had a pelican soaring between two lines, up toward a Heaven complete with a gate.

All three wore loosened ties with tight knots.

Ian remembered beginning to draw them. He picked up the pad. "You know," he whispered to his impassive companion. "There are fish in the sea. Many, I'm told." No response came. "The other guys are catching your share."

"How many?"

That question did not come from the pelican, but it stood and flexed its wings at the sound of Gabe Hubble's voice.

"Ian, you are talking trash to a bird."

"Thank God. I wasn't sure."

"'It was weak, but it was still trash." Gabe wore a Nike aqua and white polo outside white and aqua Nike shorts. His ball cap matched as well. The sunglasses bore no logo. He opened a navy captain's chair to the left of Ian's cooler.

"You saw him? Before he stood up?"

"Yeah." Gabe eased himself into the chair. "I didn't mean to wake you. Either of you. Sorry."

Two last *pro forma* flaps of its wings and the pelican slowly drew everything feathered back into itself.

"It's been like that for..." Ian checked his watch. "Over an hour. Right in that spot."

"It's funny. That's where Claire said *you* would be."

"Claire?" Ian looked at Gabe. "Oh. I don't remember telling her."

"I called her when you didn't answer. I figured you'd be at a beach," Gabe said. "She said something about stress and a glazed look. She told me you stopped rambling about Marty Pinedo and his *southpaw* and how sure you were about JJ. She knew you were going to this beach," Gabe said. "Instead of calling me."

"You're a busy guy."

"Then she started to say something *Maria the blond with the goods and the bodies* and either a knife or a nail file, but I had another call come in."

"It was both," Ian added. "Knife and nail file. I didn't see either one, but I knew they were there."

"Okay. The blond lefty? Maria Suarez?"

"Oh, no. Maria is *really* the blond," Ian said. "I have Marty Pinedo guarantee and I trust him on that. Maria's the one with the file, who has and saw a body. Marty's guy has the knife. Auturo. He's the very spooky southpaw." He tried to make a spooky gesture with his left hand, but it looked like a mermaid's tale. "And, by the way, I was not glazed," Ian added. "No one gets glazed on two shots of Makers Mark. At least, I think it was two and I think it was Makers Mark."

"You need this break, I take it." He kicked off his sandals. "Ah."

"You had official business? For whom? Nike?"

Gabe glanced toward his watch, only to make a point. "Unlike present company, I don't claim to work until dawn, which is not much of an alibi, either." He stretched his legs out in front of him and retracted them. "I haven't seen a beach sunset for about a year. Suzannah has to fill me in. The pelican lawn ball over there is an added treat she never mentioned."

"In the dream, you almost interrupted, I had just named the stump thing after JJ Amos. By the way, Maria is the blond with the goods, in many respects. She pegged JJ as our spy. I helped. Maybe, too much. It might not stand up in court."

"Do I need to remind you?"

"Oh. I guess you did."

"That gives us another fourteen percent it was JJ," Gabe said. "We are unofficially at ninety-nine percent. Officially, we are still undecided." Gabe toed the bag. "Now, you've brought in this Marty Pinedo and the wacko who works for him. Thanks a lot."

"No thanks needed. I was doing my unofficial job."

"Did Marty's guy really tail you to the blond's? Maria Suarez?" He leaned over and pried open the Velcro strip at the top of the bag. "There it is. Mountain Dew."

Collier County's park beaches had signs declaring a ban on alcoholic beverages, but non-park 34th's sign was silent on the subject. Claire had suggested the use of tinted soda bottles for non-soda beverages, "to protect them from sunlight." Because Claire preferred Lowdermilk Park's beach – with its man-made bathrooms – she deferred to the County's sensibility, if not its rule or intent.

Ian had settled on Mountain Dew green PET bottles which the gold of Chardonnay altered to a murky chartreuse.

"Yes, he did," Ian said. "And if you are on unofficial business – I'm a little confused on that – no, to the second question."

"It kind of looks like Mountain Dew."

"It kind of tastes like it, too."

"Too bad," Gabe said. "I never liked Mountain Dew."

"My formula is not much better. At first."

"It's kind of a nice bottle."

"You should have seen the blond."

Gabe sighed and looked at the Pelican. "Why did I let you do my interviews, again?"

"Well, I am non-threatening," Ian said. "Even laughable. At least to one slick Bolivian and a hot blond. Others, not so amusing."

"Are you up to repeating your report to Claire?"

Ian took a long swig of faux Dew and related his three visits, Kami, Marty and Maria, four if staring down Arturo counted. He wound up with Maria's description of her voyeur.

"So, you accept her, Maria's opinion?" Gabe asked. "Based on whose body type?"

"You should have seen the blond."

"She's sure it wasn't your pal Auturo? He was spying today."

"Maria knows Auturo. His body is not the same. And I believe her when she says she knows body shapes. He's decidedly short. I don't think he has a thing for Maria," Ian said. "He was at the salon to watch me. Marty said it wasn't for him, but I don't know. Kami and Marty are linked in several ways. We know that, but Maria's just a tenant. Besides, Auturo wouldn't spy on her from the Bog. He'd scowl by the garage or knock in a door without a hello."

"Whew."

"Yeah. He gives that impression."

"Okay. JJ was the peeping Tom but not the usual reason," Gabe said. "That supports the accident theory as much as anything."

"Essentially. And most of that was before all the *path* talk," Ian admitted. "It was collection related, but he spied on Kami's unit four or five times. I'm convinced she or her unit had a special place in JJ's heart."

"It's close to our Bog entry," Gabe acknowledged.

"It sure is."

"If his path went through Ibis Creek, it stopped near her place."

"In more ways than one."

"Why don't we find Kami in his emails or on his phone?"

"He *was* suing her," Ian said. "They were adversaries."

"He was dressed for a meeting. Back to a blackmail theory we go?"

"Kami's not illegal. She's a US citizen. You can check Maria's status." Ian held up a green bottle. "I'm willing to bet this bottle of Dew-Dew she's legal."

"It's something else. Something we still don't know." Gabe added loudly, "Damn it."

The Pelican stretched, kept his wings close and eyed them.

"Pardon the language."

"He's not judgmental," Ian said. "If he were, I'd be in the lot." He handed Gabe his notepad triple-graphic.

"For this one, you cut its throat."

"Poetic license. I just shortened the neck, a la the Naples East Bay Ibis." Ian explained the gash across the throat and the dribble down the front of the pelican. "That's a tie. They all have ties. They are actually three states of this one pelican. I think. I don't recall doing drawing in the ties."

"Really?" Gabe glanced back and for the between the drawing and the Pelican. "Your poetic brain put JJ's tie on a Pelican even on the road to Ibis Creek? And you don't remember?"

"Lines don't always mean *road*. Think *context*," Ian said. "It's his *path.* I extrapolated it to Heaven."

"You need more than a couple hours on the beach."

"It seemed appropriate. At the time." Ian explained. "This pelican is most stubborn, stumpy bird I've ever met and he is resolutely not where it is supposed to be. What's his *path*?"

"Where did you learn how to tie a tie?" Gabe asked, studying the drawings for unlikely inspiration. "You'd have to be Vin Diesel to tie them that tight."

"Vin Diesel? Why not The Rock?"

"Fine. The point is…" Gabe shook his head. "You didn't exaggerate. The knot was *pulled* very tight."

"Thank you."

"And your Pelican's ties are loose."

"That's my Post-Impression."

"No, loose as in relaxed," Gabe explained. "Loose as in *pulled* loose."

Ian finally understood. "JJ The Pelican speaks."

The two men looked at each other, then at the Pelican, back to the drawings.

"You missed the buttoned collar, Ian."

"That's Post-Realism. Or Post-Bourbonism."

"I didn't hear that."

"You're right," Ian said. "About the knot, for sure. I've seen JJ's knots. His wife, Sally? She told me he tied his own Windsor knots. I mean the best I've ever seen."

"Someone yanked it tight."

"So he met a fifth grader on his divine path?"

Gabe shook his head. "Think context. An angry woman."

"Kami? No, I don't see it," Ian objected. "She is too small and she's not…"

"The type?" Gabe asked. "She knows someone who is."

"Auturo?"

"You figure he's in the mix."

"Auturo would just take the head clean off, Gabe. He's no recess bully."

They each drank some wine to consider scenarios.

Gabe said, "That… whatever it is… isn't very good."

"Meet me more often and you'll get you used it."

"Maybe, a ginger ale bottle," Gabe suggested. "It's even more greenish."

Ian looked at Gabe with surprise and then he nodded. "You are a natural."

"What? At cracking an accident case?"

"Evading the law."

"It's not natural," Gabe said, "to make a beach *dry*." Gabe wondered if he had stolen an *Ian* line.

Ian made a mental note of the line that his *sort of Ian* character could steal from his new *Gabe-ish* character. He nodded at the Pelican. "That's not natural, either."

They fell silent again and watched the Pelican offer them and the gusts only a ruffled feather or two.

"He could double for Auturo, from what you say," Gabe said.

"No, he's not menacing enough. Unless you are a fish, I suppose. Besides, he's the one wearing the ties. I stand by my naming convention."

"Fine," Gabe conceded, "but for this case, I'm starting to like Arturo."

"Even if you do, you don't," Ian said. "You haven't met him."

Chapter 20

Among Ian Decker's his few distinguishing traits, his love of gadgets claimed a top-five spot. He was not a hoarder, he was determined to outwit hurricanes and power outages by stockpiling batteries and the LED bulbs they powered. He had battery-powered fans. He had outfitted his condo with a half dozen nightlights with battery backup. He left his kitchen overhead LEDs on at all times, usually dimmed to twenty percent.

The day had been a long one, ending with Gabe and Ian *liking* and disliking Auturo Guillen. Still inwardly conflicted over the new *Bolivian of interest*, Ian found he could not concentrate on his writing. Ian did not prefer working to sleeping, but it usually worked out that way.

That night/morning, he cut all five paragraphs he had written and copied them to a separate file. Ian *was* a hoarder of his deleted text. He logged off his computer early, at 2:35 AM, and closed up his office. He poured some Maker's Mark into a clunky Walmart snifter and propped himself up in bed to read. Every night, Ian read for at least an hour, usually choosing the kind of semi-mindless mystery he himself was writing. He tried to pick books with as little style as possible. He did not want inspiration to rethink his own style.

He turned off the bedroom lamps, leaving only the glow of his bathroom nightlight and a sliver of dim light from his kitchen. He began to read. Ian could – and usually did – read in the dark.

Ian's Naples traits and habits were known to few, except a very small circle. Someone casing his place might have missed or misinterpreted some, especially the reading in the dark.

For his bedtime reading – even when punishing himself with his own half-drafts – Ian stuck to what others called gadgetry, e-readers. He had consigned hardback or paperback books to history, planning his own novels as ebooks.

Ian read in bed, in the dark, on his backlit Kindle Paperwhite. He had sprung for it, early-retiring his previous Kindle – all of a year old – into what he called his *M&P* drawer, the lower of two in his bedside night stand.

He justified the Paperwhite purchase as a full-proof hedge against hurricanes, the economics of Ibis Creek's wiring and Florida Power & Lights. In the dark, the Paperwhite required so little energy for its lowest readable back-lighting that it would run for a week of survivalist reading. In that mode, it would have made a nightlight and Ian look brilliant and kept his eyes adapted for a low-energy bathroom break.

As with every other bulb in his unit, Ian had experimented with all the colors of the LED spectrum. He disliked the yellowish glow of LED Soft White bulbs. His choice of 5000 Kelvin bedside lamps lit up his bedroom like the beach at noon, and he often made notes as if it were. Neither Ian nor his Paperwhite was crazy about that many Kelvins for reading, so he always turned them off come ebook time.

From the outside, Ian's quiet reading appeared to be dead sleep.

Ian liked the sound of thunder, common to Naples summer nights. At 3:46, he put his Kindle face down on his lap to listen to a distant, inland rumble. Since the moon had intermittently glanced off his blinds, he figured the storm was no closer than Golden Gate Estates north and east of him, or Everglade City, wherever it was. He liked thunder best when generated east of Collier Boulevard.

At 3:47, Ian heard thunder a lot closer than Collier. It came from about fifteen feet away.

For the first time ever at that hour, Ian opened his M&P drawer for its namesake. Adrenaline – apparently building since Gabe and he left the beach – slowed time to a crawl, just as the Hun had told him it would. "Have you ever been in a fender bender? Well, it's like that. With you watching."

Ian used the term *M&P* for the drawer because it was easier to say that S&W. The peaceful, old Kindle was sandwiched between a gun case below and his Smith & Wesson M&P .40 caliber pistol.

In the elongated interval before he grabbed the M&P, Ian ran the gun's history and The Hun's tips through his mind.

On an assignment from a name partner in his firm, Ian had miraculously saved Ellis the *Hun* Hunnicutt's pit pull, Mauser, from a certain needle. The Hun was an embarrassing cousin of the partner and ultra low-profile. Mauser was the embarrassing pure-bred cross-bred American Pit-Bull Terrier named after the four vintage Mauser rifles in The Hun's arsenal.

In a portent, Evie had flown First Class to New York City on a major SEC case, while Ian had driven to Chambersburg, or thereabouts, on a partner's cousin's dog case. At least, he had represented, in Mauser, a top-dog kind of client the firm otherwise preferred. The Hun and Ian had spent some beers discussing the value of breed purity. The Hun firmly believed in *breed* purity, but only after a solid cross-breed came along. "Humans? That'll be a long wait." The Hun liked that Ian agreed with him.

Thrilled with Ian's Mauser-saving work, the Hun had insisted on a special, personal bonus for Ian. "You don't get a piece of the fee – I know my cousin – but this piece is yours." The Hun possessed more well-maintained handguns than rifles and, as the side-fee, had offered his new favorite.

"I appreciate what you did for Mauser and me," the Hun said after a hug. "We consider you a true friend and fellow cross-breed, in-progress. From here on out, we may have to rethink our attitude toward both."

The Hun, college educated in philosophy but self-schooled in gunsmithery, had previously replaced the M&P's barrel with a threaded one for a suppressor – silencer to the initiated Ian at the time – and modified the trigger pull for Ian. The M&P had fired only a few hundred rounds by the time Ian shot two thousand more into a stand of South Central Pennsylvania Black Gum trees on the Hun's acreage. The Hun's goal was the killing small branches with a single shot. It took Ian all two thousand rounds to finally do it.

So pleased was the Hun with the acquittal of Mauser that he had thrown in a thousand rounds of practice rounds and three full clips of Winchester 180 grain hollow points. He included the suppressor for free, as well, because all lawyers "lived in a nice quiet, upscale neighborhood."

Ian had returned to Pittsburgh, temporarily triumphant in his legal endeavor, fully loaded and sporting a sore elbow and a carry permit in the works. He also had a nice story line and a couple new characters.

Evie was right about Ian's lack of originality – "but that's okay, Ian. Shakespeare recycled, too" – For his second novel, Ian *created* Leslie Hummingbird and his American Staffordshire Bull Terrier, his fictionalized versions the Hun and Mauser. He nicknamed them Les the Visigoth, Les Viz, for short, and Luger.

Ian's aborted writing earlier had been a passage in that same novel's draft, adding Kami, Maria and Auturo, equally as heavily fictionalized as Les Viz and Luger.

Paranoia and keeping a loaded M&P did not require originality, just imagination, Ian thought.

In the otherwise quiet, mid-market Ibis Creek, the cheap sliding glass doors sounded almost like distant thunder when moved, but not quite.

As his predicted detachment continued, Ian made a mental note to use thunder to disguise a home invasion through a slider.

Once he had opened the M&P drawer, Ian buried the Paperwhite under his pillow. He swung his feet to cold tile, almost yelping at the cold touch. He slipped his cellphone from beside the snifter – he almost paused for a sip, which he decided would be too odd – and into a pocket and shifted his eyes to the Smith & Wesson and its suppressor. The extra clips were sealed in the case, but he did not expect to need any beyond the one in the pistol.

He quietly grabbed the M&P and the silencer and took three strides into his bathroom and pressed the door closed shy of a noisy latching.

As the Hun had said, he found himself watching his hands and legs shake to match the vibration in his chest. Adrenaline worked both ways, he thought. He took a deep, silent breath, then another, as his observant mind approved his increased body control.

He held the pistol up and prepared to rack the slide as quietly as possible.

"Racking to warn some asshole? That's fucked, brother." The Hun had handed him the suppressor. "This isn't for your neighbors. I was kidding about that. It makes it harder to tell where you are. If there are more than one, you want that."

In the years since the Hun's training, Ian had shot at Pittsburgh ranges all of three times, only once with the suppressor, and never in Naples. He had cleaned and lubricated the gun only his second week in Naples. He had purchased a few hundred rounds of hollow points the next day. The M&P had no odor to it at all.

He had a dormant pistol and stale bullets. A jammed semi-automatic didn't need a suppressor to be silent, but he carefully screwed his into the barrel. He positioned the M&P behind a hanging towel and racked the slide.

The suppressor next to his nose, Ian hesitated at a spot next to the cracked bedroom door. He recalled that height was a mistake and lowered the gun until his right hand hit his waist. He used only the balls of his feet and toes to edge toward the living wall side of his bedroom. He paused again at that sliver of kitchen light. He stepped through it quickly, putting his shoulder to the wall.

Most likely, he suspected, his adversary's back shared that wall with him.

He realized that he had been assuming only a single adversary. He had been assuming Auturo, however unfairly. For two or more, though his fourteen shots would be plenty. He doubted anyone wanted a firefight in a condominium.

Ian knew he was not, in fact, paranoid. He had found Kami, Auturo, Javier, Marty and Maria, in the space of 30 hours, and he had an intruder. He remembered their voices, but the face he saw wore Auturo's final, angry glare outside the nail salon.

Neither Gabe nor he had expected his harmless lawyer act to reach an Act Six.

He felt the wall as if the intruder would warm it.

Man, he thought, this was not his thing. He decided on listening for breathing.

When he related the story, he would not admit to being so exhilarated, so keenly aware, so steady. The shaky Ian had not survived the bathroom.

He heard nothing.

While he listened, he grew more alert. In the sluggish time, he ran through the legal consequences of using deadly force. Whoever had broken into his home – his condominium, for Christ's sake – had opened the door to his use a measure of force. Unless, the guy – he pictured Auturo – pointed a gun at him, he would shoot extra low, for the short legs. He hoped to miss the femoral artery.

His area rug and sofa would slow or absorb missed shots. His window was – or was supposed to be – ballistic resistant, but that was for hurricanes not bounced lead. The wall behind the couch was concrete. Collateral damage would be contained within his unit.

Once done with that legal analysis, Ian forced himself to tote up his theft-worthy possessions. He did not for a second believe the intruder was interested in robbing him, but a robbery carried a decent slug of intimidation: It would, at least, take the starch out of an annoying someone.

Without Evie, his paltry household had few treasures: A wedding band and a couple nice watches, gifts from Evie; a dinosaur desktop computer and a low-end Chromebook, if there was such a thing. Even his precious writing files were secure up in the Cloud. The LCD TV was a 40 inch Vizio, for Christ's sake. His drugs were scripts from Walmart. No one would target his granite countertops.

He did not own so much as one Apple product.

Not even a last-gen iPhone…

Ironically, his polar opposite, JJ did not have an iPhone, either.

Huh, he thought, but JJ did, at Blue Martini…

He thought of Samara.

If Kami had communicated his JJ, it had been through a burner iPhone.

His thoughts were interrupted by a slight sound that he could not characterize.

Ian prepared to shoot. He had never used any stance but the isosceles favored by the Hun – arms in front, equally extended but for a slight elbow bend – who also had insisted on the lock-down handed grip. Ian had not forgotten the kick of the recoil, but he had lost the impact of it. Since he intended a series of shots, he would have to be ready for the kick.

There it was again. Ian realized it was the scraping of the living room wall, getting closer to the bedroom door.

The Ibis Creek wallboard, courtesy of Barton Abbott, was the cheesiest Ian had ever seen. It couldn't block conversation let alone a bullet or –

As if completing his thought, a glint of light bounced off the door.

His mind went to *knife* and *just*. Then, it added *Auturo* and deleted *just*.

Auturo's knife could jab Ian through Barton Abbott's wall if he stayed where he was. He could not shoot from his position anyway. Ian angled away from the wall, behind the dresser. He assumed the isosceles stance and aimed low.

It seemed one-sided, gun versus knife, but Ian knew the Hun would not forgive him even one warning shot. "At least two. Three's better."

The M&P's shock wave wiped any remaining queasiness out of him. The hole was right where his knee had leaned into the wall. He followed up with three shots on either side of the first, each lower, punching a dotted arch through to the living room.

The result included two words that sounded like Spanish words to his ringing ears, followed by what may have been a hiss.

The slider roared and the lanai door banged.

Ian waited, in case Auturo – or whoever – had not come alone.

After remaing still for a minute, he moved from behind the dresser. He opened the bedroom door and led with his left side into the living room. He protected the Smith & Wesson, held by his right hip. The sliding glass door was fully open. Blood spray colored the tile and the grout.

Not much, he realized, but enough.

As he called Gabe Hubble, Ian wondered what removed stains from grout and if the Hun still drank Veuve Clicquot on New Year's Eve. The usual doggie-antlered card would not cut it for the next Christmas.

~ ~ ~

Gabe shook his head "This Ellis the Hun? He taught you to cripple an entire chorus line?"

"You were worried about grout?" Nicolina asked. "You chipped the damned tile and blew out your couch."

The CS tech took an extreme digital close-up of more blood drops on the tile.

"You're sure it was Auturo?" Gabe asked.

"No. I didn't see him. He *is* my first choice." Ian explained, "I was pretty sure he had a knife, but I had already made up my mind. That it was him. That's why I aimed so low."

"Considerate," Nicolina said. "And smart. You don't want some asshole lawyer..." She smiled at Ian. "Suing your lucky ass."

"Lucky?"

"Assuming you hit something all organic."

Ian kept his legal analysis to himself, as it made him seem cold-blooded. "I'm used to shooting trees."

A second tech finished digging a third bullet out of Ian's sofa. He held the .40 caliber up for Gabe to examine. "Two forties, Lieutenant. Every one so far. One hundred eighty-grains, hollow points, as he said."

"The Hun liked mass," Ian explained, though no one had asked. "He didn't care about kinetic energy, calculations, just *punching* weight, as he called it."

"Very scientific."

"You fired seven times, Ian?" Gabe asked. He held up the evidence bag with Ian's Smith & Wesson. "You started with a full clip? Fifteen?"

"Yes."

"It looks like at least one walked right out the slider. Slowed by the –"

Another tech interrupted him. "Here's number seven. It dug into the rug in a rust-colored spot."

"You at least nicked him." Gabe's cellphone rang, giving them all a start.

It was Hugh Barrett, who was calling from beyond the crime scene tape. "I heard about the shooting. I called Mara. We're both out here."

"It's a crime scene, Hugh. We're in the middle of –"

"I've been in the middle of your scenes before."

"Thanks for the reminder. Please wait outside."

"We're both worried. For different reasons," Hugh said. "Is he all right?"

"Yes, he's fine. I'm still not sure if he's a good shot, though. Hold on." Gabe muted the phone. He asked the CS tech. "Are you finished here?"

"No, sir, but foot-printing is not done outside the lanai, but it is in here. We got blood swabs." He shrugged. "It's up to you."

"Hugh is here?" Ian asked, surprised. "It's not like he's a beneficiary."

"Mara, too."

"Okay, that's just weird."

"Lawsuit," Nicolina said. "Lax security in a securely gated community."

"Oh. I love that one." Ian laughed. "Let them in, if it's okay with you."

Gabe unmuted the phone. "All right, Hugh. You can come in. You're at the front door, right?"

"Along with half a dozen cops and a few residents."

"Just you two."

Nicolina resumed her study of the wall. "Even this tissue drywall slowed the rounds down. Your 40s may have bounced off him or sucked some blood out just going on by."

The tech said, "I don't think it works that way, Detective Webster."

Before the dismayed Nicolina could comment, Hugh walked in, alone. "Ian? Thanks, Lieutenant. Detective Webster."

"Where's Mara?" Ian asked, disappointed. He had anticipated some sparks from Mara invading Nicolina's crime scene.

"She heard you weren't dead," Hugh explained, "she said that a word that rhymes with *just my luck* and walked away with Nolan Sanders on speed dial."

"At least I won't need a good lawyer," Ian said.

Nicolina almost volunteered a cliché about *good lawyers* but bit her tongue. She returned to the wall, nudging Ian to one side. She leaned toward the wall and illuminated a spot with her phone. "Were these here before? They look new."

Ian peered into the circle of light. Two dark slashes showed through taupe paint, defined by their white drywall borders. They were two feet apart, one a few from the bedroom doorway. "Shit. No. And no."

"It looks like a knife did that." She raised her phone, picked the photo app and fired away.

"It sure does," Hugh said, almost to himself.

"A big knife," the tech said. "Sharp. It sliced cleanly, all the way through."

As Nicolina had observed, the wallboard used in Ibis Creek was the thinnest the building code allowed. Ian had broken through with his blunt recliner twice since moving in.

"It could have been a fingernail," Ian said.

"Freddy Krueger, maybe," Hugh said.

The tech agreed. "Yeah. A left-handed Freddy Krueger."

"Nosferatu," Ian said.

"Yeah, yeah. Better. But still left-handed."

Ian stared at the tech, then at the slash in his wall. "Tell me you're sure."

The tech nodded.

Ian looked at Gabe, who nodded.

"What did I miss?" Nicolina demanded.

"A suspect," Ian said.

"Oh. The Auturo guy you like? He's left-handed." She left for the interior of the bedroom.

Hugh's mouth dropped open. "You mean Auturo Guillen? Marty Pinedo's guy?"

"How may Auturo's do you know?" Ian asked.

Hugh shrugged. "Just him. And I've seen his knife. It could do that."

Nicolina walked back out immediately. She had Ian's notepad in her hand. "And I thought *writing* was not your thing."

"I'm a multi-tasker, not a master-tasker."

"It looks like you swung this poor bird around by the tie. To get airborne."

Ian and Gabe nodded at each other. Gabe said, "Hugh, will you excuse us?"

"Sure." Hugh turned.

"But stick around." Gabe wanted to know why Hugh had called Mara, not the other way around. "You may be of some help."

They waited until Hugh had cleared the front door.

"He got here quickly," was all Gabe said. "Ian, go ahead."

"Auturo's strong enough to launch JJ into the Bog," Ian speculated.

"What? Oh, the mystery of the loose tie, again," Nicolina muttered. "He just slid it off and on and forget to slip it up. You can't use a tie –"

"It's your theory," Ian said. "Seriously. If you slide a tie down the knot barely tightens if you are careful. And JJ was careful about his ties."

"So?"

"The knot on JJ's tie was much too tight for him to have loosened it," Ian continued. "I doubt even a woman would be so gentle, present company excluded –"

Nicolina made a sound. "Dream on, Decker."

Gabe said, "Hear him out.

"It was a meeting."

"What was a meeting," she asked. "If tonight was a meeting, Ian, you should retire. Again."

"No. JJ had a meeting," Ian said. "At the Bog, right? During that meeting, whoever was at that meeting yanked JJ's tie."

"Very hard," Gabe added. "

"My launching pelican." Nicolina considered the theory. "I don't see it. Who would do that?"

Ian just cocked his head. Gabe did the same.

"Auturo? He sounds like he'd just cut our... victim's tie. Above then collar," she said. "If he were pissed enough."

"We don't have any evidence yet," Gabe admitted.

"That's an understatement, Gabe," she said. "If there was a meeting, we have any evidence of the who or why. We don't know why JJ went dark beforehand. We don't know what the last text messages said." She looked from one to the other. "You guys seem to think you've solved the case. Calm down."

Gabe agreed. "Okay. Let's take a step back. We know JJ acted as if he thought secrecy was critical for his meeting. He disabled his phone and went dark from 9:00 PM on. He did not get Mara's text at 10:15. We know he somehow got a text on his iPhone at Blue Martini. Right?"

Nicolina rolled her eyes. "Damn it. His phone wasn't an iPhone. It was a Samsung. I knew I was missing an obvious piece."

Gabe dropped his head. "We both did."

"If he had an iPhone, we can find his account," Nicolina said, rallying. "With, AT&T, maybe."

"Sure– "

"I don't think so," Ian interjected. "I think he had a burner iPhone. In the sense that he had a used iPhone with a burner sim. An unregistered sim. You can buy one or you can buy a burner phone and borrow its sim. Either way, we can't find the account."

"How paranoid was this guy?" Nicolina asked. "He'd have to be afraid of being tracked or hacked. I didn't think he was that smart to be that paranoid."

"He would have been if someone told him to be," Ian suggested.

"Someone *told* him to be a nutcase? That's just fantastic."

Gabe turned to go. "I have to talk to Barrett."

"What? Why?" Nicolina asked. She started to follow.

"One on one, for the moment."

Gabe left Nicolina and Ian, looking at each other before she stomped off the bedroom again.

Hugh was perched on the second step of the staircase opposite Ian's office. Gabe sat next to him. "You know Auturo. How well?"

"Not well. He'd be a hard guy to know well," Hugh said. "Yes, he is left handed and has a big knife. Marty uses him as a gofer and sometimes as a bully but I though he was all bluff."

"We're not so sure."

"You can be," Hugh said. "Ian just got a piece of his thigh. Not bad, though."

"Oh, really?" The off-hand style of the response angered Gabe. "He told you."

Hugh returned the glare with a mild look. "Of course not. Marty did. He called me from Bolivia."

"From Bolivia? You're close, you two?"

"Marty and I are... have been business associates for some time." Hugh was choosing his words. "I might know some of the companies and... individuals who have invested in his AMP Financing deals."

"Interesting. How well?"

"Well enough, but not too well. The point is Marty and I do exchange information, on occasion," Hugh said. "And I get to landscape his Ester View houses."

"Go on."

"He knows Ian and I are friends… fellow boggers, you might say," Hugh explained. "Marty thought I might want to get over here."

"So, it was Auturo."

"Yes."

"And Marty was behind it?"

"He said he was not. He had no idea. I believe him. It is not his style. Not at all. He's mostly a front man for a pool of investors who want to remain in the background."

"I'll have to ask him about that," Gabe said, getting up.

Hugh grabbed his arm and let it go. "He doesn't know most of them. That's the point."

"Well, I'll ask him anyway."

"You might ask Ian."

"Why would I do that?" Gabe asked, irritated again. "I gather Evie made his investments."

Hugh just raised an eyebrow."

"What?"

Hugh said nothing.

"Oh. Shit."

"Don't, seriously. I mean don't ask him." Hugh added, emphatically. "Forget I said anything. That's a distraction right now. You only need to know the three things Marty told me to tell Ian and you," Hugh said, firmly.

"And?"

"Marty is in Bolivia."

"You gave me that already."

"Two: Auturo was cashiered from the Bolivian Army for going *off the reservation*. Marty's words."

"That's a scary number two. Is this is in order of bad?"

"You decide," Hugh answered. "Three: Auturo is off the reservation, again."

Chapter 21

On Saturday's, the Sheriff's Department opened its shooting range for public use, but Gabe did not have to wait that long. He took Ian in the afternoon after the break-in, in other words as soon as Ian had gotten up.

Ian brought his M&P and Gabe provided ear and eye protection; some 165-grain range rounds; and a variety of personal defense hollow point rounds, all 180 grains in weight. Gabe put the targets and five and seven yards. "If you are shooting farther than that, don't."

After a hundred rounds of the 165s, Ian had brought his groupings of five shots to within six inches. "Maybe, I should bring the Hun down here to do some training seminars."

"I can get you his video," Ian offered. "He's very shy even when fully armed."

At two hundred hollow points, Ian had gotten to five-inch groupings half the time. He had also picked the Federal Premium HST as his brand of choice. "That's enough, Ian. You are pretty good for a retired amateur."

Once they were done, they headed to a dealer to buy a hundred of the Federal HSTs and, then, the safety of the beach at 34th. Once there, they sampled the new ginger-flavored Chardonnay in red Solo-clone cups, but no so much they could not see or shoot straight.

Auturo was off the reservation.

After half an hour, Ian's phone rang. He put his cup down and dug his phone out of the canvas bag he used for the wine. He glared at the glossy surface and immediately answered it.

"Hello, Simara."

Gabe put his hands to is ears and gave Ian a questioning look. Ian shook his head but held up his left index finger.

"Hi."

"It isn't three in the morning," Ian said, cheered just by the sound of her voice of the surf. "It must be important."

"It is." She hesitated. "You're at the beach, you shit."

He turned his phone, briefly, to the Gulf. He put it back to his ear. "What was that?" he spoke louder than necessary. "I'm at the beach. Surf's up."

"You're on the Gulf," she said, without raising her voice. "I'm familiar with what you retirees call *surf.*"

"How's your office?"

"Private, but I'm in a limo, going to a hearing," she said. "I had to talk to you. And a nice quiet limo is even more private."

"How does it feel to work for a firm with multiple limos?"

"Great," she said, "to be honest. I'd get there quicker on the subway, though." She hesitated and her voice changed to one notch above a whisper, barely loud enough to hear. "It's not a firm limo."

"Okay, now, I really can't hear you," he objected. "We have wind here, too."

"Fine. Go to your car." Her tone was no-nonsense and meant *please do it, now*. "I'll call you back in two minutes. I don't have much time."

Ian touched the phone off, with a shrug. He looked over at expectant Gabe. "I'll be back in a few minutes. I don't do phone sex in public."

With Hugh's words coming back to him, Gabe said, "Thank you for that."

Ian put the cellphone in his shirt pocket. He rocked twice to facilitate getting out of the low sling chair.

Gabe said, "Simara is not a real name, is it?"

"It should be."

"That was Evie, I take it."

"I'll have to ask her."

"I've seen you talk to her once," Gabe explained. He sipped some wine. "You are an open book, my friend. Is she?" He regretted the question as soon as it was out. "I'd like to meet her someday."

"You will, but I must go hide, now," Ian said. "She's paranoid. Me, I know Auturo's out there, but won't call first."

Gabe waved him on his way with the red cup, wondering what the hell Evie knew about Hugh, Marty and a bunch of shadowy investors. He opted to believe Hugh for now. He did not need to know and did not want to. He could read Ian well enough to know Ian was not clueless, but close and should stay that way.

Once safely in his car, Ian blasted the hot, moist air out the sunroof until the car was livable. He turned the air down, just as Simara called again. "You embarrassed me in front go Gabe."

"How did I do that?"

"I don't know. How did you do that? He reacted... I don't know." He did not know. Maybe, Gabe mistakenly pitied him. He could understand that.

Evie laughed but sounded restrained. "I heard about your... home invasion. I wanted to call..."

It had not struck him at the time, but it seemed off that she had not called within ten minutes. "Where's your source when I need one?"

"I heard you were all right," she said. "So, I decided to ask some questions."

"Come on, Evie," he said, automatically, "It was no big deal."

"Then you should have fired only three shots. Like the Hun taught you."

That statement stopped him. She seemed to know everything. "I got too excited... shooting a wall and all. It's the *board lust*, I guess."

He expected a sincere *don't joke comment*, but didn't get one. He got what felt like a minute of silence. "Evie."

"I have something to tell you. About that Ibis Creek case."

Ian suppressed a flare of frustration. "We've had enough spying at Ibis Creek, thank you."

"You could have called me, you know." She did not sound perturbed.

"Evie, I have come to assume you know. I should have."

"You didn't want me to worry. I know you." She hesitated. "But it's not why I called."

"You already know more than I do, right?"

She didn't take the bait. "Don't get mad. This is important."

"If I were to react every time someone spied on me," Ian said, with a laugh, "I'd be you."

"That's not true," she said. "But it is fair."

Ian collected himself. He could not be upset with her for two complete seconds. "Okay. What could possibly interest a hall-of-fame, New York securities lawyer in me? Or Ibis Creek? Or us combined?"

Evie was quiet for a moment. "It's a small world, Ian. Everything's connected."

Every time Ian heard or thought it's a *small world*, the Disney tune ran through his head for days."Great. You'll have to speak up. I have a God damned song in my head."

"Good."

Ian had no ready response.

"You can trust Martin Pinedo," she said. "I mean, in this JJ Amos business. Not necessarily in general."

"That's ridiculous, Evie."

"It should be. It's not."

"How could anyone in your world, however, small, know about Marty Pinedo?"

"I can't be specific – "

"Stop that!" he said, too sharply. "I'm sorry. But you have to tell me... I don't know. Something."

Evie paused again before she said, "Let's say a friend of a friend of a friend knows Pinedo and his... dealings in Naples. And Bolivia. He's small time, but... he is *known*."

Ian waited. When nothing came, he asked, "Is he in some cartel or something?"

"No," she said. "Not drugs, if that is what you're thinking. Well, not per se."

He felt a shiver go up his spine. "*Per se* means *yes, sort of.*"

"It's not like that. I have been told you can trust him," she said, firmly. "Told unequivocally. In this Amos business." She laughed, with the same restraint. "Not in anything the fuck else."

Another name popped into his head. "Next, you'll tell me I can trust Hugh Barrett and Kami Cabrera – "

"Yes, you can and, of the two, he's not the one in Bolivia, at the moment."

Ian heard the song get louder. "It's deafening."

"What?" she asked, concentrated. Then she lightened up. "Oh, the song."

"Why are you telling me this? Who cares?" he demanded. "Who cares, as in who cares *that matters*?"

"Don't I matter?"

"You know what I mean." He bit off the words. He relented. "Please, Evie."

"Yes, I do. I know what you mean, Ian. And you know I can't go into that." Evie was deadly serious. "It is imperative you get this over with. I know you won't get out, so get it over with. There are too many things, tangential things, involved." She paused. "Remember Western Dry Rocks Key Funds, LLC."

He had to think. His mind had moved on from that research. "Yes. Kami Cabrera got a loan from them. Some other... AMP..." It dawned on him. "It's money. It's about money."

"Not the Amos case, no, but yes. I'm not being indiscreet when I say that, up here, New York? My job? It's always about the money."

"And you like that?"

"I love this job, Ian. I really love it. You should know that," she said, earnestly. "It's important to me that you know that."

Her statement had the desired effect. He felt better. "So, I trust Marty Pinedo?"

"To help resolve the case, yes," She said, flatly. "I don't know what happened or who was involved – one of his circle, yes – but Pinedo can help you. He will help you. He likes you – that does not necessarily equate to trustworthiness with the Martin Pinedo and his ilk – but he's gotten the message, too. He will help you and your new friend Gabe. And Detective Webster. I hear she's attractive."

The depth of her knowledge of the piddling case should have floored Ian. He took it in stride. "We're not going there, Evie."

She heaved a sigh audible all the way from New York. Even with the extra air, she took another moment to say, "Trust Martin Pinedo. As a favor to me."

Ian nodded.

"I can't hear you nodding," she said, almost normal. "You do know that."

"Sorry," he said to her. "Okay. Can I tell Gabe?"

"Yes. He'll know it was from me, anyway. He knows I know, too."

Ian felt a flash of annoyance. "How in God's –"

"Hugh Barrett let him know," she said. "It was out-of-school."

"Is that like *off the reservation*?"

"Not even close. We both know what that means."

"Any other tips? Like who killed JJ Amos."

"Yes, but not that one. I don't know. Auturo's my guess, too."

"So, what's the tip?"

"Finish it," she said with finality. "Please. There are strings that could become undone. That would not be good for anyone. Be safe."

"I've got police protection at the beach, for Christ's sake."

"Good. Where would I be without you?"

"That's a set-up isn't it?"

"Nothing gets by you, love. I'm at my stop. Be careful. Bye."

~ ~ ~

Ian returned slowly to the beach. Evie's call left him bewildered and frustrated. He stopped halfway to his chair and looked at Gabe, who had failed to disclose his conversation with Hugh.

"I was beginning to worry," Gabe said, as Ian finally approached. "Did Evie hear about what you did to your couch?"

"Yeah, it had sentimental value. She picked it out. We were going to grow old together on it. For, maybe, five years." He sat down and let the silence stretch for a bit. "I just found out something interesting from Evie. About you."

Gabe glanced at him, saw his expression and turned as much in a beach chair. "It's not about my Biotech investing, is it?"

"Hugh Barrett told you she was clued in on Marty, correct?" Ian said.

"Yeah. He said… he implied Evie knew about Marty," Gabe admitted. "I decided not to tell you. Sorry."

"May I ask why?" Ian picked up his red cup and looked inside.

"I thought you might not want to know. That she knew so damned much."

Ian sipped the wine. "It's just spooky, what she knows. That she knows Hugh and even *of* Marty and Auturo. What the hell is going on around here that interests anyone she deals with?"

Gabe shrugged. "Hugh made it sound like we shouldn't ask. That we didn't need to ask."

"I get that a lot from my New York connection," Ian said. "And very specifically in this case."

"Hugh confirmed it was Auturo at your place and that Marty, even from Bolivia, knew you had hit him. Don't worry, Auturo's will have to limp for a few days, that's all. Your use of force was appropriate."

"Thank God. I'm a free man. Free for Auturo to hunt down while Marty is in Bolivia?"

"Evie doesn't know if he did it?" Gabe asked. "Killed JJ, does she?"

"She doesn't. She shares our guess, for what it's worth from the Far North."

"Probably a lot."

They sat and looked at the Gulf. There no pelicans to be seen. No Egrets, no Ibis. The sky was blue, with a few white swirls for clouds.

"The gist is that we can trust Marty Pinedo. Considering he's Auturo's *patron*," Gabe said, using the Spanish pronunciation, "that means something. He can help us bring him in."

"I believe that is the point," Ian agreed. "The whole message was that we can trust him in the JJ Amos case." Ian went to his phone's contact app. He dialed Marty Pinedo and put the call on speaker.

"You have reached Marty Pinedo, of AMP," Marty's voice said. "I am out of the country at the moment. Please leave me a message and I will call back."

"Can he help us from Bolivia," Gabe said before the tone sounded.

Ian raised the phone closer to his mouth. "Marty, this is Ian Decker. Please give me a call. I need your help with the Amos case. I kinda hope you are *with* Auturo, by the way." He tapped the call off.

"Somebody has to go to the Gomes household," Ian said.

"Gomes?" Gabe asked. "Oh, Kami. What are you thinking?"

"She's in Bolivia. I'm sure of it," Ian explained. "Evie basically told me as much. I think Marty took her."

"How tuned in is this wife of yours?" Gabe asked. "How is that? I mean, really, Ian, how is that?"

"She has more friends that you and I put together."

"That is a truly inadequate answer."

Ian laughed. "Bad example, but it makes the point. That is all I know. All she can tell me."

"You wouldn't tell me anyway."

"Not if she asked me not to," Ian admitted. "But I *can* tell you, this time, she didn't."

Gabe looked at his watch. "Let's go."

"To?"

"Kami's."

"And ruin my relaxing time at the beach."

"Your foot is twitching. So is mine," Gabe pointed out. He poured out the remainder of his ginger-wine and got up. "I'll drive."

Ian looked Gabe up and down. "I'd say you look like a surfer, but," he began before he looked out at the nearly flat Gulf, "you can't be."

"I have slacks and a shirt in the car. We'll stop at Kohl's and get you something," Gabe said. "It won't matter how you look, Ian. She's *not* there."

"Then why go?" Ian asked, finally on his feet. "You were kidding about Kohl's, right?"

"Yes, your place is just a few minutes out of the way."

"Leaving the *why*."

"Kami's not there, but Javier may be. He can confirm that Kami's gone. He may say if she went with Marty, maybe Auturo," Gabe added. "And, maybe, why."

They folded their chairs and headed off the beach. As they hit the asphalt of the parking lot, Ian stopped. "It's handy that I only need clothes from my place."

"Oh?" Gabe understood. "We'll leave the Smith & Wesson in the trunk for now."

"Maybe, the why is to put some distance between Kami and Auturo."

Gabe nodded. "Which means Auturo is here."

"Which also means Kami *needs* to be separated from him," Ian added. "She knows too much for Auturo's liking."

~ ~ ~

Marty had not called back.

Ian put on stone-colored slack and a solid light teal silk-linen shirt. He wore shoes instead of sandals to complete his casual professional look.

Gabe nixed both of Ian's knives, one hunting, the other scuba since they weren't doing either.

On the drive north, silence was sporadically interrupted with speculation about the reasons for Kami to leave the country, assuming she had, that did not involve Auturo, including family and vacation. The timing argued against it.

"Her trip was awfully sudden," Ian said. "Marty whisks her off to Bolivia? I don't think it was to visit her mother. And they don't even have a gulf, let alone an ocean. They have salt flats."

"How do you know that?"

"Wiki," Ian said. "Do you know they have a shitload of Lithium under that salt? More than anyone else has?"

"How would I know that?" Gabe asked. "As in batteries."

"As in *no batteries without...*" Ian recalled what Evie had said. "*Not per se.*"

"Okay."

"Evie said Marty was not involved in drugs, per se," Ian explained.

"That's a plus."

"Coca leaves are still a drug. But there's no money in it, not as Maria talked about it," Ian explained. "But there is one drug that could be. Lithium. It *is* a drug, but the money... the money is in batteries."

"Marty's a player in Lithium?"

"He's too small time, according to Evie. But he's tied into it," Ian concluded. "We are talking billions. Enough for her Wall Street pals. We want to stay as far away from that as possible. She said it's not about that, but if we hit an anode or two, it could be more dangerous than an army of Auturo Guillens."

Sobered, they fell into silence as Gabe made excellent time. Collier Barbara was, as usual, quiet in the evening. They pulled into Mangrove Hammock a little after 8:00 PM. The Sorento was in the Gomes driveway. The nearby parking area was empty, but Gabe pulled in behind the Sorento.

As they approached the front door, Ian glanced through one of the three rectangular windows in the garage door. Kami's Kia was inside. "Her car is here."

"That doesn't tell us anything. She'd get a ride to the airport. For South America, probably Miami's."

Indicating that Ian should stop just behind and beside his right, Gabe rang the bell to the left of the door's handle. He then stepped back, leaving a comfortable space between the door the two of them.

It only took a moment for Javier to open the door partway. He peered out at Gabe and looked puzzled. Then he saw Ian and frowned a little. "Hello. Hello, Mr. Decker."

Gabe said as he displayed his badge "I'm Gabe Hubble. I'm with the Sheriff's Department."

Javier's expression went dark. "What? What happened? Is she okay?"

"It's nothing like that, Mr. Gomes," Gabe said, calmly. "In fact, we were hoping we could talk with her."

"She's not here," Javier said, looking relieved, if not relaxed. He stammered out, "She went home. Visiting her parents. She left two days ago. Her father."

Ian said, "Oh, she left with Marty. I forgot."

Javier bit his lip. "Marty, yes." He did not try to hide his ambivalence. "If you are Bolivian, he can be a very good friend."

"That's fine," Gabe said. "Could we talk to you, inside, for a couple minutes?"

"Me?" Javier looked concerned and the door edge toward its frame. He looked at Ian. "I can't help you with Kamila's business with Ibis Creek. That was from before. Marty's handling it. Martin Pinedo."

"Before you were married. We understand," Gabe said. "We understand. We are talking to Mr. Pinedo about that."

Javier eased the door open. "I don't have dealings with Marty, just Kamila," he said with a shrug.

"But you know him. And Auturo Guillen?"

After a moment's thought, Javier opened the door and stepped back. "Kamila divorced him before I met her. Still, he collects her sometimes and he works for Marty sometimes, so he is around. I can't call Auturo a friend, but he comes over, to watch a game or have a beer. Too often, like an ex-husband. You know?"

Gabe took the opening while it was offered and walked in past Javier. Ian followed, nodding to Javier as he went. Javier led them left into the small dining room, its curtains closed. Javier did not offer them seats, so they just stood. Javier positioned himself on the window side of the table.

The ornate, solid oak table and its eight matching chairs warmed up the tiled dining room. On second sight, Ian recognized it as the larger model of one Evie had rejected as too expensive for their Ibis Creek condo. It was a beauty, its surface was pristine.

Javier noticed Ian's reaction to the table. "It was Marty and Peta's wedding gift," he said. "We got married in February."

"I am envious," Ian said. "We wanted a smaller one just like it when we bought down here. Our place was too small."

"It is big." Javier was trying his best to relax. "We have only used it a few times." He laughed. "When Marty and Peta comes to dinner."

"Very nice," Gabe said, with an inflection that prepped them for a return to business. "Does Kami, Kamila, still work for Mr. Pinedo?"

"Marty? She never did," Javier said, confused. "She just returned some favors. He did get her a job, maybe, two. She was married to Auturo or Mateus, Mateus Duarte. Marty is very active with the Bolivian's here... You already know that."

"Don't worry. Mr. Pinedo is not a focus of our inquiries," Gabe said. "In fact, we expect he will be of some help to us when they get back."

"She's not coming back for a while," Javier said. "I am trying to move my vacation to go for a week. Marty, though, will be back the day after tomorrow, I think. He said he was only going to help Kamila with her father's care if needed."

"Oh, that's good. Ian left him a message just a bit ago," Gabe said. "We look forward to working him. About that... You know about the lawyer who died?"

Javier's face went blank for a beat. "Oh. The collection lawyer. Kamila didn't like him, but it's too bad about him, anyway." He looked from one man to the next. "You knew him?"

"I did," Ian said. "I hate to say it, but we were not on good terms. It was the peril of his job, I'm afraid."

"No one likes the bill collector," Javier said, with the first hint of his smile. "I manage the warranty service at the Kia dealership. We use a collection agency sometimes. You would think our service was all free –"

"I learned that lesson, Ian said, with a laugh. "Back when mine only covered the drive train."

"Oh, Kia warranties are a selling point, but not everything is covered. People get angry and dispute the credit charge. That's all," Javier said. "I had student loans when I was younger. It was hard to pay them, and bill collectors called all the time. That's why I always pay ahead." He added, with a slight eye-roll. "Kamila has been, too. Except for Ibis Creek. I did not get involved in that."

"One last question, Mr. Gomes and we'll head out." Gabe glanced at Ian. "Unless Ian, Mr. Decker, has anything."

Ian shook his head.

"Good. Then, Mr. Gomes," Gabe began. "I know Mr. Guillen is not a friend, but he works with Mr. Pinedo. Did he go to Bolivia, too? With Mr. Pinedo and Kamila?"

"Auturo? No. Marty needed him to stay," Javier said. "He was disappointed."

"Marty needed him to look after things?"

"That's what he said. Rent collection, probably. There are some things he won't do, not even for Marty. He could be a handyman, but he thinks it is beneath him," Javier said, with a hint of a frown. "Maybe, we all have some of that. He says he was a foreman in Bolivia, but not here. He resents that."

"Does Marty go back to Bolivia a lot."

"Every few months. Auturo doesn't go with him. Auturo is not very good company."

"I see."

"Also, Kami said his leg is hurt. It hurt too much for the long drive to Miami."

"I'll bet," Ian said. "The Miami airport."

Javier nodded. "I volunteered to drive them. It's an easy trip."

"How did Auturo take that?" Gabe asked.

"His leg hurt, but I could tell he didn't like me doing it," Javier said. "You can always tell with Auturo. Marty said he would take the car service when he came back."

"So do you have any idea where Auturo is at the moment, Mr. Gomes?"

Javier shrugged. "No. I don't even know where he lives," Javier said. "But there are always late rents and overdue bills to be collected And, like Mr. Amos, Auturo is a damned good bill collector."

Chapter 22

If it was possible for something as non-aerodynamic as a block of granite, Auturo Guillen was in the wind. Nicolina checked the home address they had for him. She ran by the AMP office on J&C Drive and reported the place dark and locked, with no cars in the lot.

Gabe and Ian drove to Marty's house. No one was home. Marty's silver Benz was in the garage.

"Damn it," Gabe said. "We don't even know what's he's driving."

Ian pulled out his phone and dialed Marty Pinedo. He got the *out of the country* message. "Marty. Ian Decker. If I were Auturo Guillen, where I would I be and what car would I be driving? It sure isn't that reclaimed Mercedes of yours." He ended the call.

The sat in the Pinedo driveway, considering their next move. It took a while because they could not see one.

As if Evie had waved some wand from afar, Marty called. "I just got a call from Maria Suarez," he said without answering Ian's questions or even a hello. On speaker, he added, "He just left her condo. He scared her half to death, he was so angry."

"Did she have any idea what he was up to?"

"Ask her directly. In person. She likes you and she may calm down enough to remember something." Marty paused. "Auturo is basically – "

"Don't say harmless," Ian cut in, sharply.

"No, you're right. He's not. Not when he is... upset," Marty agreed. "Right now, Ian, he is very upset with you."

"Consider it mutual," Ian retorted.

"He believes, strongly, that you are a threat. Only you."

As Ia began to respond, Gabe lowered the palm of his hand. Ian got the message and ratcheted down his annoyance. "Do you any idea where he may go, Marty? What he is driving?"

"No. There many places he could go. Places I don't know about, too. Go see Maria. She might know what car he is using."

"Anything else?" Gabe asked, quietly.

"Anything else, Marty?" Ian remembered the main point. "Did Auturo kill JJ Amos?"

Marty did not respond at once. "From what little I know, I don't believe so."

Ian and Gabe shared surprised expressions.

"You don't sound sure," Ian said.

"I wasn't there when Mr. Amos died, so, no, I am not sure."

"Okay. If you think of anything –"

"I will call. I promise you that." Marty added, "We Bolivians always keep personal promises."

"Good to know. Thanks."

"Good-bye."

Ian ended the call and took a deep breath. "Fuck."

"No," Gabe said. "He said he, Marty, was not there when JJ dies. That implies Auturo was."

"I guess it does."

Gabe began to back up. "We've got exactly one lead."

"That's the bad news. The good news is that he left."

"It's good?" Gabe stopped the car

"For Maria, not us."

~ ~ ~

Gabe did not need his dome light to get south on Collier Boulevard. He took it all the way to Rattlesnake Hammock, across 41 to Thomasson. It wasn't the shortest route to Ibis Creek but it was quick and required little thought. He and Ian kicked around air-balls the whole way.

As they approached Ibis Creek going north on Naples East Bay, Gabe saw the closed gate. "Can anyone get in that gate whenever they want?"

"Auturo would have a Vendor Code," Ian explained, almost apologizing. "He can use AMP's since it is a landlord agent. Hell, in his mood, I'm surprised he didn't just drive through it."

"Yeah, well, I don't have one."

"Me, either. Hit my call-box code." He gave Gabe the code.

The police and fire departments had a central dial-up for codes, as well, but Ian's was quicker. His cellphone rang, he answered and hit nine on his virtual keyboard.

"Access granted," the Call-Box said. The gate began to open with maddeningly slow grace.

"Jesus."

"It doesn't matter, Gabe," Ian said. "Auturo's gone."

Gabe drove to within an inch of the LiftMaster arms as the gate doors finished their mirroring arcs. "If JJ had to wait this long, I'm surprised he lived as long as he did."

"Maria's building is left."

"I know," Gabe snapped. "It's Kami's. I know the address by heart." He drove fast around the corner without worrying about oncoming vehicles.

Ian cringed. He always moved through that corner, slower than the gates. There was no way to see an approaching car. He said nothing.

Gabe pulled in front of Maria's building and found no parking spaces, except for one handicapped space. He took it. "We won't be long enough to get towed." He turned off the car and restrained Ian with a hand on his arm.

"What?"

"I'm decompressing. I'm sorry about at the gate."

"Not as sorry as I am. Every day."

Gabe did not move. "You're right. He's gone. We have to be low key with this girl. Take a few breaths."

Ian sat and breathed. Gabe had been right. He *had* needed it. "Okay. I'm all oxygenated."

They got out of the car and walked, calmly, to Maria' Suarez's front door. Even so, Ian waited a full second before hitting the bell. Gabe stayed slightly off to the side, visible but deferring. She would see Ian first. She would see only him if she looked through the peephole in her door.

Maria must have been waiting by the door with a glass on vodka rocks in her hand. She opened the door immediately. Her eyes were wide, and her hair showed finger tracks. The rocks vibrated in the nearly empty glass. "Thanks." She stepped aside. As Ian passed her, she held up her class. "I started already."

"Marty didn't mention that when he called us," Ian said, as he steadied the glass in her hand. She surrendered it with relief. "He said you had a visitor, Maria."

"You have to refill my dry martini for me. I… spilled, this time," she said, leading them into the condo to the kitchen. It was the second smallest of the units in Ibis Creek, so they didn't have to go far. She pointed to the Iceberg Vodka bottle. Unless she had finished an earlier bottle, she had taken only three or four ounces, two small drink, given the ice still in the glass. "Maybe, pour out the ice."

Ian checked her eyes. They were clear enough. She had not said much, but her voice seemed clear, too. Her accent was heavier and her speech pattern somewhat broken, but he attributed that to her level of anxiety. He left the ice and poured in less vodka than he would have for himself, without the ice. "This is my favorite vodka. Hard to find sometimes."

"I like it," she said, her hand less shaky as she took the glass. She looked at Gabe and showed him the glass. "You're the *Lieutenant*. Is it okay?"

"I wish I weren't on duty," he said. "Marty told you we were coming."

"Right back. He called me right back. He knew I was scared."

"Auturo."

"Yes, sir."

"Gabe is fine," Gabe said. "We're just talking over your drink, right now."

She barely managed a smile. "Okay." She looked at Ian, looked at her glass and back. "Hi, Ian."

They parted to let her pass through and lead them to the living part of the misnamed great room. She had a small, four-seat table for the dining area so the living room could handle a sofa and three chairs without seeming cramped. She had fifty-five inch LED on one wall.

"Nice TV," Ian said.

"It's Kami's, not mine," she explained. "Marty and Kami's boyfriend installed when I moved in a couple years ago."

"Javier Gomes," Ian said.

"Kami's lucky."

"What about Marty?" Ian asked. "He seems like a hell of a guy."

Maria sighed. "Very much." Without noticing it, she fluffed her hair a little. "I liked him too much when I met him. I didn't know him in La Paz. My boyfriend did…" She looked at Ian. "I told you."

"Yes. As we were coming over, "Ian lied,"I told Gabe what you had told me. That's okay?"

"Sure."

"I always tried to mail my rent, in advance. If I was late, Marty was the one…" She grimaced. "Only twice. The next time, he sent Auturo." She shuddered. "I mailed my rent, at least the part I had. I was good, and Marty knew I was good. Twice, I was too behind. Auturo came again. Just at the door, he scared me. I told Ian. You remember?"

"Yes. And I agreed."

"Some months, when my tips are smaller, I can't pay on time. Summer is like that. My customers' tips are smaller, too."

"Summer is slow for everyone, of course."

"I try not to because I don't want to see Auturo."

"And today? It's not rent day," Gabe said.

"No. And I mailed mine last in, so I was surprised to see him."

"What did Auturo say?" Gabe asked. "How did he behave?"

"I saw him and was surprised. I opened the door," she said. "And was scared, but because he scares me, just being here."

"I've met him," Ian said.

"Then you know. But, he didn't look as mad tonight, at first. He seemed more in pain – his leg, maybe; he limped – but, I think… not sad, but something. It's hard to tell." She sipped the vodka with unexpected restraint. "I think he got mad when he saw how I looked at him." Her next sip was less restrained. "He pushed me, to get inside. He didn't use his hands, just his chest and hip. I'm taller than he is but he is very thick. He hit me against the wall only by going past, and I went *woof*, like you know when the air comes out of you? That made him madder. I asked if his leg hurt. He didn't like that."

"Did he hurt you?" Gabe asked. "Did he threaten you?"

"I felt his big knife. And when Auturo's mad? That's enough," she explained. She handed Ian her glass. "Can I have a little more martini? I did eat before."

Ian considered her body and wondered how much she could have eaten and how much she ever ate, gelato aside. He took her glass and headed to the Iceberg in the kitchen. "Do you have any Valium or anything like that?" he asked, feeling four eyes on him.

"No," she said, "and I wouldn't take it with vodka. That's stupid."

"Granted," he agreed, never having mixed pills with vodka.

With surreal forbearance – considering the tension Auturo had left behind – both Maria and Gabe waited until Ian returned with the glass. "You might want to make this the last one. You are… on the slender side."

"I know. I try. But I can't get over… One hundred fifteen pounds?"

"You don't look too thin if that worries you."

Maria brightened. "Thank you. Very much."

"Maria," Ian said, "I'll bet that is not news to you."

She tilted her head in acceptance.

"He had his knife? You're sure?" Gabe asked.

Her eyes widened. "Oh. I am. It left a mark." Without prompting, Maria pushed down her waistband to show them the mark on her hip. It was small and red on her otherwise flawless skin. "Not bad, is it?"

"The mark?" Ian asked. "No, it's not bad.

"What did he say to you?" Gabe pressed, gently. "Why was he here?"

"He asked about Marty. If he had said anything about him, Auturo. Since yesterday," she said. "I didn't talk to Marty since before you came to see me, Ian. I told Auturo that. Then he asked about you."

Before Ian could respond, Gabe cut in. "Did he ask about anyone else?"

"No. Only, you, Ian. He scared me again." She turned to Gabe. "He wanted to know what Ian told me."

"What Ian told you?" Gabe asked. "Not what you told Ian?"

"That, too. Second," she said. "I told him it was about the *voyeur*, in the back. That you, Ian, you were going to sue Ibis Creek over it. That was all."

"How did he react?"

"I could see he didn't believe me, so I said it was only about the man I saw. That's right?" She asked Ian. "Then I said we talked about my coming to the United States."

"That's it."

"Was he finally satisfied?"

"After that, he was. He wasn't mad anymore. It was that something else. I think he felt bad. For scaring me? It was something more. I don't know."

"Did you see Auturo's car, Maria?" Gabe asked. "We know he didn't use Marty's Mercedes."

"No, no. Once he left, I closed the door right away and called Marty."

"No problem. Did Auturo say anything about where he was going from here?"

Maria curled a blond strand around an index finger as she thought. She shook her head. "He didn't."

"Okay." Gabe shot Ian a questioning look and got a shrug in return. "Thanks – "

"Oh, wait," she said. "He said Kamila went to Bolivia with Marty." She nodded at the recollection. "The way he said it, I thought he was saying about Marty and Kami – you know, being together – but that makes no sense because Peta was there, too. So I said that was nice of Marty, but Javier must be lonely. I hoped they called back and forth. On Skype. I said that was free. Almost."

Gabe and Ian both stiffened well before she had finished.

"Then he said maybe Javier shouldn't be lonely. That Javier was on the way," she said. "But is it? The way he said it? I don't know where Javier and Kami live. I don't know where Auturo lives, either."

Gabe froze Ian with a glance and resisted jumping out of his chair. He rose slowly. "Thank you, Maria. We'll pay a visit to Javier and see if Auturo stopped by. That would be great. We could talk to them at the same time." He made it sound like they figured to catch Javier and Auturo during halftime at a soccer game. He handed her his card. "Call me if you... Anything. Just call. Anytime."

She looked at the card and then at Ian. "It is fancier than yours."

"Yeah, but the phone number works just as well. Call it before you call Gabe."

"I think Ian's *after* would be better, Maria."

"Yes. Probably." Maria stood when Ian did. She hadn't touched her vodka. As she walked them to the door, she no longer shook. "Thank you. Both. I feel better." As she walked them to the door, she laughed. "No Valium for me, tonight."

"Great," Ian said.

"Next time, Ian," she added, "you spill." Maria smiled, waved and closed the door.

They took matching deep breaths.

"Javier," Gabe said.

"Before we go?" Ian asked. "I have a bottle of Valium two minutes across the Bog."

"I have a feeling we don't have the time."

~ ~ ~

On the way to his car, Gabe called Nicolina first. She was farther from the Gomes house than they were. He called dispatch and ordered a couple deputy units to seal off Kami and Javier's house. "It is a cul-de-sac. Do not approach. Do not approach unless you have a clear that the occupant is at risk. His name is Javier Gomes. Otherwise, wait for me."

Gabe waited impatiently as the exit gates crawled to enough of a gap for him to shoot through. His Ford Interceptor sedan had flashing colored lights built into the grill and side mirrors, as well as along the top of the windshield. He saw only a few cars on Naples East Bay Shores Boulevard and held off on his siren until he turned right onto Tamiami. The vehicles on 41 cleared and he took a hard left onto Airport. It was the shortest way to go, and traffic appeared light enough for him make good time.

"Ian," he said. "Tell me what you think. I need a second guess, here."

"Sure."

"Do you dare call Javier?" he asked. "If Auturo is there, it might set him off."

Ian considered the options. It seemed like a possibility. "It's not like he's killed anyone. Lately."

"Cold comfort if he killed JJ."

"Marty said he didn't."

"Not quit, he didn't."

"Okay," Ian agreed. "But Javier had nothing to do with that."

"Marty took Kami to Bolivia for a reason."

"To get her away from Auturo. Shit."

"But he could have taken Javier," Gabe said, casting theories. "Maybe, Marty didn't see him as at risk."

"Good point," Ian agreed. "But it seemed like Javier was not one of his *people*, either. He's from Rhode Island."

They remained silent for a few seconds before Gabe decided. "Make it."

"Agreed."

Ian pulled his contact list. He had Kami in it. "Second guess?"

"No. Call him."

Ian put the phone on speaker and dialed the number. It rang. It rang some more.

"Hello." It was Javier, but he did not sound like the Javier they had met earlier.

"Hey, Javier. It's Ian Decker."

"Yes, Ian. Are you with your friend Gabe?" An additional hollow quality meant that Javier's phone was on speaker, too.

Javier was sending a message. "No. Just me," Ian said. He spaced the next words out, giving Javier space to respond. "I was over at Mercato and thought I'd stop over. I know you're a bachelor tonight."

"Oh, no –.

A thump was audible through the phone. Then another.

"No... I mean, yes. Good. Park in the visitor lot. Like Gabe did." The words seemed to come from deep in his throat.

"I'll be there in a few minutes."

Javier's cough sounded wet. "Good. Thanks."

The call ended on Javier's side.

Gabe accelerated. "If I had to guess?"

"Yes?"

"Auturo has his knife out."

"That was the thump?"

"Two of them." Grim, Gabe added, "On either side of the phone."

"Yeah?"

"He's asking Javier some difficult questions."

~ ~ ~

Gabe and Ian knew, without saying a word, that they were going to be too late.

They reached Mangrove Hammock in a frighteningly short time. It seemed one car after another anticipated them by blocks, even though Gabe killed his siren well before and his flashers immediately before entering the development. The stars had aligned to get them there in time.

Neither had much faith in the stars.

There were no patrol cars as they approached the cul-de-sac.

"Just as well," Gabe said, as he stopped ten feet from the far edge of the four-slot parking lot. Thanks to a six-foot high hedge bordering the curbs of the lot, they could not see the Gomes' driveway. More importantly, they could not be seen from the house.

Gabe started to get out.

"You want to walk?" Ian asked.

"I have to scope it out. Stay here."

"I –"

"Stay the fuck in the car, Ian," Gabe whispered. "I will be back in two minutes."

Gabe kept to the hedge. The undeveloped corner lot and its neighbor would hide him most of the way, as well. Much as he wanted to run, he proceeded slowly. His training kept him breathing normally.

Finally, through the brush, he caught sight of the Gomes house and stopped. He pulled out his Glock. The lights were on on the right side. He could not see the Gomes driveway. There were no cars to the right, not on the street or in any other driveway.

He inched forward until he was even with short tree until he could see the driveway. All he could see was Javier's Sorento.

He retreated to his car. Ian stood outside, but no farther than the bumper. Gabe kept to a whisper, though he knew Auturo was gone. Unless they were both wrong, Javier had telegraphed that a second car was in the driveway. "No second car. He's gone." He had a bad feeling about that conclusion.

Ian just dropped his head. He started to move quickly.

Gabe caught him by the arm. "We can't take the chance. He and his knife may still be in there."

"No way."

"Remember, he knew you were coming. He may have understood Javier's tip and moved his car."

"Okay. Yeah."

"I think he sees you as his target," Gabe said. "I don't know how much of planner he is."

"Me, either."

Gabe retraced his earlier steps. Ian stayed behind him. If Gabe's initial reconnaissance had seemed endless to both, the second was worse. Gabe stayed in the middle of the brush covering the adjacent lots, again covering the approach to the garage. The garage had no side windows, letting them get to the edge of the dining room window before they stopped.

In the pause, Ian realized that Gabe's breath remained even. He had held his own, making him a shade light-headed.

The lower frame of the dining room window was too low for them to crouch under it. Fortunately, the drapes were closed.

"The back has windows all over the place," Ian said.

"Okay. Get beside me away from the house. We'll cast one shadow. Stand up, to make it look like someone coming to the door."

Once they were aligned, they approached the front door. When Ian went to stand in front of the door, Gabe shook his head, made a knifing motion and tilted the Glock.

Ian got the message and stayed to the right side of the door.

Gabe rang the bell and pointed at Ian.

"Hey, Javier," Ian said, as cheerful as could be. "It's Ian."

They waited, both holding their breath.

Nothing happened. There was not a sound, not a shadow. Gabe rang the bell again and knocked. He cued Ian.

"Are you awake, Javier?"

When there was no response, Gabe tried the door. It was locked, but it was that type of self-locking latch. He stepped back and his foot exploded the door frame. He waited just a heartbeat and led with his Glock, in close. He held Ian back at arm's length. He looked at the floor. It was tile and gave no hint of footprints. All he could do was guess.

He guessed wrong, picking the right.

It was the left that mattered, the dining room.
Only, it didn't matter.
Auturo was gone, as Gabe had feared. "Stay put, Ian," he ordered. He quickly scanned the living room and the dining room. Both were clear, except for Javier.

~ ~ ~

The Gomes' flawlessly sealed oak table had absorbed blood only in the gouges left by a knife. Some more blood beaded on the left side of the surface. The gouges were grouped, three and four, about eighteen inches apart and a second set spread at about ten inches. They were of varying depth. An eighth gouge was under an iPhone. The blood was only in the left-hand gouges.

Someone had stabbed an iPhone through the heart. Its specks of blood obviously came from Javier's neck.

Javier still lay crumpled on the floor beside the table. The pieces of one chair lay mostly in the passage to the kitchen. Some had blood on them, too.

Nicolina had arrived and, from the edge of the living room, glared at the top of the table, at Javier and back. "Who is this guy? This Auturo? How insane is he?"

"My phone call must have done it," Ian said. "I ramped him up."

"It was my decision, Ian."

"Yeah, Gabe. But my voice. The mere sound of it..."

Nicolina turned to look at him, then Gabe, but held her tongue.

They stood in the living room side of the great room, letting the Crime Scene crew do their job. The techs had greeted Ian by name on the way in.

Fortunately for Ian, the techs had beaten Nicolina to the scene.

"Did you call Claire?" Gabe asked. "Maria's covered?"

"Yeah."

Once he had recovered from his initial dismay, Ian had called Claire. He told her just enough about Auturo and his actions to motivate her to be careful. He needed nothing to get her motivate her otherwise. "I need you and Leo to get Maria over to your place. She lives –"

"I know where she is. She's a tenant."

For a moment, Ian was further disheartened. Claire knew too much about tenants.

"She's the one who Mara Collins wishes she could be."

He blurted a laugh. "I'm not sure, but yes. And Jesus, Claire."

Ian had then paved the way with a call to Maria, scant on details.

He then called Marty to leave a message to call him, immediately, concerning Auturo.

Though he trusted her above all, Ian did not make Evie his next call. He chided himself for thinking she would know soon enough as his secondary reason. He wondered if she would call to see if he was all right. He seriously hoped she would not.

Before he could make his next call, to Hugh Barrett, Leo called in a report. "She's was safely upstairs, Ian. She certainly dresses up a place."

Ian agreed.

As he expected, Claire blew out the door, with Leo in tow, and marched to gather Maria, tenant or not, and hustle her off their townhouse. "From what I hear, Auturo can't move as fast as I can," she called into Leo's speaker.

Ian agreed with that, too.

Even with the tension high, Leo could not resist telling Ian, "Poor Maria slipped on a *criminally* unlit pile of dog poop on the way. She broke one of those nails. That's a tragedy worth telling."

Ian hesitated on that one. "She can fix it. Stick with your five acts."

"She said she could do a tip on it tomorrow," Leo said.

"Good. I have to go. Don't tell Claire, but I'll get you some back-up."

Ian retrieved the number from his contact list. He looked at it: Hugh Barrett stood right up there with Marty on Evie's trust list. Strange faiths, Evie and murder did make, he thought, as the phone dialed. He gave Hugh a capsule version of the events of the evening, including the brutal knife work.

"I know the guy, Ian," Hugh said. "I never expected that."

"We don't know what he'll do next. That's the problem."

"What do you need?"

"Reinforcements. I doubt Auturo will go back to Maria's, but we moved her to Claire and Leo's place."

"Everybody knows where that is."

"Would grab Chiky and a couple of his guys to keep watch? Even after the cops get there?" Ian asked. "Do you have, I don't know, an elephant gun?" He regretted the statement immediately. "Oh."

"I'm disappointed in your memory, Ian. I'm a felon," Hugh chided him. "I would never admit to having a gun."

"Sorry."

"I will see to to it that Chiky is at least as well armed as you."

"Thanks, Hugh. I owe you. And Chiky."

Hugh laughed. "Don't give it a thought... for now."

Ian considered omitting a key tip but did not. "You guys watch your step out there. I mean that literally."

"What did that mean?" Nicolina asked. "*Literally?*"

"We welcome pets."

"Oh, yeah. I remember."

Gabe asked, "Maria? How's she taking the move? Otherwise?"

"Leo said she can use an acrylic tip on her nail. No problem. Leo did not sound sure."

"If she's any good, she can," Nicolina agreed. She blanched. "I chip mine at the firing range. Sometimes."

"A manicure is not a sign of weakness," Ian said.

"Don't tell me Mrs. Perfect the Ex gets manicures."

Ian shrugged. "Not as good as Maria's."

The response drew a smile. "Well, well."

"Aside from that…" Gabe asked, "Maria's okay?"

"She's fine. She doesn't know about this, Javier," Ian said. "I just told her it was a good idea to stay with Claire and Leo. She jumped at it. She thanked me. You, too."

"She didn't ask about Javier?" Gabe was surprised. "She knew we were coming here."

"She didn't have to. I told her the truth: Auturo had been here and left. That we *had* Javier." Ian sighed deeply. "God, it sounded like I was lying, but she must not have picked up on it. She just she said was relieved. She didn't need to know the grisly details."

Javier had a vertical knife wound in his throat. The cut was not near his carotid artery, which explained the limited blood on the table. There were five stab sites around his heart. They had concluded – mostly Gabe – that Auturo had Javier with his torso bent back, the upper part and his head on the table. The grouped gouges had the look of *encouragement* to talk. Frustration had spurred ever deeper stabs to within inches of either side of Javier's head and neck.

The iPhone lay within Javier's reach. Either Auturo realized that Javier had tipped off Ian on the iPhone or Javier shifted too far to his left. Auturo had stabbed Javier's neck first.

"I don't know," Gabe said. "It might have been a mistake. The neck wound."

"Javier feels so much better."

"I'd guess," Nicolina said, "your Javier waited through a dozen misses to say something Auturo didn't like."

"He was braver that I'll ever be," Ian said.

"Hopefully," Gabe said, "you won't get the chance to compare."

"We'll see."

"Don't think it, Ian. He's more dangerous, now."

Nicolina shook her head. She nodded to the smashed chair. "More dangerous? Than this?"

"I've never met him. Ian?"

"I think Auturo was sure Javier knew something and was holding out on him," Ian said. "But about what?"

"Why the five to the heart?" Nicolina asked. "He's supposed to be good with his knife."

"Maybe, Javier didn't die fast enough for him. After the neck."

The senior CS tech came over to them. He had heard part of the discussion. "We'll have to wait for the ME's guy, but I'd say the victim suffered the fist chest wound as he slipped to the floor. One wound is as much a drag wound as anything. The other three…" He considered his word choice. "All are precise. This guy did not lose it and he is skilled. He bent the victim to get better access. Any one would have done it."

"Frustration? Anger?" Gabe asked.

"Not with this… it's almost surgical." The tech gestured to the chair. "Frustration afterwards would explain the chair."

"It didn't go the way he wanted," Nicolina said.

"Not entirely, no."

"What about the neck?" Gabe asked.

"Obviously, the neck strike was on the table. The victim fell to the floor from there. It's possible the neck wound was unintentional. The victim may have moved." As he turned to go back to the dining room, he added, "Given the knife's threatening pattern – call it an *interrogation* pattern – I'd say the victim held out on him. At the end, he may have resisted, cutting off the interrogation before the perp had gotten all he wanted."

When Gabe checked Ian's face, it was pale. "You should sit down."

Ian did and did it poorly. He almost slipped off the nearest chair. "The neck might have been a mistake. Auturo was good with a knife. What if *was* the call made him miss? Just my voice."

"Don't, Ian."

"Yeah, Ian," Nicolina said. "It's not your voice that's a problem."

Ian smiled wanly and took a few breaths. "Thank, Nicolina. But you know what?" The color rose in his face. "I can't wait to fucking ask him."

Chapter 23

Marty Pinedo gave Auturo Guillen the wrong day for his return to the Ft. Meyers airport. He rarely flew from Miami to Ft. Meyers, but Ian Decker balked at a round trip Miami, *under the circumstances.* Marty deferred to Ian, putting him at the Ft. Meyers baggage claim to met Ian. His only bag, though, was a logo-free bag that looked headed for a gym. He had been in Bolivia two nights.

Marty nodded to Decker as he approached.

"You travel light," Ian said.

"When my baggage is coming tomorrow, I don't need much."

They shook hands, somewhat wary of each other. Ian led Marty to Gabe's car, waiting at the curb, and, per arrangement, being ignored by airport security. "Mr. Pinedo," Gabe said as a greeting. "Thanks for meeting with us."

"It was my intention – call me Marty, if you would, Lieutenant Hubble – but I should not have considered delaying. Javier Gomes was not part of... He was never part of anything. Kamila is devastated." His accent had become more pronounced.

"I'm sorry to hear that. The name's Gabe."

Gabe drove a couple miles to the Airport Hilton on Alico. Gabe and Ian filled Marty in most of the details of Javier's murder on the way. "It looks like he just lost it," Ian said, summing it up.

Gabe asked, mildly, "Did you or Kami know he was going there? To the Gomes house?"

"Not at all. I assure you, he was on his own. He and Javier are not friends," Marty insisted. "He did call me to tell me Javier was dead. Much after you called me." Marty hesitated.

"What did he say?"

"He blamed you, Ian. You were asking questions of Kami. She was afraid, so he was worried…"

"Afraid of what?" Gabe asked. "What is Kami in all this?"

"I will explain," Marty said. "But for now, Auturo said it was a mistake. Mr. Amos was a mistake. He then mistakenly thought he could intimidate Javier to keep the first mistake from you, Ian. He blamed everything on the three of you, for being *obcecado*, blindly, stupidly stubborn, for fighting battles not meant to be."

Ian asked, "Does he get that he described himself more than anyone else?"

"No. He is the victim," Marty said. "It is common for some – who have been victims much of their lives, who have had to fight for everything – to see the world that way. Auturo is such a case."

"He's a case, all right."

Gabe added, "For me, he's now two cases." As he pulled into a Hilton slot, he said, "How many of them are Kami's?"

"Just the one. Mr. Amos. She was present, but she did not kill Mr. Amos. It was an accident."

"Auturo killed Javier to cover up an accident?" Ian asked.

"Stranger things happen," Gabe said. "But I'm having a problem with this one."

They said nothing more as Marty checked into his suite. He paid cash. The next day, he planned to return to the airport by shuttle for his scheduled pickup by Auturo.

Not until, the three were in the suite, did Marty speak. "It is not much of a suite." He dropped his bag and surveyed the separate bedroom and small living room, which had an alcove for a desk and office chair. There was a small balcony off the main room, which was big enough for their purposes, with a love seat and two upholstered chairs. Marty checked out the balcony and said, "I can smoke one of Chiky's Cuban cigars out here. Either of you interested? I have half a dozen..."

He remembered where he was, how he got there and where his cigars were. He looked at his small carry-on. "Well, that's inconvenient." Disappointed, Marty took the love seat.

Ian and Gabe took the chairs.

Gabe started. "Is there anything in your baggage tomorrow we need to know about?"

"Not a thing. Customs, ICE, Homeland, they are used to me. I travel to Bolivia quite a bit. The Caribbean," Marty said, with more of an accent than Ian had heard before. "I do not import anything, you know, like fruit."

"You know it was Auturo," Gabe said.

"Javier. Yes. He felt he had no choice."

"How so?"

Marty stretched his long legs. "Long flight," he apologized. "He knew you two had... visited Javier, looking for Kami. Javier had told her, and I made the mistake of telling Auturo. He had been worried about Kami and Javier already. You've seen her. She appears delicate. She and Javier were too close, too in love, for Auturo. He was the odd man."

"He'd be the odd man in doubles team."

"It was a matter of time," Marty continued. "Of course, he was right."

"So, you are saying," Gabe said, "that Auturo meant to kill Javier all along."

"He wasn't sure. He needed to make an example of him. Scare him. Hurt him. As a warning… to Kami." Marty nodded toward Ian. "And to you, Ian. Javier was a message to you. He blamed you, more than Javier. You brought the police with you. He could not tolerate that. Here, you Americans don't realize how much the police cannot be trusted in Bolivia, in most countries. The government is not trusted, its rules are seen as only for those in power. His time in the army reinforced that feeling."

"Marty," Ian said, "you are one of the *you Americans*. You're from San Bernadino."

That drew a hearty laugh. "Born and partly raised," he acknowledged. "But my father – he was from South Africa originally – he did not consider himself American."

Marty's father was a mining engineer brought from his native country to Bolivia to work in silver and tin mining operations There he met Marty's mother. He then got a good job in California Mountain Pass Rare Earth mining, located in San Bernardino County, very near Las Vegas. That mine was the leading mine for rare earth metals in the United States. Eventually, the mine was mothballed due to low-priced Chinese competition.

"When I was… what? Fifteen years old, we went back to Bolivia.

"Do we need to hear this?" Gabe asked.

"As background," Marty said. "My father was hired by a man to help him sell shares in a company with plans to pursue mining for Lithium in Bolivia. A *great* opportunity, he said, for a man with my father's background. He paid our way."

"I thought no one mined Lithium to speak of in Bolivia," Ian said.

Marty looked at him with surprise.

"Wikipedia. I've been doing a lot of research into Bolivia," Ian explained.

"He does that a lot," Gabe said.

"Then, you probably know of the Afro-Bolivian culture there."

Ian nodded.

Marty's mother was a genuine princess, but his father was a tall, very dark, very handsome engineer with what they thought was an Australian accent. Her family did not like the British but liked the Australians. The reason for that, Marty had never learned.

His father had so much money that the family assumed he owned part of a tin mine. He never implied that, but Marty's mother freely hinted as much. Her family readily approved of the match. She was a third daughter, after all. Still, it surprised he that they approved so quickly.

"She felt that, even though she was a lesser princess, the family should have objected, if only for show. She felt disgraced. Emotions are funny things."

"Not to prattle on," Marty added, "She left her family, Mururata – that is in the Yungas." He glanced at Ian.

"Yes, I know a little of it. East of the Andes and south of the rain forest."

The area was very poor but culturally rich. Part of the culture was coca, but definitely not cocaine, pitting her family against cocaine interests.

She grew up on the edge of the Salar – Bolivia's huge salt flats – which were a major tourist attraction and a holy place for some, but not her. When tin hit a bad time, Marty's mother was more than ready to leave her home for better opportunities, California, as it turned out.

Because she knew the Salar, she knew the Lithium company was more scam than real. Under the salt layer, Lithium was there for the taking, along with a ton of salt water. Commercially very viable, the Lithium was politically untouchable, then and to the current date.

"It was except to bring in tourists and or breed Flamingos."

"Then and now," Ian said, nodding. "How about next year?"

"Not that soon. Maybe, not soon at all," Marty said. "But batteries? Cellphones. Electric cars. They need Lithium."

"Go on," Gabe prodded.

Fake or not, the Lithium offer was too good an opportunity to pass up. Marty's father was part of a traveling dog and pony show to sell stock. His mellowed mother was anxious to take Marty and his siblings home. If nothing else, the family's savings would go much farther."

"After we were settled in La Paz, my mother convinced my father that the mining in the Salar would not happen in their lifetime. He tipped off some of the big investors he had met in pitches. They were very grateful to my parents."

"What about the promoter?" Gabe asked.

"The US wanted to extradite him. That was not possible," Marty said, "given the state of the body."

"I see."

At seventeen, Marty left *that* home and came back to live with his father's uncle in California for a year to qualify for in-state tuition. Once he graduated, he moved to Miami. He found very few Bolivians with any clout in Miami. Bolivians did not care for Cubans who felt very superior to everyone in South America. "

"The Bolivians consider themselves superior to everyone in South America," Marty elaborated. "Not a good fit.

Besides, I was not Cuban. And cocaine? My mother would kill me. So Miami was useless to me."

As he related the story, Marty had inched forward on the couch. He realized is and leaned back. "Long, short, I had feet in both worlds – three if you count Lithium – and was seen as a good conduit for Bolivians seeking opportunity in Florida. Both people and money."

"That brings us back to Kami and Auturo," Gabe said. He had listened with interest to Marty's background but wanted to move on.

"Not Javier. As I said, he was never... a Bolivian." He hesitated to cool some obvious anger. "Only Auturo and Mateus. Kami was an American citizen." He shrugged. "She knew Auturo in Bolivia. They worked in the same company for a while. They planned to be married as soon as they got here."

"They planned?"

"A minor point, Gabe. Yes, I *encouraged* it," Marty said. "Like many in Bolivia."

"Encouraging for visas and Green Cards," Ian said.

"Most marriages don't work out, do they, Ian?" Marty retrieved the first wink-smile of the day. "Each is a pity, but hardly a sin."

"You arranged for Auturo and Kami to come to Naples?" Gabe asked. "To work for you?"

"Not to work for me, no. Kamila was an American with skill in office work. Auturo was very skilled in concrete work. He did some odd jobs for me. That's all. He had plenty of work until the bottom dropped out of everything."

"And kept dropping," Ian said.

"I found an out-of-work Auturo was a humiliated Auturo. Frustrated on his best day. I didn't want him using that knife of his."

"Look how that turned out," Ian said.

Gabe cut in. "It turned out that he is a suspect in two homicide cases."

Marty refrained from comment, but his expression could have been impassive – he had that level of control – but it was not.

"What about the Ibis Creek buys?" Ian asked. "Like Kami's? What was the point of all that?"

"Cheap investments that boomeranged." Marty stopped. He clarified, "Investment money from the Lithium interests. It was idle in Bolivia. In the Caribbean. Money wants to be where it can be used. Your LLCs make investment simple and opaque."

He tried the wink-nod but missed. "As for Ibis Creek, Barron Abbott needed to sell his subsidized units, *the Affordables*, as you call them. No one was buying, even at the peak. We approached him and made a deal." Marty opened both hands flat. "Our investors would provide initial financing, discretely, one unit at a time. Not surprisingly, the demand raised the prices and all but the last unit could be refinanced for twenty percent or more than originally paid."

"Nice," Ian observed, "until it wasn't."

"We were out by then, the money in the hands of our LLCs. The banks were in. We had planned to flip the units, but the foreclosures actually worked faster. The money *waited* in the hands of Kami…" He wink-nodded to each listener in turn. "And the LLCs. When prices bottomed, the money could be invested again at much lower prices or used elsewhere."

"So Kami and Ibis Creek was a very small part…"

"Of a much larger… *program*, yes," Marty said. "It was designed well and was legal. No one intended to walk away from the mortgages. That just happened."

"Price manipulation?"

"Your interpretation, Ian. Caution requires continuous reevaluation. That is not sinister." Marty shrugged.

"Fair enough," Gabe said. "My interest is limited to Ibis Creek."

"Mr. Abbott liked the idea of increasing demand that he asked to do more of it for him, with more expensive units here. We helped out there as we; He sold many units at higher than list price toward the middle of 2007, believe it or not."

"So Abbott's part of this, too?" Gabe asked.

"Not as you think. Part of the deal was that both Kami and Auturo would get jobs for the Ibis Creek contractor. Kami would report back to Barton Abbott about anything odd on the job. As Abbott's eyes and ears."

"I beg your pardon?" Ian asked. "They both worked for Abbott?"

"Indirectly."

Gabe followed, "When?"

Auturo started early on, with the pouring of concrete footers. He took exceptional pride in his concrete work and was very disappointed at what he saw. Kami began a few months later. Abbott saw material prices climbing thanks to the Chinese market sucking up building materials. Subcontractors were trying to pull out or substitute.

Like Mara using JJ inside Sanders Tilden, Abbott used Kami and Auturo to alert to any changes, poor performance and anything odd. Kami had the run of Burkle Lehane and became Lehane's trusted assistant.

Marty used a genuine smile. "You've met Kami."

"She is awfully... aware," Ian said. "That petite ingenue look doesn't hurt."

"So, you see."

"What about Maria Suarez?"

"She is a rare blond from Bolivia," Marty said. "She was very popular in La Paz and latched onto an earnest fellow – on I knew through my mother – who was sent to lobby the UN for coca as coca. She loved Naples and wanted to stay. She likes men, and they like her even more. Not hard to understand. Aside from her being Kami's tenant, she has nothing to do with any of this. Aside from meeting you, Ian."

"But you three, you do, correct?" Ian felt that twang of chagrin over his causal role. Maria was his fault, too. "Pardon my lawyer hat, but are you looking for immunity for yourself? Maria? Kami? Me?"

Marty laughed, but not too much. "You and I don't need immunity. Poking a hive is not a crime, Ian. And, as for me, it is early, yet."

"Yet?" came from Gabe.

"Maybe, later," Marty added. "Maria, of course, not at all. Kami? She's home in La Paz."

"What about JJ Amos?" Gabe finally got to the nub. "Who wants immunity for that?"

"That is up to God, I think," Marty said. "I understand that it was his own fault."

~ ~ ~

Marty placed the Skype call on his laptop. He did not use the hotel wifi because it was iffy. He used cellular data. Kami answered right away.

"Hi, Ian," she said without a smile. Her eyes were red. "You must be Lieutenant Hubble."

"Yes. What do you have for us, Ms. Gomes?"

Skype could render poor facial images. Even allowing for that, Kami was barely recognizable. Her eyes were swollen and red, her face puffy, drained of color. The transmission effect of Skype robbed her voice of its musical quality. Ian thought it a shame that Gabe had to meet her from three thousand miles away.

"It is hard for me," she said. "I have a video you can download from my cloud account. It shows some of what happened. I took it."

Though prepared by Marty, Ian was dismayed. "You were there."

She nodded. "I didn't tell Javier. He didn't know anything."

Gabe asked, "What was it about, Kamila?"

"I worked for Mr. Abbott," she began. "I was a spy for him. Auturo, too. Mr. Lehane, Fred Lehane – not his brother Will, I didn't work with him – he trusted me. I became his administrative assistant, though I was paid as a secretary."

In a halting monotone, Kami went on to explain the workings of her (Abbott) Burkle Lehane responsibilities. She liked working for Fred Lehane. Naturally, he liked her working for him, though she encouraged him very little. He entrusted her with an increasing range of work. Ultimately, she was monitoring change orders and substitutions of material.

Kami did not approve anything, but she did triage for Fred. As such, her signature appeared on much of that kind of paperwork – and on one piece in particular – to be ruled on by Fred.

Barton Abbott was thrilled. She reported important changes and took photos – with the most recent iPhones Abbott could supply her – of key records. The first bonus, though, came through Auturo. He noticed the concrete was either badly mixed or included off-spec, inferior materials, such as fly ash; much of the concrete block looked like *seconds* and, as building went along, like recycled blocks; rebar was not tied properly. He reported to Kami, who reported, in turn, to Abbott. Auturo kept his eyes open.

The ingredients of the poured concrete were below specifications, but, in Auturo's opinion, not too far off, just *wrong*. The test samples given the inspector – the private contract engineer hired and paid by Burkle Lehane – came from a better, on-spec batch. The engineer passed it, though it was borderline.

Barton Abbott was stymied at first. Ibis Creek was to be his jewel, but he knew what was happening to material and labor costs. Even the subs' undocumented labor had grown scarce and pricey. Burkle Lehane was not a fault any more than he. His own lender, Orion Bank, was having its own problems. He asked Kami for Auturo's opinion.

"You're kidding?" Ian interrupted.

"He was a concrete foreman in Bolivia," she explained. "He's very proud of his work."

Auturo was used to such chicanery from his days in Bolivian construction, but not when *he* was foreman. Auturo opined that the concrete and block would be adequate for the Ibis Creek buildings, but not for one with an additional story.

Those were just the first substitution. The substitute windows for all the buildings after building three had certification – as hurricane impact-resistant – for a window half the size of the Ibis Creek windows. Kami's signature was on the window receipt, initialed by Fred Lehane as accepted. As Fred explained to her, it was the batch of glass that mattered, not the window size.

Again, Barton Abbott was disappointed, but the proper windows were, by then, thirty percent more expensive. It was happening with many of the materials.

Copies of these types of records were produced as demanded by Sanders Tilden's Graham Chapman early in the Abbott defect case. Of course, Kami was not involved in the case. Fred Lehane had let her go when the Ibis Creek project was complete. The lawsuit started more than four years later. Graham took forever to schedule depositions, and Kami was not on his deposition list. Her signatures were buried in the tens of thousands of scanned, pdf-formatted records. Graham, himself, did not review the records. He had a paralegal and a first-year associate skim the records. Graham was relying on his experts to force a settlement, making the Burkle Lehane records production a costly affair for the contractor and a fee-builder for Graham Chapman and his firm.

Even when JJ Amos joined the Abbott case team, he had no role with the Brukle Lehane records. They required endless reading, at task for which he was not then suited. Besides, JJ was still busy suing Ibis Creek delinquents like Kami. She had no lawyer and never got any papers. Marty told her about the lien on her unit and, later, about the two process servers who had come to Maria with papers addressed to Kami. Maria did not take the papers, but Marty knew JJ had filed a foreclosure lawsuit.

Late in 2012, according to JJ, he began his own study of the Burkle Lehane documents. He spotted the familiar signature of Kamila Cabrera.

"He told me to thank Mara Collins," Kami said. "She gave him the power to read at some fast rate."

Gabe raised an eyebrow at Ian.

"Yeah, yeah."

"I don't know how he found them," Kami said, via Skype. "There were so many pages."

"But he did," Gabe said.

"Yes, not many, but he thought I was approving bad building materials," she added. "He found me. I don't know how. There he was on our phone, demanding I talk to him. I said no. He said I would be personally liable for all the back dues at Ibis Creek. I didn't know that."

"That is true," Ian said, knowing the state of their home's title. "But –"

"Javier and I bought our house before we were married," she said. "He said since we didn't have married title, that he could take our house. He scared me. He said Javier would be sued, too."

Gabe and Marty looked at Ian. He nodded. "It could happen. He could get at Kami's half of the title and force a sale or buy-out on Javier."

"I couldn't tell Javier. You see that."

The way JJ said it, it made it worse to Kami. She had received calls from bill collectors – mostly for work – and knew their bullying voices were not real. JJ Amos's phone demeanor did not match her experience. He sounded sorry, like a man who had no choice in the matter of hurting her. JJ's tone alone made Kami believe him.

Javier knew she was behind on her mortgage payments, but left her Ibis Creek business to her and, mostly, Marty. Javier understood the impact of the 2008 recession. Many of his customers and friends had lost investment properties. He had not indulged.

Suitably rattled, she agreed to meet him. It was in March. JJ did not want Kami anywhere near his office. He said their dealings had to be kept secret until the right time. He claimed Graham Chapman was jealous of JJ and may have refused to forgive her personal foreclosure liability.

They could not agree on where to meet. She wanted some place neutral. She knew Maria Suarez worked in the evenings twice a week, Tuesdays and Thursdays. She had a key. JJ liked that idea.

"It was *appropriate*." Kami shrugged.

"Little did he know," Ian said.

"He said he would come from behind, to keep it secret," she said. "Even that scared me, made me think it was so real. I let him in the lanai. We talked inside, with the door closed."

He had some pages, invoices, receiving records that he showed Kami. On half, her signature was only in the *Received* stamps. She laughed at those and then worried he would get mad. JJ did not, because he did not care. He said Kami knew that she was involved in the *wrong-doing*, that she was *morally responsible*. Ibis Creek's flaws might eventually kill someone, and her complicity would come out. Her only way out was through him. His certainty rattled her.

"I finally said, *It was Fred.* That was stupid of me."

"He had a witness," Gabe said. "You were a witness."

"Yes. His eyes got very big. And he smiled. Not a mean smile. He looked... satisfied. He nodded at me."

JJ handed her one-page affidavit. In it, she stated that she knew – from her own personal knowledge – that many of the materials used in Ibis Creek project were substandard and that Fred Lehane knew, it as well. She refused to sign it. He did not want her to sign it there; she had to do it at a notary. She continued to refuse, and he let her continue for a few minutes. Finally, he said, calmly, she did not have to. It was up to her and Javier.

Kami got the message as if he had slapped her. He would tell Javier and drag him into Kami's mess. Javier might not love someone like *that* Kamila, the one she *was*. More than anything, Kamila could not allow that.

"I told him he would have to rewrite it," she said. "Because Baron Abbott knew, too. I told him so myself."

"Oh, brother," Ian said. "No way, he'd let you walk back from that. Why?"

She sighed. "I liked Fred Lehane. He was nice. I didn't like Mr. Abbott."

JJ insisted on redoing the affidavit to reflect Barton Abbott's involvement. Kami thought the rewrite would buy her time, so she gave him some details to include. Because of JJ's desire for complete secrecy – it was clear to Kami that he intended to spring it on Graham Chapman and Nolan Sanders at some precise moment – she suggested using burner phones. She had done the same thing with Barton Abbott. JJ and she could exchange the burner numbers in a week or so.

"I told him to call Marty when he had one."

Gabe and Ian looked to Marty for confirmation.

He nodded. "She told me it was just for negotiating her foreclosure case."

"I did," she said. "From the beginning, JJ insisted on secrecy. He did not want anyone else involved."

To help delay, she told him to get a pre-paid *burner* phone. Many people coming into Naples from South America – they had no credit for a Verizon or AT&T account – used them. They were private, too. Some immigrants needed secrecy, too – Cash-only day jobs often required it – He could buy one at a Circle-K. That was the example she used, the one that sprang to mind. They could communicate as much as necessary with the phones and JJ could even attach a document to a text.

"What kind of phone did he buy,?" Gabe asked.

"He said it was an iPhone. From a flea market. He was not happy about that," she said. "He said something about a snake and a tree. I didn't know what he meant, but he seemed resigned to it."

With their communication issue resolved, Kami felt better, certain she could string JJ along. For a time, her plan worked well. The Abbott case was making no progress and JJ seemed patient.

Suddenly, in mid-July, JJ demanded the executed affidavit. He even had a definite date for a final meeting: Tuesday, July 23rd. He attached a new affidavit to a text. Kami printed it out and had it notarized by AMP's Bolivian-born translator and notary, who knew Kami well and could not read mangled legalese in any language.

"He said that was the day. After 10:30. He wanted to meet at Maria's. I told him no. Maria would be back by then. He didn't care. He said behind it would be good enough. He wanted it on that date, no other day."

The explicit nature of JJ's demand convinced Kami that she had to do something to stop JJ. He had painted her as so guilty that she started accepting the fact that she was a party to fraud and possibly injury or death.

JJ's ploy had worked too well. Kami became afraid to reveal how involved she had been in the Ibis Creek construction deceit. She feared that her part in Marty's Ibis Creek...

"Sorry, Marty."

"It's fine, Kamila. They know enough," Marty said. "I told them we had a *program* for Ibis Creek and other places."

She looked relieved. "Oh. Okay."

"Go on." Marty preempted her. "She came to me.

"He was blackmailing me," Kami said. "Marty said there is only one thing blackmailers like JJ want, no matter what they say."

"Money," Gabe volunteered.

Marty said, "Yes, money."

"You were wrong," Ian said. "Weren't you?"

Kami nodded. "And I didn't have money. Javier and I only had joint accounts."

"Raising cash is not difficult for me," Marty said. "For the right cause." He shrugged. "As you say, Ian, I misread Mr. Amos. I thought he wanted a partnership. That required buy-in money. So, we'd give it to him."

The plan was simple. Marty asked Hugh Barrett to find out what it would take for JJ to buy into a partnership at Sanders Tilden. Hugh got the answer from Mara Collins. She knew JJ desperately wanted – and she wanted for him – a partnership. Mara had even asked Roy Collinf they could swing the $50,000.

Roy had met JJ and did not believe any amount of money would gain him a partnership, not even in Sanders Tilden. He did not share Mara's interest in Ibis Creek, the Abbott case or JJ Amos.

Once Marty knew the amount he assumed would satisfy JJ, he had some cash *washed ashore* from one of the LLCs he had… benefited in the past.

"I told Kami to just pay him the fifty," Marty said. "If he demanded more later, we would deal with it later. That's the sum total of my role."

"It was," Kami readily agreed. "It was. He just helped me." She realized her words were ambiguous. "With the money. Only with the money."

"If you say, so," Ian said.

Marty looked Gabe, in the eye, deadly serious and then Ian. "You can *trust* me on this. I just supplied the cash, period," he said. "I didn't – and don't – want to get into any more detail on its journey here. My word."

He had used *trust*, Evie's magic word, so Ian said, "It's good, Gabe."

"Go on, then."

Kami related how she had struggled with how best to handle JJ and the money. She decided to wait until they met that Tuesday. Then she changed her mind. She texted an offer of money rather than the affidavit. JJ refused. After she persisted, on Monday, July 21st, he shocked her by demanding what had not occurred to her: The money in *addition* to the affidavit.

"*Penance.* That's what he called it."

"I suggested she offer more money," Marty said, with a weak shrug.

JJ said no to more money. The fifty thousand was the *appropriate penance.* He texted that Kami was running out of time, that late Tuesday was the time. He texted that it was *ordained.*

"That's the word he used, *ordained,*" she said, sniffling. "When I heard that, I decided that it was just him making a point, shaming me. Marty was sure he couldn't turn down the money once he saw it. We thought it, the money, was the partnership."

"You didn't know," Ian said, "that money alone wasn't enough to get him that partnership."

"No. I don't know how those things work."

"I do," Marty interjected. "I thought JJ had earned it because of his relentless collection work. It never occurred to me that he would reject the money. I gave bad advice."

"So, finally, late Tuesday, I agreed to meet him behind Maria's... my condo."

"I told her not to go alone," Marty said. "I thought the right kind of *support* would help JJ accept just the payment."

"Enter Auturo," Ian said.

Her eyes grew defiant. "It was fair. Auturo would protect me if JJ... I don't know."

Whatever the mood of the Skype confession to that point, it darkened with the addition of Auturo.

"JJ may have looked fearsome, "Ian said. "But he would never have touched you."

"How would I know?" Her expression belied her question. She knew.

She took a deep sigh and looked toward Marty. "At the last minute, I realized that blackmail is illegal. That blackmailers can be blackmailed," she said. "I would use my iPhone take a video of him taking the money."

The recording plan was only a slight wrinkle. Kami would show JJ the Affidavit, as she had planned, but not give it to him. She would have Auturo approach JJ with the cash, to let him see it, become seduced by it. She would begin filming, catching JJ with taking the cash. Since he was blackmailing her, it would be easy to edit the recording to show the payoff, leaving the affidavit out.

Her alternative would be to accuse JJ of taking a bribe to throw the Abbott defect case. One or the other would neutralize JJ's threat.

Gabe said. "I take neither one worked."

Kami nodded. "He was crazy."

It had gone as Kami had expected, at first. She controlled the pace, and he seemed contained but excited. She showed him the executed affidavit. He grinned and started to approach her. Auturo stepped in, pushing JJ back. JJ slipped but caught himself. Auturo stepped back, with the bag of cash between Kami and him. He opened the bag but only glanced into it.

It was very dark, under full cloud cover and with very few lights on.

Kami held out her iPhone to light up the bag, to tantalize JJ. He appeared pleased. Kami pulled the iPhone back and, surreptitiously, began her video recording. She said she'd keep her light on so they could see better.

She stopped her narration. "Do you have it, Marty?"

"I downloaded it before the call." Marty shrank the Skype window and opened the video in another window. Neither window was particularly big. He hit play.

Kami's iPhone light illuminated JJ fairly well, eyebrows, suit, reddish tie and all. The tie was cinched at the buttoned collar. He wore a suit jacket.

Ian and Gabe exchanged confused looks.

"What happened to the jacket?" Gabe asked. "He wasn't wearing –"

"It came off."

The image rotated as Kami moved her iPhone for a wide shot. JJ was not looking at her. He was looking to the side, presumably at Auturo. He looked perturbed.

"I just wanted to see it," he said to Auturo.

"Stay back," came Auturo's voice.

Kami's voice was next. "He has your blackmail money, Mr. Amos."

JJ shot her an affronted look. "It is not blackmail, Ms. Cabrera. I thought of it as your penance, but that is the wrong way to look at it. It is part of God's plan, but you should think of it as your request for His forgiveness."

"It is a one-time thing, right?"

"Yes, for your past sins."

"Auturo," she said with her perfect diction, "give him his filthy, God damned blackmail."

JJ's eyes flashed with anger, but then it was gone, replaced with disappointment. He picked up the open bag and tried to toss to Auturo. "If that is how you see it, it can not help you if you do not offer it in the right way."

Suddenly, the video blanked. When it resumed, it was clear something was wrong.

"I stopped it. The recording," she said. "What he said? I didn't understand. He was giving the money back?" Then she said, "I had to put them together. The two parts of the video," Kami said to them. "The videos In one file. I was going to delete it, but I was afraid to. It shows it didn't happen –"

"That's fine," Gabe said.

"And I made a mistake. Instead of video, I hit text."

As the video continued, a buzzing came from inside JJ's suit jacket. The vibration was audible, but Kami seemed not to notice. "Take the money. It's best for all of us. It's your one bite at the apple, for God's sake."

JJ got a strange look on his face. "Oh?" *His hand moved in slow motion. He took the burner iPhone from his inside breast pocket, presumably to cancel Kami's inadvertent text, but that was not what he did. Instead, he stared at the back of the phone. Then he turned it over. He tapped the screen and Kami's voice came from his burner iPhone, nice and clear. He let the conversation play without comment.*

"You recorded us?" Kami whispered. "You ruined everything."

He began to say, something very odd, "The ruin *is yours,*" *he proclaimed.* "I was wrong. Your money is the fruit of the serpent. My path is the Truth."

Her voice cooled. "Mr. Amos, give Auturo the phone. He'll give you the money."

He shook the iPhone at Kami. "This is the Truth. It can not be bartered." *He sounded like a preacher at the end of his sermon.* "This Apple *holds the* Truth. *I didn't see it, but the* Truth... The Truth is my path."

"Oh, shit, JJ," Ian said, as they were all there with him. "Don't see it, now. Not now."

"The iPhone holds the truth?" Marty asked. "The recording?"

Auturo appeared in the frame, grabbing for the iPhone. "Give it to – "

JJ turned away from Auturo and, with a grand flourish, put the phone back his jacket's inside pocket. "This does not belong to me –"

Auturo seized JJ by the lapels and spat, "Good. So, give it to me."

JJ shook his head, firmly. "I am its Keeper."

Two two squat men tussled. It looked less like fight than a fabric-tugging contest. The stronger, Auturo succeeded half-way, getting the right side of JJ's jacket free. He also held up something that glinted even in the dim light.

"The knife," Gabe said. "Auturo pulled the knife."

JJ stopped resisting. He had managed to pull the iPhone out of his jacket pocket. Auturo did not see that motion. JJ conceded the suit jacket. Auturo backed off a few steps, sheathed his knife and patted the coat for the offending cellphone.

As the jacket search continued, JJ's expression became smug. He displayed the iPhone for Kami one last time and put it his right pants pocket.

The camera moved in closer as Kami approached. "He has it," she said, quietly. "It's in his pants."

Auturo moved in and reached for JJ's pants pocket. The force staggered JJ. He fought to retain his balance. He slipped backward and flew out of the frame. The splash and a discernible thud were heard.

"Oh," Kami said. It was too short to characterized.

On Skype, she said, "He fell in. I didn't... We didn't push him in."

The camera angle changed radically. Kami was no long pointing. She just held it in the hand at her side. "Can you get him?" she asked.

"Let him stay," Auturo said.

"I want his phone."

Splashes of water were heard.

"He doesn't need my help," Auturo said.

The camera caught a part of JJ pulling himself, crawling on the grass. The camera moved to frame him.

"He was fine," Kami said to the three viewers. "He was just wet. I wanted to see it on the video. That he was fine."

"Mr. Amos," her voice said on the video, "give Auturo your phone. Please."

"No. You know the Truth *is not* mine."

"Please. You can have the paper." *A quarter of the affidavit entered the frame.* "You can have the money."

Auturo and JJ struggled again. JJ ended up in the shallows of the Bog again, face first. For a moment, he did not move.

"Oh, God."

"Humph," *was all Auturo had to add.*

JJ pushed himself slowly to his knees. It seemed surreal when he came out of the Bog again. He stood and stood as tall as his stature would allow. "I didn't see it. In your temptation. I was confused. You can be forgiven. You helped me see my* path."

Ian whispered, "Enough with the path, JJ. Give them the damned phone," as if he could change the outcome. "Come on."

JJ did not hear Ian. He did not hear Auturo grunt in frustration. Auturo moved into JJ, his thick chest making contact. JJ leaned away. Auturo's hand swung up with a flash of red, JJ's tie.

Auturo pulled at the tie, sliding the knot. The force turned JJ enough to his right that he was ninety degrees to the Bog.

Of all things JJ could have tried to grasp, he chose the distorted Windsor knot. He used his left hand to try to center it. He even fought to tighten it again while yanking his left shoulder further. He succeeded only slipping the tie over his shoulder and bringing Auturo's left foot between his.

JJ kept resisting, tipping more forward, but Auturo held the tie, in the process holding JJ at an increasingly dangerous angle.

Auturo was digging into JJ's pocket. His next word was garbled but the second was clearly "it."

JJ must have heard the phrase as give it, *because he said, "I can't."*

Auturo laughed and set the tie free. The iPhone swung up in his right hand.

JJ did not even know he had lost the phone.

He crashed face first into the Bog. This third time, he stayed.

The video ended.

"Damn," Ian said, "did I have JJ half-wrong."

"I just wanted the phone," Kami said, dismally. "Auturo tried to hold him, Marty. I told you –"

"No." Marty's voice was oddly neutral. "No, Kami. He didn't."

Having found himself leaning toward the computer screen, Gabe straightens. "So, you took his coat to his car and put it in the back seat."

"'I didn't know what else to do...'" Kami began. Through her sobbing, she explained, "Javier couldn't know. He didn't. He couldn't say anything." She kept repeating it as if a mantra. Then she suddenly stopped. She raised her head and fixed fierce red eyes on Marty. She said nothing.

Marty nodded to her.

Kami's face disappeared.

"What was that, Marty?" Gabe asked.

"About Javier. I told Kami I'd take care of him, to treat him with the respect he deserves."

"I can help you with that."

"Just ask," Ian added.

"Thank you, both" Marty said. "I promised her."

~ ~ ~

The mini-bar was half empty, no thanks to Gabe. He just watched.

"What about Auturo? Your ride tomorrow?" Ian asked. "Are you nuts?"

"He still trusts me," Marty said. "It is that way with us here. We are a small community."

"You got fifty grand pretty easily," Ian replied, "*you* have more reach than I do."

Marty drained the last of the Jack Daniels and shook his head. "You and I? We both have *friends*. Most of mine, I can trust only on *a minute by minute* basis. Believe me."

Gabe let them wear themselves out and finally asked, "How is this going to work, Marty? As much as it seems like a good idea, I'm not letting Ian be bait."

"It is the only way to get Arturo to a place where the public is not at risk."

"What about the car on the way from the airport?"

"Or me," Marty said.

"Fair enough."

"The site I am suggesting is empty. Ester View is familiar to Auturo and you, Ian, you have been in all three versions."

"I have. Nice job, by the way."

"Thank you. Because we own the vacant land, there are very few houses nearby. It is safe."

"Wherever Auturo is, is not safe." Gabe stood up. "For all we know, Auturo has been staying on of them."

"He will pick me up," Marty said. "You'll know he is not there."

"So you can control when he gets there. We can get in position."

"Absolutely." Marty smiled. "The *goat* first, then the *puma*."

"I'm not the *puma*, I take it," Ian said.

Marty shrugged. "We all have our parts."

"The goat will be awake this time," Ian insisted.

Gabe nodded. "As bad an idea as it is, you'd better be armed."

"Yes," Marty agreed. "Arturo knows about your Smith & Wesson. If you don't have it, he may charge you."

"Bring him on."

Marty added, "Bring Detective Webster. An attractive woman will embarrass him. A moment hesitation is all you'll need. To take..." He hesitated. "Auturo Guillen is not a bad man. He has been loyal to me. He just has his own way of looking at things. We can use that against him."

"With Ian," Gabe said.

"Yes. It is a matter of pride for him, now. He thought he had defended Kami, successfully. And me," Marty explained. "Ian, you have opened up this closed wound for him. I will tell him that you and I have agreed to meet, that I will mislead you. He knows I am good at that."

"How reassuring."

"The important part is that I will be bringing the *open wound* to him. He wants to close it, for good, with his knife. We all have our individual senses of honor."

"Just his knife?" Gabe asked.

"Since the army, Auturo does not like guns. The knife is a weapon of personal courage," Marty said. "I am not so brave and will need a 9 millimeter. He will feel that difference." He looked Ian in the eye. "You will be fine. I promise you."

"All right," Gabe said, reluctantly. "Ian, maybe you don't need your Smith & Wesson."

"Dream on," Ian said. "And this place has no sofas in the way."

Chapter 24

The afternoon that Auturo picked up Marty in the silver Mercedes at the Ft. Meyers airport, the plan Gabe, Ian and Marty had devised was set in motion. Marty had added his own *two for the price of one* adjustment, unbeknownst to his allies.

During the first half of the forty-five minutes of the return drive, Marty learned that Auturo had been staying in the west-most of the three Ester View shells. He asked Auturo to bring the keys to the middle house. "No need for you to remove your belongings." The choice of site for the confrontation with Ian Decker pleased Auturo. He knew the layout of the house and, Marty told him, Ian had never been in it.

"Did you bring both Sigs?" Marty asked. "I'm sure he'll bring his pistol."

Auturo lifted the center console as he drove. Marty lifted the Sig-Sauer P229 DAK 9 millimeter semi-automatic and checked the magazine. It was full, with ten Speer Gold Dot +P 124-grain, hollow point rounds, Marty's ammunition of choice.

Auturo lifted his shirt to flash the butt of the second of Marty's twin Sigs, holstered and tucked into the small of his back.

"I'm sorry to insist," Marty said. "I know you dislike guns."

He shrugged. "I have my knife. In case."

"How is your leg? Where Decker shot you?"

"It hurts. Good for me, he is a bad shot." Auturo made a show of crossing himself.

They laughed.

Auturo fleshed out the limited details – from his point of view – of both the JJ Amos and Javier Gomes incidents. To him, the two men had brought the results upon themselves. It was their defiance and bad luck.

"And Ian Decker," Marty said. "He was responsible for intruding where he shouldn't."

Auturo gobbled that bait whole but instead of enraging him, it calmed him. "He is a devil," Auturo said, with venom. "If not for him, I would not have had to hurt Javier."

"No, you wouldn't," Marty readily agreed. "Kamila told Javier nothing. It was Decker who put ideas in his head."

"She would have." Auturo shook his head, disappointed. "She was safe back home."

"Decker had me worried," Marty explained. "He would have kept after her. I had to take her home."

"I hadn't decided." Auturo described, again, how Javier had proven his treachery, tricking Auturo during the call from Ian. "He said something about the driveway. He meant my car."

"Decker's idea of a secret code, no doubt."

"I was asking questions," Auturo said. "The knife work was for convincing."

"And after the call…"

Auturo shook his head. "I never trusted him."

"That's when you hit his neck, by mistake."

"That was a mistake. I didn't think he had courage. After that…" Auturo shook his head. "She's free of him, now."

For the rest of the drive, Marty continued to build up Ian as the culprit, on what he and Auturo had to deal with: They and all of Marty's affairs were at risk because

Ian Decker had found out too much while investigating JJ Amos's death. Ian Decker, like JJ Amos, had proposed blackmail.

"Decker calls it a retainer," Marty explained. "He wants me to pay him one hundred thousand dollars for a lot of legal work he has no intention to perform. That will not be the end of it. He will never stop."

Marty praised Auturo for his work in fending off Decker but more was needed. Marty had a plan to deal with Ian Decker.

Auturo felt ever more assured in his mentor's confidence in him, Marty's approval of his actions.

As Marty had told Gabe and Ian, a confident Auturo was a predictable Auturo.

Marty talked about their *code*, a proud Bolivian's *way*. Marty kept any hint of irony from his voice.

The three enclosed shells on Ester View were partially well lit in front. The three different layouts each had a side-facing, two-car garage in the front, with a pass-through to the kitchen area behind. The recessed front door of the middle house was in shadow.

The land had been completely cleared for the construction process. The Quadrant-designed landscaping remained strictly on paper. The windows and doors had been installed, but no finish work had been started inside or out. Each garage door was operational. In all three, the electrical contractor had run the wiring through the walls, but only a few circuits were active to allow interior work. At night, only the several standing lamps provided light for the great room and kitchen. The bedrooms and bathrooms had no lights.

During the day, sunlight combined with bare windows to illuminate most of the interior quite well, if casting many shadows.

Outside, the street was dead quiet.

To Auturo, it would be the perfect place to neutralize Ian Decker.

Auturo stopped the car in front of the garage. He began to get out.

"Save your leg," Marty insisted. "I have the code on my phone." He retrieved the code from his phone, tapped at the keypad and the door began to move. The garage's overhead light came one.

Auturo pulled the Mercedes into the slot created by building materials and tools. He checked the security of the Sig's holster as he got out.

Marty retreated to the car and opened the trunk. He opened his cabin trolley and pulled out a small blue camera.

Auturo was waiting at the opened pass-through door first. Marty held up his camera to wave Auturo through the door.

The kitchen and great room were monuments to concrete block. A large work table sat in the middle of the great room. On it lay a set of plans. Some stacks of bags were the only other furnishings.

Auturo limped to the sliding glass door to the lanai. It was locked and had an off-white plastic pipe in its track to prevent break-ins. "He can't get out this way."

"Not quickly, No."

Marty led Auturo on a tour of the three small bedrooms, their closets and the two bathrooms, all starkly gray. There were no interior doors. While in the master bathroom, he picked up two blue electrical boxes. He poked his index finger through the largest hole. He took a small blue camera from his pocket and placed it in the blue box. "And they're color coordinated."

The camera, set to begin recording video at 6:00 was a perfect fit. Marty had purchased it a few years earlier to secretly film of some suspicious subcontractors. The junction box rig had worked perfectly before, too.

He set the two boxes on top of one of the stacks of bags. He repositioned them to make them look like part of the woodwork. "Let's get a few things from the garage to make them look less lonely."

After they had finished, Marty admired their handiwork. "It makes the bags look like an impromptu shelf. He won't notice any of it. Good play?"

Auturo frowned. "The same play didn't work with Amos. And you are shorting Decker."

"The players make the play, Auturo. That was you, Kamila and a lunatic lawyer," Marty said, heading to the stack of bags. He set down the two boxes. "This time, it will be you, me and a practical, if crooked, lawyer. As far as the half-price, he won't know how much is in the bag, until we have him recorded, will he?"

"That is true."

They walked toward the short hallway that led to the front door. "The only way in or out for him will be through here," Marty said. "And you'll be between it and him."

Back in the car, Marty reiterated the simple plan. Marty would lure Ian Decker to the Ester View house on the pretext of giving in to Ian Decker's blackmail demands. "Decker is a sane man. A sane blackmailer is a businessman. Don't worry about a repeat of Amos."

"He is friends with a cop," Auturo said, thoughtfully. "He hasn't told him?"

"Decker gains nothing by telling anyone. If he does that, he gets no money from me. That's all he wants. He didn't like Amos. He didn't know Javier, so revenge is not a concern, either."

Auturo nodded. "I hope he does not cooperate."

Marty clapped him on the shoulder. "It would be more final." With a serious look, he said, "He will cooperate. If not, you have your Sig."

~ ~ ~

At 5:40 on the night of the Auturo take-down, Nicolina and Gabe relaxed in Ian's condo. They had coordinated with six deputies to seal off the Ester View street on Gabe's cellphone signal. Only the three of them would be inside the house.

Before Marty's return, Ian had shown them through the middle house. The layout was more than adequate, with the walls providing solid cover.

Ian would stand on the far aide of the plans table. They wanted Marty and Auturo to seem him when the entered, making him Auturo's sole focus. Marty would have Auturo carry a bag with the fifty thousand originally intended for JJ. Marty would be attempting to short Ian, adding to the credibility of the approach. The combination would fit with Auturo's mindset and make him less suspicious.

Ian had mocked up a retainer agreement he could wave about, to distract Auturo. Ian realized that JJ Amos would not get the irony of the plan had he been present: The document and cash combination had not worked out well for JJ, but JJ had not been dealing with Marty.

"Besides," Ian observed. "There's no water and no tie."

"Yeah," she said, "don't mention that to him."

"I know. I'm so two days ago."

Gabe wore light gray suit and sand colored shirt. Nicolina paced about in a silver silk blouse and form-fitting dark gray slacks that were tactically eye-catching. The point of her outfit was to put Auturo's machismo in play.

Ian looked thick in orange shorts and a yellow and orange striped golf shirt with one button buttoned. He looked as threatening as melting two-scoop gelato.

"That's the point," she explained, deadpanned. "We want him looking at you."

"What about you?" Ian asked. "He's going to notice you, for sure."

She glared at him. "It's a costume. Yours isn't."

After Gabe ran through their roles, Nicolina said what they all were thinking. "This is a damned stupid plan. I mean, the guy just carries a knife. We can take him anywhere."

"He has access to significant firepower," Gabe said. "He had two Sig-Sauers when he picked Marty up at the airport."

"Shit," Ian said. "What happened to the knife."

"He'll still have it. Marty told me he had talked Auturo out of the guns. Marty will be armed, but Auturo will just have his knife."

"That *just* means he throws it. And this glowing button makes that a *can't miss*. Thanks to my *dresser.*"

"I *selected* it for you. You own it," Nicolina said. When Ian glared at her, she added a smile and, "Oh, I'll bet your sainted Evie didn't pick it out."

"They aren't supposed to go together."

Nicolina patted his waist. "A little tight."

"You're saying this Kevlar makes me look fat?"

Gabe responded first. "It makes you look safer. You two can compare figures later."

"I'm not doing that," Ian said.

Nicolina kept her view of the respective self-images to herself.

Standing, Gabe said, "Ian if you can extract a confession from Auturo that would be good. He's confessed to Marty, but, let's face it, Marty is about as credible as Hugh Barrett."

Nicolina stage-whispered to Ian, "That's *Hubble-speak* for *not at all*."

Ian wondered how far Evie's endorsement on trust went. No matter, as he knew no jury would have Evie to back up Marty's testimony. "Okay. But he doesn't talk much above a grunt."

"Let's get moving," Gabe said. "We want to be in position first."

~ ~ ~

At 5:55, Auturo pulled the silver Benz alongside the red Audi parked in front of the house. They both recognized as Ian's.

In the back seat of the Mercedes sat the bag full of cash that Marty harped on as Ian's *retainer*.

"Damn that arrogant bastard," Marty said. "At least, I have the camera set up," he added. "But it won't start to run for a few minutes. I'll have to stall. Pull up to the garage. I'll get the door and go on in."

Auturo did as instructed, and Marty hopped out. He keyed open the garage door and hurried to the pass-through. He motioned for Auturo to pull in. As soon as Auturo was out of the car, Marty pulled the Sig from his hip holster. He made a show of ejecting and restoring the clip. "Wait here."

Auturo mimicked Marty with his Sig-Sauer. He prepared to rack a round into the chamber.'

Marty gestured him to stop. "Not yet. Let me feel him out, first. Decker is all words. That is all I should need. That and the cash." He reached in and displayed his phone "Use your phone. Wait Until 6:01."

Auturo took out his phone and touched the face. It said 5:57. He nodded.

"Much as I would like you to remove Decker from our lives," Marty said, "his death would be even more complicated for both of us."

Auturo nodded reluctantly.

Marty went through the door and closed it, firmly.

~ ~ ~

Inside the house, Ian leaned against the sliding glass door. He envied its solid feel. Indeed, everything about Marty's project had better materials and workmanship than Ibis Creek. Marty may have been a fraud, but Ian thought he might move., if Ian came out of this, he thought, he might move.

He had to survive the night first.

Gabe was positioned inside the doorway to the second bathroom, its wall blocking the view in and out. Nicolina was in the smallest bedroom, the one in the front of the house. That room, unfortunately, led to the small hallway that would block her view of Marty and Auturo at first. On the plus side, she could slide forward ten feet without being seen.

Gabe had to suppress his bad feeling about the whole plan. Nicolina had doubts of her own.

The door from the garage opened. Marty entered.

"Well," Ian said. "Mr. Pinedo."

"Mr. Decker." He dropped to a whisper. "We have a couple minutes until my camera is ready." He gestured for Ian to speak and at higher volume. He did the same. "You are early."

"Is that still impolite?"

"Auturo wanted to be able to greet you."

Ian rolled his eyes. "You brought your muscle?"

Marty strode through the kitchen and then turned sideways, to let his voice carry in both directions. "Men like Auturo carry the load, Mr. Decker. You and I make phone calls."

"I can handle a deposit slip with anyone," Ian said. "If that's that you're getting at."

Marty waved him forward and to Ian's left. *The camera,* he mouthed, as he dug out his cellphone.

Ian walked to a position at the end of the mid-room table until Marty's extended palm stopped him.

Marty looked at his cellphone. It displayed 6:00 PM. He led up one finger.

"Come on, Marty," Ian said, loudly. "I have things to do."

"I thought you were working for me, now."

"Not quite yet."

Marty waited, checked his phone. 6:01. He nodded and the door from the garage opened.

~ ~ ~

Auturo grew frustrated, stuck listening through the door, watching his phone, with the cash bag at his feet. He took out the Sig-Sauer. He looked at it. He resisted the temptation to triple check the magazine. He had banged it home thirty seconds earlier. Marty had ordered him to keep his Sig's firing chamber empty. He had been shot once by Decker already. Marty wanted him to keep the chamber free, but his code, his sense of honor would not allow Ian Decker to shoot him again without dying in the process.

He racked the slide.

He kicked at the bag. His leg stung.

Ian Decker had done that.

If Marty's plan worked as well as Kamila's, Auturo was just as ready.

When 6:01 came, Auturo picked up the bag. He opened the door and walked into the kitchen area.

The first thing, the only thing, he saw was Ian Decker. Auturo forgot, in that moment, that Ian Decker was dangerous, that Ian Decker had shot him.

He forgot because the coward Ian Decker looked like a *clown*.

~ ~ ~

When Auturo entered the first door, his eyes unmistakably fixed on Ian and he actually laughed out loud.

Gabe sent his text to the deputies.

Marty spoke first, "Auturo, you remember Ian Decker."

"We meet again," Ian said. He resisted the temptation to add a comment.

Auturo's laugh became a distant memory. He scowled into silence.

"It's all right, Auturo," Marty said. "We're all going to be friends tonight."

"And going forward," Ian agreed, with the touch of sarcasm he knew Auturo would expect.

"We can let the past be the past. We three will be working together, according to Mr. Decker."

"One can never have enough lawyers."

For a second, no one spoke. Marty broke the silence, "Auturo has your retainer, Mr. Decker."

"And I brought my... our retainer agreement. My hourly fee is $1200 an hour."

"That is robbery territory," Marty said, genuinely surprised. "Or blackmail."

"But privilege has its privileges," Ian responded. "Legal representation brings confidentiality and silence."

"Is it wise to have a written blackmail agreement?"

"Florida Bar ethics require a written agreement." Ian supplied a smirk to match his tone.

Marty laughed. "That's too absurd to be false. What do you think, Auturo?"

It took Auturo a moment to realize that Marty had addressed him. He narrowed his eyes and said, "Honorable men don't need a piece of paper."

"But, Auturo," Marty said, with a slight laugh, "Mr. Decker is an ethical lawyer."

Ian looked at Auturo. "A piece of paper didn't help JJ Amos, did it Auturo?"

Auturo's eyes opened wide. "Javier? Before?"

"Yes," Ian continued, "Javier told me about it before you killed him. He also said you didn't have the guts to kill JJ Amos outright."

Auturo started forward until he was even with Marty, who stayed him with a gesture. "Past is past," Marty said. "It is time to let both Mr. Amos and Javier rest in peace."

"No," Ian said. "I'm risking a lot, *representing* someone like you, agreement or not. The crowd you're in. I want to know who I'm dealing with. If I can depend on your… muscle if things get dicey going forward. That means *rough*, Auturo. You're kind of short. Maybe, JJ Amos is your idea of *rough*."

Marty objected. "Auturo can handle himself. He handled Amos and, regrettably, Javier Gomes. Right, Auturo?"

Auturo throat rumbled.

"Was that grunt your affirmative one?" Ian asked, sarcastically. "You know, Auturo, like *si* or, as we say in America, *yes*?"

"Both," Auturo growled. "Both of them."

"Both words or both men." Ian had ramped up to mocking. "Maybe, you are better with words than men."

"Both men."

Marty said, sharply. "Enough. We know what is past, now. Can we move forward?"

"Yes," Ian said, flatly. "I am as satisfied as I'm going to get."

Marty glanced down at the bag in Auturo's hand. "Auturo." He nodded toward the bag. "Put the money on the table and push it toward our new friend."

Auturo stepped forward – Marty matched him, to his right – and swung the bag into place on top of the plans. He gave it a shove, but it didn't go far. He shoved it harder.

"I have our agreement," Ian said. He began to reach his left hand his jacket's inside pocket.

~ ~ ~

For the second shove of the cash, Auturo went badly off balance. Pain shot up his leg, the one Ian Decker had damaged, hiding behind a wall.

He glared at Decker in his clown suit.

But Decker was not laughing. He was reaching –

~ ~ ~

"Gun!" Marty called out, a flash before Auturo went for his Sig.

Ian threw the retainer agreement on the table and looked up in surprise.

Gabe sprung into the room from Ian's right. His Glock trained on Auturo.

From behind Auturo, Nicolina advanced in the shadows of the short hallway. She kept her Glock close to her side and trained on Auturo. She crossed behind Auturo and edged forward. She motioned for Marty to step toward her.

He did the opposite. He moved to the end of the table, but along the wall. As he did so, Ian edged diagonally away.

Nicolina took a position to Auturo's right, Ian's left, along the same wall as Marty's. Auturo was flanked on both sides.

Marty pointed his pistol at Ian.

Auturo's head swiveled from Gabe to Nicolina, but his Sig remained on Ian. He did a serious double-take on Nicolina. He glared at her briefly before eying Ian again. He saw Ian's Smith & Wesson coming from behind his back.

Auturo took a couple steps back in reaction to the appearance of the Smith & Wesson. He gave his version of a smug smile and retook his ground. His smile faded into the usual scowl as he glanced at Gabe. He then looked Nicolina up and down, quickly, then again.

Once his went forward, everything froze. Until Auturo cocked the Sig's hammer and said, "The coward brings his woman."

Nicolina bit her tongue.

Auturo smiled ugly. "Of course."

Ian raised his 40 and pointed it full at Auturo's chest.

About the same time, Marty pointed his Sig at Ian, too. "Auturo, I have Decker covered."

The block of granite that was Auturo Guillen did not flinch. It was clear he had a favorite outcome.

Gabe used his most mild voice. "All right, everybody. Take a breath. That means you, Ian. Auturo. Marty. No one has to do anything."

"Si," Auturo said. Then he put on a different nasty smile. "That means, *yes*," he added, glaring at Ian.

"Auturo." Marty matched Gabe's tone. "We can't get all three of them. Look how they are spaced apart." The words seemed to have no effect at first.

As the words registered, Auturo swung his gun to Nicolina. "The insult is the woman."

Marty said, his voice sharper, "You know men of honor can't shoot a woman, Auturo, but women... She has no code."

Auturo centered his gun on Ian, once again, but moved his head through the arc that brought him to Gabe's eyes.

Marty kept talking. "You see. There are three." He inched toward Ian, still well away. He pointed at Gabe. "I have Decker."

Auturo nodded, but said, "No." His head turned away from Gabe, facing Ian.

"Auturo! There are three!" Marty said, suddenly, very sharply. "Stop! We surrender!"

The word stunned Auturo. It was unmistakable. His eyes blinked rapidly.

Gabe, Nicolina and Ian all stiffened.

"We surrender," Marty repeated, sounding positively craven. "Don't shoot us. Please."

If *surrender* had shocked Auturo, *please* made his head and shoulders turn toward Marty. The Sig followed. He caught himself and abruptly re-targeted Ian.

Marty's shot Auturo close enough to his heart.

The expanding Gold Point round jerked Auturo backward, but his low center of gravity held him upright. As a sudden reflex brought him forward, Auturo dropped the Sig. For a strained breath or two, he teetered on the balls of his feet before he fell stiffly face-forward, just as JJ Amos had done.

Instantly, Gabe and Nicolina swung their Glocks to Marty. Marty dropped his Sig-Sauer before they made the switch. Ian just dropped his pistol to his side.

"Shit, Marty," Ian said.

Marty held out his hands. "You can thank me later."

Nicolina, her gun still on Marty, asked Gabe, "Now, the fuck what?"

~ ~ ~

Gabe had not answered Nicolina's question. No one had.

He had lowered his gun and reran the events in his head. Then he had said, "Well, first, we ask Mr. Pinedo when he changed the plan."

Marty had nodded toward the piece of paper on the table. "I wanted Ian as my lawyer."

"Hilarious." Nicolina had kept her weapon level for another minute.

"He's got a point," Ian said, reluctantly. He quickly read the retainer agreement. "A pretty good one, if I do –"

"You both had guns pointed the same dead guy," Nicolina said.

"We all did," Gabe said just before he called in the shooting.

The deputy cars roared down Ester View and skidded to a stop on either side of the driveway. Since Gabe's text, they had sealed off the street. They quickly secured the scene on the otherwise deserted area. Marty pointed out his camera.

Gabe, Nicolina, Marty and Ian had no choice but to wait for others to process their own scene. Auturo had no choice, either.

None of them wanted to sit on the stack of bags. They went outside. Ian and Marty leaned against the hood of Marty's car, the other two against a patrol car next to it.

Gabe sighed. "So, let's play this straight."

"How do we do that?" Nicolina asked.

"Well," Ian said, "you can speak to Marty through me."

"Really?" Nicolina got off the car and paced.

"Okay," Gabe said. "Auturo had a loaded gun? Why is that, Mr. Pinedo?"

"Marty, don't answer that."

Marty waved off Ian. "Auturo can be – was – insistent. Ian had shot him once already. He assumed that Ian would be armed had no intention of letting him have that advantage, again. Could I object strongly without compromising the plan?" He shook his head. "And Auturo knew my Sigs too well, I had no choice but full magazines. I told him not to chamber the first round."

"That worked like... a God damned charm," Nicolina reminded everyone.

"He did that against my orders."

"So, he was serious when he cocked the hammer," she said. "Good to know."

"He didn't fire," Marty replied.

Ian interjected, "And I'm not dead."

"Nothing is perfect."

Gabe said, "Seriously. Marty, you all but told him he had one shot."

"That was reality," Marty said. "I told him I had Ian."

"Yes, thanks for pointing me out."

"A tactical decision, Lieutenant."

"You knew he wouldn't, "Gabe said. "It seemed you were goading him to shoot Ian."

"Believe me, that was not necessary," Marty said. "No offense, Ian."

Ian held up his hand. "We all know who Auturo wanted to shoot. Let's leave it at that. I can replay that for you in my dreams for the next few years."

"I'll pass," Nicolina said. "Thank God, we have it on camera."

"Thank Marty."

Marty flinched, slightly. "I'll leave the video to you. Auturo was a friend, and I mourn his death." He sounded somewhat sincere. "But I also see if for what it was."

"And that is?" Gabe asked.

"Under our... code In Bolivia –"

"Where we aren't," said Nicolina.

"In Bolivia," Marty said. "we would call it *mantener una promesa.*"

"*Keeping a promise,*" Nicolina translated.

Epilogue

In the end, Marty Pinedo released Ian from his ethical obligations, and Ian returned fifty thousand cash in retainer.

Gabe took one afternoon and laid out the entire plan for the State Attorney for Collier County. That official had decided in the AM that Marty Pinedo was justified and, under the standards of his office, a near-hero.

Marty received that happy news at noon and returned by car service from Miami's airport.

The affidavit of Kami Cabrera Gomes remained in Bolivia, as did Kami. As a consequence, the Ibis Creek v. Abbott, Burkle Dehane construction defect case continued to generate legal fees without interruption.

At the suggestion – to use the polite term – of Mara Collins and Hugh Barrett, Sanders & Tilden made JJ Amos a posthumous junior partner, without equity participation.

Ibis Creek president Kenny Becks proposed the association's Clubhouse bookshelf niche be designated, however incongruously, the JJ Amos Memorial Reading Room. No motion was made but it passed unanimously. Mara bought ten new audio books – with her own money– and had Jenny Moreno quietly shelf them the very next day. Mara did not submit the cost for reimbursement from Ibis Creek.

Maria Suarez continued her career as a premier manicurist, with Claire and Leo as new clients. She moved into an Ibis Creek townhouse, just like Claire and Leo's, at the same rent she had been paying Kami. Her new LLC landlord was owned by another LLC based in Antigua, which, in turn, was owned by an unknowns Nevis Trust. Her landlord also used AMP Management's comprehensive services.

Ian still owed Claire three Ibis Blogger posts, though both agreed use of his *nom de Blog* was a bad idea, temporarily; he would just his own name for a time. Claire agreed to cut him some slack because... "I'm glad you're safe. Even I can't fight a war on only two hands."

Another plus, Leo appointed Maria as his new *muse*. "She's closer. Evie's all yours... Sorry, I mean muse-wise, she's all yours."

The insurance company stuck with a half million dollar policy on the life of JJ Amos refused to pay. It claimed the facts showed that JJ had committed suicide by throwing himself face first into an unnamed body of water. The company was mysteriously acquired, two days later, by a private equity firm, with offices down an Antiguan street from Maria's landlord. The new claims VP reversed the Amos decision in under five minutes.

Most importantly, Mara broke down and replaced Leo's outside carriage light.

To cap a busy week, Gabe and Ian finally convinced Nicolina to join them on the beach at 34th. She wore gauzy slacks and a linen blouse, both off-white and loose-fitting, with no Kevlar. She looked and felt very cool, Naples weather notwithstanding.

She would not go so far as to sit beside Ian, landing Gabe in the middle.

"I have to admit," she said, sipping Chardonnay from a 7-Up bottle. "I'd forgotten how nice this was."

"7-Up?" Ian asked. "Or to be friends."

"That, too. And, not." She laughed. "You did surprise me. Though, I am left to wonder if you could have hit anyone above the leg."

"Lot of loose ends," Gabe said. He had developed a taste for ginger wine and used his own bottle. "What is Marty really up to?"

"Drugs," Nicolina insisted. "Gotta be."

"Lithium, you mean?" Ian asked innocently.

"Cocaine," Nicolina said. "Come on, genius, it's Bolivia."

"I don't think so." Gabe believed Marty's story but wondered how much Evie Decker's *trust certification* went.

Ian's cellphone rang. "Samara," he said to Gabe. He got out of his chair. "I told her to call about now." He started toward the parking area.

"Lucky you," Gabe said, getting up as well. "While you do that, I'm going in the water."

Nicolina asked him, "Who the hell is that? The name sounds bogus."

"I'll let Ian tell you that."

"And I'm back," Ian said, phone still to his ear. "Simara wants to congratulate us all and thank you for not getting me killed."

"Simara who?" Nicolina raised an eyebrow.

"You're welcome," Gabe called, halfway to the water.

"We all make mistakes," Nicolina said, loudly.

"You heard that," Ian said into the phone. "Good. Yes, that's Webster. Gabe says she wasn't always like that." Ian listened, then said to Nicolina, "I'll be back."

He could not wait more than four paces before he asked, "Do you know any insurance companies?"

"I had nothing to do with that," Evie said.

"You know what I'm talking about, though."

"Oops." She laughed that laugh of hers. "Seriously, I had zero to do with that and I don't know *exactly* who did. That's the truth."

"Okay. Okay."

"A good result, though, don't you think?"

"The first claim rep was insane, so, yes." When she did not comment, he said, "You were mostly right about Marty Pinedo. And Hugh, of course."

"You can still trust Marty, but not in anything about investments or money. Or Bolivia. Hugh, either, except the Bolivia factor. Keep me posted."

"Why don't you come down here and you can spend a day or two telling me what all is going on where I live."

She sighed. "I would, but did you notice who called?"

Ian sighed back. "Oh."

"You live in a town more complicated that it looks from where you are sitting," Evie said. "Not like here, but… money, money, money."

"True." He started walking the few steps to his chair.

"Gotta go. Love you and miss you."

"I love you, too. Always will."

"Bye."

Nicolina waited until the call ended. Ian had not gotten all that far away, so she had heard his end. "So, Who's the lucky girl? This Samara?"

Ian said. "But since you asked nicely, she is my favorite person in the entire world. Present company included."

"That's half an answer," Nicolina said. "We have enough of those already."

"Her name is Evie."

"Wait. Samara's your ex-friggin-wife?"

"Yes, she is."

"She's from Pittsburgh, too?"

"From. She was from an Irish neighborhood. Right next to the Polish and Italian neighborhoods," Ian said, sitting down. "Me, I'm a suburbanite, so I never bought into the glory or ethnic neighborhoods. I know a guy who says we are all mutts hailing from someplace else. We humans have not yet reached the purity and usefulness of the American Pit Bull Terrier."

Nicolina stared at him. She started to speak twice, her expression angry, at first. She gulped some Gulf air. "*Mutts* is not a nice way of describing us."

Ian was taken aback. "Sorry. Evie felt the same way. You're both right. How about GMOs?"

"That sounds familiar," she said, "but I am going to hear about it now, aren't I?"

"Genetically Modified Organisms. Like every Homo Sapien, ever."

"That's even less politically correct."

Ian finally sensed her sensitivity. "I shouldn't have said that to you."

"Me? Now, I'm special?"

"Gabe said you took your Cuban ancestry very seriously."

"Yeah, I did. Very much." She looked away. "Do you know Ancestry dot com?"

"That never interested me. Evie used it. I asked her if the first Celt was born in Ireland. She was not amused."

"And she divorced you."

If Ian expected a *good for her*, he did not get one. "Yes, Nicolina, but one did not descend from the other."

"Hm."

They sat, listening to the surf, watching Gabe emerge from the water. He was in much better shape that Ian.

"How far does Ancestry dot come go?" Ian asked, finally. "Go back?"

"Too fucking far." She did not elaborate.

Gabe reached them, and Nicolina threw him his towel. As he toweled off, he looked at her. "What's wrong?"

"Nothing," she said, barely above the surf.

"I was gone two minutes. You two faced down a Sig-Sauer together and l can't get along for three minutes?"

"I thought we were," Ian said.

Nicolina nodded. "Who knew?"

Gabe sat between them, looking at each twice. He decided to skip to what had been bothering him enough to pull him out of the water. "So, Ian. Did... Simara have any other answers? She doesn't seem to need questions."

"Oh, please. It was Evie Decker," Nicolina said. "I mean *Evie*, since we're all *friends* here."

"Did she have answers? Or did she tell me?"

"With you and Evie, I guess that's a valid question."

"She does everything but electronically alter her voice, Gabe," Ian said, pleasantly. "So, yes, it is a valid question."

"Damn. I was hoping, I don't know, for something on our loose ends..."

Nicolina asked, without any edge, "How does this work? You and Evie?"

"Pretty well. For us."

"Better than when you were married?" She laughed. "That's not my experience."

"No, definitely not better," Ian said. "Second best." He sipped his wine. "We are who we are and where we need to be. We like the symmetry of it."

"Jesus." She paused. She looked from Ian to Gabe to Ian. "I was wrong about you. You are not an asshole, just tragic," she said, sarcasm still absent. "After, what five years, you're in love with your ex-wife?"

"Tragic? Me?"

"I mean, it must be hard, knowing you are still in love with her."

Ian had the thought, as he often did, but he hesitated for the phrasing. "The hard part," he said, "is knowing I never was."

~

Acknowledgments

The Body in the Bog, was initially inspired by a very real, very slowly draining, and, hence, flooded preserve. In that sense, the real bog deserves some credit here. The planned Ian Decker/Death by Condo series was inspired, if that he word, by living in a condo, the less said of that being the better.

In the Acknowledgment section for my epic 750 page novel *The Girl in the Coyote Coat*, I made the mistake of acknowledging the help of my sisters, Janet Nave and JoAnn Kiburz and friend Julie Kimball, for their alpha reading and editing assistance. Somehow, my compulsion to introduce two errors for every correction and rewrite they suggested may have made it impossible for them to get another similarly frustrating and non-paying gig.

So, *no one* helped me with *The Body in the Bog*. Honest. And if anyone secretly did so, do not admit it.

I should add that this book is not autobiographical. I did endow Sebastian Decker with a few bits of my own background, more for fun than laziness, but Ian is his own man. Every other character or event in the novel is my own fabrication.

About the Author

Born in 1950, John Nicholas Datesh lived mostly in and around Pittsburgh, Pennsylvania until early 2009. At Brown University, he took many courses in writing as an institutionalized rationale for doing just that. Then, at Boston University School of Law, he learned to mix in words and phrases like *It Depends* and *Hereinafter*. It is unknown when he learned to use italics every third paragraph.

In Spring 2009, he moved cats Lila and Lucy Liu to a condominium one mile in from the east side of Naples Bay in Florida. He left his Pittsburgh career in law, business and product development in favor of concentrating on writing fiction, winging blogs and cultivating beach chairs, presumably in that order of dedication.

He began writing fiction with a pencil and published, on paper with actual ink, his first three books, the SF/Mystery novel *The Nightmare Machine*; the Softboiled Detective novel *The Janus Murder*; and the International Suspense novel *The Moscow Tape*. All three novels are currently *evailable* in virtual ink at e-book stores on the Web and in trade paperback.

Also widely *evailable* are the short stories *The Pro Station* (WWII), *The Final Equation (SF)* and *Reruns ad Infinitum* (SF/Fantasy). They join the author's definitive Christmas short story, *You Could Call It a Christmas Story* as works published after the move to Naples.

He concocted a humorous and/or satiric blog at EmptyGlassFull.com shortly after moving. His *Christmas Story* started out as post to the blog, and he has e-published a collection its other early posts, grandly entitled *The Very First Blog Posts of All Time*. As novel writing began to take more of his time, he sent blogging on long vacation.

His 2013 novel, *The Girl in the Coyote Coat*, came to ignore the boundaries of mystery/suspense genre for which it was originally intended. No one would call it a romance, either. With a real estate and finance backdrop, the novel exposes how love, sex, money, scams, drugs, house-breaking and -shopping and fur coats can affect the lives of complex and intriguing characters and even kill a few.

November 2016's *The Body in the Bog* is a Sunset Noir mystery novel. It is the first in the author's planned *Death by Condo* series starring prematurely retired lawyer Ian Decker.

His screenplay *The Last Three Minutes* was the first piece written partly on the beach and entirely in the Naples Bay scenery, though it is not set there. *The Last Three Minutes* has been adapted as a novel, if not a movie, by the author and was published in December 2016.

Author's Note on the novel
The Girl in the Coyote Coat
and *A Need Apart*

That heading is not an error. They are the same novel. So, why? To double sales? Not likely.

The novel *The Girl in the Coyote Coat* had a long, tortuous road to its final form, right down to the cover and the very title. It was published under that title after some serious consideration. The novel had gone through any number of working titles, as time allowed, from the 1979 original *The Real Estate Novel. The Girl in the Coyote Coat* was always my favorite, inspired, as it was, by an actual coyote coat on an actual model. In the end, that was the title I chose, in a close call (if only to me) over number two, *A Need Apart*, but I did not use the photo that initially inspired the title.

In 2016, I decided to try a little Amazon Kindle advertising. Amazon would not accept the somewhat racy cover. That rejection got me thinking. The novel had grown into what I must loosely call a literary novel, if only because it does not fit into any genre. Why not try a different cover for an ad? Then, I thought, why not try a different, more literary-sounding title. The result is the identical novel with a different name, *A Need Apart*, and a different cover.

Ironically, the *A Need Apart*'s cover uses the shot that originally inspired the working title *The Girl in the Coyote Coat*. Fortunately, I love both titles and both covers, equally. Oh, and both the coat and model, too, if not quite so equally.

Made in the USA
Lexington, KY
04 June 2017